FATAL RECKONING

FATAL RECKONING

RUTH SUTTON

HOAD
PRESS

First published in United Kingdom
by **Hoad Press** in 2016
2 Lowther Street, Waberthwaite, Millom, Cumbria LA19 5YN
www.ruthsutton.co.uk ruth@ruthsutton.co.uk

ISBN–13: 978-0-9929314-1-4

A CIP catalogue record for this book is available from the British Library.

Prepared for publication by Aldridge Press
enquiries@aldridgepress.co.uk

Editorial: Charlotte Rolfe
Design: John Aldridge
Cover design: Kevin Ancient
Cover photo: Whitehaven harbour, PeteG, Fotolia
Typeset in Bembo 11.5/14.5pt

Printed and bound in UK by TJ International, Padstow

Acknowledgements

All the usual suspects have been invaluable in the development and production of *Fatal Reckoning*: my thanks to John Aldridge, Charlotte Rolfe and Kevin Ancient for their publishing, editing and design expertise. I also had the benefit of specialist insider knowledge about the story's setting and content, through conversation in Whitehaven with retired Detective Inspector Terry O'Connell, MBE. Many thanks to him. And as ever, I'm grateful to my partner, Mick Shaw, for his continual encouragement and support.

RS, Waberthwaite, November 2016

CHAPTER I

Rattling rain woke him. The boy burrowed deep into his bed away from the cool March air, but there was something else, a different sound. He got up and looked out of the window. The street lamp glowed through raindrops that seeped down the glass like orange tears, and a small tree at the end of the garden thrashed in the wind. Suddenly there was movement below him. As the boy struggled to see he heard the back door open and close. Someone was in the house.

He wanted to shout out, but no sound came. Fear propelled him out of the room, across the narrow landing and into his mother's bedroom. 'Mummy,' he whispered. 'Wake up.'

Elspeth stirred and turned. 'Tommy?' she said, stretching her hand towards him. 'What is it?'

'Someone's downstairs, in the kitchen.'

Elspeth kicked back the covers and pulled the child towards her. 'Get in the bed and don't move,' she whispered. Tommy reached for her. 'Don't go,' he said. His mother wrapped a pink dressing gown tightly round her body and put a finger to her lips. 'Stay here,' she said. The boy nodded, his eyes wide.

Elspeth saw the line of light under the kitchen door at the foot of the stairs. The telephone was down there, by the front door. As she reached the last stair the light disappeared. She

1

stood still for a moment, adjusting to the darkness, listening. Nothing. Silence. She waited. Could she ring the police, or would it take too long? A large umbrella stood by the front door and she reached for it: too light to do much damage, but better than nothing. She gripped it tightly. Turning back towards the kitchen door she planned the movement in her mind, then flung open the door and reached for the light switch on the wall just to her left. The neon strip flickered into life. 'Don't move!' she shouted. 'The police are coming.'

A man looked, startled, across the small room. Familiar eyes blinked at her, framed by a dark beard and long hair.

'Sam?' The umbrella slipped from her grasp onto the floor.

'Sorry,' said the man.

She held up her hand, turned towards the door and called out. 'Tommy, it's all right. It's Uncle Sam. Come down and say hello.'

'You frightened us,' Elspeth said to her brother. 'And you look terrible. Where have you been?'

Tommy stood at the door, squinting into the harsh light. 'Look who's here,' she said to the child. 'It doesn't look like Uncle Sam, does it? But it is.' Sam held out his arms and the boy ran to him, hugged him tightly for a moment and then pulled away. Elspeth smiled. 'I think Uncle Sam needs a wash, don't you?' Tommy nodded. 'But the first thing is a cup of tea, right?'

'Please,' said Sam.

Half an hour later the first pot of tea was empty, the smell of bacon and egg lingered in the air, and Tommy had been coaxed back to bed before the day dawned.

'So where *have* you been?' she asked. 'Why didn't you call us, instead of turning up in the middle of the night and scaring us half to death?'

Sam groaned. 'What a mess,' he said, wondering where to start. 'Did you get my card from Germany?'

'That was weeks ago, and not a word since.'

'We were on a construction site miles from anywhere. When the job finished I'd had enough, so I headed back to Manchester. I was going to stop with Ian – one of the blokes from the site – just for a few days, so I could get cleaned up, call you, sort out a few things.'

'And what happened?'

'It was my birthday…'

'I got you a card,' Elspeth interrupted, 'but there was nowhere to send it.'

'Well, all I wanted was a bath and a shave, but as soon as I got to Ian's place he dragged me off to the pub before closing time. No chance to get changed. And then it all went wrong. Most of the people in the pub I didn't even know, but Ian kept going on about it being my birthday and they were buying me drinks.'

'But you don't drink,' she said.

He shook his head. 'When we got back to the house I just fell asleep. Didn't wake up till mid-afternoon. The place was a tip and I felt awful. Just wanted to get out of there, so I went for the last train up here.'

'But that would have got in about seven, hours ago.'

'Sunday engineering work or something. We crawled along for a while outside Chorley, got as far as far as Arnside and stopped. They were working on the viaduct and we had to get a bus round to Grange. It took ages. They said we'd get to Roose about ten, and I was going to ring you from the station, but then the train stopped again just outside Dalton. Tree on the line.'

'Oh no!' said Elspeth, fighting the urge to laugh.

'By this time I'd had enough. They made us walk down the line to the station and then I just kept walking.'

'You walked? From Dalton?'

'Seemed like the best idea.' He hesitated. 'Or it would have been if I hadn't got lost.'

This time Elspeth laughed out loud.

While Tommy ate his breakfast downstairs two hours later, Sam Tognarelli wiped the steam from the bathroom mirror and looked at himself. Dark hair that was usually clipped, combed and neatly parted to one side hung in damp curls round his neck and forehead, and the lower half of his face was hidden by a wiry beard. Only the broad nose and greenish eyes under heavy brows reminded him of young Sam, the way he'd been over a year ago, before he'd resigned from the police and left Barrow. He'd escaped into anonymity, ending up in Germany where the money was easy and no one asked any questions. It had been a good place to hide from the guilt and the failed promises. He'd come back because he was lonely, unbearably lonely, but what now?

For a few precious hours Sam slept in Tommy's narrow bed. When he woke the rain had stopped and the house was quiet. A note on the kitchen table told him that Elspeth and Tommy would be back after school. He made himself a sandwich and then put on his coat and set off into the town, towards the docks and the Walney Bridge. He knew Barrow, had walked its streets and recorded its crimes, but he'd never liked the place, and he still didn't. On the far side of the bridge, the road curved across the narrow island to the open coast. Here, specks of sandy spume blew round his feet from the tide that crashed along the shore. Salty wind rasped his face, but Sam opened his mouth and breathed in, letting it fill his lungs and empty his brain.

On the way back to Roose he stopped at the barber's to lose the beard and long hair that he no longer wanted.

'OK,' said his sister after their evening meal, when Tommy left them to watch TV. 'Now you look more like yourself again, I need to give you something.' She reached for an envelope from the top shelf of the dresser and handed it to him. 'It came last week,' she said. 'You read it in peace. I'll go and sit with Tommy for a while.'

Sam looked at the familiar writing and his stomach turned. He opened the envelope slowly, afraid of what it might bring. Inside were a birthday card that made him smile, and a letter.

Dear Sam,

I'm sending this to Elspeth because I don't know where you are. She said she'd had a card from Germany, but that was a month ago. I've been stuck at home in St Bees all this time, since you went away. I remember promising to keep in touch when we met that day in Silecroft, but then it all fell apart. I had a sort of breakdown. Dr Albright said it was delayed shock. I thought I was too strong for all that, but I was wrong. I thought I was going to die that night, and I couldn't get it out of my head. I meant to call you before you went away, but I was too late. And I wanted to go back to the Furness News, but Mum and Dad wouldn't let me, and they were probably right. I was a mess. I've been working at Sellafield, in the press office, like Mum had wanted me to all along. It was all right at first, but now I'm bored, and living at home is driving me crazy. I feel much better these days. You've got the number of the St Bees house. Can you ring me when you get back?

All the best, Judith

Sam put down the letter and leaned back in his chair. He'd been trying not to think about her, but now memories flooded his mind. The Judith he remembered was free and bold, taking risks, making mistakes. This Judith sounded different. He re-read the letter, remembering the smell of blood in the room when they'd found her tied up and helpless, with Thornhill's body slumped in the chair. He closed his eyes. Tommy's footsteps on the stairs tugged him back to the present as Elspeth put her head round the door. 'I'm taking Tommy up to bed.' She looked at her brother carefully. 'You OK? How is she?'

He shook his head. 'I'll tell you later,' he said.

There wasn't much to tell, and Elspeth wanted more. 'You two were so close,' she said, sitting down beside him. 'I thought, you know, that you were getting on really well. Was I wrong?'

He shrugged. 'For a while I thought she was keen. And afterwards, we talked about keeping in touch, but then … well, it sounds as if she had a bad time.'

'She came down with her dad to collect her scooter, must have been about this time last year. I thought she looked thinner, less confident. Mr Pharaoh was fussing too much, and she let him. I was surprised.'

Sam shook his head. 'It's not surprising really, with what she'd been through. Thornhill gave her that job at the paper, and his wife was friendly, or pretended to be, and then they turned on her. She was trussed up like a bloody turkey while Thornhill waved his gun at her, did you know that? No wonder she couldn't get over it.' He turned away.

Elspeth persisted, 'Maybe it would have helped if you'd stuck at it, not given up. Was there nothing more you could have done about Montgomery House? The place is still running, Sam. The kids there now might be hurt, too. What about the police doctor, Dr Hayward? You said he might help.'

Sam shrugged. 'He's dead. Sergeant Morrison's gone. I gave up. And now I don't know what to do.' He pushed back the chair and stood up. 'You remember I went to Hayward's funeral, just before I went away?'

'Something upset you, I remember that.'

'Well, before he died he gave me some information about what had happened at Monty House, and how he'd been blackmailed.'

'Blackmailed? Who by?'

'Morrison, and his boss. Inspector Cardine, did I tell you about him?'

'Not much.'

'It was Cardine who told me I was finished as a policeman in Barrow. Looks like a professor, tall, white hair, but he's bent. He fixed the sergeant's job for Morrison and made him do the dirty work, including blackmailing the doctor, making him change his reports to suit them. Once the doc had given way to that pressure, they had him. Hayward knew he was dying, and there was nothing more they could do to him. He gave me all the details he could manage.' Sam struggled with the painful memory. 'It was awful listening to him fight for breath. I wrote down what he said, and he signed it, like a proper statement, and I left it with his wife. I thought it would be safer with her.' A forgotten detail jumped into his mind. 'She said she would hide it in the sugar jar, with all the notes she'd made about what happened. By the time I thought of going back to get it, the old man was dead and she was gone. And what could I do with the doc's statement anyway? Take it to the police? I couldn't see how I could take it any further. I still can't.'

'You could find Mrs Hayward, surely? She probably still has

the statement if it was so important. And she could testify to what had happened, back you up.'

'OK, but then what? Nothing's changed. Cardine is still there as far as I know, and he could block everything.'

'So is that the end? Is there nothing you can do?'

'I don't know,' he said. His mind was too full. 'And I'm exhausted.' He turned and smiled. 'Thanks for putting me up, by the way. It's good to be here.'

Sam heard Elspeth and Tommy downstairs in the morning, but he didn't want to speak to anyone and waited until he heard the door slam behind them before he got out of bed. His sister's insistent questions had stirred up things he'd been trying to put behind him, and now they swirled in his head. He yearned to be far away, with nothing to think about but hard, physical work, food and sleep; now he was faced once again with uncomfortable choices. He badly wanted to see Judith, but feared that she saw him as a friend, nothing more. He'd come back to be part of a family again, but didn't want questions about the past. The Haywards, Sergeant Morrison, that bastard Cardine, all part of a bad dream that didn't fade with the morning light.

The day stretched ahead of him. Early rain gave way to sunshine, and he set off from the house towards the town without planning where to go, just needing to walk. Waiting on a corner for traffic to pass, he realised that the Haywards' old house was just a few hundred yards away, and his feet took him there before he could resist. On the opposite side of the street he stopped and looked across. The house looked even more neglected than he remembered. Ann Hayward had moved out just after her husband's funeral: maybe whoever lived there now had a forwarding address. He took a deep breath, crossed over and walked up the mossy driveway to the front door. Memories hit him hard – the smell of sickness, the old man's cough, his wife's tears. Sam rang the bell and waited. The door opened and a young man in a stained shirt stared at him. 'What do you want?' he asked.

Sam hesitated. 'I'm looking for Mrs Hayward.'

The young man looked puzzled. 'Moved out last Christmas gone. The old man died, she went off to live with family. I've got tenants 'ere now.'

'Do you know where she went?'

'No idea.'

'What about all the contents, furniture?' Sam asked.

'How should I know? Sold, cleared out. What's it to you? Who are you anyway?'

'Just a friend. Do you know where she moved to?'

'I told you, no idea.'

Sam hung his head.

'That's it, right?' asked the young man, before he turned back into the dark hall and closed the door. Sam turned away and walked back to the house in Roose, where anxiety and exhaustion overwhelmed him and he slept fitfully through the afternoon.

'Do anything interesting today?' Elspeth asked as they sat together at the table after supper. 'And have you decided how long you want to stay?'

Sam looked up. 'I know,' he said. 'You're wondering what happened to the busy, optimistic brother you used to have.'

'No,' she began, but he cut off the denial and got up. 'I'm wondering that too, actually. I thought I was ready to come back, but now I'm not sure. It's all crowding in on me.' He turned back to face her. 'I went to the Haywards' house today.'

9

Elspeth's face brightened. 'You did? Have you found her?'

'I thought whoever lives there now might know where she'd gone.'

'And did they?'

Sam shook his head. 'I felt a right idiot, burbling on about what happened to the furniture. Of course the bloke didn't know. Why should he?' He turned away.

'Enough,' said Elspeth, impatience obvious in her voice. 'Look, if you really want to find Mrs Hayward, you can do it and you will. You might have to talk to some people you haven't seen for a while. What about that bloke you used to work with, the other DC. Is he still around?'

'Harry Grayson,' said Sam, remembering. 'Yes, he's probably still here, and he'd know everything that's happened since I went away.'

'Well then?'

'But I don't want to see him. I don't want to see any of them.'

Elspeth held up her hands. 'Oh, for heaven's sake, Sam, pull yourself together. If that's how you feel, then get out of Barrow and get on with your life. I'm happy you're back, and you can stay here as long as you need to, but moping around like this isn't good for you or us either. If you don't want to go back to the police force, there must be something else you could do, and away from here.'

Sam hung his head. She was right. He had to start again.

CHAPTER 2

It had rained heavily all night, but with morning the rain had eased to a fine veil that drifted across the brick walls and red tiles of the estate and dripped from the peak of Sam's cap. After the walk up from the main road, he adjusted the heavy mailbag on his shoulder, stood for a moment to breathe, and looked down the street ahead of him. They called it an avenue, but only a few of the trees were left. Some hadn't survived infancy, trampled by feral children who roamed after dark. The remaining trees drooped, heavy in the sodden air.

Damp or not, Sam was glad to get out of the sorting office, where the mood was as gloomy as the day, infested with anger and recrimination. Blame hung in the confined space like smoke, aimed at the strike, the bosses, the union, everything and everybody that had left their lives in such a shambles. Sam wasn't sorry he'd moved up here from Barrow, but neither was he really happy to be on this bleak Whitehaven estate, delivering final demands to people who had nothing.

Above his head, invisible seagulls screamed, but other sounds were muffled by layers of mist. He had walked only a few steps before he stopped and looked around him. It was eight-forty in the morning, but no one was about. Where were the kids trudging down to school, and the mothers with prams and pushchairs who chivvied them along? Where was the old van that usually blocked the pavement on the other side? Years in the army and on the beat nudged Sam's senses and triggered questions that raised his heart rate. Something wasn't right, he could feel it.

A sudden movement in the weeds on the other side of a low garden wall caught his eye. Sam put the bag down on the wall and looked more carefully. A fledgling sparrow struggled vainly, and beyond it, flat to the ground, a white cat, oblivious to everything except the fluttering movement, waiting in ecstatic anticipation of the warm morsel in its mouth. Sam didn't wait. He picked up the bag, shrugged it into place and walked on, holding the envelopes in his hand, counting doors. At number 19 he opened the letterbox carefully and pushed the envelope in just far enough to avoid the snapping terrier teeth on the other side. But the familiar high-pitched bark of the terrier didn't happen. Instead, further down the street, another dog began to howl.

Again Sam turned to check behind him, listening for footsteps, or the sucking of tyres on wet road, but there was nothing but the tuneless whine of the dog. Across the street another movement snagged his eye. A curtain twitched and was still, and he noticed that all the curtains in all the windows within sight were drawn tight.

The persistence of the dog drew him forward, into the mist that swirled with his passing and closed behind him. At the end of the tattered row of houses was a corner, where the next artery of the estate turned off into the gloom. The sound of the dog grew louder. Sam knew this dog, and feared it. Around the litter-strewn garden of the corner house was a fence, with just enough gap between the rough vertical planks for the dog's teeth to show. Sam rarely opened the gate, and if he did it would be only a fraction, while he checked that the animal's chain was looped around its neck and short enough to protect him from attack. But this morning the sound of the dog was different.

Sam stood on tiptoe to look over the fence. The green front door, scratched and scoured by the dog's claws, was closed. To the right, out of sight, Sam knew there was an old garage, with a wide, peeling door. The dog was still whimpering, and another sound, lower, caught Sam's ear as he moved to his right, dropped the mailbag to the pavement by his feet and strained upright again to peer over the fence.

He noticed the dog first. The chain was taut, the dog's eyes dark and round, watching. A thin trickle of blood stained one side of its mouth. Then Sam saw the naked man's outstretched arms against the garage door, hands white and fingers drooping like dying flowers. At the centre of each pale palm was a dark hole with something protruding from it. Below the bent head, matted black hair on the chest and belly, shrunken genitals, legs bent, grey toes resting on tarmac and weeds.

'Jesus,' said Sam.

The man moaned but did not lift his head. Sam's mind raced, caught between compassion and curiosity. He found gloves deep in his coat pockets and put them on to open the gate, pulling the heavy mailbag into the yard after him. Treading carefully, and keeping well away from the dog, Sam bent his face to the man's head, listening for the rasp of his breath.

'Who did this?' he asked. There was no response and Sam straightened up. 'I'm going for help,' he said. The man's head moved slightly and the dog growled.

Sam closed the gate after him and looked up. He needed a phone and traced the phone wires that ran to some houses but not to others. Across the street he chose a house that was a little less dishevelled than some and knocked on the door. 'It's the postman,' he shouted through the letterbox. 'I need help.' The man's name came to him. 'Are you there, Mr Jones? It's Sam, the postman.' Putting his ear to the door, he could hear movement and the soft shuffle of feet down the hallway.

'What d'you want?' said an elderly voice.

'Do you have a phone? I need to call an ambulance.'

'Don't want no trouble,' said the voice.

'You're not in trouble. But there's a man across the road who needs help. Please.'

A chain rattled, a key was turned, and slowly the door opened. Bernard Jones hid behind it, gesturing for Sam to come inside. When the door was shut again, he pointed to the phone on a small table and then shuffled back to the kitchen. Sam picked up the phone and dialled 999.

A young uniformed constable was the first to arrive. Sam was offering water to the naked man, holding his head up with one hand, when the policeman opened the gate and peered in.

'Christ,' he said. 'Is this how you found him?'

'Yes, about ten minutes ago. I called the ambulance. Should be here by now. The dog was still alive,' Sam said without turning round. 'I think it's dead now. Be careful though. It's vicious.'

'You the postman?' asked the constable. 'New, aren't you?'

Sam turned around, Mr Jones' cracked cup of water in his hand. 'Sam Tognarelli,' he said. 'Been on this round about three weeks.'

'PC Benson,' said the policeman. 'I'll call this in.' He unclipped his radio and spoke into it. 'One for DC Holmes up here, 31 Grange Avenue, Hattingham,' he said. 'Someone nailed to a door. And check the ambulance, they were called ten minutes since.' The radio crackled in response. PC Benson took out a small notebook.

'Just tell me the basics,' he said to Sam. 'Ten minutes, you said, so that makes it about quarter to nine when you found him. Was the gate open? How did you know he was 'ere?'

'I heard the dog,' said Sam, 'and it sounded odd, not like normal. I looked over the fence and saw him. Then I went across to Mr Jones, number twenty-eight, and called it in.' PC Benson wrote carefully in his notebook. The rain was heavier now, dripping off Benson's helmet. 'Did Mr Jones hear anything?' he asked. Sam shrugged. 'He says not.'

'See anything?'

Sam shook his head. 'You'll have trouble finding anyone round here to tell you anything,' he said.

The throb of a diesel engine came closer and Benson went out into the street to flag down the ambulance. Doors banged, and the ambulance man said, 'Bloody 'ell, hope we can get them nails out.'

It took several more minutes before the nails were carefully pulled out, and the man lowered onto a stretcher, covered with a blanket. Just as they were lifting the stretcher towards the open gate, another figure appeared, tall, in a long macintosh and a brimmed hat pulled down against the rain. Benson nodded his head. 'OK, Benson,' said the man. 'Start at the beginning.'

When Benson pointed at Sam and explained his presence, the tall man held out his hand. 'DC Holmes,' he said. 'Whitehaven police.' He fumbled for his warrant card. Sam looked at it carefully. 'Sam Tognarelli,' he said. 'Postman.' He pointed to the badge on his lapel. 'Not been here long. I was first on scene. Tried not to disturb too much, but I couldn't just leave him there. I gave him some water.'

The ambulance doors banged shut and the sound of the engine reverberated in the quiet street as it pulled away.

'How was he when you found him?' said Holmes, pulling a pad out of his pocket.

'Nailed by his hands to the door. Crucified, but feet on the ground, so he wouldn't have died, unless from shock and cold. Might have been hours before anyone checked. The dog was still alive, but I think it's gone. Blood on its mouth. Could have been kicked. I asked the poor bugger what happened, who did it, but he didn't speak. Apart from the nail wounds his hands look unmarked, and no facial injuries. Doesn't look as if he put up a fight before … you know. Might have known whoever did it, or been threatened. More than one person would need to do this.'

Holmes wrote on his pad, then looked up at Sam curiously.

Benson interrupted. 'No-one's been near us,' he said. 'None of the neighbours. They must've seen summat.'

'Too scared,' said Sam.

'That's the idea,' said DC Holmes. 'Seen this before. Gets people's attention, tells them what to expect if they don't pay up.' He looked at Sam. 'You finish your round. I'll need a full statement, but later will do. You know where the station is, in the town?'

Sam nodded.

'Come down when you're done up here. We'll get the scene-of-crime blokes up here first, so no rush.'

Sam pointed to the marks of his boots on the mud among the weeds. 'That's where I came close to him. I tried to go back the same way, keep disturbance to a minimum. And I used gloves when I opened the gate. Might lift some prints off it. No sign of a hammer – I looked.'

DC Holmes looked carefully at him. 'Sounds as if you know

what you're doing round a crime scene.'

'Should do,' said Sam. 'I was a DC like you once, a while ago.'

Holmes raised his eyebrows. 'Really? Well, well. Tell me more about that later. Come down around noon, OK?'

Sam picked up the heavy bag with difficulty and eased it back onto his shoulder. He was suddenly very tired, but didn't want to show any sign of it to the detective. Yet again he felt the tug of fear and guilt that had plagued him since he had walked away from that bastard Cardine's threats. He remembered Inspector Cardine cornering him, at a funeral for God's sake, and then that brief meeting in his office. 'Resign or go back to uniform and be shunned'. That had been the only choice on offer. Sam knew he could have fought it, but he was exhausted and depressed and he'd taken the easy way out.

Judith. Sam thought about Judith too as he trudged the familiar round for the next couple of hours. He thought of her pale face, and the long auburn curls that surrounded it. He still wasn't sure about her. Maybe she was like Christine during their short marriage, who would say one thing, but do something else.

The inside of Whitehaven police station was depressingly familiar, smelling of cigarette smoke, wet clothes and disinfectant. Sam had left his cap and coat at the sorting office, but he still wore the shirt and tie, tweed jacket and grey trousers that had been his normal work clothes since he had graduated from the blue police uniform into plain clothes three years before. There was a mirror on the wall of the reception area and he checked his hair, smoothing it down with his hand. No sign of the curls, or the beard from five weeks ago. Sometimes he looked like his father, older than his thirty years. Today he looked too young to be taken seriously, and too short to be a real policeman. His height, just a fraction over the minimum required for the force, had always bothered him. Over the past year he'd got fit and he liked the depth and strength of his shoulders, which compensated for his short legs.

Despite the nickname of Nelly that had haunted him since school, Sam had no doubts about himself as a man, but plenty about his worth as a policeman. Why else would he feel so ashamed at the prospect that DC Holmes might find out about his past? 'Can't be trusted,' would be the word on the Barrow police grapevine. 'Picky, by the book, a right prig. Shopped his own sergeant. Don't touch him.' Would any of that percolate up the coast? Barrow was in the Lancashire force, and this was Cumbria. Maybe that would protect him, for a while at least.

A door opened behind him, a voice called his name and Sam followed DC Holmes into the familiar CID room full of desks and papers and typewriters. Somewhere a phone rang and rang. Holmes pulled out a chair and Sam sat down.

'So where were you?' Holmes asked.

'Barrow, central,' said Sam. 'Not for long. Before that in Chorley.'

'Barrow hooked up with Lancashire didn't it?' said Holmes. 'That must've been cosy.'

Sam smiled. 'They all hated it,' he said. 'And I was the new boy. I took the training seriously, by the book. I didn't like them and they didn't like me.'

'Nice,' said Holmes. 'That why you quit?'

Sam looked at him. The phone began to ring again. 'Had trouble with my sergeant,' he said after a pause. 'He pushed off to a job in Hong Kong, but the DI said they'd never let me make sergeant.'

'You did the exams?'

Sam nodded. 'Fat lot of good it does if your face doesn't fit. And mine didn't. And there were some other problems too. Anyway, I quit, over a year ago.'

'Big step,' said Holmes. 'Any regrets?'

Sam looked away. 'Some. But maybe I needed a break.'

'And now you end up falling over a body. Just like old times.'

'How is the bloke? Do you know who he is?'

Holmes looked down at the notes on the messy desk. 'Arthur James Paling' he read. 'Aged 43, unemployed. Lived alone. House is a tip. Rotting food in the kitchen, not much furniture. There was a wife apparently, but long gone. He'll survive now they've warmed him up, got some fluids into him. Nasty wounds in his hands, possibly some nerve damage. His embroidery days may be over.'

Sam wanted to smile, but Holmes didn't look up. Sam felt the man didn't trust him. Why should he? 'Did you get anything out of the neighbours?'

'Not a thing,' said Holmes. 'Heard nothing, saw nothing. That's what happens when you nail people to doors. Shuts everyone up very nicely, but the word gets around anyway. There'll be a few on the estate paying their debts this week, any way they can. Thefts will go up. Cars, bikes, anything that's not nailed down.' He hesitated. 'Sorry. Figure of speech.'

'Any prints?' asked Sam.

'Nothing on the gate, and the rain hasn't helped. We could see your boot prints, but just a lot of mud and mess around the body. Dog was just alive, it's gone to a vet. Was it you who reckoned it'd been kicked? Looks like internal injuries.'

'How long had they been out there?'

Rob Holmes shrugged. 'Hospital said he wouldn't have lasted much longer. Shock and hypothermia. It was wet but not that cold last night. Maybe early hours of the morning.'

'Do you think you'll get him to talk?'

'Doubt it. That's how it works. Not worth killing the guy or they'd never get their money back, but there are worse things than being killed quickly. Poor bastard knows they'll come back, and if he talks it'll be worse, or they'll go after other people, anyone he cares about.'

'How did he get in such a mess?'

'Betting, probably, dogs, horses, football, cards. Punters lose more than they afford, can't pay, then the debt gets sold on to people who make a living out of getting the money, fair means or foul. Happens all the time.'

'Did you say you'd seen this crucifixion thing before?'

'Gang in Workington with links to a Glasgow mob. Some of the enforcers come from Northern Ireland, but they have different MOs, not like this. They're real psychos up in Glasgow. All sorts going on that seems to be leaking down to here, God help us.' He turned to a fresh page of a large notebook. 'OK, I'll take a proper statement, so let's start at the beginning.

Sam walked home from the police station later, wishing he could spend the next day helping to track down Arthur Paling's assailants, rather than trudging around streets still numbed by violence. He was thinking about Cardine too … and then, Judith's hair.

CHAPTER 3

The adrenalin of the morning had worn off, leaving Sam empty and low, and the prospect of another evening in his drab lodgings did nothing to cheer him up. He had three rooms on the first floor of a narrow terraced house on a steep hill that ran down towards Whitehaven harbour. From his bedroom at the front of the house he could catch just a glimpse of the sea, but the room was noisy with traffic rumbling past. He had a second room at the back that caught the morning sun, with enough space for a tiny table and a couple of gas rings, and the bathroom and toilet completed the arrangement. It was enough, just. There was money in his bank account from years of living frugally, but he'd never wanted to spend much money on himself.

He pulled a chair away from the table in the kitchen and sat down, closing his eyes. The image of the spread-eagled man with blood-streaked hands sat stubbornly in his head, refusing to move. He stood up, grabbed his wallet and a bag and set off down the hill towards the shops. An hour later he was back, refreshed by the wind in his face off the sea and the brisk walk back up the hill, but still feeling as if his life had stalled.

Christine's leaving had set him back, but that was three years ago. Surely he shouldn't still be fretting about her going as she did, taking every stick of furniture with her. It was the shock of that day he couldn't shake off. Maybe that was one reason why he just walked away from the Barrow job when Inspector Cardine gave him the ultimatum. Young Sam would have fought back, but this older, anxious Sam had given up. Judith had been disappointed in him, he was sure of that, although she hadn't said so. And Elspeth, too. She thought he'd given up too easily. Maybe he had, but it was done now.

It wasn't being on his own that made him feel bad, but the sense that there was nothing ahead of him.

Food might help. He made himself a corned beef sandwich and a mug of tea and leafed through the local paper. More adverts for engineers to work in Libya: £300 a month. Good money, and it sounded exotic, like joining the French Foreign Legion, but he didn't have the skills. Further down the same page was another advert. Cumbria Constabulary was looking for recruits, minimum height five foot eight – he knew that – salary £1300. Then it said, 'Every rank in the police, and right to the top, is open to you. Promotion is by ability and experience alone.' Sam put the paper down and snorted in disgust. That's how it should be, but not how it was. He knew he'd been a good DC, but that counted for nothing when the people you reported to were just looking after themselves and their cronies.

Judith's birthday card caught his eye from its place on the shelf. He'd rung the house in St Bees and spoken to her, but it had been stilted and awkward. He'd thanked her for the card and told her about the new job, but she'd shown little interest and it had made him nervous. He couldn't tell what she was thinking. Three weeks had passed since then, and the uncertainty was weighing heavily on his mind. He had to do something. It was nearly four o'clock. There were plenty of trains going south to St Bees. If he left now, he could claim he'd just come down for a walk on the beach, or up to the lighthouse on a fine evening. At least it was something to do, better than sitting here, feeling sorry for himself.

When the door of the Pharaohs' house in Beach Road opened Sam wasn't expecting to see Judith, and he stepped back. She looked at him, her head on one side. He looked for a smile, but didn't see one. 'Good heavens,' she said. 'What are you doing here?'

'Well, it's a lovely evening,' he said as innocently as he could, 'and I fancied a walk on the beach, or up to the Head.'

Behind her Vince appeared at the bend in the stairs. 'Sam?' he called out. 'Is that you?' Vince pushed his sister to one side and stretched for Sam's hand. 'Know that voice anywhere,' he said. 'How's it going, Mr Postman? Come in, come in.' Sam noticed that Vince's eyes seemed just the same, open but blank. Since his childhood accident Vince had seen little except light and shade, but it never seemed to hold him back.

Vince pulled Sam up the step and past Judith into the hall. 'It's Sam,' he called out, as a middle-aged woman in an apron appeared in the doorway at the end of the passage. Judith's mother Maggie had the same red hair as her daughter, but with grey strands in it now. Her welcome was less enthusiastic. 'Well,' she said, wiping her hands on the apron, 'You're a stranger. Stop hanging on to him, Vince. Front room.'

Sam was steered into the front room. Not a good sign, he thought. The front room was hardly used by the family, just by visitors; he was being put in his place. Judith followed them into the room and leaned against the doorframe. Sam glanced at her, but she didn't look back at him.

'Well then, Sam,' said Maggie, taking charge of the occasion. 'What's brought you down here to see us? John's not back yet, but he won't be long. You can wait, if it's him you want.'

Sam looked up, wondering how to explain himself. He'd come to the house before, just after he'd moved to White-haven, but Judith hadn't been there, and he'd pretended that it was just a social call. 'No special reason,' he said. 'It's such a lovely evening, and I fancied a walk. Won't be dark for hours yet. And I wanted to see you all, of course,' he added. 'It's been a few weeks, hasn't it?'

'Ages,' said Vince. 'You came to see us that Sunday, before you started the new job. How long ago was that?'

'Three weeks ago, middle of April' said Sam. 'Taken me a while to get used to the hours as a postman. Early starts, early finish. Not much evening when you have to get up in the middle of the night.'

'Good steady job, though,' said Maggie. Sam noticed she was still wearing her apron; if he'd been really welcome she would have taken it off. 'Judith's in a good job too, aren't you, pet?' Maggie went on. 'Plenty to do at Sellafield these days, but none of those silly hours like at that dreadful *Furness News*. She needed rest and routine after all that ... all that carry-on, and Sellafield's the perfect job. Well paid, too, for a girl. Nearly a year now, isn't it Judith? She's doing ever so well.'

Judith stood away from the wall. 'Mum's a great believer in routines,' she said. 'Trouble is, they drive me round the bend.'

'Judith!' said Maggie. 'That job's been a godsend for you.' She turned back to Sam. 'If she'd stuck at university she could have been a teacher by now, good pay, long holidays, but you know what she's like. Me and my mother never had those chances.'

'I'll come for a walk with you,' said Judith suddenly. 'And he could stay for supper, couldn't he, Mum?'

Maggie sniffed and took a handkerchief from the pocket of

her apron. 'I expect there'll be enough for six.'

'Six?' said Sam.

'Gran's here now,' said Vince. 'Getting pretty crowded.'

'I'll tell Sam all the news,' said Judith. 'We won't be long. Supper at half past six? We'll be back by then.'

Nothing else was said until they had closed the gate and turned towards the beach. Judith caught his arm and turned him towards her. 'Let me look at you. They said you looked the same, but I think you're different. You look thinner, and you've caught the sun.'

'The wind, more like,' he said. 'I've been working outdoors a lot of the time.'

'Vince told me what you've been up to, working on a building site, plastering. I didn't know you could do all those things.'

'Picked up some stuff in the army, and learned the rest on the job.'

'Funny, isn't it,' she said. 'You think you know someone, but you don't. It's hard to imagine you doing all that. Dad was funny about it. I think he envies you.'

'He was a climber, wasn't he?'

'And now he's a pillar of the community.' She smiled. 'Did you have a good time, really?'

He shrugged. 'Some of it was pretty uncomfortable. The money was good.'

'Well, you've had more fun than me.' She turned away and held her hands up to her face. 'God, Sam, I don't think I can stand it much longer. You know what Mum's like. All she cares about is me having a safe respectable job, or better still getting married and having babies. I'm thirty already and it's getting worse. I could write the script. And now Gran's moved in, I'm banished to the boxroom in the attic. Only just enough space for a bed, skylight instead of a window. I'll go crazy.'

'How is Violet?' said Sam, trying to stem the torrent of Judith's frustration.

'Old, and dotty,' said Judith. 'She's had a hard life, I know that, but she and Mum are so alike, it feels like they're ganging up on us. I know Vince feels it, too.'

'Didn't your brother Frank move in to look after her?'

'Yes, but he didn't look after her really, more the other way round.'

'Not sure I ever met him.'

'He was never here much when you were around. And he's not at home in West Row much either apparently. I reckon he was staying out just to avoid her, and she was on her own too much. She was talking to the photos on the wall, wandering around at night. Mrs Barstow, the old lady next door, she tried her best, but she's getting on a bit, too.'

'When did Violet move here?'

'About two weeks ago, not long after you were here last. That put the lid on it for me, actually. I have to get out. The job's tedious as ever, and I really don't like working so close to my dad. He's OK about it, but it feels like I've never grown up.' She turned to Sam. 'Am I moaning a lot?'

He laughed. 'Yes,' he said. 'Come on, we'll see how far up the cliffs we can get before we have to turn back.'

There was a wooden bench by the path at the top, looking out over the shining sea below. Judith and Sam sat side by side, watching the ceaseless movement of birds and waves.

'How are you, anyway?' she asked. 'How's the new job?'

'Deadly, most of the time. Doing the round is all right, but I'd never thought about being in the sorting office and that's pretty awful. All those weeks on strike and then they went back for a deal that nobody wanted. The new boys like me keep our heads down, but the old fellers just moan all the time.'

'Sounds like the Barrow police,' she said. 'That wasn't exactly a bed of roses, was it?'

'True, and I got dumped in the nettles at the end.'

Judith was quiet for a while. 'I know it's a long time ago now, but we've never really talked about it. You didn't really have to leave, did you? You could have stayed. After all we'd been through, why did you just decide to pack it in?'

Sam looked down at his hands. 'I've thought about that a lot this past year,' he said. 'It just felt as if there was no point fighting any longer. You and I knew what was happening at Montgomery House, but no one would believe us. None of the boys would give evidence, and Iris Robinson convinced herself everything was fine. Captain Edwards was still in charge and would never admit any wrongdoing, Cardine protected him, and Morrison just did as he was told. When things got difficult they shipped Morrison off to Hong Kong and carried on.'

'Do you remember Doc Hayward?' said Judith. 'It might have been the strain that made him drink.'

'And the drink killed him.' Sam thought about telling Judith about his efforts to contact Ann Hayward, but he decided not to until he had something more to say.

Judith was watching children playing on the beach below. 'Is there nothing we can do?' she said, turning to look at him. Sam shrugged. 'I don't know,' he said. A gull swooped over their heads. Suddenly she stood up, stretching her arms towards the clouds passing close above their heads. 'I've made up my mind, Sam. I'm going to ask for my old job back, at the *News*. The new editor's from Yorkshire, and he's doing OK, apparently. I met Andrew, the young office lad, in Barrow when Mum and I were shopping. Do you remember him? Skelly's still there, apparently, but Andrew says things aren't good. I'm hoping Skelly won't stay much longer and then they'll need someone. That's a proper job, not writing good news press releases about nuclear power. I can't do 'upbeat' any longer, it's exhausting.'

Sam laughed again. He loved the way Judith came straight out with things, even if she did it for effect. 'You wouldn't go back to that flat in Cannon Street, would you? Too many memories, surely.'

'I have a plan,' she said. 'Now that you're up here, do you think your sister Elspeth would have me as a lodger, in your old room? We've been friends a long time, from before you moved in with her. And I could help with Tommy, like you did.'

'Oh,' said Sam. The idea upset him. It was as if the two women had pushed him out.

'Oh what?' Judith asked, looking at him. 'Are you feeling left out? That's how I felt, when they decided to move Gran in, without even asking me and Vince.'

'But she's old and ill by the sound of it,' said Sam. 'It wasn't a choice really, was it?'

'Could be a good thing actually,' said Judith, 'if it makes me get out. And I have to do it, soon.'

'Poor Vince,' said Sam. 'He can't really go anywhere, can he?'

'He's amazing,' said Judith. 'His sight is still bad, but Dad got him a job in his office at Sellafield and he has loads of friends who take him around. He's got a better social life than either of us.'

'You going out much?' Sam ventured.

She smiled. 'Me? I told you, I live like a nun.' She jumped up from the bench. 'Come on. I'm hungry.'

He didn't ask again. They walked back down the steep path

to the beach and home. Sam wanted to tell Judith about his role in the incident on the estate that would be in the news the following day, but he couldn't bring himself to do it. Nor, after the conversation they'd had about giving up, could he tell her about the idea of going back to the police force. That made him sound indecisive as well as pathetic. He would tell her, but only if and when he'd made a definite decision. Going back to Barrow was out of the question anyway.

The smell of dinner in the house made Sam's mouth water. John Pharaoh was in the kitchen putting an extra leaf into the table when Sam and Judith arrived back. He greeted Sam much more warmly than his wife had done. An elderly woman with tight hair, pinched face and large round glasses was sitting in a small armchair in the corner. 'Violet, this is Sam,' said John, loud and slowly. 'He's a friend of Judith's from Barrow.'

Sam leaned down. 'How do you do,' he said. He couldn't for the life of him remember what Violet's surname was.

'Violet McSherry,' said Judith, sensing his hesitation. 'My mum's been married twice, so she's had three surnames. No wonder people get confused about names sometimes.'

John smiled. 'Violet lived in the house in West Row, where I met my Maggie all those years ago. Frank lives there too now. Very handy for working at Marchon. That's the big chemical works, Sam. You can't miss it, huge place on the south end of the town.' He turned back to Violet. 'Frank looked after you well, didn't he, Violet?'

Violet smiled. 'Frank's a good boy,' she said. 'He's always been good to me. Where is he?'

John said patiently, 'He'll be on his way home from work, I expect.'

'Or maybe straight to the pub,' said Judith.

John frowned at her. 'I'm sure we'll see him at the weekend,' he said, patting Violet's hand.

Maggie put a large cottage pie on the table, followed by dishes of red cabbage and carrots, and the family assembled, chairs scraping on the floor.

'Where are you living now?' asked John as he passed the plates round.

'In digs,' said Sam, nodding to assure them all what a good life he had.

'He hates it,' said Judith.

Sam hung his head. 'It's fine,' he said. 'Not as comfortable as living with my sister in Barrow of course, but better than some of the places I stayed in while I was away. And it's close to town. I can see the sea.'

They ate in relative silence for a while. Then John put down his knife and fork and sat back. 'Well now,' he said. 'If you would like to consider this, Sam, I know of a house with a wonderful view of the sea, also close to town, with one current tenant who's quiet and tidy.'

Maggie looked at him. She said nothing, but her eyebrows asked a question.

'I own the house,' said John, 'and I get to choose who lives in it. There's a vacant room there since Violet moved out. What do you think, Sam?'

Judith gasped. 'Sam living at West Row? Are you serious?'

'Why not?' said her father. 'Two single, hard-working young men sharing a house. Sounds pretty sensible to me. Maggie?'

Maggie stared at her husband. 'It's your house, dear,' she said finally. 'You must do what seems right.' Even if I disagree, was the unspoken addendum.

It was still light at nine o'clock when Judith walked with Sam back to the station. 'Will you take Dad's offer?' she asked.

'I'm not sure,' he said. 'What's Frank like? I don't remember him at all.'

'He's seven years younger than me, and I was never that close to him. He was a funny kid, very quiet. I was fairly noisy and Vince was too when he came along. I think Frank felt a bit squeezed between me and Vince. He always claimed that he was the responsible one and Vince and I were spoiled. Could be true, looking back. I just thought he was grumpy. Nothing was ever right for Frank.'

Judith thought a little more, walking along beside Sam, the low sun lighting her hair. 'Vince's accident made it worse. After that he was even more the centre of everyone's attention.'

'So Frank's about twenty-three is he? That's a tough job for a young man, looking after his gran.'

'It's only since Christmas that's she's been going down,' said Judith. 'Before that she kept the house spotless, did all the cooking and Frank's washing, and never asked any questions about where he was. Life of Riley. And it was all free, of course. Dad said it was worth the rent to have Gran in her own home, close to her own church and her friends. We didn't really notice for a while that Gran was going a bit strange. She was still looking after the house but Mum noticed she was mixing up the days, getting confused about money. Nothing serious. Then one day Gran got lost, couldn't find her way back from town to the house she'd lived in most of her life. Mum was really upset, but there was no point getting cross about it. Poor Gran. It was Dad's idea she come and live with us.' She laughed. 'Frank will have to do the housework now Violet's gone,' she said. 'Don't let him dump all that on you.'

'So you think I should take it?' Sam asked.

'You'd be a fool not to,' Judith replied. 'Go down and have a look at it. See what you think. Have a look at Frank, too, before you decide. He's still grumpy.'

As the northbound train rumbled into the station, Sam turned to Judith, but she was looking the other way. He had so wanted to see her, but it hadn't helped. She was moving on with her life, and he would not be part of it. He should have told her about the crucified man, but now it was too late, and he boarded the train without saying any more. As the train pulled out of the station he looked back, but she was already walking away, her hair blowing in the breeze off the sea.

CHAPTER 4

'I'm not in,' said a low voice through the front door. 'Go away.'

'I've a parcel for you, Mr Jones,' said Sam quietly, bending his head to the letterbox. 'You need to sign for it. Can you open the door, please?'

Silence.

'What sort of parcel?'

'A big one.'

The door opened slightly.

'Can I come in, please?' said Sam. He looked around. The high gate on the house across the street was closed, and there was no one about. The image of what had happened behind that gate flashed in his head. He needed to know more, and Mr Jones could tell him.

Finally, the door opened enough for Sam to ease into the hall, holding the large brown box in his hands and the heavy mailbag on his shoulder.

'Thank you,' he said. 'Actually, Mr Jones, this isn't a real parcel. I needed to speak to you, and this way no one would know.' The old man looked at him open-mouthed. 'The police came, didn't they?' Sam went on quickly. 'And I'm sure you told them you know nothing about what happened across the street. But I think you do, and you might talk to me. And no one would know, do you see?'

'Did the police send you?'

'No, they wouldn't do that. But things like this shouldn't happen, should they, and it'll happen again if we can't find out who would nail a man to his own garage door.'

'You tricked me,' said Bernard Jones.

'Only a little,' said Sam, smiling. 'I think you can tell me something about Mr Paling. He didn't deserve what they did to him. If you can tell me about it I won't need to stay long.'

'I could report you.'

'Yes, but you won't.'

Bernard Jones lowered his eyes and sighed. 'He gambled,' he said. 'Betting shop down the street. He were there all the time. He used to 'ave a car, but that went about three month ago. Said he didn't use it, but I knew he needed money.'

'Any family who might help?'

'Daughter in Cleator. Doreen. Married, kids. Why should she help 'im?'

'Did you ever see anyone come to the door?'

'Couple of weeks since,' said Bernard. They were standing close together in the hall. Bernard's shirt was stained and Sam could smell the dog that was scrabbling against the back room door. Bernard spoke again after some thought. 'Car came, two fellers. It were sunny, not like today. One of 'em had a tattoo right up 'is arm. T'other feller was older. Bald.'

'Do you know them?'

Bernard shook his head.

'Any road,' he went on, 'they 'ammered on't door, and Arthur opened up and they pushed in. Two minutes later they were away again. Noisy.'

'What kind of car was it?'

'Van, no windows at back like. Grey, dirty.' Bernard Jones

raised his head, leaned round Sam and opened the door behind him. 'That's all,' he said. 'Now, bugger off.'

There was still no one in the street when Sam carried on with his round, but that didn't mean no one had seen him. He'd left the empty box wrapped in brown paper at the house, so to all appearances he'd delivered a parcel, and that was Bernard's story if he needed it. He wondered if the old man would report him, but he concluded that he wouldn't. No one on this estate would draw attention to themselves if they could avoid it. What Bernard had told him was more than a policeman on the doorstep would ever have got. Sam went over the information again in his head. He liked writing everything down, but he would remember this time.

At the end of the day he would walk down to the police station, or better still call Rob Holmes and meet him somewhere else. It wasn't much information, but better than nothing, and he thought Rob would be pleased. Sam stopped as the thought struck him. He'd tricked his way into that man's house, and it wasn't about truth and justice, was it? It was about impressing Rob Holmes. Or Judith. The pleasure he'd felt about getting the information drained away.

The other plan for the day suddenly looked depressing, too. He didn't much like his current digs, but he didn't want to move into John Pharaoh's house in West Row and feel beholden to him, or become a cosy house-mate for a grumpy young man he'd never even met. Why should he? He liked his own company. He could make his own decisions about where to live. If it didn't suit Judith or her family, so be it. And anyway Judith wanted to go back to Barrow, so the distance might help him forget about her.

Released from work, he went home first and called the police station from the phone box near the sorting office.

DC Holmes was out, he was told, but had to be back by five o'clock so Sam might catch him then.

Sam felt restless. Maybe he could kill time before then and have a look at the Pharaohs' house in West Row. It meant walking down into town, round by the harbour and then up the steep steps to Kells, but the day was warm and walking without the heavy bag was a pleasure. He had a rough idea where he was going, to an old area of housing built for the pit workers. Like much of Whitehaven it was laid out neatly in squares. The High Road formed the east side of the square, with North, South and West Row the other three sides and Middle Row across the centre. Sam realised that West Row would be the side overlooking the sea, but he was still unprepared for the scope and beauty of the view that opened up as he walked down the hill from the main road.

The Irish Sea and the Solway Firth lay before him, winking in the afternoon sun. Across the firth were the low hills of Galloway, and beyond them, towards the horizon, more blue shapes of the Scottish coastline further to the west. Below the cobbles of West Row were narrow gardens, some with vegetables and a few windblown flowers. Beyond the end of the gardens a field sloped down to the edge of the cliff above Saltom Bay. In the winter it would be wild, but now, in the softness of early summer, it took his breath away.

It occurred to him that he didn't know the number of Violet's house. A woman was coming down the road with a child and Sam walked across.

'Excuse me, missus,' he said. 'Do you know which house is the McSherrys, Violet McSherry?'

The woman pointed to the centre of the row. 'Twenty-three,' she said, 'that's Violet's. But she's not there now, tha' knows. Gone to live with 'er daughter, St Bees.'

'Yes,' said Sam, 'I saw her there yesterday.'

'All right, is she?' asked the woman. 'Tell 'er Ivy was asking after 'er.'

'I will,' said Sam. 'Have you seen Frank around today?'

'Works at Marchon,' she said, pointing towards the south. 'They chuck out around four. He should be back after that.'

The child tugged at her arm.

'Have to go,' said the woman. 'See you later.'

Sam stood staring out across the water for a few minutes before he walked down to number 23. The house looked solid. It would have to be, to withstand the force of the wind up here when a storm came in off the sea. And no traffic, he realised, apart from the few cars of people who lived here. If it was windy, he might be able to hear the waves on the beach far below. Compared to the dingy rooms he had now, this place was heaven. If he moved, it would be because he wanted to be here, not to please anyone else or to do Frank's housework.

He found his notebook and pencil in the back pocket of his trousers, and wrote a brief note: *Can you contact me about renting your spare room? Your dad suggested it.* He added his name and the phone number at his digs and pushed it through the letterbox. Making sure he wasn't noticed, Sam also peered into the front window, shielding the light so he could see more clearly. It was a small square room, with two easy chairs and a television and not much else. Sparse, but that was OK. The bedrooms would be small, too. He guessed that Violet would have had a front bedroom, so that might be his. What a view to wake to every morning – it made his heart lift just to think about it. The air was warm and still and smelled of the sea. Sam walked back into town with a lighter step.

The conversation with Rob Holmes later in the day,

however, left him puzzled and frustrated. They met for a pint at a pub near the Castle around six, and Rob seemed distracted and annoyed right from the start.

'You did what?' was his first response when Sam told him how he'd managed to get into Bernard Jones' house. 'Isn't there some code of conduct for postmen? You can't just con your way into people's houses with fake parcels.'

'Let me worry about that,' said Sam, anxious to offer the information he was sure Rob wouldn't have. 'Jones told me there'd been a van outside, and two men banging on Paley's door a couple of weeks ago.'

'So?' Rob said, not looking up from his pint.

'So I thought you'd be interested. These could be the same blokes who nailed him up.'

'Maybe, maybe not.'

Sam ploughed on. 'Well, of the two blokes, one was older and bald, and the other had a tattoo right up his arm.'

'Which arm?'

Sam shrugged. 'Does it matter?'

Rob put down his pint and looked up. 'Look, Sam,' he said. 'I can see you're missing the police work, but this Miss Marple stuff isn't going to help. Two blokes, one bald, one with a tattoo. Could fit dozens of villains round here. In an old van, I suppose.'

'Yes, and it was grey,' said Sam quickly. 'See I told you, they'll be on your books somewhere.'

'A wild guess,' said Rob. 'Paling isn't talking, but he might in the end and that's going to be information we need, not some old bloke telling you what you want to hear.'

'But why would he lie?' said Sam. He couldn't understand why Rob was reacting like this.

'Any number of reasons. You're new round here. Old feuds,

stuff going back years. People who have nothing turn on each other. You're trying to help, but it doesn't, so leave it alone. I told you before, I do things by the book. So you do your job and I'll do mine. OK?'

Sam stared into his pint.

'Right?' said Rob. 'Now I'm off. Haven't seen my kids for days.'

Sam sat alone on the bench, deflated and confused. He either had to be a policeman or forget it. Clearly nothing in between was going to work.

He'd been looking forward to the chance of a pint with someone he could talk to, but that wasn't going to happen and the evening stretched ahead of him. Just gone six. If he headed back up to West Row, he might just catch Frank Pharaoh at home and check with him about the room. Something today had to go better than this, and the prospect of watching the evening sun sink towards the Irish Sea was enough to make him move.

There was no indication that anyone was home at 23, West Row, but Sam knocked on the door hoping that the walk wouldn't be in vain. Out of the corner of his eye, he saw the edge of the curtain in the front room twitch. He knocked again. Behind the door, just inches away, a voice said 'Who is it?'

'Sam Tognarelli,' Sam called back. 'I left you a note.'

The door opened a little and a young man looked round. Then he opened the door further and checked up and down the street. 'On your own?' he said.

'Yes,' said Sam. 'I just walked up from town. Thought I might catch you and save a phone call.'

'Come in,' said the young man, turning back into the hall.

He walked ahead of Sam into the front room. Evening sun filled the small space, and dust hung in the air. He gestured towards one of the armchairs Sam had noticed earlier, and sat down, wary, on the edge of the seat. Sam noticed his long fingers, the nails bitten down. His face was quite long too, with clear grey eyes and a sharp nose. Brown curly hair gleamed in the orange light. Sam was struck by how handsome the man was. From all he'd heard about Frank, he hadn't expected that.

'I got the note,' said Frank. He stretched forward and shook Sam's hand. 'I'm Frank Pharaoh, but you've probably worked that out.'

'Yes,' said Sam. 'I came up earlier and one of your neighbours told me which house it is.'

'Who told you?' Frank's question was sharp.

'A woman. I think she said her name was Ivy. She had a child.'

'Oh, aye,' said Frank. 'She's OK.' He looked at Sam, squinting against the light. 'So Dad suggested you might have Gran's old room?'

'I was at their house for supper yesterday, and John mentioned it. I might have said something about looking for a place. I've got digs up near St John's but it's noisy. I'm a postman. No car, so I walk to the sorting office. That would be OK from here.'

'Aye, useful being close to things,' said Frank. 'Not far for me either, Marchon.'

Sam nodded. There was a silence. Frank looked uncomfortable.

'Could I have a look round?' Sam asked.

Frank got up. 'Place is a bit of a tip,' he said. 'Gran did everything, before she, you know... All the cleaning, washing. I got used to it. Now it's down to me, and I've been busy.'

'Long hours?'

'Aye, and another job, too, behind bar at the Legion. I'm not here much.'

'Suits me,' said Sam. 'I like my own company, right enough. Early starts, early finish. I can help with stuff round the house if you like.'

Frank smiled for the first time and his face lit up like a boy's. Maybe he was grumpy with Judith, but not all the time. Sam was relieved. Things looked as if they might work out.

Frank was right about the state of the place. In the small kitchen, dirty plates and mugs were piled in the old sink and on every surface. Empty beer bottles stood in a corner and the room smelled stale. Frank picked up some old wrappers off the floor and stuffed them into a half full rubbish sack.

'I've been clearing up a bit,' he said. 'Gran's only been gone a couple of weeks but stuff piles up, you know.'

'Upstairs?' said Sam.

'That's really messy,' said Frank. 'You'll have to give me a chance to clean up. You don't want to move yet, do you?'

'I have to give two weeks' notice if I want my money back,' said Sam. 'Which room would I have upstairs?'

'The bigger one at the front,' said Frank. 'That was Gran's. I'm at the back. There's a bathroom up there, too. Dad had that done when he bought the house. Gran and Grandad rented before that, but Dad, well, he's not short of a bob or two. So he bought the place.'

'Yes, your dad's done well,' said Sam.

'Good with money,' said Frank. 'Lucky for some.' He seemed suddenly agitated. 'I'm due out again shortly,' he said. 'Start work at eight on week nights.'

'Two jobs,' said Sam. 'Must wear you out.'

'Got to be done,' said Frank. 'Bills to pay, you know.'

Sam wondered, but said nothing. None of his business. He

was going to be a tenant, not a nursemaid.

'Talking of money,' said Sam. 'Do I sort out the rent with your dad?'

'Good idea. Nowt to do with me.'

Frank was edging towards the hall, and Sam moved to let him through, taking the hint that Frank wanted him to go.

'I'll walk up with you,' he said, as Frank took his jacket from a peg on the wall and followed him out of the front door.

They walked in silence for a while. As Frank swung his jacket onto his shoulders, Sam caught a sweet smell, not after-shave, a woman's scent.

'Still on your own then?' he asked.

Frank snorted. 'More trouble than they're worth, women,' he said. 'You?'

'All alone,' said Sam. 'Married once, that was enough.'

'Bad one, eh,' said Frank.

'Bad,' Sam agreed.

Frank stopped suddenly. 'Hang on', he said. 'Are you the copper that our Judith was mixed up with, that business in Barrow? She was in a right state after that, by all accounts. Our mum and gran talked about it all the bloody time.'

'Yes, that was me.' They were walking up North Row now and Sam noticed that Frank was slower, and breathing hard. Too much smoking probably, while Sam was fit from his daily round with the mailbag.

'So you were a copper,' Frank said.

'Detective,' said Sam. He expected further comment, but there was none.

When they parted, Sam watched Frank walking along the High Road towards the Legion, his hands pushed into his pockets, his long back bent. Every instinct told Sam that Frank was troubled, probably by the woman whose perfume was on his jacket. She must have expensive habits, thought Sam, to make her boyfriend need two jobs.

CHAPTER 5

Judith waited until Maggie and Violet had gone out before she picked up the phone and dialled the familiar Barrow number. '*Furness News*,' said Hattie Sim's sing-song voice. 'Can I help?'

'Hattie, it's Judith, can you talk?'

'Judith!' squealed Hattie. 'Where are you? Andrew said he'd seen you. Are you coming back?'

'Can you keep it down? I don't want people to know I'm around, not yet at least. Just tell me what's happening, if you can.'

There was a pause. Judith could see Hattie in her mind's eye, standing up to look over the low partition that divided her space from the rest of the office.

'Andrew's out, Ed Cunningham's at a meeting and the editor's in his office with Bill Skelly, and the door's closed, so we're OK.'

'Bill still there?'

'Not for much longer,' Hattie was whispering now. 'He's never got on with the new editor and it's mutual. That's probably why the door's closed, but when they start rowing I can hear them anyway.'

'What's the problem?'

'Bill's old school, well you know that, and Mr Springrice

is from away, Yorkshire or somewhere, and they don't work the same way, at all. It was rumbling on all last year and nearly came to a head a few weeks back. Bill managed to wriggle through, but this time I think he's had it.' She lowered her voice even further, and Judith strained to hear. 'I reckon he'll be out any time now.'

'Really?' said Judith. Neither of them spoke for a moment. 'What's he like, the new bloke?' Judith asked. She knew all there was to know about Cunningham the sub-editor, and Andrew was just a junior who kept his head down. 'Clifford Springrice,' Hattie whispered. ' "Call me Cliff",' he says. Yorkshire accent, I can't do it. He's all right with me, very respectful, not roaring and bellowing like Bill.'

'It must have been hard for everybody after – you know.'

'It was a mess,' said Hattie. 'Bill was in charge for a while, just until Cliff arrived. He was terribly shocked by it all, we all were. And you – you were there, Judith, when it happened. It must have been worse for you.'

Judith remembered the feeling of total helplessness, trussed up, watching Thornhill drinking brandy with the gun in his hand. 'I closed my eyes,' she said. 'It was so loud when the gun went off. My ears rang for hours afterwards.'

'But you're all right now, aren't you?'

'Yes, I'm fine now, and going mad with my mum fussing, and the job at Sellafield is so dull, Hattie. I have to get away.'

'Back here?'

'If I can.'

'Hold on, the door's opening,' Hattie whispered, and then her voice changed. 'The editor's just finished a meeting, madam, would you like me to put you through to his office?'

Judith understood, and thought quickly. 'Yes, please.'

There was a pause before a new voice came down the

phone. 'Cliff Springrice here,' it said. 'I didn't catch the name?'

'It's Judith Pharaoh, Mr Springrice,' said Judith, as brightly as she could muster. 'I used to work for the *News*, a year or two ago.'

A pause. 'Miss Pharaoh, good heavens. What can I do for you?'

The following day, Judith left the St Bees house early. Working part-time meant she could take the day off, and she told her mother only that she was going down to Barrow to see Elspeth and Tommy, and would be back in the evening. She'd taken care with her appearance, but Maggie always got dressed up to go anywhere, and approved when she noticed Judith in a skirt and heels rather than the jeans she usually wore at home. 'You should put your hair up like that more often, dear,' she commented as Judith left the breakfast table and headed for the train.

Just thinking about a proper job in journalism and moving back to Barrow made Judith both nervous and excited, as if she were leaving home for the first time.

When she walked into the familiar *Furness News* office, the first thing that hit her was the cigarette smoke. No one at her home in St Bees smoked now that Frank had left, and she was unprepared for the bitterness of the smell, and the way the air was thickened by it. Ed Cunningham, the sub-editor, smoked almost continuously in the small cubbyhole he liked to call his 'office', and which Judith had learned to keep out of. When she first started work at the paper, his lewdness and straying hands had been a constant irritation.

Andrew's head went up as Judith walked in, and he gave her the same incongruous thumbs-up gesture that sufficed for all occasions. Hattie was at her most formal: 'The editor's expecting you, Miss Pharaoh,' she announced, guiding Judith unnecessarily towards the familiar door at the far end of the room.

In the editor's office, Clifford Springrice was on his feet and round the desk to greet Judith, even before she'd closed the door behind her. His handshake was firm and he propelled her towards one of the two chairs that faced each other. Judith was interested to see that he chose to sit next to her, not behind the desk as Thornhill had always done when he wasn't standing, looking forlornly out of the window.

'Very good to meet you after all this time,' said Mr Spring-rice, looking directly at Judith. 'I've heard so much about you.'

She noticed that the smile and the eyes didn't quite reflect each other.

'All good, I hope,' she said. She was determined to behave as if nothing untoward had happened, thankful that Thornhill had blown his brains out at his home, not here in this office.

'Of course,' he smiled. 'It took determination and courage to do what you did, whatever the final outcome.'

What does he mean by that, she wondered. 'Yes,' she said, 'I was a bit shaken up for a while, but it's a long time ago now, and I think I'm ready to do a real job again, not the magazine stuff they were giving me at Sellafield.'

'Well whatever you did there, they think highly of you,' he said. 'I called your boss there, Mr…' he checked a pad on the desk beside him, 'Mr Simpson, and he was very pleased with your work. I believe you'd mentioned to him that you wanted to get back into "proper" journalism again?'

'I didn't put it quite like that,' said Judith. She wondered what old Simpson had actually said about her.

Cliff Springrice looked her. 'Well, this is very timely,' he said slowly. 'We may have a vacancy quite soon, as it happens. You remember Bill Skelly, of course?'

'Of course.'

'Well, he and I agree that it's time for him to move on. His wife's been poorly for a while, and …well, he's decided to leave at the end of the week.'

'Ah,' said Judith. The man knew how to pick his words carefully.

'And so all this is very timely,' Cliff continued quietly, with the unmistakable vowels of West Yorkshire. 'Would you consider replacing Bill, I wonder? Bring some fresh thinking to the job?'

Judith waited. The conversation with Hattie had alerted her to the possibility, but now she had to control her excitement and think about how it would be to work with the man she was looking at. 'There'd need to be at least one other reporter,' she said finally. 'Is Andrew ready to take that job on?'

'I'm prepared to give him a trial period,' said Cliff, smiling again. 'We'd have to see how it worked out, you and I.'

This time she turned her attention to the window, determined not to sound too eager. 'And pay?' she asked.

'We'll talk about that too. You have less experience than Skelly of course, but I'm sure we can find an agreement.'

It was enough. Judith sat up straight in her chair and said, 'Well, Mr Springrice, subject to that conversation, I'd be happy to accept your offer. When did you have in mind for me to start?'

'Monday next?' he said.

Judith's heart bumped in her chest. 'If we can work out the details by the end of the week, that would be fine. I'm sure that Mr Simpson would be prepared to let me go.' And he knows who my dad is, she thought, which would definitely help.

Outside in the street, her heart still pounding, Judith checked the time. It was over an hour before Elspeth would be back from school for lunch, and just time to check around the shops for a suitable outfit for the paper's first female chief reporter. She knew how Bill Skelly would react, and she didn't care. Cunningham would mutter about women taking over the world, but he could sod off, too. There was one person who would support her: Elspeth was Sam's half sister and she and Judith had always encouraged each other, even when things with Sam had been difficult.

An hour later, Judith and Elspeth hugged on the doorstep of the terraced house in Roose, twenty minutes walk from the *News* office in the centre of town. Over tea, and cheese on toast, Judith recounted her meeting with Springrice and admitted how much she wanted the job, and her relief that the offer had been made. 'Chief Reporter, Elspeth,' she said laughing. 'Me!' Judith hadn't even had to ask about taking Sam's old room before Elspeth asked if she would consider it.

'You'll have your own place soon,' she said, 'but could you live here for a bit, while you settle back in? Tommy and I would love it.'

'So would I,' said Judith, delighted. 'Thought you'd never ask!'

Judith stayed at the house while Elspeth went back to school for the afternoon. Sam had taken some of the furniture with him to Whitehaven, and Judith made a list of things that would need sorting out – curtains, cushions, bedding, a desk and her typewriter. None of that took very long, and she decided to pass the time before Elspeth's return by taking a bus out to Rampside to watch the tide for a while.

It was a mistake. She wasn't prepared for the panic that suddenly welled up from nowhere. Just there, out on the sands in the fog and cold she'd tried and failed to save a man's life and almost lost her own. And up on the hill behind her was the house where she'd come close to death again. Only the brandy and the shock of his wife's betrayal had made Alan Thornhill turn the gun on himself, not her. For a week or two she'd held it together, but then the world had crashed and sent her home to be cared for by her anxious family like a sick child. She felt the wind of the incoming tide on her face and let the tears creep down.

'Judy!' Tommy shouted as he burst into the kitchen an hour later and discovered her nursing a cup of tea. Only Tommy ever called her that. Judith managed to smile and pull him into her arms, feeling the boy's warmth. When Tommy pulled away finally and went to watch his children's programme on the TV in the other room, Elspeth put an arm round Judith's shoulder. 'I wondered if the memory might affect you,' she said.

Judith sniffed. 'It did. I went out to the shore at Rampside and it all came back. I couldn't do anything, just stood by the side of the road and cried. I'll be all right in a minute. Seeing Tommy helps, brings me back to the here and now.'

'He's a joy,' said Elspeth. 'Do you want more tea, or something stronger?'

'God, no!' Judith smiled. 'Can't start drinking at four o'clock. Tea would be good, thanks.'

For an hour and more the two women talked, while Elspeth moved around the kitchen making a meal for them.

'How's Sam?' said Elspeth.

Judith smiled. 'You know Sam. He soldiers on, but I think

he's unsettled.'

'What about?'

'The new job mostly. I think he wants back into the force but knows it'll be a battle. Whitehaven's well away from here, but rumours travel. And there's the Lodge connections of course. Heaven knows what the men in aprons are saying about him, with Cardine dripping the poison down here.'

'Is Sergeant Morrison back from Hong Kong?'

Judith shook her head. 'No, thank God. He made Sam's life a misery, but he was only acting under orders. It was Cardine at the bottom of it all, and Captain Edwards from Montgomery House behind him. Or maybe Cardine called the shots for all of them. Hard to tell.'

'And they're both still around.'

'Sam tried so hard to get to the truth, but he couldn't get anyone to tell him what was really going on at Montgomery House. He thought that man in Lancaster prison, Bill Noakes, would do it but then he backed off.'

'What about that boy who helped you?'

'Mikey Bennett? I don't know what happened to him. He'll be sixteen or so now, old enough to go out on his own. He could be in trouble already, Borstal or something. They were all scarred by Monty House, one way or another.' Judith closed her eyes. 'And there's still nothing we can do. It rips me up. That's why I can't think about it, and when I do, like this afternoon, I feel the anger coming back. It makes me feel sick.'

Elspeth asked, 'Can you find out more about Monty House, now you've got your job back?'

Judith thought for a while. 'That depends on smiling Mr Springrice. Don't know enough about him yet. He could be in Cardine's pocket, or just unwilling to rock the boat.'

'Or upset the Lodge,' Elspeth added. 'What will you do?'

Again Judith thought about it. 'Get my feet under the desk, then ask a few questions and see what response I get.'

'Does Springrice have to know?'

Judith drew in a breath. 'Carry on digging behind his back, do you mean?'

'It's a big story,' said Elspeth, 'or it could be. The national papers might be interested. Surely any editor would like that?'

'You'd think so, but it could ruin him. A few rumours, that's all it takes in a place like Barrow, stuck out here on the end of a headland. Things fester. They could make life very difficult for him.'

'And for you.'

Judith said no more. The thought of chasing such a big story filled her mind for a while, despite the dangers it might bring.

Chapter 6

'You can't go back there, Judith' said Maggie. 'Tell her, John. She's safe here with us, and at work with you. I should have known something was going on this morning, when you were all dressed up. And not a word to me.'

'I knew what you'd say,' said Judith. 'And you're saying it now.'

'Why, Judith?' said her father.

'You know why, Dad. I'm thirty years old, I can't just stay at home like a teenager. This is what I've trained for, and it's a good job, what I've always wanted.'

'You don't need the money,' Maggie's voice was raised in frustration. 'Your father has always looked after us, right from the start. He rescued me from that screen shed. You remember what that was like, Judith? The dirt, and the baths by the fire. We don't need to do that any more.'

'I'm a reporter, Mum, not a screen lass.'

'But your job nearly killed you,' Maggie sat miserably at the table. John put his arm round her shoulders.

'It wasn't the job that nearly killed me, it was those bastards trying to shut me up.'

'Judith! Language!' Maggie shouted at her. 'Tell her, John. Tell her she can't go back. Look what it's doing to her.'

John knelt beside his wife, and stroked her hair, speaking softly to her. 'We raised her to be part of the world, pet, not hide from it. And we can't make her do anything, not at her age. If she wants to work, and she has a job offered, a good job, then she must decide.'

Judith smiled. 'That's it,' she said. She turned to Vince, who was standing by the kitchen door, listening. 'You agree with me, don't you, Vince?'

Vince smiled. 'If I could leave home, I would,' he said. 'I'm OK, but I need to be here, and you don't. You went through hell with that business in Barrow but you're still the same stubborn cow you've always been.' He laughed, 'Give up, Mum, you'll never change her mind.'

Maggie sniffed and blew her nose. 'Well, you're not going back to that flat in Cannon Street.'

'No, I'm not,' said Judith. 'I'm going to live with Elspeth, Sam's sister, and her little boy. It's all fixed. I'll take the first lot of stuff down on Sunday.'

Maggie sniffed again. 'Elspeth's a nice woman, but...' she hesitated.

'But what?' said Judith. 'But she's got a child and no husband, is that what you're worried about? Short memory, Mum. Look at our dad. What about his mam? What about Jessie?'

Maggie sniffed again. John intervened. 'All right, that's enough. Leave it, Judith. You've got a job and a comfortable place to stay, only a train ride away, and we're happy for you. Go and tell your gran about it. Vince and I will help Mum wash up. When do you start, by the way?'

'Monday.'

'Monday!' Maggie looked up. 'How are we going to get everything ready by then?'

The following morning Judith was keen to get out of the house for a while. She rode over to West Row on her Vespa, wondering how Sam and Frank would manage living together. It was a good idea, but she couldn't imagine how such different people would get on. Sam was tidy and well-organised; and Frank? She realised that she probably knew Sam better than she knew her own brother. She'd been away from home since he was just a boy. And after he'd moved into West Row she hadn't seen him at home much either. Granny Violet thought the sun shone out of him, and Maggie always said what a steady young man he was, but Judith wasn't so sure.

As she was parking the scooter, Sam appeared round the corner at the far end of the street, carrying a suitcase. 'Checking up on me, are you?' he called. He dropped the suitcase by the front step and delved in his pocket for the key.

'Give me the key,' she said, 'and you carry the bag. Let's see what the house looks like without Violet doing all the work.'

Sam handed over the key and watched as Judith opened the door.

'Frank,' she called as she went into the narrow hall. 'Are you in?' The house was silent and smelled of dust and old food. Sam followed her in, struggling to navigate the bulky suitcase round the phone hanging on the wall by the front door.

'Which bedroom are you having?' Judith asked.

'The front,' he said. 'Where Violet used to be.'

'Pity it's cloudy today,' said Judith. 'Amazing view from up there.'

'I saw it the first time I came here. It's one of the reasons I said yes to John's offer.'

'The view's not that important, is it?'

'It's the sea that's important. I never really saw it when I was a kid, and Morecambe Bay's different isn't it? This is like the sea at Walney, wild and open. And I love seeing Scotland across the Solway. Reminds me of my dad.'

Judith smiled. 'And how are you going to get on with Frank?'

'OK, I reckon. He keeps to himself, doesn't he, like I do. We're both working. Makes sense to share the space, making meals and such.'

'Where is he, I wonder?' asked Judith. 'And don't get too excited about meals. The kitchen's tiny and Violet did all the cooking. I bet Frank lives on pie and chips.'

Sam took the suitcase upstairs and was hanging up his few clothes in the cupboard in the front bedroom while Judith searched the messy kitchen for a cloth to start cleaning up. In one of the drawers she found various scraps of paper, took a handful to the kitchen table and was trying to piece them together when she heard the front door open. Suddenly Frank was standing in the kitchen doorway, his eyes wide.

'Oh, it's you,' he said. 'What are you doing? Those are private.' He pushed her aside and began gathering the papers with both hands. 'What are you doing here?'

'Well, hello to you, too,' she responded. 'I came to help Sam move in. He's upstairs. I was looking for a cloth, and found this stuff. Are these betting slips?'

Frank snorted. 'You've no idea, have you? It's just rubbish. And none of your business. You should have told me you were coming, not just turned up out of the blue. I've cleared up Violet's room, but not in here.'

'Obviously,' said Judith. 'You're right. Nothing to do with me.'

Sam was standing at the door. Two people in the kitchen

was cramped, and three was impossible. 'I was telling Judith I haven't had time to clear up down here yet,' said Frank, without looking at Sam, 'but I can do it now while you're sorting things out upstairs.'

'I'll make a brew, shall I?' asked Judith.

'No,' said Frank firmly. 'I'll do it. Make yourself useful and go and get some milk.' He pushed the handfuls of paper into his jacket pocket and looked anxiously round the bare room. Sam and Judith exchanged a glance and Sam passed Judith some money. 'Get some biscuits as well,' he said. 'Chocolate ones.'

Judith took the money, unlocked the back door and stepped out, pulling the door closed behind her.

'Judith can be a real pain,' Frank said. 'Ruled the roost when we were kids, and she still treats me as if I was about ten.'

Sam decided to agree with him. 'She's a bit bossy, that's for sure, but that Thornhill business knocked the stuffing out of her for a while.'

'Not that I've noticed,' said Frank. 'Still seems as pushy as she ever was.'

Sam noticed that Frank looked tired and pale. 'Things OK?' he asked.

Frank bridled. 'Fine! Don't you start. Bad enough with the rest of them. Not the same without Gran here to do things, but it's fine. Quieter. I told you, I'm not here much.' He looked around again. 'You've got your own key, right? So you don't need me here. I'll make the tea, clean up in here a bit, then I'm going out. People to see.'

'Fine,' said Sam.

When Judith came back the three of them sat in the front room with their tea and biscuits; nobody said anything much. After a few minutes Frank drained his mug. 'Right, I'm off

57

then,' he announced, and was gone. They heard the front door bang behind him.

'Where's he gone now?' Judith asked Sam. 'Did he say?'

'No idea,' said Sam, 'none of my business – and none of yours either, Judith.'

Judith turned her annoyance on him. 'What's he said?'

'That you treat him like a kid.'

'And you obviously believe that. What makes you an expert on our family all of a sudden?'

Sam held up his hands to ward off the anger. 'I'm going to live here, and it won't help if you're winding him up.'

'Winding him up? He's wound up enough already. I think there were betting slips in one of the drawers. Lots of them.'

'So he has a flutter,' said Sam. 'He's a working bloke, no dependents. He can spend his money how he likes.'

'He lives here rent free, did you know that?' she said. 'OK when he was looking after Gran, but what about now? Dad's always been soft with him. Treats him like the prodigal son. And Gran thinks he's God's gift. Makes me sick to hear her going on about him.'

'He's been good to her. Nothing wrong with that.'

'Oh, leave it,' she said. 'And don't give me all that "honest working man" stuff. He works no harder than anyone else.'

'Two jobs, he told me.'

'Two jobs? Where's the other one?'

'At the Legion, behind the bar.'

'And then he blows it all at the betting shop. Crazy.'

Sam helped himself to another biscuit. 'I can handle him,' he said. 'You'll be back in Barrow and we'll get on fine.'

Judith took the mugs back into the kitchen. 'I thought he said he was going to clear up in here,' she said. 'He looks a mess, don't you think? Never used to have those bags under his eyes. He's only twenty-three. And he's jumpy as hell.'

Sam called back from the front room. 'I asked him if he was OK and he told me to back off. Must have something on his mind. Or maybe he's just tired with doing two jobs.'

'That's what I mean,' said Judith, exasperated. 'He wouldn't need two jobs if he didn't waste money on betting.'

When the phone rang a few minutes later the noise made them both start. 'That's loud,' said Sam. 'Do you want to answer it? It's more your house than mine.'

Judith picked up the receiver. 'Hello?' She listened. 'No, he's just gone out, sorry. Who's calling?' A pause. 'Say that again,' she said, gesturing to Sam to come closer. 'How long? So you've not seen him all week? Are you sure?' She put her hand over the receiver. 'Frank's not been in work all week.' She handed the receiver to Sam. 'You try.'

Sam said, 'I'm Sam, I'm living here with Frank. Did you say he's not been at work all week? Have you tried the Legion?' He waited. 'Hang on, Ron, before you go. Any idea where he might have been? We've just seen him and he didn't mention anything … Well, if you do, can you let me know? Yes, here. Thanks. 'Bye.'

'What's all that about?' he said, putting the receiver back. 'Must be a mistake. Did Frank say anything about work?'

Judith shook her head. 'Did that Ron bloke know where he's been?'

'No, that's why he rang here. Apparently Frank was supposed to report to someone on Friday, and they asked Ron to find out where he is.'

'What should we do?' Judith asked. 'Should we tell Mum and Dad? Feels like telling tales.'

'But what if something's up that we could help with?' said Sam. 'He looks pretty washed out.'

'As if he's been up half the night,' she said. 'Hasn't had a proper wash either, by the smell of him. Granted I haven't seen much of him the past few years, but that's not the Frank I remember.'

'Are you going back to Beach Road now?' Sam asked.

'I only came out to get away from Mum for a few hours. She's stopped crying about me going away, but she still fusses.'

'Let me finish up here and I'll come with you,' said Sam. 'I think they need to know that Frank's gone AWOL from work. Even if none of us can do much about it.'

The sky had cleared when they pulled the front door shut a short while later, and the sun was high in the sky, blurred behind a thin veil of cloud but out to sea it was sparkling bright. Sam stopped and looked, breathing in the salty smell. 'Look at it,' he said. 'Maybe people who live here take all this for granted, but I think it's wonderful. And now I can see this every day, all the different lights and weathers.'

'You're just a romantic, Mr Tognarelli,' said Judith, smiling. 'Must be your Mediterranean heritage coming out.'

Sam climbed on the scooter behind Judith and held on to her jacket. On the way they called in at the Legion, which was filling up with lunchtime drinkers. Sam went to the bar to get them both a drink. Judith saw him ask the barman something, and the man shook his head.

'He hasn't seen Frank either,' Sam said, balancing their drinks on the small table. 'He doesn't work Monday and Tuesday, but he was due in on Wednesday and didn't show up, and they haven't seen him since. He'd better turn up tonight or he'll be in trouble with them, too.'

They drank in silence. In the corner above the bar, the television showed a boxing match that got the drinkers shouting enthusiastically for a few minutes before the jukebox resumed its background thumping.

On their way out, Judith pulled on Sam's arm and crossed the street. 'Down here,' she said. 'We'll try the betting shop. Could be where Frank spends all his time.'

The betting shop was further down the street, between an off-licence and a hairdresser. Judith pushed Sam in ahead of her. The air was blue with cigarette smoke. Three men stood at a high bench that ran down the side of the small room, but no one looked up. Copies of the newspaper racing pages lined the walls, and a curious barking sound began from a speaker high up in one corner. The men turned around to face the speaker, listening intently, imagining the horses thundering round a grassy course, manes flying in a fresh wind, a crowd cheering them on. In the gloom of the betting shop no one spoke.

At the far end of the room was a formica counter and a mesh grille, and behind it a man sat, a cigarette at the corner of his mouth. He looked at Sam and Judith curiously. 'Yes?' he said.

Sam went to the grille. 'We're looking for someone, thought he might be in here.'

The man didn't respond. 'He lives round here,' said Sam. 'Frank Pharaoh, lives in West Row.'

'Not seen 'im,' said the man, lowering his eyes.

Sam tried again. 'When did you last see him?'

The man shrugged. Judith stepped towards the grille. 'He's my brother,' she said.

'Lucky you,' said the man. 'If you don't want anything else, I'm busy.'

Sam turned away, pulling Judith after him. 'Waste of time,' he said. 'Needle in a haystack.'

'They know him,' Judith said.

'They know most people round here I should think. No help to us. Come on.'

When they got back to St Bees and the house in Beach Road, Sam whispered to Judith that they shouldn't say anything until John returned. 'Your mum's upset enough about you going,' he said, 'without worrying about Frank as well.'

Judith busied herself upstairs, sorting out what to take to Barrow the following day, while Sam talked to Vince about football. Despite his sight problems, Vince didn't seem to miss anything. He was the kind of man who'd make a good police collator, Sam thought, able to hold a great deal of information and make connections that could be vital in police work.

Thinking about that made Sam yearn to be back in the force, but the brush-off he was getting from Rob Holmes worried him. Would the police ever have him back?

'Dad's home,' said Vince as John's familiar step sounded in the porch. Sam opened the door. John was surprised to see him.

'I was at West Row,' Sam explained, 'and, well, Judith and I wanted to check something with you.'

'Tea first,' said John. 'Is Judith here too?'

Judith came down the stairs carrying a pile of clothes. 'We need to talk to you, Dad,' she said. Vince followed them into the kitchen, but Sam looked at Judith and shook his head.

'Vince,' said Judith, 'could you take Sandy out back while we talk to Dad?' Vince hesitated, then called the dog, opened the back door and left them alone.

Sam closed the door.

'It's about Frank,' he began. John put the kettle down and looked up, then at Judith. 'He came back while we were there,' Sam went on. 'Seemed a bit distracted, then he went off again.'

'After that, there was a phone call,' Judith picked up the

story. 'Someone called Ron, from Marchon. He said that Frank hasn't been at work all week.'

'Maybe he's been sick,' said John.

'Frank didn't mention anything about missing work,' Judith went on. 'He looks pretty bad, Dad, tired and scruffy. And the place is a tip.'

John put the kettle on the gas and sat down. 'I thought this might happen when Violet moved out,' he said. 'She's done far too much for Frank. Maybe he just can't cope on his own.'

'But why stay off work?'

'And he's not been to his other job either,' Judith added. 'We went and checked.'

'Went where?' John was puzzled. 'What other job?'

'The Legion in Kells,' said Sam. 'They haven't seen him either. He works behind the bar.'

'Since when?' said John. 'And why does he need two jobs?'

'I found a pile of betting slips in the kitchen,' said Judith.

John groaned and rubbed his hands down his face. 'Does your mother know?'

'Not yet, That's why we waited until you got back.'

'Wait here a minute,' said John. They heard him in the hall, on the phone. When he came back he looked more worried than puzzled. 'I know someone who works in Frank's section at Marchon. Apparently they rang West Row a couple of times on Thursday but there was no response. So if Frank was sick, he wasn't at home. Where's he been?'

'He just said he had people to see and went off,' said Sam. 'We had no reason to worry about it, not then.'

John went to the door again and called, 'Vince.'

Vince appeared. 'What's up?'

'Do you know where Frank is?'

Vince shrugged. 'I know where he usually is on a Saturday

night, before he goes down to the Legion.'

'Did you know he was working at the Legion?'

Vince looked surprised. 'Not working, just drinking. He's done that ever since he's been at Marchon. Saturday night starts at one of the pubs in town and ends up at the Legion, so he can walk home.'

'Where in town?'

'The Nelson, or the Three Tuns.'

Sam said, 'The Three Tuns, that's the bikers' pub isn't it? What's Frank doing there?'

'Maybe he likes bikers,' said Vince. 'All that leather and ponytails.'

Sam looked at Judith and raised his eyebrows. 'Are you thinking what I'm thinking?' he asked.

'Probably,' she said. 'Have you got a leather jacket?'

That evening, she was astonished to see that he did.

Chapter 7

They met at the station at eight, when the long May evening was fading but light lingered in the sky to the west. Soon the street lamps would flicker on, announcing that Saturday night had definitely arrived. The streets were already busy, and a steady stream of people came off the northbound train.

Judith noticed Sam standing waiting for her. He looked quite different, more relaxed than usual. 'You're dressed for it,' she said. 'Where did that leather jacket come from?'

Sam shrugged. 'Had it a while. Christine bought it.' Sam rarely mentioned his ex-wife, and regretted it immediately. 'Don't wear it much.'

'You should,' she said. 'Suits you.'

'What've you done to your hair?' he asked.

'Thanks,' she said. 'Great to have a positive response.'

'You know what I mean.' When she teased him, he didn't know how to react. 'It's different. It looks, well, you look, you know, glamorous.'

'Glamorous,' she smiled. 'That's the right word, Sam. What a handsome couple we are to be sure. Where do you want to start?'

Sam asked, 'Have you got a picture of Frank?'

'Yes,' Judith searched in her bag. 'Not the best. Mum took

it last summer, at church.'

'Didn't know Frank went to church.'

'High days and holidays, that's all. For some reason, he liked Father Price. Must have caught that from Gran, and she would push him to go to Mass with her. Anyway, there he is. I've folded it back so it's just him, not Gran as well.'

Sam held the photo towards the light. Frank was wearing a suit, looking young and healthy, smiling, his curly hair blowing round his face.

'Hard to believe that's the same person we saw this morning,' he said. 'What's happened to him?'

'Something drastic. I'm worried about him now. He can't just hide like this. And why did he come back to the house this morning? He must have known we'd find out that he hasn't been to work.'

'Maybe he wants help, but daren't ask for it,' said Judith. She pulled her blue cardigan closer. 'Come on,' she said, taking Sam's arm. 'Let's try the Nelson, it's the nearest. I'm not quite ready for the bikers yet.'

The Nelson was quiet. 'We're too early,' said Sam. 'Serious drinking probably doesn't start for an hour or so yet.'

Judith let Sam buy the drinks; she knew that even when it was quiet she might have trouble getting the bar staff to take any notice of her. They sat in a corner, so that she could see the whole room.

'Anyone you recognise?' Sam asked.

She looked around and shook her head. 'I'm realising how little I know him,' she said. 'I've no idea who his friends are. I might remember a face from the kids he used to hang around with, but I was away most of the time at that boarding school Mum sent me to. I'd see some of his friends in the holidays, but that was ages ago. They grow up.'

'They might remember you,' said Sam.

They sat for a while in silence, listening to Paul McCartney singing 'Let it Be' on the jukebox. 'I wonder why he left the Beatles?' Sam asked. Judith didn't answer. She was watching a group of young men who'd just come into the pub and were standing at the bar. 'The one in the grey jumper,' she whispered to Sam. 'I think he's called Harry.'

'Do you want me to ask him?' said Sam. He felt self-conscious in the leather jacket.

'Wait here,' Judith said, getting up. He watched as she walked over to the bar, and as the young men turned to look at her. 'Hello gorgeous,' said one of them. 'Fancy a drink?' Judith turned towards Sam, and gestured. He saw her ask something of the tallest man in the group, who looked down at her, smiling, and then bent a little closer. 'Judith Pharaoh,' Sam heard him say. 'Well, I never.' Judith's back was still turned, but Sam guessed that she'd asked him about Frank. The young men turned to each other, but no one nodded. They don't know, he thought, although they might want Judith to stay and talk. These men seemed to find conversation so much easier than he did, but maybe that was because they were in a group. He wondered why he'd agreed to this uncomfortable strategy to find someone who might be trying hard to disappear, but how else could he spend Saturday night on the town with Judith?

The music was suddenly louder. The man Judith had called Harry put down his pint and took Judith's arm, pushing her towards a space while the others started to clap in time. Judith was laughing. Sam sat still wondering what to do. Should he get up and claim Judith back? Is that what he would do if they were a proper couple? Mercifully, Judith pulled away, still laughing, and came back to him, patting her hair back into place. 'That was Harry,' she said, picking up her drink. 'He hasn't seen Frank for weeks he said, and his mates haven't either. He's certainly grown up since I last saw him.' She waved across to Harry, who waved back while the young men lowered their voices and laughed.

'They're laughing at us,' said Sam.

'They're all right,' she said, looking at him. 'Do you want to dance?' He shook his head.

Half an hour and another drink later Sam had stopped worrying about tall young men, especially now that Harry and his mates had gone. Saturday night saw many White-haven drinkers progressing round their favourite haunts in an unspoken ritual before ending up at the final destination, chosen for some long-forgotten reason and now enshrined in habit. New groups of drinkers had come in. Judith scoured their faces without seeing anyone worth approaching. Finally Sam said, 'Give me the photo.' He took it and pushed his way to the bar, waiting until the most senior of the bar staff looked up at him. 'Have you seen this bloke around?' Sam said, thrusting the photo across. The man turned it to the light. 'That's Frank, isn't it?'

'Aye' said Sam. 'Frank Pharaoh. Seen him, last week or two?'

The man shook his head. 'Used to come in Saturday nights, early on, but not for a while. Hang on.' He pushed the photo under the nose of another man pulling a pint alongside him, who also shook his head. 'Sorry, mate,' said the barman, returning the photo. 'Can't help. In trouble, is he?'

Sam smiled. 'No trouble,' he said. 'Thanks.'

'Come on,' he said when he got back to Judith at the table by the door. 'Waste of time. Let's try somewhere else.'

Outside they looked up and down the street, lit by sodium lamps now, not the sun. Judith shivered. 'Should have put a jacket on,' she said. 'I'll be OK if we keep moving. Where next?'

Sam smiled. 'Three Tuns and the bikers. I reckon. Are you ready?'

Thank God for the leather jacket, thought Sam as they pushed through the men thronging the pavement outside the Three Tuns and spilling across the street. The tweed jacket he often wore would have stood out in this crowd like a neon sign reading 'off-duty copper' or 'history teacher'. Heads turned as Judith followed him through the open door. Sam felt her holding the back of his jacket as he pushed towards the bar. Here the noise was loud, and Sam caught sight of the small band in the far corner. He changed direction, to the opposite corner where conversation might just be possible, found two spare stools and parked Judith on one while he went to the bar. It was several minutes before he could get back, and noticed that his stool was now occupied by a large man with a ponytail.

Sam hesitated. With a warrant card in his pocket he knew exactly what to do, but now he had to think. Did he try and stake his claim to this woman, as might be expected here, or feign cheerful indifference? The necessary hint of possession was satisfied by leaning right round the man to place Judith's drink on the table in front of her. The man turned his head and Sam caught the whiff of tobacco and beer from a bearded face very close to his own.

'This seat's taken,' said the bearded man. 'Piss off.'

Sam stood up, wishing he was taller. To his surprise Judith stood up too, and leaned towards him. 'Sorry, mate,' she said to the bearded man. 'I'm with him.'

The man turned, looked Sam up and down and laughed. 'Why?' he asked. 'Half pint of piss, isn't he?'

Judith smiled, 'Black belt,' she said, raising her arms to a martial arts stance. 'Low centre of gravity.'

'Fuck you,' said the man, getting up. He was bigger than Sam, but Sam kept his gaze steady until the man turned and disappeared in the direction of the gents. Judith sat down and Sam followed, breathing out with relief as he did so. They looked at each other, and laughed.

'Where did you get that black belt idea from?' he asked.

'Just came to me,' she said. 'Now we have to hope he doesn't want a demonstration.'

Sam had done some judo at the police training college. A voice in his head said, 'Tell her,' but nothing came out of his mouth and the moment passed.

Judith looked over his shoulder and her eyes widened. 'Over there,' she said into Sam's ear. 'He's called Dave, I think. He and Frank were mates at school. I saw him once at Gran's, last year sometime. Stay here.'

Sam watched as Judith approached a man who might have been around Frank's age but looked ten years older, with a gut that spoke of serious drinking. Sam shifted on the stool, aware of the heads turned towards Judith. This time the man's face showed recognition, and he followed Judith back to her seat. Sam got up, 'Sit here, mate,' he said, 'so you can talk.'

This is Dave,' said Judith. 'He's at Marchon, with Frank.'

'I've been at work all week,' said Dave. 'Where the hell is 'e? I called round at his place the other night, no one there.'

'We don't know where he's been,' said Judith. 'We were at West Row this morning and he dropped in for a few minutes and then left again. That was before we knew he'd not been to work.' She hesitated. 'He looked rough, Dave. Is he in trouble? Do you know?'

Dave rubbed his hand down his face. 'He's not right, but

not sure you'd call it trouble. Hang on.' He was swallowed by the crowd for a few minutes and came back with another man. 'This is Jeff,' he said. 'Tell them what you 'eard.'

Jeff looked at Judith. 'You Frank's sister?'

'Judith' she said.

Jeff turned to his friend. 'Should I tell 'er, Dave?'

Dave shrugged. 'She's a big girl, she can stand it.'

'It's a woman, see,' said Jeff. 'Frank's got a woman.'

'What's wrong with that?' asked Judith, trying not to think about Frank with a woman.

'Well she's not a woman like you, love,' he said. 'This one's trouble.'

'What kind of trouble?' Sam asked. He was thinking the worst already, drugs, prostitution.

'Well for a start, she's older. Second, she's married, and third the husband's a problem.'

Sam waited. Judith looked puzzled. 'He's coming out, soon,' said Jeff, lowering his voice. 'How long's 'e been inside, Dave?'

'Two years, thereabouts,' said Dave. 'Got off lightly I reckon. Broke that bloke's arm.'

'Hang on,' Sam said. 'The woman who Frank's been seeing has a husband who's in jail for assault, and he's coming out?'

They nodded. 'Right, and 'e's a big bastard, sorry love, and 'e doesn't bother about 'urting people.'

'Who is this bloke?'

'Shorty,' they answered in unison.

'Shorty what?'

Dave shrugged. 'Just Shorty, That's what they call 'im, allus 'ave.'

'And what's the woman's name?'

'Gloria summat,' said Jeff. 'Don't know 'er name neither. "Gloria," I ask you. She used to sing with a band, years back.

71

Still a looker, mind. Frank's not the only one who's been sniffing around. Shorty'll be busy when he gets out.'

Judith looked up at the two men standing beside her. 'What's he like?' she said. 'I mean Frank, not Shorty. What's Frank like?'

'E's your brother, love, you should know.'

'But I don't,' she said. 'The brother I know lived with his Gran, took her to church, went to work, came home, couple of pints at the Legion of a Saturday. How did he get mixed up with this Gloria? That doesn't sound like my Frank.'

'Well you know nowt, love,' said Dave. 'The Frank we know is a cocky sod, sorry, chucks his money around, loves the gee-gees. Life and soul of every party, our Frank. Met Gloria in 'ere likely, or maybe up Mirehouse near 'er place. He drinks up there sometimes. How long's 'e been seeing Gloria, Jeff?'

'Must be about six months since he got stuck into 'er, sorry, and 'e's changed, 'asn't 'e? Tired all the time.' They both laughed out loud. 'Sorry, but you know, like 'e's out all night. And spending money like water. She likes money, does Gloria.'

Dave looked at Judith. 'Your Frank's gone crackers, love, no offence but 'e 'as. No wonder 'e's shitting himself.' He looked into his glass before draining it and wiping his mouth with the back of his hand.

'How will this Shorty bloke know about Frank if he's been inside for two years?' Sam asked.

'Every nick's full of gossip – 'e's in Haverigg, just down the coast – 'e knows what's going on, no bother. And 'e'll be out pretty soon.'

Sam saw the alarm in Judith's face. 'We'll find out about that,' he said. 'We need to find Frank, quick. Any ideas, lads?'

'Could be with 'er,' said Dave. 'And 'e said summat about working extra, on the side like.'

Judith nodded. 'At the Legion.'

'Nay. Had to be summat that pays more than that.'

'What then? Where?'

Dave shook his head. 'You're family. Ask 'im yourself. Sup up, Jeff, we're off.' He turned round before they got to the door, came back and leaned over to speak into Judith's ear. 'Nowt to do with us, love, and we told you nowt, right?'

Judith clasped her hands together and bit her thumb. 'Oh God,' she said. 'What's he got into, the stupid sod? Angry husbands, moonlighting. And all the time Gran and Mum think he's Mr Dependable. They'd have a fit if they knew all this.'

'Well they're not going to, are they, not until we've tracked him down. We have to keep this to ourselves, Judith.'

'What about Dad?' said Judith. 'He knows a lot of people. We might have to ask him to buy Frank out of something.'

'Not even your dad,' said Sam. 'Not yet. Let me make some enquiries, on the quiet. And you ask Violet, casual like, if she knows where Frank might have been this week. No good pretending he's been at work, but don't make it sound like a big thing. We need to know more about who he hangs around with, and she might know.' He looked at Judith. 'Are you worried about him?'

'Of course, aren't you? And it's bad to find out stuff like this from strangers. "You're family," that's what Dave said. Well, I am family, and I haven't a clue what Frank's been up to. That's awful.'

'He's a grown man,' Sam said. 'He's making his own choices, bad ones by the sound of it. But it's just gossip so far. We need to dig around a bit, see what else we can find out.' He was thinking of how to broach it with Rob Holmes, who clearly didn't want to talk to him. 'You ask Violet about any other friends Frank has, names, where they live. We need to find people who know him better than those two.'

The sour tang of bodies in the pub mingled with another sweeter smell that Sam recognised. He looked around for its source and saw the familiar reefer being passed round a group sitting on the far side of the room, close to the band. 'Come on,' he said to Judith. 'I need to get out before our friend with the ponytail comes back for more conversation.'

She nodded. 'Too hot and smoky for me in here. I must be getting old.' He put his arm round her shoulders and shepherded her towards the open door and into the street. They stood still for a moment, collecting themselves, thinking.

'Don't go home yet,' he said. 'Let's have a look at the sea.'

They walked slowly down towards the harbour side, where the export of Marchon phosphates had all but replaced coal. The quayside was littered with tracks and equipment, while fishing boats sat quietly on flat black water that shimmered with reflected light from the sky. Further out, at the end of the curving sea wall, the lighthouse stood silhouetted against the twilight. In just a few weeks the sunset would reach its most northerly point and start the slow return to the south. They stood for a while, watching, listening to the low rumble of traffic and voices in the streets behind them.

'I still think of him as a boy, but that boy's gone,' said Judith. 'We have to find him, Sam. It would break Mum's heart if anything happened to Frank.'

'We will,' said Sam. 'He's bound to go back to West Row sometime, for clothes, or food, or a place to sleep. If that woman's husband is coming out, she won't want Frank around. And if he has another job, he still has to sleep somewhere. He'll be back, and at least there'll be someone around when he does.'

Judith looked sideways at him. 'You don't need to do this,

you know,' she said. 'It's our problem.'

Her eyes were shining. Sam looked away. 'I can help,' he said. 'I'll walk you back to the station. Will you be OK from there?'

She smiled. 'I think I can manage the walk home at the other end,' she said. 'And I'm going back to Barrow tomorrow afternoon. Elspeth will look after me there, if I need it.'

They waited on the platform together saying nothing more, and Judith shivered in the breeze from the sea. Sam took off his leather jacket and draped it round her shoulders. 'I won't be needing this again for a while,' he said. 'Leave it at Elspeth's. And good luck with going back to work.'

'Thanks,' she said. The train rattled in. He leaned towards her, but Judith turned away, stepped into the carriage and found a seat by the window, raising her hand to him as the train pulled out.

As he walked back to Kells, Sam went over things in his head. It was too early to panic about Frank. He could be anywhere, with this woman Gloria, or another woman. Dave and his mate didn't know much really, just hints and gossip. There were some things he needed to ask about, if he could get Rob Holmes to speak to him over the weekend.

The West Row house was empty, as Sam had thought it would be. No sign that anyone had been there since he went out. He picked up the phone and rang the number that Rob Holmes had given him on that first morning when he'd found the crucified man. He asked for the CID office, and then for Rob by name, but the young woman he spoke to said that DC Holmes wouldn't be in until Monday morning. Sam took a chance. 'Can I ask if you know of a local man known as Shorty?' he said. 'I think he's currently in jail in Haverigg.'

'Who's speaking?' said the young woman.

'My name's Sam Tognarelli. I'm a witness in one of DC Holmes' cases, and this man's name has been mentioned to me.'

A short pause. 'I couldn't give you that information, sir, but I'll give DC Holmes your message and ask him to phone you. Does he have a number for you?'

'Yes, he does, thanks,' said Sam. It was the best he could do, but he doubted Holmes would call him back. Why should he?

Sam put down the phone and stood for a few minutes on the front doorstep, watching the final glow in the sky. Frank was Judith's brother, but she hardly knew him. How could one man have two lives so at odds with each other?

CHAPTER 8

Judith woke with a start, hearing pinpricks of rain on the skylight of her bedroom, under the roof of her parents' house. It was already light, just a few weeks before the longest day, and the dawn came early. No sounds filtered up from the sleeping house below. She lay still, thinking, watching rain-drops stutter down the incline of the glass. She pictured Sam in the leather jacket his wife had bought him. Judith couldn't imagine Sam as a married man, loving a wife, having sex with her, being hurt and betrayed. He seemed so closed down, but sometimes, when she least expected it, he did something that surprised her. She should know him well, after all they'd been through together, but she didn't. Images from the previous night in Whitehaven were sharp in her head, and she went over them, to hold them and remember. The jacket that outlined his shoulders; the way he walked, fluid and easy, moving his hips. Maybe that walk came from his days in the army, or his policeman's boots. She liked it.

Sam was still a surprise, but her brother Frank, Judith realised, was a mystery. All it had taken was a few minutes' conversation with his mates in the pub and her image of her brother fell into fragments. 'Life and soul of the party' one of them had called him, but the abiding memory she had of Frank was his complaints to his mother about Vince teasing him when they were children, clinging to her apron, his face twisted with resentment and blame. Then another image appeared, of Frank standing at the graveside at Grandad's funeral, holding Violet's arm, his gloved hand on hers. Had something happened to him, or had he always had these conflicting sides? And what about the girlfriend they'd mentioned, Gloria? Who was she? Was Frank with her when they all thought he was living quietly at West Row and going to work every day? Maybe men are wired differently, thought Judith. Is it just sex that draws them to unsuitable women, like dogs to a bitch on heat? She shook her head to break the thought.

The creak of a door downstairs caught her ear. It was from her old bedroom, the one she gave up when Violet moved into the house. Then the toilet flushed. Violet was awake. Judith got out of bed, pulled on her dressing gown and went quietly down the steep stairs from the attic. Violet's door was open and Judith knocked on it as softly as she could. Inside Violet was sitting up in bed.

'Do you want tea?' Judith asked.

The old woman nodded and smiled and patted the bedclothes. 'We can have a little talk, pet,' said Violet. Judith held a finger to her lips.

A few minutes later she put the cup and saucer carefully down on the bedside table and perched on the edge of Violet's bed. A wisp of steam from the hot tea rose into the air. Judith walked to the window and drew back the curtains. The sun had already risen and light slanted down, catching the side of Violet's lined face.

'Can I talk to you about Frank?' Judith asked. She wondered how much Violet really knew about his life.

Violet smiled. 'He's a lovely boy,' she said. 'So good to me.'

'Yes,' said Judith. 'He's looked after you well, hasn't he?'

'Always,' said Violet. 'And now there's another nice young man, what's his name again, dear?'

'Sam?' said Judith.

'Yes, Sam. He has another funny name doesn't he? Foreign.'

'Tognarelli,' said Judith, smiling. 'His dad was Italian.'

'He's going to live with Frank, isn't he?' Violet went on. 'That's a good idea. Frank needs company his own age, after being with me all the time.'

'Yes,' said Judith, still trying to decide where to start.

'I've been helping Sam to move in,' she said. 'But Frank doesn't seem to be at home much these days. Sometimes he doesn't come home at night.'

Violet frowned, but said nothing. Judith went on. 'And someone from Marchon said he's not been at work.'

'Not at work?' said Violet. Judith hoped she would keep her voice down. The last thing she wanted was her mother asking questions.

'We thought that maybe he was ill and staying with someone else. But I don't know about his friends. Who might he be with, Gran? Do you know?'

'Not at work?' Violet repeated. 'That's not like him. He was always there, doing overtime, coming in late. Sometimes he was up and away before I woke up.'

'Does he have any friends?' Judith persisted. 'Anyone he might be with?'

Violet shook her head.

'What about a girlfriend, maybe? Does Frank have girl-friends, do you know?'

'Of course he does,' said Violet. 'He's a good-looking boy, isn't he, and he's got a good job. Real catch for someone.'

'Anyone special? Did he ever mention someone called

Gloria? One of his mates said he knows a girl with that name.'

'Gloria?' Violet looked puzzled. Then her face cleared. 'Yes, Gloria,' she said. 'I do remember. It's a funny name for a girl these days isn't it? Gloria, like an old film star.'

'Do you know where she lives?'

Violet looked down. 'Let me think,' she said. Judith watched, wondering about the tumble of half-remembered shreds in her grandmother's mind. 'Was it Mirehouse?' she prompted. Violet looked up. 'That's it,' she said. 'Near St Benedict's. She knows Father Murray.'

'Have you met her?' Judith asked, surprised.

'They'd been somewhere,' said Violet. 'They called in. It was hot and they wanted a drink.' She paused. 'She's older.'

'Older than Frank?'

'But you can't tell these days, can you?' said Violet. She was looking out of the window, and the window in her mind seemed to have clouded over.

Judith waited, sipping her tea and watching her grand-mother. Sometimes the old lady hardly knew her own name, and then, from nowhere, reality peeped out, for just a few moments. Did she really remember a woman called Gloria who lived near St Benedict's, or was she thinking of someone else?

Judith tried another idea.

'Sam and I met some other friends of Frank's, down in town, last night.'

'That's nice, dear.'

'They were called Dave and Jeff.' Violet didn't respond, still looking out of the window. The tea had cooled, but she hadn't touched it. 'They were asking about Frank.'

'Are they in the club?' asked Violet, turning to look at her. 'What club?'

'The club that Frank runs.'

Judith stared. 'Frank has a club? Where people go?'

Violet laughed. 'No, not that sort of club, silly. It's a Christmas club that you put money in, like a savings club.' She tapped Judith's hand. 'Frank says we could make a lot of money.'

Judith waited, her mind struggling. 'How does it work?' she asked.

'You know,' said Violet. 'You put money in every week, and then when you need it, you draw it out. You had a piggy bank didn't you, when you were little? John always encouraged you to save up, when he married your mam and there was spare money at the end of the week. Well, it's like that. Frank put my money away every week. He says when I need it there'll be more. He invests the money, you see. Lends it out and gets more money back. He calls it the Future Club. Hasn't he told you about it?'

'Where's your money now?'

'In the club,' said Violet triumphantly. 'All I have to do is ask for it at Christmas. Now I'm living here, I won't need it until then.'

'Have you paid more money in, since you came here?' Judith asked.

Violet thought about it. 'No, actually, I haven't. Frank used to pay it in every Friday. He must have forgotten to ask me.'

'Is it your pension money?'

'Of course, dear. Frank looked after me, you see. I didn't need it all, so some of it went in the club, every week.'

Judith stared. 'That's been going on for a while?'

'Yes,' said Violet. 'Not sure how long.'

'Have you talked about this with Mum and Dad?'

'Well, they never asked,' said Violet. 'And it's my money, and I'm saving up to help them out with Christmas things. It'll be a surprise, won't it?'

Judith didn't dare to ask any more. Her mind was racing. How much had Frank taken from her? And where was that money now?

'I'll get us some more tea, Gran,' she said. 'You stay here. Sunday morning, no rush.'

Downstairs in the kitchen, she filled the kettle and tried to decide what to do. She wanted to tell someone, but who, and what? Maybe Violet was wrong: however clear and certain she sounded, her mind was muddled. That's why she was here, because she simply couldn't remember how to live her life any more. Judith had no way of knowing with any certainty what had been going on, and she couldn't accuse Frank of stealing from the grandmother he'd volunteered to care for. But maybe that care was just a sham, a ruse to get at her money. The kitchen clock showed just after eight. Too early to do anything. She needed time to think, and she needed advice.

She was standing in the hall, the phone in her hand and her back to the stairs when she heard her mother's voice behind her.

'Good heavens, Judith,' Maggie called out, 'You can't be phoning anyone at this hour on a Sunday. Put it down, dear, and come and have some breakfast. Have you made tea already?'

'Just for me and Gran,' said Judith, putting the receiver down. Here was her chance to share her fears with her mother, but she decided against it almost immediately. Too many loose ends. Maggie would want more, and there was nothing to tell.

'I might go out later,' Judith said as she followed her mother back into the kitchen. 'Looks as if the rain is clearing. I'll go and see a few friends before I go back to Barrow this afternoon. Are you and Granny going to church?'

'Dad'll run us up to St Mary's,' said Maggie. 'Mum wants to see Father Price, and we could call in at West Row.'

'Don't go there today, Mum,' said Judith. 'Sam's moving in and it's such a mess. Give him a chance to get settled. Maybe next weekend.'

'Good idea,' said her mother. She looked at Judith. 'Did you have a good time last night, dear? We heard you come in. It wasn't late, was it?'

'No, it was busy and noisy in town,' said Judith. 'Sam doesn't drink much, and I only had a cardigan and I got cold. So I came home.'

She looked across at her mother, defying her to ask more, but Maggie thought better of it, and went to fetch eggs from the pantry.

An hour later Judith was sitting on the bus as it wound through the Mirehouse estate. She didn't take the Vespa, not knowing where she might have to leave it. When the bus passed St Benedict's, she got off and looked around. The rain had stopped and the still air held the fumes of the bus as it pulled away. Cars were parked on the street, spilling over from the car park beside the church. Judith remembered Father Price's sermons at the church in Kells and the guilt she still felt about not being at Mass on a Sunday morning. Did her mother and grandmother feel that pull, or did they really enjoy it? Going to church was about the people of course, as much as their duty to God. Judith remembered suddenly the day her grandfather, Frank McSherry, had died. Father Price came to the house and they were on their knees in the small front room at West Row, listening to him praying for the old man's soul when Maggie had reached over, pulling her daughter towards her. Judith was only young, but she had pulled away, resisting her mother's pressure, and she had pulled away ever since. Would Frank's Gloria be at church, she wondered? She looked around and saw the pub. It would be easier to ask questions there than in the church, and if she waited, it would fill up soon, as the women headed home from church and the men came to snatch an hour's drinking before lunch.

Inside, it was quiet. Smoke curled towards the low ceiling from behind a newspaper in the corner. As she approached the bar, a man appeared from the back, a tea towel over his shoulder. 'Yes, miss,' he said. 'On your own?'

'Yes, just a half of shandy please,' said Judith. 'Quiet, isn't it?'

The barman looked at the clock behind him. 'Give it half an hour,' he said. 'Place'll be heaving, unless there's a christening or summat to slow them down.'

He placed the glass of shandy on the bar and looked at her, waiting for payment.

'Do you know someone called Gloria who lives round here?' Judith asked. 'She used to sing with a band.'

The barman smiled. 'Everyone knows Gloria,' he said. 'Pinched your bloke, did she?'

Judith felt herself blushing. 'No,' she said quickly. 'Nothing like that. It's just...' Her voice tailed away. She had no idea what excuse she might use for wanting to find Gloria that didn't provoke more questions. She handed over the money and waited for change.

'She might be in later,' said the barman. 'Often in here around lunchtime, now her man isn't around to keep an eye, you know.' He winked, and Judith felt herself blushing again. 'Do you know where she lives?' she asked.

'One of the mountain roads, you know, the ones named after mountains. God knows why they called the streets round here those names, but they did. Scafell, is it? Down the road, on the left.'

Judith shrugged. The barman called across to the person in the corner with the newspaper. 'Alf, where does Gloria live?'

The newspaper was lowered and an old man in a flat cap looked across.

'Bowfell,' he said. 'Top end.' The newspaper returned to its place. 'There you go,' said the barman. 'I told you, everyone knows Gloria.'

Despite the earlier promise of clearing skies, the rain had started again when Judith left the pub and walked to Bowfell Road, round the corner and up towards the 'top end' as the man in the flat cap had described it. All the houses looked much the same, semi-detached boxes with small windows and an air of neglect not helped by the rain that was falling straight down from a leaden sky. Judith pulled up the collar of her coat, and tucked in as much of her hair as she could, but she could feel a cold trickle down the back of her neck as she walked. She asked herself why she'd come out on such a fool's errand, but still she walked on, determined to find Gloria now that she'd come so far.

As she neared the end of the road, a woman with a push-chair emerged from a house on the other side of the street and set off down the hill, her head down. Judith ran across to her. 'Excuse me,' she said. 'I'm looking for a woman called Gloria who lives round here. D'you know –'

The woman reacted before Judith had finished her question. Her mouth twisted in an expression of disapproval. 'Thirty-one,' she said, jerking her head towards the end of the street. 'Always has the curtains closed, lazy cow.' With that she turned away and walked on, without a second glance.

Judith found number 31 and looked at the house. It was less care-worn than some of the others, but still needed fresh paint on the front door, and someone to cut the long grass that straggled beyond the low wall. The curtains were indeed closed, but that didn't signify very much, apparently. She knocked on the front door and waited. Nothing. Judith put her ear a little closer to the door and listened.

'Who is it?' came a voice from inside.

'My name's Judith. I'm looking for Gloria.'

'She's not here. Judith who?'

'Judith Pharaoh.'

Nothing happened for a few moments. Judith pulled up her shoulders against the damp and caught the twitch of the curtain to her left. Then the front door slowly opened, just enough for half a woman's face to peer round at her.

'What do you want?' The voice was throaty and low.

'I'm looking for my brother, Frank. I thought he might be here.'

'Christ,' said the voice. 'You'd better come in.'

The face disappeared and Judith pushed open the door. She stepped into the dark hall that reeked of cigarettes and dog. At the far end of the hall stood a woman in a dressing gown. Behind the woman was a closed door and behind the door a creature of some kind scratched and whined. The woman banged on the door with her fist. 'Shut up, Kaiser,' she shouted and the dog fell silent. 'He wants to protect me,' said the woman. 'Go in the front room. Move stuff if you want to sit down. Give me a minute.'

Inside the room there was enough light through the curtains for Judith to see the litter of papers and bottles across the floor, and various items of clothing on the chairs. She moved some things carefully from a chair onto the low table and sat down on the edge. She could hear someone moving upstairs and wondered if Frank was here himself, cursing his sister, angry, embarrassed. When the woman came into the room she was dressed in a pair of jeans and a red blouse. Judith's eyes had adjusted to the gloom and she noticed the woman's hair, white-blond and down to her shoulders, and the bright pink slippers on her feet. She was quite short, but the neat hourglass of her body was belied by the tired face, drawn and pale, with dark smudges around the eyes.

Judith stood up. 'I'm sorry to impose on you like this,' she said. 'I'm trying to find my brother and I heard…'

'What? Who from?' asked the woman. 'If it's Gloria Tennant you want, you've found her, but who said owt about Frank?'

Judith struggled to explain. 'We were asking if anyone had seen him.' she began. 'We?' Gloria interrupted, looking round. 'Got someone with you?'

'No, just me, but I met some people in Whitehaven, last night, and they said that Frank might be… with you.'

'Who said that?'

'Friends of Frank, from Marchon.'

'Fucking typical,' said Gloria. 'They're all like kids in a playground, tattling on. What did they say, exactly?'

'That you and Frank are, you know, seeing each other.'

Gloria sat down heavily in a chair. 'Christ Almighty,' she said.

'Is Frank here?' asked Judith. Gloria didn't answer. She groped among the debris on the floor, found a packet of cigarettes and pulled one out. Then she felt in the pocket of her tight jeans for a lighter and lit the cigarette, drawing in the smoke deeply. When she ran her other hand through her hair Judith could see the dark roots. Gloria closed her eyes and said nothing for a while, while Judith watched and waited.

'I used to be a singer,' said Gloria finally. 'Clubs, pubs, you know. Big beehive hair, short skirt, the lot. Fellers all over me.' She pulled on the cigarette and went on, as if she was talking to herself. 'Always picked the bad uns. Need my fuckin' head examined. And 'im, worst of the lot. Big lad, big wad of notes, promising me everything. Car, all the stuff. Rough as shit, but most of them are round 'ere.'

'Frank?' said Judith. 'You're talking about Frank?'

Gloria didn't respond, just laughed. She opened her eyes and looked at Judith. 'You got a feller?'

Judith hesitated. 'Sort of,' she said. 'We, you know, go out sometimes.'

'Good in bed is he?' asked Gloria.

Judith stared. 'I, we —' she stuttered.

'That's a good start, love, if they're good in bed. They don't rush at it, don't hurt you. But if they do hurt you, bit late then in't it? If you say no after that they just get mad, hurt you some more. Reflects on their manhood or some crap like that.'

'That's not Frank, is it?'

Gloria laughed again, deep and throaty, and started to cough. 'Good God,' she cried, 'not Frank. God no.' She laughed again. 'Frank's a pussycat.'

'Is he here?' Judith asked again.

'Not seen 'im for a week or so. I thought he'd got wind of it, you know.'

'Wind of what?'

'The big feller, Ray. He's coming out, but the bastards won't tell me when. Frank's your brother, right?'

'Yes,' said Judith. 'He's a few years younger than me.'

'Baby-snatcher, that's me,' said Gloria. 'Always did like 'em young. Should have stuck to that, but the young uns don't 'ave much, you know, apart from being pretty busy in bed. All that energy, can't beat it. But not enough money, most of 'em.'

Judith hesitated. 'Are you older than Frank, then?'

Gloria drew on the cigarette before she leaned over to stub

it out against the fireplace. 'Not much. Younger than I look probably.' She sat up in the chair and looked across at Judith. 'He's all right, your Frank. Bit, you know, tight, wound up. Lives with his granny, that right?'

Judith nodded.

'Poor bugger, no wonder he goes a bit wild.'

'Does he?'

'You've no idea, 'ave you?' said Gloria. 'Want some tea? You wait 'ere. Kitchen's a bit of a mess, and Kaiser'll kick off again if 'e sees a stranger.'

Judith looked around the room. She couldn't hear the rain any longer and the room was lighter than before. On the shelf over the fireplace was a photo of a woman in a tight black dress and heels, her white hair piled up on her head, standing at a microphone. There were three or four men behind her, but they were insignificant compared to the woman. This was Gloria in her heyday. Judith picked up the photo. On the back it said, *Egremont, 1968.* Just three years before.

When Gloria came back with two mugs of tea, Judith looked at her carefully. The body was still there, and with makeup and her hair up she could still be the same woman as in the photo.

'How long have you known Frank?' Judith asked when Gloria sat down again and pulled up her legs, sitting in the chair like a cat.

'Year or so,' she said. 'He'd come in the pub, buy me a drink, you know. Then he started flashing money around, so I took more notice. And with the old man away, you know.'

'Your husband?'

'He thinks 'e is. But I'm not the marrying kind, not any more. Tried it once. That was enough. Wish 'e was staying inside. I like it on my own. Got a bit of money set aside now, don't need 'im like I used to. And I could do without the temper. It gets worse – 'e can get nasty, you know.'

'Did you say he's getting out?'

'Out of Haverigg nick, love. That's probably why Frank's scarpered. You'd think 'is mates would keep their traps shut, but they don't, do they? Like kids.'

'What might happen?'

Gloria shrugged. 'God knows. Depends what mood 'e's in. Last one got 'is arm broken.' She leaned forward. 'Look, love. When you find Frank, tell 'im to stay away, right? And tell those mates of his to shut up, for Christ's sake.'

'You said Frank was flashing money around. Where did it come from?'

'God knows, could've been betting on the horses, or cards. Big wads of cash. I asked, but 'e didn't let on.'

'Could it have been from a job? His mates said he was working somewhere, not at the Legion, something else.'

'Didn't mention any names, did they?'

Judith shook her head. 'But it must pay more than he gets at Marchon, or the Legion. Don't know where he'd earn more, not round here.'

Gloria smiled. 'You really don't 'ave a clue, do you? Plenty of places to find big money if you don't mind the risk.'

'What risk?'

'The risk of losing, or getting caught, of course. Christ, love, grow up.' Gloria unwound herself and got up. 'You'd better push off. People round 'ere gossip enough as it is. They'll start thinking I'm batting for the other team. Tell Frank to disappear for a bit, right, for 'is own good. With any luck, Ray'll blow it again and go back inside.'

Judith tried once last time. 'Where might Frank hear about ways of making more money?'

Gloria looked at her. 'Sometimes a few fellers play cards, in a pub down near the harbour, but you didn't hear that from me, right? Now, bugger off. And sort yourself out, love. Sex is great when you find the right man. Time you got on with it.'

'One last thing, please?'

Gloria looked askance at her. Then she lit another cigarette and the smoke curled up from the side of her mouth.

'Your, um, boyfriend, the one who's in prison. Do you really think he'll go after Frank?'

Gloria shrugged. 'Done it before. Always wants to hit someone. If it weren't some feller, it'd be me. And I cop it too, sometimes.'

'He hits you?'

Gloria shrugged. 'That's what they do. I can handle 'im.'

'What's his name? Ray what?'

Gloria blew out another stream of smoke. 'What you up to?'

'Nothing. We just want to find Frank.'

'There's that "we" again,' said Gloria, opening the front door. 'Just leave it, right? Forget you've been here. Wherever Frank fuckin' Pharaoh's got to, he's a big lad and won't want 'is sister running around after 'im. Right?'

On the doorstep Judith turned to look at Gloria again, but the front door was shut in her face. Despite the rain, she walked slowly back towards the main road and the pub, and sheltered in the porch until the bus came. The encounter with Gloria Tennant had disturbed her world, and she couldn't think clearly. All she wanted to do now was escape to Barrow, to the sanity and safety of Elspeth's tidy house and the new job. She needed to talk to Sam, but it would have to wait.

Chapter 9

Sam woke early on Sunday morning after a restless night worrying about Frank and Judith and a future full of questions. He felt as if he'd hardly slept at all, and for a moment he couldn't remember where he was. The light was the wrong colour, and his bed the wrong way round. He needed the toilet but didn't know where to find it. He sat up and looked around, remembering that he was in a different room. The curtains in this room were a dark pink, filtering rosy light onto flowered wallpaper which must have been Violet's taste, but certainly wasn't his. The bed was comfortable enough, but narrower than he was used to, and when he found the bathroom the smell of it made him heave. Yet again he regretted the decision to move in, and it was only when he opened the curtains and looked out that he remembered why he'd been so keen. Even on a dull morning the sight of the sea lifted his spirit.

He stood for a while, watching the movement and colours of the water and listening for any sound of movement elsewhere in the house. The previous night he'd lain in bed, wondering if Frank would come back, but today, when he checked the back room, the unmade bed was empty and cold. He must be somewhere, but nothing they had learned last night had really helped. No one they'd met who knew Frank had seen him for a week or so, nor did they have any idea where he was. Dave and Jeff had mentioned a woman, what was her name? Gloria, he remembered, and there was a problem about her husband. Maybe he could ask around, but why should anyone tell him anything? He had no right to know. He was just a friend of Frank's sister, and he wasn't even sure about that. Judith was a puzzle to him.

Sam was adrift in a sea of uncertainties. Only a few days ago he'd found a man nailed to a garage door, but he still had no idea how or why that had happened. He thought the local policeman had welcomed his interest, but it looked like that had cooled. He'd moved into this dirty house, which he now realised was probably about getting closer to Judith, who didn't seem to care. She had moved back into her old life in Barrow and here he was, stranded, flapping on the shore like a beached fish.

He'd just found the energy to go and make tea when he heard a noise, faint and high-pitched, which seemed to be beyond the bedroom wall. Was it a baby crying, or a gull swooping past outside? He stood still at the top of the narrow stairs and waited. It came again, from the house next door. It was a cat, mewing insistently. Then a door opened and Sam heard a woman's voice, just a few words he couldn't make out, but the mewing stopped. He tried to remember if he'd heard anything about the neighbours. Then he remembered something Judith had said about an old lady, what was her name? Barnett? Maybe she might know more about Frank's activities. Too early to call round there yet, but it sounded as if she was wake.

It was less than an hour later when Sam knocked on the door of number 25, next door. The dull morning was turning damp and Sam felt exposed on the doorstep, wishing he'd put a coat on.

'Who is it?' a voice called from inside.

'It's Sam, from next door, Mrs Barnett,' Sam shouted, his mouth close to the door. 'Can I have a word?'

The door opened. A woman stood inside. She was wearing a brown overcoat and brown velvet slippers, and her grey hair was pulled back away from a lined face. In the corner of her mouth was a cigarette that waggled as she spoke. 'The name's Barstow, Eileen Barstow,' she said. 'Who are you?'

'Sam Tognarelli,' said Sam. 'I'm a friend of the Pharaohs. Violet's daughter, Margaret Pharaoh, you know?'

'Maggie, you mean. Violet doesn't live 'ere any more.'

'Yes, I know. She's moved to live with Maggie, and I've moved in with Frank.'

'You'd best come in,' said Mrs Barstow. 'Don't want Charlie getting out. He runs off, I think someone's feeding 'im.'

'Thanks,' said Sam. Inside, the hall was dark, with glossy dark green walls and a strip of carpet.

'Front room,' said Mrs Barstow. 'This is Charlie. Come to see the visitor, 'ave you?'

The large black and white cat stood at his mistress's feet, back arched, weighing up the new arrival. Sam bent to stroke it, but the cat slid away, tail raised.

'I think I heard your cat, this morning,' said Sam. 'Wondered what it was.'

'Sounds like a babby. He knows 'e can't come in my room at night, but these light mornings 'e stands outside and wails till I let him in. Done it for years. All right when I was getting up for work, but no good now. I've told 'im.'

'Where did you work?'

'At pit, down road,' said Mrs Barstow, 'like most folk round

94

'ere. Violet did too, long time ago, before her lass married that rich feller. All right for some. D'you want a cuppa? Kettle's on.'

The tea was dark and too sweet, but Sam sipped at it gamely, still wondering how to ask the questions he wanted answers to.

'What was that name again?' the woman asked. 'Sounded foreign.'

'My Dad was Italian, Tognarelli, but I was born here.'

'Aye lot's of I-ties ended up 'ere after the war. And you're living next door, you said?'

'Mr Pharaoh suggested it, now that Violet's moved out.'

'Worried about 'is lad, mebbe?'

'Frank? Should he be?'

Mrs Barstow shrugged her shoulders and looked towards the window. 'I mind me own business,' she said. 'But that lad's up to summat.'

'What makes you think that?' Sam asked.

'Not 'ere much, is 'e? Comes and goes at all hours. Violet said 'e were working shifts, but I reckon he were up to summat. And now she's gone…'

'Where do you think he is, Mrs Barstow?'

'Eileen, call me Eileen. Beats me where 'e is. Woman probably. None of my business.'

Sam waited. 'Does Frank get any visitors, do you know?'

Eileen Barstow looked at him. 'Nay, not that I 'eard. Legs aren't so good, you know, but I can hear things, voices like. Mind you, a bit back, there was summat up, shouting an' that. Saw the bloke when he left. Looked a right 'ard case.' Sam waited. 'Tattoos, like them biker fellers 'ave, all up 'is arm. It were cold, but he'd just a black T-shirt and them tattoos. Nasty piece of work.'

'Was it him who was shouting?'

'Both of 'em, 'im and Frank.'

'And how long ago, do you remember?'

Eileen thought about it. 'Mebbe two weeks? Not seen much of Frank since then.' She looked at Sam. 'And what do you do, then?'

'Postman,' said Sam.

'On strike, were you?'

'No, I joined after it was over.'

Eileen shrugged again.

Sam drank the rest of his tea. 'I think the family are a bit worried about Frank,' he said. 'If you do hear or see anything and I'm not around, could you let me know?'

'Want me to spy on 'im, do you?'

'Not spying,' said Sam, 'just being neighbourly. Thanks for the tea, Mrs Barstow. Don't get up, I'll see myself out.'

Sam was cleaning the bathroom when he heard the front door open and footsteps heading down the hall. 'That you Frank?' he called out. 'It's Sam, I'm coming down.'

Frank was in the kitchen, washing his hands at the sink and he turned as Sam came to the door. He looked exhausted, Sam thought, and as if he hadn't washed for a while. Frank dried his face and hands on the clean towel. 'Any food in the house?' he asked.

'You OK?' Sam asked.

Frank shrugged. 'Been better,' he said. 'Hungry.'

Sam said, 'There's some bacon and a few eggs, and some of your Mum's bread. You look tired. Go in the front room and have a sit down and I'll make you something. Won't take long.' He stood aside as Frank passed him. The man smelled like a tramp. 'Or there's hot water, if you want a bath.'

'Aye,' said Frank. 'Thanks.'

Twenty minutes later Sam knocked on the bathroom door. 'Food's in the kitchen,'

'OK,' said Frank after a pause. 'Down in a minute.'

As Sam stood watching, Frank wolfed down bacon, two fried eggs, two slices of fried bread and a mug of tea. 'Needed that,' he said. 'Got any cigs?'

'Don't smoke,' said Sam. 'Sorry. Do you want more food?'

Frank shook his head. 'Thanks.'

'Where've you been?' Sam asked. 'We've been worried about you.'

Frank shook his head again. 'Out, things to do.'

'All night?'

'Work, you know.'

'But you've not been at work, not at Marchon, or the Legion.'

'Who told you that?'

'Everybody we asked, Judith and me. We went downtown last night to see if we could find you, but no one knew where you were.'

Frank frowned. 'What's our Judith doing, poking her nose in, or you come to that?'

'Your dad asked us,' Sam said. 'Are you in trouble?'

'Why?'

'Well, things aren't exactly normal, are they? Where are you when you're not here.'

'None of your business, is it? I can look after myself.'

Sam picked up the empty plate from the table. 'OK,' he said. 'But maybe there's something I could help with.'

'This is Sam the copper talking, is it?'

'Ex-copper,' said Sam. 'But yes. If I was still a copper I'd say you were in trouble. And if you are, I might be able to help.'

Frank pushed back the chair, walked out of the room and went upstairs. A minute later he was back, a cigarette in his hand. This time he didn't sit down but stood leaning against the doorpost. 'What makes you think I'm in trouble?'

Sam looked at him steadily. 'You look like shit, dirty, hungry, tired, that's for starters. Not been to work, rumours of some woman whose husband's trouble, I'm guessing there's a money problem too. That enough?'

Frank stared out of the kitchen window, then pulled out the chair and sat down again. For a while there was silence in the small room. Sam knew enough to realise that Frank was thinking hard and he left him to do so, uninterrupted.

After a moment or two, Frank reached into a cupboard and pulled out a half full bottle of whisky.

'This early?' said Sam.

'Shut up and listen,' said Frank, pouring the whisky into a glass off the shelf.

'This is between us, right. Not the St Bees lot, not even our Judith. Right?'

Sam nodded.

Frank took a sip from the glass, put it down and wiped his mouth. 'I needed money, more than I could get from two poxy jobs. So I've been playing cards, you know, to make some more.'

'More money for what?'

'To pay off the bastards I owe it to, before they come after me.'

'And did you make some money?'

Frank shook his head.

Sam said. 'I thought it might be something like that.' He waited a moment, and then asked, 'Who's the guy with the tattoo?'

Frank looked up. 'Has he been here?'

'Eileen next door told me about the shouting match, two weeks or so ago. Who is he?'

'You don't want to know. Seriously, leave it.' Frank drew on the cigarette before he stubbed it out. 'Can't stay,' he said. 'Cards are calling. My luck'll turn, has to. Don't fret about me, I'll be OK.'

Sam had to ask more, it couldn't wait. 'That man with the tattoos,' he said. 'I've heard about him before. Police think he attacked someone who owed him money.'

Frank stared at him. 'Who, where?'

'On the estate where I do the post,' said Sam. He couldn't be sure that this was the same man, but he wanted to make Frank think, to get past the veneer of confidence. 'I found a man nailed to a garage door.'

'Was he dead?'

'No, but it was bad.'

For a moment Frank was silent, taking another mouthful from the glass. 'I'll be all right,' he said finally. 'Just leave me alone.'

'You should stop,' said Sam.

'Not yet,' said Frank. 'Just one big win, that's all I need. It'll come.'

'And if it doesn't?'

Frank shrugged. 'Just leave me alone, right? And not a word to the folks. If I need help, I'll ask them myself.'

'What about Gloria?'

'Who the hell told you about her?'

'Someone in the pub. They said she has a husband.'

Frank laughed. 'Shorty. He's inside.'

'Maybe, but for how long?'

Frank took a step towards Sam, raising his hand. His face

was flushed. 'Look, copper, just back off. It's my life, and I'm having more fun than you've ever had, you poor sad bastard. More sex, more everything. So it's hit a bad patch, so what? Tell that to our Judith and all. When I want help… Right?'

Sam put up his hands. 'Your life.'

'Aye, it is that. See you around,' said Frank, and he was gone, slamming the back door behind him.

Sam made a coffee and drank it, trying to think what he needed to do. Frank was in deep and couldn't stop. Sam feared what might happen. It was mid-morning on Sunday and he wondered where Judith would be. He couldn't tell Frank's parents anything without talking to Judith first, but when he called Elspeth's number in Barrow there was no response. Maybe she was still at St Bees, but the phone there rang out too. There was nothing he could do for now, so he carried on clearing and cleaning the kitchen, turning over in his mind how to help someone who seemed intent on putting himself at risk. It reminded him of a dreadful hour he'd spent trying to talk a man down off the parapet of a bridge over a railway line. Just when he thought he'd got through to him, and the whine of the police car in the distance said that help was nearly there, the man had stood up, smiled, raised his hands and dived off the bridge. They managed to get his body off the line before a train hit him. Sam wished he didn't remember it so clearly. It was still in his mind when he went back to bed and fell asleep.

It was the smell of smoke that woke him. For a few minutes Sam lay still, trying to clear his head. There was no fire lit downstairs. Maybe there'd been a fall of soot down the chimney. Maybe someone had made a bonfire outside. He put his feet to the floor and sat up. It was still light outside, but hard to tell the time with cloud covering the sky, and his watch was on the side of the sink in the kitchen where he'd left it. Then he heard the sound of someone knocking on the wall, and a voice calling. 'Help! it said. 'Help me! Fire!'

Sam pulled on his shoes, ran down the stairs and opened the front door. Looking to the side he could see wisps of smoke seeping under the front door of Mrs Barstow's house, and when he put his hand on the door it was hot. He covered his hand with the sleeve of his shirt and lifted the flap of the letterbox. It was too hot to touch for more than a moment, just long enough for smoke to pour out until he let it drop again.

Back in Frank's house, the wall behind the phone was warm too, but Sam dialled three nines and waited. 'There's a fire,' he said when the woman's calm voice answered. He gave the address. 'There's an old lady in the house, so send an ambulance too.' Then he put down the phone, ran to the back door and out into the yard. He could see the haze of smoke at the back kitchen window next door, but no sign of Eileen Barstow. The back door was locked. 'Eileen!' he called, 'Open the door! It's Sam. I can get you out.'

Peering through the window, he caught sight of pale legs and the brown velvet slippers in the doorway of the kitchen. Sam put his shoulder to the back door but it didn't budge. He looked around the tidy backyard. Nothing. Beyond the back gate, at the edge of the drying greens, were some bricks. Sam picked one up, stepped back into Eileen's yard and hurled the brick at the kitchen window with all his strength. Glass splintered and he pushed at the jagged remains around the window frame, feeling the sharp bite of broken glass on his arm as he did so. When the lower edge of the frame was clear, he heaved himself up onto it, and pushed himself head first into the room, landing among the shards on the floor. At the edge of his hearing was the faint bell of the fire engine.

Inside, he stood up, pulled another piece of glass from the waist of his trousers and turned to unlock the back door. Thank God, the key was in the lock, but the rusty top bolt stuck for what seemed like minutes before he could prise it free to open the door. As air rushed in he heard the noise of flames from the hall and he pushed the door closed again before he turned to pull Eileen clear. At the other end of the narrow hall the front door was alight on the inside, flames flicking up and round towards the bottom of the stairs. Eileen lay still at his feet. Sam bent over to see her face. Her eyes were open, and the smoke was less overpowering close to the floor. She moved her head slightly. 'Charlie,' she whispered. 'Upstairs.'

Sam spoke into her ear. 'Eileen, I'm going to lift you,' he said. 'Don't try and get up. Leave it to me.'

Pulling her back into the kitchen across the floor would risk more damage from the broken glass. Sam bent and pulled the prone woman up at the waist, struggling to get his hands around and underneath her. The heat from the hallway was fierce on his head, and he could see Eileen's hair beginning to singe. Urgency brought strength. He heaved Eileen onto his shoulder and turned towards the back door. Propping her against the table, he pulled open the door and pushed her out into the yard, across the concrete and onto the edge of the worn muddy grass at the back. He wanted Eileen to sit up, but she leaned sideways and slumped on to the grass, moaning. He lurched into Frank's kitchen, wetted a towel under the tap, filled a mug with water and went back outside. The clang of the fire engine stopped suddenly and Sam heard raised voices in the street. A man came running across the green towards them. 'Firemen are here,' he cried. 'Is she all right?'

Sam sat back on his haunches and handed the mug of water to the man, who bent over Eileen and held the mug to her mouth. Rubbing the cold wet towel down his own face, he noticed the spreading crimson stain on his shirt sleeve and the steady drip of blood at his wrist.

Chapter 10

'Stay with her,' said Sam to the man, 'I'm going back inside.'

As he reached the kitchen door, Sam heard the front door splinter and a fireman holding the nozzle of a hose stepped through the gap, spraying water on the burning fragments of the door. 'Out of the way!' he shouted to Sam. 'Leave this to us.'

'There's a cat,' said Sam, 'upstairs.'

The man directed the water onto the smouldering staircase, then turned and handed the nozzle back into the hands of someone behind him. 'Going up,' he shouted over the throb of the engine. 'You stay here,' he said to Sam. 'Where's the occupants?'

'Out back,' Sam said. 'She's OK, there's someone with her.'

The fireman nodded, stepped over the damaged lower stairs and disappeared, his heavy boots shuddering on the floor above. The smoke was clearing now, blown through the house by the breeze off the sea. The fireman clattered back down the stairs, the heavy body of the black and white cat over his arm. 'Under the bed. Smoke, I think it's gone. Take it,' he thrust the body at Sam. 'Outside, see if it comes round.'

Sam held the cat close to him. It was warm, with green eyes open and staring. He carried it across the broken glass on the kitchen floor and out to where Eileen was sitting with the man, a red blanket draped round her thin shoulders. 'The cat was upstairs,' said Sam. 'He's caught the smoke. Do you want to hold him?' Eileen stretched out her arms, her red eyes watering. She took the cat and held it gently on her lap, stroking it, calling its name.

Sam couldn't watch. He turned and went back into the house where the air had cleared and he could see the dark shape of the fire engine in the street and the sky beyond. He picked his way over the pieces of the charred door and went outside.

'You the owner?' said one of the firemen, who'd taken off his heavy black helmet and was scratching his head.

'I live next door,' said Sam, pointing to the front door of number 23, which was untouched by the fire but running with water. 'I heard Mrs Barstow shouting through the wall.'

'Hear anything else, before that?' the fireman asked.

'I was asleep upstairs,' said Sam. 'The smell of smoke woke me.'

'Might be hard to spot,' said the fireman, 'but this looks like arson to me. Someone's put summat through the letterbox, flared up the inside of the door, up into the stairwell. Petrol likely, still smell it. Sure you didn't hear anything?'

Sam shook his head. 'Someone did this deliberately?'

'Seen it before, many times. Could be kids. Who lives here?'

'An old lady,' said Sam. 'Eileen Barstow. She must be in her seventies. Who'd want to hurt her?'

'Local bobby's coming down,' said the fireman. 'Should be here in a minute. He'll need to talk to Mrs Barstow, and to you too, so stick around. Can you get someone to board up this door?'

'I'll sort that out,' said Sam. 'I'm just a lodger, but I'll call the owners, they'll take care of things I'm sure.'

'Right-oh,' said the fireman. 'We'll make our report and pass it on direct. Rest is up to police. OK? Cat dead, is it? They can't deal with smoke.'

'Don't know,' said Sam. 'Hope not. Thanks.'

'We'll be off soon,' said the fireman. 'You were lucky. Fires like this can spread really fast.'

Sam walked slowly back through the house. Someone had found a chair for Eileen, and arranged the red blanket over her head and shoulders. She was holding a mug of tea, but there was no sign of the cat. Sam's heart sank. 'Where's Charlie?' he asked. Eileen smiled, and pointed. The man who'd looked after her was holding Charlie in his arms, and the cat was butting into his chest, enjoying the attention.

'This is Geordie, from back over,' said Eileen, 'I thought Charlie had gone but then he coughed and shook his head and came back to me.'

'That's good,' said Sam. 'There's a policeman coming to talk to you, Eileen, about what happened. Try to remember all the details if you can. I'll see if I can find him. Go in my kitchen if you want.'

'I heard the fire engine,' said Geordie, 'then I saw you break the kitchen window. I live over there, South Row.'

'Geordie used to know my man, Colin,' said Eileen, 'from way back.'

'I'll tek her back to mine,' said Geordie. 'Number twenty, South Row. Bobby can come round there, tell 'im.'

'He's here now,' said Sam, watching as the familiar figure of a beat policeman in his helmet strode down the alley towards them. Sam went to meet him. 'Sam Tognarelli,' he said, putting out his hand. 'I live next door. Mrs Barstow's shocked obviously, but she's OK. Take her in my kitchen, next door, if you want to get her statement.'

PC Kelly from the Kells police station on the High Road preferred to stand rather than sit in Sam's kitchen. It had taken him a few minutes to wrest control of the situation back from Sam, and for Sam to revert to being the concerned neighbour rather than the officer on scene. Geordie had taken the cat back to his house, out of the way. PC Kelly pulled his notebook and a stub of pencil from his top pocket.

'I can handle this, thanks,' he said pointedly to Sam. 'Can you see about getting that door boarded up?'

Sam took the hint, and went into the hall to try once again to call Judith, and then John Pharaoh. He'd almost given up hope of finding Judith when a voice said, 'Elspeth here. Who's speaking, please?'

'Elspeth, thank God you're there,' Sam said. 'I've been trying to find Judith.'

'Your voice sounds funny, Sam. We've been out for lunch,' said his sister. 'Just got back. What's so urgent?'

'Can you put her on, please? It's about Frank, her brother.'

'Sam?' said Judith, after a short pause. 'What is it, what's happened?'

'I've seen Frank,' said Sam. 'He's in trouble, money, gambling. He came back this morning. He had a bath and had some food and then went again. He wouldn't stay here, I did try.'

'So where he is now?'

'I don't know. There must be a big card game going on somewhere. Said he was going to win his money back. I couldn't stop him.' He paused. 'And there's something else.'

"What? Tell me.'

'The house next door, looks as if someone tried to burn it down, or send a warning or something.'

'Next door, in West Row?'

'An old lady lives there, Eileen Barstow.'

'Eileen's a friend of Gran's,' said Judith. 'What's any of this got to do with her, Sam? It doesn't make sense.'

'I know. The local copper's come, and he's talking to Eileen in the kitchen. Didn't want me hanging around.'

'Have you told Dad?'

'I'm going to call him. I didn't want to talk to him until I'd checked with you.'

'Well, call him now,' said Judith. Sam could hear the anxiety in her voice. 'Should I come back?'

'No, stay there. Get on with your job, there's nothing you can do here. Frank's in a mess, but he's a grown man. John needs to know, and we need to secure Eileen's house. I'll have to tell him about Frank, but there's not a lot any of us can do.'

'Did he tell you about Violet's money? About the club?'

Although Sam was puzzled, he didn't respond; he was desperate to talk to John. 'It'll be all right,' he told her hastily 'Stay there. I'll call you when I know any more. Put Elspeth back on, will you?'

'What's going on, Sam?' said his sister.

'Judith will tell you,' he said. 'Don't let her come back here, Elspeth. She really needs that job, and there's nothing to be done here. It's up to the rest of the family now. It'll be OK. I'll call you again later. 'Bye.'

The second phone call was harder. John Pharaoh answered the phone himself. Sam explained the basic facts, said he needed to speak to him personally and soon about Frank and the house, and after only a moment's hesitation John said he was on his way to West Row and would be there as soon as he could. He asked Sam to get the policeman's name and that of his sergeant and rang off.

Fifteen minutes later, after PC Kelly had finished talking to Eileen and she'd gone across to Geordie's, John Pharaoh's car pulled up outside the house. Sam was waiting. Kelly had taken some details from Sam, and was keen to get away. Sam wondered if DC Holmes would pick up the connection. He introduced John to PC Kelly, and made sure to mention John's job at Sellafield. Kelly was in no doubt by the end of the brief conversation that he would be expected to take the incident seriously.

When Kelly had left, John arranged for someone to board up Eileen's door and broken window until proper repairs could be made, and then he listened without interrupting while Sam told him everything that had happened since Frank had appeared at the house several hours before.

'Come and have a look at the house,' Sam said.

John was dismayed by the mess and obvious neglect in Frank's room, as Sam knew he would be. They went from room to room, John's anxiety increasing all the time. Back on the street, staring out at the familiar view, John turned to Sam. 'This is where we had our wedding meal, Maggie and I.'

'Here, in the house?'

'No, right on the street. It was a beautiful afternoon in August and we set up tables and chairs on the cobbles. Violet thought her brother Tom had been killed in a dreadful pit accident but then he turned up; he and a few others just walked out of the pit, hours after the explosion. It felt like a miracle. Judith was with us of course, and Frank too, actually, although we kept quiet about that. He was born early the following year, 1948. And now this.' He looked at the house, puzzled and clearly upset. 'What do you think, Sam?' he asked. 'You must have come across situations like this before, haven't you?'

'To be honest, Mr Pharaoh –' Sam began.

'Call me John, please, Sam.'

'Well, John,' Sam went on, 'it doesn't look good. I would

guess that Frank's been getting into serious debt for quite a while now. Probably horses to start with, then cards to try and make some bigger money to pay off his debts. He said he was going back to a card game when he left here this morning.'

John shook his head. 'Who does he owe money to?'

'Hard to say. Probably the bookies to start with, but if someone doesn't pay up, the debts get passed on to people who put a lot of effort into getting the money back. And the debts keep going up because everyone Frank is borrowing from will be adding interest to the original, lots of interest. It gets out of control really fast.' He hesitated. 'And it gets ugly too. "Enforcers" they call them. They get called in finally, and they stop at nothing. I've seen some...' The image of the crucified man flashed into Sam's mind. 'They could have done what happened next door.'

'But why next door? Why not here?'

'They want to scare people into paying up. No point in harming the person who owes the money, they have to be able to keep on getting more. And no point in damaging property that might be part of the debt.'

John stared at him. 'But I own this house.' he said. 'I bought it years ago for Violet. Frank lives here as my tenant.'

Sam said what had been on his mind for a while. 'It's possible that Frank has told the people he owes money to that he owns this house himself, and he's made it part of his debt.'

'He's put this house on a bet?'

'It's possible, yes. It's been done before.'

'So rather than attack this house, whoever is after Frank has attacked the house next door?'

'Could be,' said Sam. 'Or they could have been after Frank and just got the wrong house. That can happen too. Some of the people who make a living this way are pretty dense.'

John leaned his long body against the wall. 'Oh God,' he said. 'This is awful. I can't believe Frank's got himself into this. He has a good job, a place to live, a quiet steady life.'

Sam remembered the conversation with Frank in the morning. He didn't want to talk in the street, where people were passing, curious about what had been going on.

'Let's go back in the house,' he said. 'Bit more private.'

John sat on one of the rickety chairs at the kitchen table while Sam made them both a drink.

'I've known some young men like Frank,' he said, putting two mugs of tea on the table. 'They crave excitement, and the things that you and I might value mean nothing to them. Frank could have started gambling because he was bored.'

John shook his head. 'I don't know him at all. None of us do. This could be a compete stranger we're talking about, but he's my son.'

'I'm sorry, John. You asked what I think, as an outsider, and that's what my policeman's mind is telling me. I wish I could have stopped him this morning, but I couldn't. Even if I'd been a policeman I had no reason to stop him doing what he wanted to do. You can't arrest someone for being a fool, not unless you've got some evidence.' He could see John's distress. 'Can I get you something? I think there's some whisky, or more tea?'

John leaned forward, looking hard at Sam. 'We have to do something,' he said. 'No. *I* have to do something. I'm his father, and I've let him down. I just assumed, you know, that everything was fine. I've got money. Frank could have asked me any time to help him out and of course I would, if I'd known.'

'But he didn't ask, did he?'

'What about the police? Can we report Frank missing, get

111

them to find him and bring him back, away from whatever trouble he's in?'

Sam shook his head. 'I told you, the police can't go and get him unless they're sure that the gambling he's into is illegal, or he's been harmed, or is under duress. That's not what I saw this morning. He was exhausted and hungry and he needed a bath, but he was going back wherever it was of his own accord. When I tried to stop him, he threatened me.'

John leaned his head on his hand, looking first at the table, then out of the window. 'Do you have any idea where he may have gone, where he's playing cards?'

'I could probably find out, just by asking around. Or DC Holmes might have an idea, if I can get him to talk to me. It may not be illegal, but I know what trouble those games can cause. They've got a case already, a poor bloke in trouble with debts, up on the Hattingham estate. Someone nailed him to a garage door. I found him there.'

John looked up. 'That was in the paper. Was it you who found him?'

Sam nodded. 'They kept my name out of it. The man was terrified, still refuses to talk. That was the idea, to scare him and anyone else who owed them money.'

'And that's what Frank…' John's voice tailed away.

Sam wished he could tell John that it would be all right, that Frank would see sense and ask for help, but he wasn't sure that he would.

'I could take a few hours off,' Sam went on, seeing John's anxious face. 'Ask around, see if I can find him. Would that help?'

John rubbed his hands down his face. 'There must be something we can do,' he said. 'I can't bear just waiting for something to happen. It makes me sick to think of it. And now this.'

He looked up at Sam. 'How much notice would you need to give, at your job?'

Sam shrugged, puzzled.

John went on, 'Look, I want you to give up that job and work for me. I'll pay you what ever you want. I have to do something, and this is the best I can think of. Could you do it, Sam? Could you find out what's been going on and get Frank out of it, before he gets hurt? For us, as a family? Please?'

'Work for you?' Sam was struggling with the idea.

'Why not? I could go and find a private detective to do it, but you're a detective, and a good one. I know you left the force and I've a fair idea what made you do it, but you could do this for us, Sam, as a proper job.'

Sam began to think it through. He could leave the job at the Post Office. They'd be unhappy, and it might cost him, but what John was suggesting couldn't wait. His mind raced through the possibilities. He would need transport, and some kit, a camera maybe. And what about the real police, how would he work with them?

John was watching Sam carefully, and could see his hesitation. 'Think about it overnight,' he said. 'I know I'm asking a lot and it's all very sudden, but from what you've told me we can't hang around. I could pull some strings with a senior police officer I play golf with, but he might not have much clout up here. And I don't want someone dealing with this because he feels he's been bullied into it. You're close to our family already. You know what it means to us.'

Sam rinsed their mugs under the tap. 'I'm not sure,' he began, but John held up his hand. 'Don't say anything yet, think it through, and if you can help us just make a list of what you need. Anything. I've worked hard all my life and what's it all for if I can't help my son when he needs it? Sam, do you understand what this means to me? Call me tomorrow morning before you go out, at work, not at home. Is that OK?'

Later that evening, when John had gone home and Eileen's house was secure, Sam sat on a bench across the street, on the strip of ground that once been a garden, looking out over the Irish Sea. Fears and uncertainties tumbled in his brain. Part of him was afraid, and he knew it: fear of failing and sacrificing John's trust; fear of the people that he would need to get Frank away from; fear of what could happen to him.

The fire next door was nothing compared to the violence he knew could be facing Frank and anyone who tried to help him. The image of the man nailed to the garage door stuck behind Sam's eyes and would not be shifted, even by the whisky that he had sought out as soon as John had gone.

And Judith. What would she think if he turned away from John's desperate pleading? She was bound to find out. He had promised to call her back this evening and had no idea what he could say to her.

The sun sank below a bank of cloud near the horizon and flashed across the water into his face, making him blink. All around him golden light bounced off brick and sandstone, cobbles, chimneys, and the burnished sea. This was his chance, to prove himself and to face his fears.

He heard the phone ringing in the hall and ran across to answer it.

'Sam?' said Judith. 'What's happening? I need to tell you what I found out today.'

'Today, where?'

'I found that woman we heard about on Saturday night,

Gloria. She lives in Mirehouse. I talked to her. She's not a nice woman, Sam. Heaven knows what Frank's doing with her.' She paused. 'Sam, are you there? Are you listening to me? What happened at West Row? Is Eileen all right? We put the local radio on, but there was nothing. And that Gloria has a husband, well he's not her husband, but he's in Haverigg prison. He's coming out soon, and he might go after Frank.'

Sam shouted down the phone. 'Judith. Slow down. There's lots of things to tell you, and for you to tell me. So calm down, let me take it all in.'

'OK, OK,' she said. 'Tell me what happened up there.'

'The fire's out, the house is boarded up, Eileen's OK, she's staying with friends in South Row, and the cat's all right too. Your dad's been here, and we had a good talk. We're going to talk again tomorrow about Frank, and what to do.'

'Is Dad upset?'

'Of course, but he's fine. Don't tell him about Gloria and all that. He's got enough on his mind already.'

'I want to come back,' she said.

'Please, stay in Barrow,' said Sam. 'There's nothing you can do here. Give me Gloria's address in case I need to see her myself.'

Reluctantly Judith gave him the address in Bowfell Road. 'I didn't like her, Sam. Don't go there.'

'No decisions yet about what we're going to do. That's why your dad and I are talking tomorrow, when things have calmed down a bit. You need this new job Judith, so go for it. We can handle things here. Frank looked much better with some food and a bath. He can look after himself.'

'I do need this job, but you have to tell me what's going on. Promise me you will. Shall I phone Dad?'

'Not tonight. He may not want to tell your mum or Vince until we know what to do next. Just leave it for tonight.'

Silence.

'Judith?'

'I'm here,' she said. 'I'm glad you're there, Sam.'

CHAPTER 11

The whisky didn't help. Sam fell into bed, his head swimming, but three hours later he was awake again, aware of every sound. This time it was a barking dog that woke him and he felt the adrenalin bump in his chest. He lay quite still, his senses twitching, the bitter smell of smoke still infesting the air. It would linger in the curtains, the bed, his clothes: the thought depressed him utterly.

He had a final decision to make before he spoke to John, and then he might have to see his boss at the sorting office for another awkward conversation. He was still on probation but did that mean he could leave or just that they could sack him? Why did he feel as if he would be letting them down? If he was sick, or some vicious dog had taken his fingers off, they would have to do without him, so what was the difference?

Sleep came again for a while, but was broken when the daylight strengthened. Beyond Violet's pink curtains the sea gleamed like mother of pearl. As he drew the curtains back, Sam realised that his mind was clear and made up. This was his chance to do something important, more important than trudging round the dreary estate with letters and demands for money that would just add to people's misery. He was angry with people who were happy to take Frank's money and then pass on his debt to others who would bully it out of him without compassion or compunction. He was angry with Frank too, for not recognising that the family would always help him if they could.

Sam wondered how much he could ask John to pay him for taking on the work of rescuing Frank from his predicament. It felt uncomfortable discussing money in these circumstances, but he had to live on something. He found the advertisement in the paper with the salary figures for a constable in the Cumbria police, which was slightly more than he was getting as a novice postman. Maybe that would be fair, if he could work out a daily rate. Then he made a list of what he would need: some form of transport was definite, preferably a car. He might ask to borrow Judith's Vespa, but she would need it herself now she was back at work. And a camera; if he was ever going to convince the police to take action they would need hard evidence, not just rumours and speculation. He was going to be a private detective and that's what they did in all the old films, sit in a car for hours with a big camera, taking incriminating photos of people being unfaithful to each other. An image of himself in a big hat and a trenchcoat swam into his head and made him smile. But anxiety made him get up and dressed and go for a walk, just to get the smell of smoke out of his nostrils. He needed to strengthen himself too, before heading to the sorting office to tell them he was leaving. He had no idea whether they would expect him to finish his shift, but he didn't want to do so. Now that the prospect of John's offer was in front of him, he found it irresistible.

The sun was already high and climbing before seven. He set off along the well-worn path that led from the south corner of West Row towards the old mine workings. He wanted to get out on to the cliff tops overlooking Saltom Bay, but after a few hundred yards he found his way blocked by the hellish vista of the Marchon chemical plant that sprawled over the crest of the hill and down the slope towards the sea. He'd seen it from the main road into Whitehaven but not realised the full extent of the plant. Smoke and steam curled into the quiet air from dozens of stacks, and the air was heavy with unnatural smells. What must it be like to work here, he wondered. The noise of rushing water caught his ear, and looking to his right he saw the huge Marchon waste pipe, several feet across, out of which a steady stream of unclean water poured down the cliff towards the beach and the sea. The sandstone headland of St Bees lay beyond, but cut off by the rush of contaminated water. There were steps leading down towards the beach, but they were fenced off and too close to the pipe to be inviting. If he wanted to get down to the beach, he would need to find another way, and avoid whatever perils the waste water would carry. Sam looked for a while, taking in the sounds and smells before he turned and retraced his steps to face what lay ahead.

It was just after eight when Sam called John's office at Sellafield, hearing him pick up almost immediately. It was too early for the secretary who usually fielded his calls and John was expecting him.

'I'll do it,' said Sam, immediately, before he had the chance to back away from risk.

'Thank you, Sam, thank you so much,' said John. 'I won't interfere. You know what needs to be done, and how to deal with the police. I spoke to my golfing colleague who's a police inspector but he's based in Workington, and he wasn't sure how much influence he would have with the Whitehaven people.'

'Not sure how much clout I'll have either,' said Sam, 'I'll do my best. It might not be easy to convince the police that

Frank wants to be found. The last thing they want is to get hooked into a domestic dispute and a prodigal son.'

'Do you think Frank's in danger? Be honest with me, Sam.'

'He may be. It depends how bad his debts are and who's taken them on.' Sam thought again of the crucified man. 'If we can find his debts and clear them, he should be fine. It's not in their interest to harm him. They just want the money.'

'Can you meet me today?' John asked. 'There are some things we need to sort out obviously, and I'd rather we didn't do that at home. I could come to West Row, but why don't we have lunch in Seascale? Easier for me to leave the site than you to come to the office.'

'I'll go and sort things out at work before that,' Sam said. 'You're sure, aren't you, before I burn my boats?'

'Oh, yes, we have to do this. I can't rest while Frank's out there, however much he may have brought all this on himself. Do what you need to do, Sam. Meet me at the Scawfell Hotel in Seascale at one and we'll work out the details.'

Sam's train to Seascale meant he was early for his lunch date with his new employer and he had time to gather his thoughts. The early morning meeting with his supervisor at the sorting office had been easier than he expected. Apparently the probation period worked both ways, and it hadn't been too difficult to extricate himself from his commitments. He'd told Mr Yearsley that there was a family crisis that he had to respond to immediately, which wasn't far from the truth. He sacrificed the two weeks' pay they owed him, picked up a few things from his locker and walked away without regret. It had been useful to do the job for a few weeks, to get fit again and put the strain of the Barrow experience behind him, but he had no real desire to stay on. His nocturnal anxieties seem to have smoothed into a hum of anticipation about the challenge of rescuing Frank and making himself feel useful again, even without the comfort of a police warrant card in his pocket. And he trusted John. Anything Judith had ever told him about her father was reassuring: he had worked hard all his life, people respected him, and Sam couldn't think of anyone he'd rather work for.

They shook hands when John Pharaoh found him in the corner of the bar at the Scawfell Hotel. Sandwiches were ordered, and as they waited Sam explained that he was free to start work straight away. John agreed without demur to pay for the two weeks Sam had lost, and the daily rate that he'd worked out. Sam had always worried about money, but John's working life revolved around it quite comfortably. He urged Sam to find a second-hand car, and buy whatever equipment he might need, no questions asked.

'Do the rest of the family know what we're doing?' Sam asked.

John ate his sandwich without responding for a few minutes. 'I haven't said anything, actually. Didn't want to worry them yet if you weren't able to help, in which case I would have to go straight to the police and try to convince them that we weren't just using them to do family business.'

'That would have probably been their reaction, the police I mean,' said Sam. 'Frank's twenty-three, old enough to be out there on his own.'

'Maggie still thinks of him as a teenager, and Violet — well, she'll struggle to take any of this in.'

'What about Vince? Do you think he might know more than he's telling us?'

'I doubt it,' said John. 'He's as worried about Frank as we are, although he's not showing it. I'm sure he would have said if he had any idea what Frank's been up to.' John hesitated. 'I

121

will have to tell them about it, I know that. Tonight? At least now I can give them some positive news, that you can help us. Do you want to be with me?'

Sam thought about it. 'Yes, I think so. There's something I need to ask Violet about, and I'd rather you and Mrs Pharaoh were there when I do. It was something Judith mentioned, but I didn't ask her for the details. And I'll need all of you to think hard about anything that might point us in the right direction.'

John finished off his half pint of shandy. 'We'll feel really foolish if Frank just turns up again at West Row.'

'From what I saw and heard yesterday, I don't expect that to happen,' said Sam. 'But we can always hope.' He raised his glass to John. 'And thanks for asking me to help. It means a lot to me.'

'And to us,' said John.

By the time Sam walked down to the house in St Bees later that evening he'd already ticked some items off his list. He'd found a cheap car at a yard in Corkickle that would be ready for him in the morning, and bought a camera with a telephoto lens, a Polaroid camera that could be very useful, a new notebook and some file cards. The old routines of detective work were coming back to him fast, and it felt good.

One thing hadn't gone well, although he'd never expected that it would. He'd finally managed to track down DC Rob Holmes in a café close by the police station in town and explained that he was being employed by Frank Pharaoh's family. When he mentioned that Frank might have gambling debts, Holmes rolled his eyes.

'You telling me he's going to end up like Arthur Paling? I saw Kelly's crime report. The fire could just be kids messing around,' he said.

'It's too much of a coincidence, isn't it?' Sam replied. 'I

know you think I'm just playing at this, but it's serious for the family, and they asked me to help.'

'Proper little boy scout, aren't you?'

Sam was expecting to be patronised and didn't rise to it. 'What if I went above your head, to your inspector?' he said. 'John Pharaoh's well-connected, not "on the square", but people know him from when he worked at the Haig.'

Rob wasn't impressed. 'If you want to try Inspector Williams, be my guest. He'll ask you the same questions I've asked and you'll get the same response. Your lad's a grown man making his own mistakes, and there's no hard evidence of criminal activity. We're not the bloody Salvation Army rounding up lost sheep. When you've got some evidence of wrongdoing, away we go. Before that, my ex-copper marra, you're on your own.' He pushed his chair away from the table and got to his feet. 'Real work to do,' he said. 'See you around.'

Sam was about to ring the Pharaohs' doorbell, when Vince opened the door. 'Knew it was you,' he said. 'Your shoes sound different to everyone else's. Dad's being very mysterious. Just said he had something to talk to us about when you got here. You and Judith getting married or something?'

Sam felt himself blushing. 'Bit more serious than that I'm afraid,' he said. 'Back room or front room?'

'Back,' said Vince. 'Kitchen table job. Mum's just clearing away. Give us a hint, Sam. What's going on? Is it about Frank?'

'Come in, come in,' said John when Sam pushed open the back room door. 'Good timing, just finished supper. Have you eaten?'

'Yes, thanks,' Sam lied. He was hungry but didn't want to waste time with Maggie fussing about food.

'Are you ready to sit down with us, Maggie? And Violet, too. Sam and I need to tell you what's going on.'

'About time,' said Maggie. 'You've been like a cat in a thunderstorm the last couple of days. It's about Frank, isn't it? Why is he avoiding us? Have you talked some sense into him yet?'

She has no idea, Sam thought to himself. She thinks Frank's playing some kind of game.

John took his wife by the hand and pushed her gently into a chair. 'Maggie,' he said, 'Listen to me. We still don't know where Frank is, or why he hasn't been at work for over a week now. It's serious, love. The last person to see him was Sam, at West Row yesterday,' he hesitated. 'From what Sam found out, it looks as if Frank's been gambling.' He took both Maggie's hands in his and made her look at him. 'He's lost a lot of money.'

Maggie's face registered relief rather than surprise. 'Well, we can pay whatever he owes, can't we?' she said. 'We're not short of money, never have been.' John looked away and shook his head.

'If we knew how much, and who he owes, you could pay, of course,' said Sam, 'but Frank wouldn't tell me. He was still intent on winning back the money he needs. I think he may be in serious trouble, more than he can handle.' He turned to Violet. 'Mrs McSherry, did you say something to Judith about Frank having a club?'

'Did I?' said Violet.

'What kind of club?' Maggie asked.

'I think it was probably a savings club,' said Sam.

'That's it,' said Violet, her face brightening. 'Like a Christmas Club, Frank said. I can take my money out to buy you all presents at Christmas.' She beamed and looked round the table. Vince put his head in his hands.

John reached for his mother-in-law's hand. 'Did you put your money into this club, Violet?'

'Frank put it in,' Violet went on. 'He gave me some money out of my pension every week, and put the rest into the club.'

John and Maggie looked at each other across the table.

'When did the club start?' Sam asked. Violet looked up at the ceiling, trying to think. 'Long time ago,' she said.

'Oh, Mum,' said Maggie. 'Why didn't you tell us?'

'But then it wouldn't be a surprise at Christmas would it?' Violet said.

Maggie ran a hand over her hair. She knew there was no point in asking Violet any more about it. 'What else did Frank tell you?' she asked Sam.

Sam hesitated. 'He didn't tell me anything much, but when Judith and I were in town on Saturday we met some of Frank's mates. They said that he…' Sam hesitated again, 'he has a girl-friend, in Mirehouse, and she might know something. I'm going to see her tomorrow.'

'You are?' said John.

'What about your work?' Maggie asked.

'That's the other thing we need to tell you,' said John. 'Sam's going to give up his job for a while, to help us find Frank. I asked him to do it, and he agreed.'

Maggie, Violet and Vince all stared at Sam. He felt his face reddening. 'So I've taken leave from the Post Office for a little while,' he said brightly, 'just until we sort this out. It's the kind of thing I would have done as a detective, and I wanted to help when John asked me.'

'But you're not a detective any more, are you?' said Vince. 'What do the real police say about you being involved?'

John turned to Sam. 'Did you see DC Holmes?'

Sam nodded. 'And he said what I knew he'd say, that until

they have some evidence of wrongdoing, or Frank's officially a missing person, there's nothing they can do.'

'What do you mean, wrongdoing'?' Maggie asked. 'Frank's done nothing wrong. He's just made a mistake.' She looked at her husband. 'He's just a boy.'

John stood up. 'Thanks for coming down, Sam,' he said. 'I'm sure you've got things to do, and we need to talk, as a family, you know.' Sam took the hint and followed John out to the front door. 'Sorry about that.'

John whispered to Sam. 'Maggie's going to need some time to get to grips with all this. We all are. Are you going to see this woman? How do you know where she is?'

'Judith asked Violet, got a few clues and tracked her down. She gave me the name and address. It's the best lead we have at present. Judith clearly didn't like her, but I might be able to get her to talk to me. I'll let you know.'

'Are you going there now? Do you want me to drive you down to Mirehouse?'

Sam pictured John's car causing comment on the estate and declined. 'I'll get the bus down, thanks. Less obtrusive.'

Gloria Tennant had no idea who the serious young man knocking on her door could be, and assumed it was someone from the council. She opened the door with her story ready.

'Gloria Tennant?' Sam began.

'It wasn't me making that racket at the weekend,' she said. 'Blame them over the road. It was that cow from number eighteen complaining wasn't it? She needs to mind her own frigging business.'

Sam took a step back, ducking away from the aggression that poured out of this small shapely woman with white hair piled into a precarious beehive.

'No,' he said. 'That's nothing to do with me. I'm a friend of Frank Pharaoh.'

Gloria stared at him. 'I've had his sister round already. So what do you want?'

'Could I come in, do you think?' Sam ventured, trying to smile. 'I'm sorry to bother you, but we need some more information, if you could help?'

Gloria looked at him. 'Not the police, are you? Or probation?'

'No, neither,' said Sam. 'Just a friend of the family. Frank's dad asked me to come.'

She stepped back from the door without another word and walked into the front room. 'Frank's a lucky lad to have people who care that much about 'im,' she said, clearing papers off a chair and sitting down. 'Nobody in our 'ouse gave a shit about me.' She looked up at Sam. 'Sit down, for God's sake. Make me nervous standing there like that. What's your name, anyway?'

'Sam Tognarelli,' he said, holding out his hand, which Gloria ignored. Instead she reached for a pack of cigarettes on the hearth.

'Togna-what?' she said, when the cigarette was lit and the first stream of smoke curled across the room.

'Tognarelli. It's Italian,' he said. 'My Dad was Italian.'

'So you're a friend of Frank's? Then you probably know that stuck-up bitch who came here the other day?'

'His sister, Judith, yes I do.'

'Didn't like 'er,' said Gloria.

Sam didn't respond, and Gloria looked at him carefully, wrinkling her eyes against the smoke.

'You're quite a looker, aren't you, in a serious sort of way. Not like most of the blokes I know. How old are you?'

'I'm thirty,' he said, conscious of her dark eyes, and the sweet scent she was wearing.

'You at Marchon, too?'

Sam hesitated. 'No, I'm a postman.'

'I like uniforms,' she said. 'Used to work on a cruise ship. Sailors. Delicious.'

He coughed, and fumbled for his notebook. 'Judith said you saw Frank a week or so ago. That right?'

'Something like that.' Gloria got up from her chair and Sam flinched. 'Look at you,' she said, laughing. 'I just want to show you something.' She took a photo off the mantelpiece and handed it to him. 'I was a singer, that's me with the band, do you see?'

Sam turned the photo to the streak of light where the curtains didn't quite meet. He could see the white hair piled up, the tight black dress and high heels. She held out her hand for the photo and he returned it without comment. 'We 'ad a ball,' she said. 'Ever been on a cruise?'

Sam ignored the question and looked down at his note-book. 'Can you think of anyone that Frank might be staying with? We think he may be involved with a card school some-where, trying to win some money.'

Gloria laughed, standing on the hearth, looking down at Sam. 'More of a fool than I thought he was. They'll fleece him blind.'

'Who will?'

She hesitated. 'Did that Judith woman tell you about my feller?'

Sam shook his head. He wanted Gloria to talk more, and didn't move from his chair.

'He's in Haverigg nick,' Gloria went on. 'At least I think he is. When he comes out he might 'ear about Frank, – not from me, mind – but people round 'ere talk too much.'

'You mean he might go after Frank?'

She shrugged. 'Well, he could. Done it before, got 'im banged up last time.'

'So he wouldn't do it again, would he?'

'You mean, 'e'd remember what happened last time, and do summat else? Not very bright, my Ray. Anyway, 'e's got to defend 'is reputation, 'asn't 'e? That's the only thing that 'e really cares about, what people think of 'im.'

'Are you afraid of him yourself?'

'He'll shout and throw things around. Might even 'it me, done it before. I can 'andle 'im.'

Sam wondered how this small woman would deal with a violent, jealous man, and whether her confidence was just bravado, put on for his benefit.

'Will you tell him where Frank is?'

'Don't know, do I? And just as well. Frank might 'ave to disappear for a bit. So much gossip – 'e's probably gone off to hide already, before Ray gets out.'

'When's his release date?'

'Wish I knew. Have to get me nails done.' She took a step towards Sam. He noticed her feet in the fluffy slippers. Her voice was very close. 'Could you find out for me? Please, Mr Postman?'

Sam closed his notebook and stood up. 'You'll have to call the prison or the police about that,' he said. 'Anything else you can tell me?'

Gloria pouted, then looked up at him and smiled. 'I'll trade you,' she said. 'Don't get something for nothing, do you?'

Sam wrote his address and telephone number on his notebook, tore out the page and handed it to her. 'I'm up in Kells, at Frank's house,' he said. 'Do you know where that is?'

She smiled. 'I certainly do, Sam.'

'If you think of anything else, get in touch,' he said, moving towards the door.

'Sure you won't stay a bit longer?'

'No, thanks for your time. I have to go.'

'Pity,' she said.

Sam opened the door and went out without looking back. He walked quickly to the corner, then stopped and took a deep breath. Now he had Gloria's boyfriend's full name he could find out more about him. 'Ray Tennant' he wrote in his notebook. 'Release date?'

CHAPTER 12

Judith felt as if her life were beginning again. The *Furness News* office looked much the same, but her place within it was different, more central, more respected. *It isn't about who I am*, Judith realised during her first few days back at work: *it's about what I do.* 'Chief Reporter', the very title carried authority of a kind she had never experienced before. She wanted to flaunt it, and especially she wanted to rub it in the face of the sub-editor, Ed Cunningham who squatted in his cubbyhole like a spider in its lair. Every time she caught sight of him, she was gratified by her change of status, knowing how much he must resent it.

On Wednesday morning, after two days of adjusting to her elevation, Judith told Andrew that she would do the routine morning check of the overnight book at the police station. It wasn't to save him time, but to make sure that people there knew about her promotion. After a windy, wet night, the streets were damp, and she picked her way through the puddles on the short walk from the office to Barrow's central police station. Nothing much had changed, although the high counter opposite the main door seemed less high. Sergeant Clark, whose kingdom this was, looked up and smiled in a way she didn't recall.

'Well, if it isn't Miss Pharaoh herself,' he exclaimed, 'gracing us with a visit. What's happened to Andrew? Have you frightened him to death already, poor lad?'

'Andrew's fine, Clarky,' said Judith, pleased with the reaction. 'I just wanted to come over myself this morning. It's ages since I was here last. I had the strange idea that some things might have changed, but clearly I was wrong. How are you?'

'When you get to my age,' Sergeant Clark began, and Judith interrupted him. 'I knew you'd say that,' she said. 'You're not that old, but you've been around for ever.'

'Someone has to know where all the bodies are buried,' said Clarky, as he always did.

He looked at his watch. 'Come through for a cuppa, Judith. I'll get someone out 'ere for half an hour. Call it "intelligence gathering", God knows we could do with a bit more of that round 'ere.'

'So, how have you been?' he asked, as a young woman in uniform put two dark cups of tea in front of them. 'How long is it since all that stuff kicked off?'

'Almost eighteen months,' said Judith. 'Funny, isn't it? For a few weeks after it happened I felt OK and then it was like someone had pulled my plug out. I couldn't do anything except sleep, but then there were nightmares, flashbacks. My brain went to mush. For a while I didn't even want to go out. When it was really bad I was too zonked to realise how bad it was.' Clark nodded. 'I honestly thought I'd never work again. Life over at thirty, that was pretty depressing. My dad got me a job at Sellafield in the press office about a year ago, which was OK, but not what I really wanted. And it felt like I was dependent on him, do you know what I mean?'

Sergeant Clark nodded again. 'What happened to Nelly?' he asked. 'He just disappeared. One minute he was a smartarse young DC and the next minute he'd gone. I asked someone and got an earful about him, and didn't ask again.'

Judith hesitated. She'd often wondered how Barrow police had explained Sam's absence, and it seemed they hadn't bothered to do so at all. She wasn't sure what Sam would want her to say. 'He resigned,' she said. 'I think he got the clear idea that his face didn't fit and he'd never make sergeant.' That much was certainly true. 'And he was pretty shaken up by it all, like me. We both needed a break.'

'So what's he doing now?'

'Not sure,' she lied. 'Up in Whitehaven, still deciding what to do next.'

'Different force up there,' said Clark. 'Lancashire doesn't talk to Cumbria. He could probably slot back into policing if he wanted.'

'Yes, we'll see,' she said, hoping that was the end of questions about Sam. 'And what about here?' she went on. 'Morrison went off to Hong Kong, didn't he? Still there?'

Clark shrugged and looked around the room. No one was in sight, but it was hard to tell who might be sitting quietly behind one of the low partitions, listening to the conversation. He leaned forward and lowered his voice. 'Not seen or heard anything of that bastard since he left. And not sorry either. He was a miserable git. Upset all the WPCs, shouting and swearing. It's been much better round 'ere without him.'

'So who's the new DS?'

'Harry Grayson,' said Sergeant Clark, smiling. 'Obvious really, once Nelly was out of the picture. Nice enough bloke.' Clark lowered his voice again. 'Not as sharp as Nelly, I reckon, but good enough, and at least he's pleasant. Gets on with everybody.'

Judith made a square shape with her hands and raised her

eyebrows. He knew she was asking whether the new DS was a freemason. 'Oh aye,' said Clark. 'No surprise there. Him and DI Cardine seem very pally.'

Judith couldn't wait to tell Sam. Harry Grayson had been with Sam when they had rescued her from the Thornhills, but she had the impression he hadn't been keen to get involved in the case.

'Is Harry in?' she asked. 'I'd love to say hello.'

Harry Grayson stood up and smiled broadly when Judith walked into the CID room. She noticed that he'd put on some weight, and looked older and more at ease with himself than the last time she'd seen him. They shook hands, and Harry leaned forward to give her a kiss on the cheek. 'Look what the cat dragged in!' he said. 'Great to see you, Judith, looking as lovely as ever. Rumour has it you're back at the *News* in Skelly's old job. Vast improvement I would say.'

'And rumour has it you're the new DS,' she countered. 'And a vast improvement on the old one, too, if I may say so.' Harry looked around. 'Dave?' he called. No response, but Harry still lowered his voice. 'Not a word about our former colleague has reached my ears,' he said. 'Supposed to be a secondment, but I don't think he'll be back. He'll be scaring some poor Chinky coppers half to death.'

'I only came in to check the overnight book,' she said. 'All the same stuff. Nothing meaty, like we used to have.'

'I think you came in to see me, Judith,' he said. 'Couldn't keep away. And you wanted to show us your new stripes. That new editor's got his head screwed on, getting you back. Thornhill would never have had a woman in that job, for all the stuff his wife spouted about equality and women's rights.'

'Did you ever track her down?' Judith asked. She still couldn't work out whether Irene Thornhill's support for her had been genuine to start with, or just a ploy to keep an eye on what Judith was finding out about Montgomery House.

'No sign of her,' said Harry Grayson. 'She probably changed her name, new passport from somewhere, off to Spain with all the other villains we can't touch.' He looked at Judith carefully. 'You must have been really upset by all that business.'

'I was,' she said.

'Well, it's behind you now,' he said, putting his hand on her arm. 'And leave it behind you, Judith. You did your best, but Monty House and Captain Edwards still have a lot of support round here, you know that, don't you?'

Judith said nothing, wondering how close Harry really was to Inspector Cardine. 'Best left alone, the whole thing,' he went on.

She nodded. 'Probably right,' she said. 'OK, back to work. They'll be wondering whether I've had enough already and gone back to Sellafield.'

'Is that where you were? Barrel of laughs, eh?'

'I'm glad to be back here, Harry.'

'And we're glad you are, Judith. Where are you living now?'

'With Nelly's sister Elspeth, in Roose. Didn't fancy living alone, not just yet.'

'You need a man,' he said. 'Come on, I'll walk you out.'

'You wouldn't believe how Harry Grayson's changed,' Judith said to Sam later when he rang the office. 'He can't be taller, but he looks it somehow. Filled out, very confident.'

'That's what getting to DS does for you,' said Sam, 'and not having Morrison around any more. I'll give him a ring myself, now that I'm half back in the business.'

'What does that mean?' she asked.

Sam told Judith that he'd given up his postman's job and was working for John.

'What? You're a private detective now, Sam? Sounds a bit rum. Why did no one tell me?' she asked.

'That's why I rang,' he said. 'And a few other things.'

'Well, I'm at work, Sam, not doing my own thing like you seem to be. I've got to go.'

'But I went to see Gloria.'

'Well, lucky you. Got to go. Tell me later. Or I'll call you. 'Bye.'

The line went dead. Sam swore under his breath and wished he didn't care. He went into the front room and sat down on the little chair, wondering about the decision to take this job on. Had he done the right thing? No wonder Judith sounded sceptical about it. He found some paper and began to make a list of things he needed to do. Most of them meant more phone calls, and he took the chair into the hall to be nearer the phone. Almost immediately the phone rang again.

'You're still there,' said Judith. 'I rang off 'cos someone came into the office. Thought you might be out sleuthing by now.'

'I know it all sounds a bit odd,' he said, 'but John was very persuasive.'

'He's worried,' she said. 'And it could work. What will you do first?'

'I told you, I've been to see Gloria,' said Sam.

'Ah yes, what a piece of work she is,' Judith said. 'I wouldn't trust her further than I could throw her.'

'She wasn't keen on you either.'

'Men first, last and all the time with that one,' Judith went on. 'Bet she was all over you.'

'Did she say anything to you about where Frank was playing cards, to try and win money?'

'I think she said something about down near the harbour. I was pretty disgusted with her by that time, couldn't wait to get out.'

'How come?'

'Personal stuff, questions,' said Judith after a brief pause, remembering. 'The woman's obsessed with sex.'

'She must be worried about her man coming out,' he said.

'Serves her right,' said Judith. She was quiet for a moment. 'While you're here Sam, can I ask you about something?'

'What?'

'I'm still wondering if I can do anything with the Monty House story, something to get the nationals interested. I just need an angle.'

Sam was horrified.

'For God's sake, Judith, leave it alone! That place is fire-proof. I tried, believe me, but there's no story, not yet. May never be, not with Cardine watching Edwards' back.'

'Yes, but Harry Grayson's here now, not Morrison.'

'Harry Grayson? The man's weak as water. He kept telling me to keep my head down, just follow orders. I bet he's halfway up Cardine's trousers already.'

Judith hesitated. 'Well, he was very pleased to see me and I like him,' she said. 'And it's my work and my story and you mind your own business. Just focus on finding Frank, right, and leave my job to me.'

The line went dead. Sam swore under his breath. Grayson. He could always turn on the charm when he needed to. He looked down at the list on his lap and made another call.

Harry Grayson's voice reached him almost immediately. 'Nelly, I was just thinking about you. How are you?'

'Judith told me she'd spoken to you,' said Sam, 'and I could do with your help with something. Congratulations on making DS, by the way. Enjoying it?'

'I'm enjoying not having Morrison breathing down my neck,' said Harry. 'Judith was here not long ago, looking as gorgeous as ever. I thought you and she were seeing each other.'

Sam managed to sound amused. 'No chance,' he said.

'Well I wouldn't mind giving it a go,' said Harry. 'Always fancied her.'

Sam didn't know what to say. The thought bothered him, and he changed the subject.

'Actually, Harry, I want some advice. I've taken on a job, for Judith's dad. It's a family problem they want help with, finding a relative who's disappeared. I need to talk to CID here in Whitehaven about it but I can't get them to take me seriously at all. I can check around on my own well enough, but without a warrant card there are limits. It's not a missing person case yet, and they just keeping fobbing me off, not replying to messages, you know how we avoid dealing with people who are a nuisance. Well, looks like I'm the nuisance.'

'What the DC's name? Might have come across him, even in a different force.'

'DC Rob Holmes,' said Sam. 'When I first met him about something else he was quite pally, but now he won't talk to me at all.'

'Name means nowt to me, Nelly, but not surprising really. We just deal with Lancashire. Seems odd that he was pally and then stopped.' Silence. 'Is this job you're working on already part of some investigation?'

'Not as far as I know,' said Sam.

'If it is, they might be worried about you queering the

pitch, so to speak. They can't come clean about it, but they can ignore you and hope you'll go away.'

Sam wondered about that himself, but said nothing.

'Can you tell me any more?' Harry asked.

'Not really, sorry. Confidential information, you know.'

'Aye, right. Sorry I can't help. Good to talk you, pal. What do they say up there, "marra"?'

'That's the word,' said Sam. 'You know it came from the Vikings? Getting used to it now. Thanks anyway.'

'Keep in touch,' said Harry. 'I'll keep you posted about my progress with the fair Judith.'

'OK,' said Sam. Damn, he thought.

Stymied. Blocked. Sam groped for the right word for his frustration. Even as a humble postman he felt more in charge of his life than he did now. The house in West Row was quiet and he sat in the relatively clean kitchen and went back over the little information he had. The only line of enquiry open to him seemed to be the vague detail about Frank's card playing. If that's what he returned to after the brief respite on the Sunday, maybe that's where he was still, hiding out somewhere. Sam knew that these games could sometimes go on for days, with players coming and going. The stakes might be high, far higher than Frank could manage. With mounting debts and desperation what might he do? 'Come home, Frank,' Sam whispered to himself.

A card game in a pub near the harbour, that was all Gloria had said. At least it was somewhere to start. Sam took the car, just in case the enquiries there led him further afield, and parked near the market square. He would ask around all the pubs in that part of town, show Frank's photo and see if anything turned up. That was his job now, and at least he was doing something.

One or two doors were still shut ahead of the lunchtime opening but Sam decided not to take a closed door as a barrier. He banged hard on the door of the Rose, to no avail. At the Salutation he did the same, and after a few moments heavy steps approached from the other side and the door opened. 'Too early,' said the red-headed man who put his head round the door. 'Half an hour.'

'Wait,' said Sam, thrusting the photo of Frank under the man's nose. 'Seen this bloke around?' The man squinted and shook his head. He was closing the door again when Sam asked. 'If I was looking for a card game round here, a big one, where would I go?'

The man hesitated. 'Try the Dog,' he said, looking at Sam's fresh face and neat appearance. 'You a copper?'

'Nay,' said Sam.

'You look like one. No one wants a copper playing cards. Makes them nervous.' The red-headed man shut the door in Sam's face.

Sam turned away and looked round the square. The noise of vehicles and trains blew in from the harbour and bounced off the tall buildings. Anywhere else, he thought, this place would be in guide books, but this was industrial West Cumberland and Whitehaven was a working town. He should have asked the man where the Dog was, but didn't want to sound more amateur than he already felt. Some parts of the town he knew like the back of his hand, but not down here.

He walked towards the main street, and spotted the three-story pub with 'Dog and Partridge' on a swinging sign. It looked promising – he'd already surmised that card playing would be done in an upstairs room, allowing the players to come and go without being noticed. The front door was open. The sound of a vacuum cleaner assailed his ears, and a short broad-shouldered older man was standing behind the bar, reading a newspaper.

'I'm looking for the game,' said Sam, leaning over the bar so that the man could hear him.

The man put the paper down a fraction. 'What game?'

'The card game. The big one,' said Sam, reaching into his jacket for a wad of five pound notes he was keeping there. 'Gloria told me to come down here. Gloria Tennant.'

The man hesitated. 'See Dermot.' He looked at the clock. 'Café, down the street.' The newspaper returned to its previous position.

Outside, Sam looked around, and this time spotted the front of the café across the street and to his left. The door-bell jangled as he entered, and a young man in the far corner looked up briefly. Sam ordered tea and toast and sat down at the table next to the young man, who took no notice of him. 'Are you Dermot?' he asked. 'The landlord at the Dog said you'd be here.'

'Who's asking?'

'My name's Sam. I'm looking for a friend, and Gloria Tennant said to try here.'

Dermot Hennessey smiled. 'You know Gloria? She OK?'

I wonder if he knows about the violent husband, Sam thought. 'Just the same,' he said.

'We were on the cruise ships together,' Dermot said, smiling. 'Good times.'

'She's fine,' said Sam. 'The bloke I'm looking for is a friend of hers, too.' Sam pulled the increasingly frail photograph from his inside pocket and handed it to Dermot. Tea and toast arrived.

Dermot said, 'Have you come for his stuff?'

'You know him?'

'It's Frank, isn't it? Looks better here than the last time I saw him.'

'When was that?'

'Yesterday morning. The game broke up around five. Frank was too tired to go anywhere so he crashed on my couch, upstairs.' He gestured to the pub across the street, then looked again at the photo and handed it back to Sam. 'You a friend of his?'

'Family friend,' said Sam. 'They've asked me to find him.'

'He needs help,' said Dermot. 'In way over his head. I'm the croupier, by the way. Never bet, mug's game. They get me in when I'm home from the cruise ships. It's a job. I see too many idiots like Frank.'

'Didn't know it was so, you know, organised,' said Sam.

Dermot sipped his coffee. 'You have no idea,' he said. 'So, do you want Frank's stuff? Haven't seen him this morning. When I woke up an hour ago there was no sign of him. If he tries to run, they'll find him. Finish your tea and I'll take you over. That's what you want, right? You don't want to play?'

In the Dog the broad-shouldered man was still reading his newspaper. 'He's with me,' said Dermot, and they walked through a door at the far end of the room and up narrow wooden stairs, right to the top of the building. Sam looked at the cluttered space as Dermot went into a neighbouring room and came back carrying a plastic holdall. 'This is all he had,' he said. 'You might as well take it. Don't think he'll be back, and if he does turn up I'm going to push him down those stairs.' He handed the bag to Sam. 'Now piss off,' he said. 'They don't like anyone poking around, asking questions.'

Sam carried the bag back to his car and opened it up in the

relative privacy of the front seat. Underwear, a crumpled blue shirt, and a wallet. He opened the wallet. No money inside, but tucked into the back was a photo. Sam stared. A young woman smiled back at him, short, petite, with white hair piled onto her head, wisps of it blowing round her face. She was leaning on the rail of a ship, and beside her stood the man he had just met, Dermot the croupier. 'Gloria,' Sam asked the image. 'Where's Frank?'

Chapter 13

Not far from the house in West Row, at Birkhams sandstone quarry perched on top of the cliffs near St Bees Head, George Flynn, quarryman, decided at noon to take his bait box and eat his lunch outside. The May morning was warm and soft, after heavy overnight rain that had muddied the site and the road from Sandwith that he'd walked down five hours before. The sun was high and the southerly breeze didn't reach a sheltered spot where he liked to sit on days like this. If there was any of his pie or sandwich left over, he could amuse himself by watching the gulls dive for it.

He walked south for a few yards from the quarry entrance and perched on his favourite rock, facing across Saltom Bay to the north and the hazy hills of Galloway. A crowd of noisy gulls drew his eye down to the beach below. Some of the birds rose on a gust of breeze and George noticed a dark shape, too big for a rock or a pile of seaweed. He strained to make it out, but his middle-aged eyes were not that good. One of the younger blokes would see more clearly, but it could wait. He finished his lunch, threw the crumbs to the wheeling birds, and walked back to the quarry. It wasn't quite time to start work again, and George asked his marra, Jacob, to walk back with him to the spot where they could look down at the beach. There was nothing to see from the quarry because the slope was too steep to get close to the edge.

'Down there,' he said to Jacob. 'Just under the cliff, on the high tide line.'

The younger man took a moment to see what George was talking about. 'Looks like a person,' he said. 'I can see his legs, spread out.'

'Someone lying down?' asked George.

Jacob turned back towards the quarry. 'We need the cops, or the coastguard,' he said. 'I reckon that's a body.'

Sam had just reached home to make himself some lunch and consider what to do with Frank's bag, when the phone rang. It was DC Holmes. 'You still looking for Frank Pharaoh?'

'Why?' Sam asked. His stomach churned.

'Call from the quarry, on the cliffs near St Bees Head. Something on the beach below the cliffs, they say it looks like a body. I'm guessing it could be your man. We're taking the small lifeboat boat out, easier than along the beach below the Marchon pipe. Want to come out with us? Quicker we get an ID the better.'

'Where, when?' said Sam.

'Wellington Lodge, harbour, twenty minutes.'

Sam parked near the square for the second time that day and ran down the quayside towards Wellington Lodge, part of the old pit buildings that still dominated the south side of the harbour. He heard Rob Holmes' voice before he saw his head above the wharf. A black rubber dinghy was moored at the bottom of some slimy steps. Rob helped Sam into the boat, already crowded with three other men. 'Sergeant Braithwaite,' said Rob. One of the men nodded. 'And Dr Jennings,' he added, indicating an older man with grey hair looking awkward in a bulky orange life vest. 'We need to have a good look before we bring the body back to the mortuary, if it is a body.'

'Not much chance of survival if he's come off the top,' said Dr Jennings. 'And the two men who spotted him saw no sign of movement. Hope the gulls haven't got him already. They go for the eyes first.'

Rob turned to the man at the stern by the tiller. 'OK, Will,' he said. 'Let's go.'

It took only a few minutes to get round the end of the outer harbour wall and the boat speeded up, turning back towards the south. Sam could see the line of houses on West Row as they passed hundreds of feet below. Round the headland lay the town of St Bees, and the Pharaohs' house on Beach Road just a few hundred yards from the shore.

They could see the dark shape on the tide line under the cliff when the flock of gulls rose squealing at their approach. The tide was low and the skipper took the boat as close as he could. The others were wearing sea boots but Sam took off his shoes and rolled up his trouser legs before stepping out into the water, struggling to keep his balance on the slimy rocks. The nausea he'd felt since Rob's phone call had intensified, a churn of anxiety and anticipation that he remembered all too well from the night when they'd rescued Judith from the Thornhills.

Sergeant Braithwaite was the first to reach the body, which lay face down on the rocks below the cliff. Pebbles scattered around, with gobbets of dark red earth pockmarked by the heavy rain of the night before. By the time Rob and Sam joined him Braithwaite had lit a cigarette and stood looking at the ground and then up at the cliff that towered above them.

'What's the story, sunshine?' Braithwaite said to the inert shape at his feet. 'Who are you, and did you jump or were you pushed?'

'May I?' asked Sam.

'That's what you're here for, lad,' said the sergeant. 'Ex-copper aren't you? You know what to do. Don't touch owt until the doc says so. Just have a look at his face, round this side. We need to know who he is, right?'

Sam walked round to where the head twisted awkwardly sideways and crouched down. He saw the closed eyes, the dark curls, the line of the jaw.

'Frank Pharaoh,' he said. Sadness and regret swept over him, and he looked away. Why hadn't he made him stay in the house on Sunday, or encouraged him more to get help? He was just a lad, twenty-three and desperate. Suddenly Sam understood what might have brought him to these cliffs in the middle of a rainy night: he was trying to get home to St Bees, to safety.

The doctor knelt by Frank's body, moving the head slightly, feeling the limbs, while Holmes and Braithwaite looked on. Sam turned away. The boatman stood in the shallow water, holding the boat. He'd seen this all before, and was planning how to get the inert form on board for the brief ride back to the harbour and then on to the mortuary.

Sam said to no one in particular, 'His parents live just round the headland, in St Bees. Maybe he was trying to get there.'

'All sorts of maybe's,' said Braithwaite, 'and all of 'em our business, not yours. Do you want to tell the family, or shall we?'

'I'll do it,' said Sam. 'Are you taking Frank to the mortuary? What if they want to see him?'

'It'll be there a few days before the PM,' said Holmes. 'How long. doc?'

'Wednesday today,' said Jennings. 'Can't get to it before Monday.'

'So tell them end of next week for the funeral, if we can release the body by then,' said Holmes. 'And give the mortuary blokes a few hours to clean him up before anyone comes to view,' he added.

Sam nodded. 'Any ideas, Dr Jennings?'

'You related?' the doctor asked, aware that Braithwaite clearly thought that Sam's status as an ex-copper didn't count for much.

Sam lied quickly. 'Sister's fiancé,' he said. 'Frank's dad asked me to give up work to look for him.'

The doctor nodded. 'Can't tell what happened. He fell, obviously, but that could have been an accident, or deliberate, or he could have been helped on his way. PM should give us a time of death, and an idea about the sequence of injuries. From what I can see, rigor and so on, I'd put time of death late last night or early this morning, but don't quote me on that. Various lacerations, broken leg, probably ribs, and damage on the right side of the head, but I won't know more than that for a while.'

'High tide was at four this morning,' said Rob Holmes. 'Sounds like he was in enough trouble to be roaming around at that hour in bad weather. Easier ways to do it though.'

'Do what?' Sam asked.

'Top yourself,' said Rob.

'Or he just slipped,' Sergeant Braithwaite added, flicking his cigarette butt into a pile of seaweed. 'Much the same, either way.'

'Not to his mother,' said Sam.

They watched while Dr Jennings looked closely at the bruised face and checked the sodden pockets of jacket and trousers. 'Nothing,' he said. 'No note, no wallet, no keys, nothing.'

Sam fished in his inside pocket for the photo he was still carrying, and handed it down to the doctor. Jennings looked carefully at it and then back at the face at his feet. 'Looks like this young man, that's for sure. How old?'

'Twenty-three,' said Sam.

'Shame,' said the doctor.

Braithwaite was all business. 'Finished, doc? Let's get him back to the mortuary.'

Between them they carried Frank's broken body back to the small boat and sat around it in silence as they returned to the harbour. The surface was calm and glassy, and the salty water on Sam's cheeks was not sea spray. Back at his car in the square, he sat thinking for a long time before he started the engine. He could go straight to Sellafield to find John, or he could do what the police showed no inclination to do, not yet at least, and check the spot where Frank might have spent the last few minutes of his life.

He drove to Sandwith, a small village only two miles from the centre of Whitehaven. Frank could have walked there in less than an hour, down the track to the coast and then along the cliffs into St Bees. In the centre of the village, Sam turned right and followed the road towards the quarry, going over his crime scene training in his mind. When he reached the end of the road at the quarry gate he made a mental list of what he could do with the few resources he had, before police boots and carelessness might compromise the place. All he had to work with was the camera, the long lens, the Polaroid, a tape measure, his notebook and the sharp pencil he always kept in the inside pocket of his jacket along with some small paper bags. Even in his days on the force he wouldn't have had much more than that. We can put a man on the moon, he thought, but we still can't do much more with a crime scene than Sherlock bloody Holmes.

With any luck he might find the spot he was looking for and examine it himself before anyone else arrived. The quarry was to his left, dark red sandstone blocks glowing in the afternoon light. High chain-link gates were open: presumably the blokes who called it in were still there. He'd try his luck there next, but the first essential was to check the cliff edge. He looked over the edge immediately ahead of him and realised that Frank must have fallen further south to have ended up where they had found him. He walked the narrow track between the quarry fence and the edge to a point where the cliff fell sharply away. The path was muddy, flanked by patches of low gorse flattened by the wind and a few stunted bushes. He caught the sweet coconut scent of the gorse flowers on the soft May breeze. Further on bluebells nodded among the long grass.

Sam dropped to his knees, feeling the damp seep through the legs of his trousers, searching for any signs of what had happened. At the edge, where the sandstone fractured into shards and the air opened up below, he fumbled for the camera, adjusted his weight to avoid tipping forwards and took a picture of the ragged earth at the very edge. Standing carefully, he backed away from the danger and looked down at the track. There was a clear imprint. A boot maybe, but it was hard to tell. He crouched down and searched for the tape measure, his notebook and the pencil. The boot mark, if that's what it was, was over eleven inches long. That was a size 11 in shoes, if he remembered correctly. But Frank's feet weren't that big, he was sure. Size 8 maybe, an inch or more shorter than this one. He wrote the information in his notebook, then got carefully to his feet and walked back to the mud and gravel where the quarry track met the clifftop path.

More boot marks, more photos, more measurements, size 11 again by the look of it, and here another pair of boots, slightly smaller. Sam looked carefully at the marks of the sole, started a fresh page in his notebook, and sketched what he saw as accurately as he could, as the gulls screeched over his head and four cormorants flapped determinedly south towards their nests on St Bees Head.

He moved further back, to the other side of the path and onto the track that led away from the quarry gates. He was looking for tyre marks, and found fresh ones that didn't lead towards the quarry gates but stopped short, facing towards the sea. On either side of where the vehicle had stopped the earth was scuffed and scarred by overlapping prints; leading away towards the track to the cliff edge were clear signs of two grooves, a few inches apart. Sam bent low, moving carefully around to get as much light as he could. The inside edges of the grooves were smooth, the mud raised a little on either side. Another photo. Someone could have been dragged, the toes of their shoes scraping through the mud, towards the darkness where the ground fell away, and a final lurch into oblivion.

A picture was forming in his head, but he fought it. Assumptions were the curse of good policing, he knew that. He must keep looking, and avoid the temptation to see only what he wanted to see, not what was actually there. Clearly a vehicle of some kind had stopped here, in the very recent past. At least one person other than the driver had stepped out. Something appeared to have been dragged down the track, but it wouldn't have been the first time that people had tipped unwanted household rubbish over the edge rather than take it somewhere else. Had he seen anything down on the beach? An old chair or table, maybe, something that could have made those two lines in the soft ground? After one more close look and feel over the disturbed ground Sam stood back, making sure that he had all the photos and notes that he needed.

He trod carefully backwards, retracing his own steps, and walked towards the gates of the quarry. Work seemed to have been suspended for the day, probably in anticipation of the police arriving after the activity on the beach. Sam knocked on the door of a hut at the side of the yard, walked in and found two men smoking, looking up at the new arrival.

'Police?' the younger one asked. Sam nodded. 'You were right, it was a body. Thanks for calling it in. Doc's had a look and they've taken it to the mortuary.'

'Aye, we saw the boat,' said the older man. 'I saw the body first.' He extended his hand which felt tough as leather in Sam's. 'George Flynn, quarryman,' he said. 'D'you know who it is?'

'Can't say yet,' Sam replied. What was the point of complicating the issue with a story about what kind of policeman he actually was, or sharing Frank's name with these strangers? He turned to the younger man. 'Jacob Doolan,' said the man. His hand was warm and rough. 'George got me to 'ave a look, younger eyes you know. I thought it were a body, right from the off. Gulls were on it. Did they make a mess?'

'Not too bad,' said Sam. 'What time did you first notice it?'

'Bait time,' said George, 'noon.'

'And what time did you start work?'

'Normal, 'alf seven,' said Jacob. 'Later in the winter like, but 'alf seven today.'

'Notice anything unusual?'

The two men thought for a few moments. George shook his head. 'Looked pretty much same as always. Not much comes down 'ere, tha knows. Track doesn't go anywhere, only 'ere. Walkers sometimes, heading off round the cliff to St Bees, but they can use a shorter path to Fleswick Bay, not all the way down to 'ere.'

Sam made a mental note to look at the large-scale map he had at home. 'Any signs of a vehicle, something that wasn't coming here to the quarry?'

They both shook their heads. 'You mean last night?' said Jacob. 'We knock off before four. If anything came down here before seven thirty this morning, we wouldn't know.'

Sam took the hint: it was nearly knocking off time. 'Anything else you noticed? Not just today. Seen any cars or vans, anything in the past few weeks?'

They shook their heads again.

'Well, thanks,' said Sam. 'I won't keep you. I'll write both your names down in case I need you again. Is there a phone here?'

Jacob pointed to the phone on a cluttered table. 'Good job there is, or we'd've 'ad to leg it back to Sandwith to call the cops.'

'What about old Cleggy, downaways?' asked George. 'He might've seen summat. Just beyond the quarry gate, on the right. Isaac Clegg. Mind, I've not seen 'im for a bit.'

Jacob said, 'I heard 'e were in hospital, but that were a while ago. Might've heard summat, if 'e were about. Worth a try.'

Both men on their feet now, packing up their bags, ready to go. Sam went ahead of them across the yard.

'Do you want a ride back to Sandwith?' he asked. 'Just need to stop at that house on the way past, in case someone's there.'

But there was no response from the cottage, and when George and Jacob walked away into the village, Sam turned off the car engine and waited. He needed to think, and to brace himself for the worst conversation of his life.

CHAPTER 14

It was after four o'clock. Sam wanted to see John before the rest of the family; he couldn't bear the thought of telling Maggie that her elder son was gone, not after her stoic refusal to recognise that he was in serious trouble. There was a phone box in the village and Sam found change, asked for the Sellafield main office number and finally got through to John's office.

'Mr Pharaoh's at a meeting. May I ask who's calling?' said John's secretary, whose voice revealed childhood elocution lessons.

'It's Sam Tognarelli, I'm a friend of the family and it's very important I speak to him, about a personal matter.'

'Oh,' she said. 'Let me see if I can find him. Can you hold the line, please?'

There was a long pause. Then John said, 'Sam, what is it?'

'I need to see you,' said Sam. He couldn't face telling John over the phone that his son had been found dead. 'Could you meet me at the main gate?'

'Can it wait till I get home, I'll be there by six?'

'I'd rather not.'

'Is it Frank?'

'Please John, let me come and see you now.'

The main gate at Sellafield was a bleak place for bad news, but John ushered Sam into a small office and asked the security man who was sitting there to leave them for a few minutes. John's face and reputation were well known, and the man left them without a word.

'It's Frank, isn't it?' said John. 'Have they found him? Is he hurt?'

Sam took John's arm and eased him into the chair. 'We found him earlier this afternoon, John, on Saltom beach.' John stared at him. 'I'm afraid he's dead. I'm so sorry.'

Still John stared, incomprehension in his face, until his eyes filled with tears and he leaned forward, shoulders bent in pain. Sam wanted to touch him, hold him, but he stood still, listening to the convulsive sobs.

'What happened?' John said finally, looking up.

Sam told him what he knew, the phone call from the quarry to the police, the lifeboat, what they found, what Dr Jennings had said. John listened without interruption, watching Sam's face.

'Where is he now?' he asked.

'At the mortuary. Do you know where that is?'

John nodded. He remembered the hours he'd spent there after the William pit disaster many years before, the silent families identifying their husbands, sons, brothers, and then the funerals, hundreds of funerals.

'Do they want me to go there?'

'Only if you want to. I was able to identify him, and I had the photo of him, too.'

John thought for a moment. 'Maggie has to know. She might want to come with me.' He paused. 'And Vince. He's lost a brother.'

'What do you want me to do?' asked Sam.

155

'Come home with me. They'll have questions, and you can help.' John put his hand to his mouth. 'Judith,' he said, choking. 'I need to tell Judith.'

'Do you want me to do that?' Sam asked.

'No,' said John. 'I'll do it from home.'

Sam closed his eyes for a moment. It would have been unbearable to tell Judith himself.

He waited while John went for his car, then followed him back to St Bees. The traffic was heavy. A life had ended but the world went on, people going home from work as usual, back to their families and their normal routines. The Pharaoh family would always remember this day but to everyone else it was just another day, like yesterday and tomorrow.

Vince was at the door as he always was, recognising John's footfall on the path. He could not see his father's face clearly, but he sensed that something was wrong. John held his younger son close. 'Where's your mother?' he said. 'I need to speak to you all, can you go in the front room with Sam?'

'What's up, Sam?' Vince whispered. 'Is it Frank?'

Maggie came in. 'Mum's asleep,' she said to John. 'Do you want me to wake her?'

John shook his head, put an arm around his wife and sat her down. Sam held Vince's arm, and they sat looking at John who was standing by the fireplace, clutching a handkerchief in his hand. His long handsome face was pale.

'Frank's dead, dears,' he said. 'They found him on Saltom beach.'

Maggie's mouth opened and she yelled, a short unnatural sound. John knelt down beside her, holding her head. Vince looked at Sam, his face full of questions, but Sam waited until the first storm was over. 'Shall I fetch Father Price?' he asked.

Maggie nodded dumbly, still clinging on to John. 'Yes,

please,' John said. 'You know where the presbytery is, next to the church, on the High Road?'

'I know,' said Vince. 'I'll go with him.'

'We should have phoned,' said Sam, as he guided Vince across the road to his car. 'No, I wanted to get out,' said Vince. 'I feel so helpless.'

'We all do,' said Sam.

Vince fidgeted in the passenger seat. 'It could have been me who died when I fell off that wall. Frank was always the steady one, that nothing happened to.' He turned to Sam as they set off towards the top road. 'What did happen, really?'

'They don't know,' said Sam. 'Truly. The doctor will be able to tell us more, and the police. It could be an accident.'

'He was in trouble, wasn't he?' said Vince.

'Yes, I'm afraid so. More than we realised.'

'He couldn't have, you know, done it to himself, could he? That would be the worst thing.' He thought for a moment. 'Just tell Father Price that Frank slipped and fell, nothing more,' he said to Sam.

Sam nodded. 'I know,' he said. 'He has to comfort your mum and Violet, not upset them. If we find him.'

They did find the priest, eating his supper alone in the large bare dining room of the presbytery, as he'd done most evenings since the place was built, next to the massive church. He'd been in Kells for many years and knew everything and everybody. Sam persuaded the zealous housekeeper to interrupt his supper, and Vince listened quietly as Sam explained and asked the priest to come back with them. Father Price left his supper, picked up his jacket and a small black bag and came with them without hesitation.

John greeted them at the door of the house, where the front room curtains had already been drawn. Violet was in the front room with her daughter, both of them sitting with their hands in their lap, waiting for Father Price to say what needed to be said. John ushered Sam out of the room, and Vince followed them. 'Don't leave me in there,' he begged. 'Are you going to tell Judith?'

'I'm going to call her now,' said his father. 'Take Sam in the kitchen and make tea for everyone will you, Vince?' He took his younger son in his arms and held him very tight. Vince's arms stayed at his side for a minute before he put them round his father in return.

In the kitchen, Vince said. 'Why don't I feel more? I thought it would be bad. I thought he might die. Why, Sam? Why aren't I shocked and crying, like I should be?'

'Things like this hit people differently,' said Sam. 'And at different times. You'll feel it. There's nothing wrong with you, Vince. It's OK.'

Judith's grief was different too, dry-eyed and bitter. On the evening train from Barrow she'd had time to feel shocked, mortal, sad, and now angry that no one had stopped this, found Frank, saved him, pulled him back from the brink. John met her off the train, and by the time they reached the house, Father Price had gone, the family doctor had given Maggie something to help her sleep, and Sam and Vince were sitting silently together at the kitchen table.

Sam was not prepared for the visible anger that hung around Judith like a thorny cloak. Vince saw it, hugged his sister, said he would see her in the morning, and left them alone.

'What happened?' Judith asked Sam. 'I want to know everything, not just the version you gave Dad before.'

'I told him everything,' said Sam.

'But what about before today?'

Sam hesitated. He looked at John, who nodded. 'Tell us,' he said.

Sam took a deep breath. As he told about the visit to Gloria, the information about Frank's losses at cards and the encounter with the croupier, John's sadness intensified. 'Do the police know all this?' he asked.

'Not yet,' said Sam. 'I'd only just found Frank's bag when I got the call from the police. That was around one o'clock. Then I went out with them, like I told you.'

Judith turned on him. 'You've done nothing, have you? Dad paid you to stop work and find Frank, and he was here in Whitehaven all the time and you didn't find him until he turned up dead on the beach.'

'Judith,' said John. 'Keep your voice down, and don't talk to Sam like that. He's tried to help, that's all I asked.'

'You don't know him like I do, Dad,' she hissed. 'He thinks too much, does nothing. You're too trusting.' Sam didn't respond, stunned by the force of her energy, and by the possibility that she might be right, that he should have done more, been more urgent, more insistent.

John came to his rescue. 'We can't blame Sam,' he insisted. 'It sounds as if Frank was deliberately avoiding all of us. He thought he could manage on his own. I had no idea he was betting like this, did you? What did we miss?'

'What did *he* miss?' Judith said, implacable, pointing at Sam. 'You paid him to find Frank, and he didn't until today when it was too late.' She rinsed her mug under the tap, her back to them. 'You never liked that job, did you, Sam? Couldn't wait to give it up. Well, lucky you.'

John got up. 'Stop it, Judith! That's enough, for pity's sake. This is not Sam's fault. I asked him to take this on, for us.

Frank was our son, your brother. If anyone's to blame, we are.' He turned to Sam. 'I'm sorry, Sam. We're all so sad, we don't know what to do or say. Judith doesn't mean it, really.'

Judith stood at the sink, her back still towards them. Sam pushed back his chair and nodded to John.

'I should go,' he said. 'Tomorrow I'll talk to the police. Good night, Judith.' She stood motionless, silent.

John followed him out into the hall. 'She doesn't mean it,' he repeated. 'It'll look different in the morning. I know you did your best.' He opened the front door. 'But there is something you could do, if you can.'

'Anything,' said Sam.

'You know how much their faith means to Maggie, and her mother, more than me and Vince.'

Sam nodded, 'I know.'

'Suicide's a mortal sin for them, and for Father Price,' John went on. 'If there's any suspicion of that, if the coroner decides that Frank took his own life, it would be dreadful for them, you know what I mean?' He ran his hand through his greying hair. 'Years ago, Father Price refused to marry Maggie and me, because I wasn't a Catholic, did you know that? If Frank's death is ruled a suicide, he could … well it could be awkward and worse, much worse, than it is now.'

Sam nodded. He understood.

'Try and find out what really happened,' John went on. They were standing at the front gate, and Sam could see Vince staring out from between the closed curtains. 'We need to know. It won't help Frank now, but it could help us as a family. We nearly lost Judith not long ago, and Vince may never see properly again. I need to understand what happened with Frank.'

Sam shook John's hand. 'I'll do whatever I can,' he said.

❖ ❖ ❖

He could hardly bring himself to go into the house in West Row. Mrs Barstow's house next door was still boarded up, and the smell of smoke still hung in the air. Sam stood for a few minutes at the door of Frank's bedroom, looking at the messy bed, the clothes thrown over a chair and on the floor. He picked up a jacket, held it to his face and caught the smell of Gloria's perfume. He found a hanger and put it away, closing the wardrobe door firmly. John hadn't asked about Frank's friendship with Gloria and he hadn't offered any details. Did the police know, he wondered. Did they even want to know? Braithwaite's mind seemed to be made up as soon as he saw the broken body. Frank had slipped or had jumped; that was the easiest conclusion and it might be hard to change his mind. And what the sergeant thought, the DC would follow, unless DC Holmes was stronger and braver than Sam had surmised.

He was exhausted, but sleep wouldn't come. As dawn began to glimmer, he was still hurting, stung by Judith's anger and his own sense of uselessness. When he woke with a start, cloud and rain had spread in from the west. It was time to decide what to do, and do it. Downstairs at the tiny kitchen table, Sam made a list. He would take the bag to the CID team and tell them about Gloria and the jealous husband. They might try to get more information out of her, but Sam knew he would probably do better himself, if he could keep the woman at arm's length. Maybe he should keep Gloria to himself for now? He would go back to Dermot the croupier, too. Mirehouse could wait, but he had to get to Braithwaite and Holmes before their minds were made up. He groped for the name of the man in the house behind the quarry. Isaac Clegg, that was it, and the name was added to the list. Then he remembered all the notes he'd made at the cliff top, and the photos that would need to be developed. Evidence. Above all, he needed to prove that Frank had not taken his own life and condemned his soul to damnation.

Sam looked around the tiny room, found some drawing pins in a kitchen drawer, and took them with an old newspaper up to his bedroom, where there was plenty of light. He spread sheets of paper over Violet's pink wallpaper and began to pin up the notes and sketches he had made. He didn't think hard yet about where to put each one, that would come later. He tore pages out of his notebook with names, dates and details and pinned them up too. He was making his own incident room, where he could gather and collate what he knew and think about it. It was what he used to do as a DC and it made him feel useful. Seeing how little hard information he already had gave him energy to go out and use it, and find more. Breakfast could wait. He got dressed in his detective's tweed jacket and grey trousers, picked up the bag with Frank's meagre belongings, and went out.

At the police station, a young WPC showed Sam to Sergeant Braithwaite's office, which was separate from a long narrow space, more like a corridor, where the DCs had their desks. It made the sergeants seem like old-time bosses, overseeing their minions. That's about right, Sam thought to himself. If he ever went back into the force, he wanted to make sergeant as quickly as possible.

It had taken fifteen minutes after Sam's arrival at the main police station for his request to see Braithwaite to be acknowledged and for him to be collected from the reception area. He'd decided to go to the police first, despite the thought that Dermot might be a more useful source of information. That would wait, but making contact with the police, the real police that Sam was no longer part of, would not. He'd also decided to keep quiet about Frank's relationship with Gloria Tennant. She would be far more open with him if the police weren't sniffing around.

Braithwaite was on the phone and pointed at Sam to sit. When the call was ended, Braithwaite turned to him. 'Well,' he said with a faintly smug expression, 'we've already found where young Frank had been spending his time, since the weekend.'

'Yes,' said Sam. 'He'd got involved in a card game in an upstairs room at the Dog and Partridge, near the market.'

The sergeant looked surprised, which Sam found very gratifying. 'When did you work that out?'

'I had a tip-off,' said Sam. 'I asked around, found where it was happening, and talked to the bloke who was acting as croupier.'

'Don't tell me, it was Dermot Hennessey,' said Braithwaite. 'Whenever he turns up in town there's trouble.'

Sam went on, enjoying his clear advantage over the pompous sergeant. 'Frank was sleeping on Dermot's couch on the top floor of the pub. Card game went on for days, apparently.' He picked up the holdall from the floor and put it triumphantly on Braithwaite's desk. 'This is Frank's,' he said. 'Dermot gave it to me. He told me Frank was finished, must have owed so much they wouldn't let him carry on.'

'Have you gone through it?'

Sam shook his head. 'Police business, you said. So it's here. I haven't even told the family I have it.' All that was true.

'How did Frank's folks take it?' Braithwaite asked.

'Badly,' said Sam. 'They're big Catholics, still go to St Mary's, at least the mother and grandmother do, so any idea of suicide is as bad as it gets.'

'Bloody Father Price,' said Braithwaite. 'He's been putting the fear of God into that lot up in Kells for twenty years, more. Don't know how they stand for it.'

'Father Price was at the Pharaohs' place last night,' he said. 'He was a comfort, as far as I could see.'

'He's a smug bugger,' said Braithwaite. 'Let's have a look at this bag. You're an ex-copper, CID, right?'

Sam nodded. He wondered what else DC Holmes had said about him.

'So you know the drill. You haven't messed with it?'

Sam shook his head. Lying was coming more easily. Braithwaite pulled a pair of thin rubber gloves out of a drawer and unzipped the bag. They both peered in, Sam for the second time. Carefully Braithwaite picked up the first item. 'Thank God for the gloves,' he said, as a crumpled pair of underpants emerged, followed by a shirt, and a pair of socks and the sour smell of stale sweat. He picked up the wallet and opened it carefully. It was empty. 'Nowt in it,' said Braithwaite. 'They must've cleaned him out, poor bugger.'

The sergeant leaned back in his chair and looked at Sam. 'Don't much like dealing with ex-coppers. Holmes said you had trouble with your sergeant, in Barrow, wasn't it?'

Sam nodded, but said nothing. 'Funny buggers down there,' said Braithwaite. 'Don't 'ave much to do with them, if we can 'elp it. They're Lancashire, we're Cumbria. That's it. So I couldn't much care what did or didn't go off with you and your sergeant. You're here, and you're trained, so you can sit in on this for a bit, right? Save us time and pestering the family when they've got enough to deal with. Do they know you're poking around?'

'They asked me,' said Sam, remembering Judith's tirade against him. 'There were words last night about it. I saw Frank at the house on Sunday, and they reckon I should have stopped him leaving. He was coming back to town to the card game, but I didn't know that.'

'And they blame you? Bit harsh,' said Braithwaite.

'Well, Frank's dad didn't blame me, just someone else. They were all upset and things got said, you know.'

Braithwaite didn't let family matters detain him, and turned his attention back to the holdall. 'We'll see what else there is, then I'll get Holmes in. He's out getting statements from the blokes at the quarry, the ones who called it in.'

Sam felt a sudden rush of anxiety, but didn't let it show. He'd told those men he was a policeman, and no doubt they'd told Holmes that, too. Damn.

There was nothing else in the bag. Sam thought of the photo of Gloria Tennant tucked in his inside pocket, and was pleased he'd taken the risk of removing it. She didn't need the police turning up at her house, and he still had more information to get from her before she clammed up.

'No keys?' said Braithwaite. 'Didn't find any on the body, did we?'

'Maybe the doc did, when they got him back to the mortuary. I'm staying at Frank's place myself. Two keys, front door and back. Might have missed them in his pocket yesterday.'

'You're living there? Take Holmes up there for a look round. You haven't cleared up or anything?'

Sam shook his head. 'Moved a jacket off the bedroom floor, then I left the rest.'

'Notice anything?'

'No, nothing helpful. Looks like Frank led a double life, dutiful grandson and hard worker on the surface, and something else underneath. Heaven knows how that started. He could have been bored to death, needing excitement.'

'Well, he got more of that than he could handle. Lost control of things and took the easy way out.'

'He didn't kill himself,' Sam said. 'I went up to the top of the cliff, above where we found him. Tyre tracks, footprints, signs of something dragged towards the edge. I took photos, measurements. The shoe size was bigger than Frank's.'

Braithwaite raised his eyebrows. 'Playing detective, are we?'

This time Sam let his annoyance show. 'I am a detective,' he said. 'Done the training, I know what to do. And the first rule is keep an open mind, isn't it?'

'Don't lecture me, sonny,' said Braithwaite. 'We –'

There was a knock on the door, and it was pushed open before Braithwaite said anything further.

'Can I 'ave a word?' said a plain-clothes man. Sam noticed he was considerably younger than the sergeant, but didn't get shouted at for coming in uninvited. Braithwaite got up without a word, went outside with the intruder and closed the door behind him. Sam strained to hear, but could make out only a murmur of voices before Braithwaite came back into the room.

'Make yourself available at the house in West Row late this afternoon,' he said. 'The bag stays here. Don't touch anything at the house, OK? Now push off, I've got work to do. Holmes'll be in touch when he gets back.'

Standing outside in Scotch Street, Sam couldn't work out what had happened there. He remembered something Harry Grayson had said, about some other investigation that might make the Whitehaven police see Sam as a nuisance. There was something going on, he was sure of that now.

CHAPTER 15

The Whitehaven police station in Scotch Street was only a few minutes' walk from the Dog and Partridge in the market place. The same barman looked up when Sam entered, and recognised him. 'You were with Dermot the other day,' he said.

'Is he still around?'

The barman shook his head. 'Gone, not long after you were in before,' he said. 'Dermot comes and goes, you know. Paid for the room for a week, so I thought he'd be here that long, but it's nowt to do wi' me, is it? Any road, he just went. Had his big bag with him, so I guess he's gone back to the ship. Liverpool probably.'

'Did you ever see him with anyone?'

'Well, there were the blokes in the card school. They were in and out.' Sam pulled the photo of Frank from his inside pocket. 'Was this bloke here?'

The barman looked carefully. 'Aye – 'e looked younger than most of the others. Nervous like.'

The man's memory was obviously good, and Sam pressed on. 'Ever see a man with tattoos right down his arm, with this card playing group?'

'Youngish bloke?'

Sam nodded. 'Could have been with someone older, bald.'

'Oh them two,' said the barman. 'Can't miss 'em. They don't come in 'ere, I barred them.'

'What for?'

'Nasty bastards, both of them. Threatened one of my regulars, so I threw 'em out.'

'Know their names?'

'Older one's called Baldy, but not to 'is face. Him with the tattoos?' he shook his head. 'Know what I'd like to call 'im. I could find out for you.'

Sam held up his hand. He didn't want it spread round town that he was looking for them. On the way out, he looked round carefully, hoping that no one had overheard the conversation or even noticed his presence.

Sam made some notes after he left the pub, then walked back up to West Row; he needed to walk now that he wasn't doing his post round. Back in the house, he pinned up the notes he'd got from the barman and rearranged the information on the wall. Arthur Paling was now in one corner, and Frank Pharaoh in the centre. He put Baldy and the tattoo man together in another corner and drew a line from them towards both Paling and Pharaoh. At least two pieces of the picture seemed to connect with each other. Sam wondered whether Rob Holmes would actually turn up to see the house. He could take it all down before Rob arrived, but why should he?

Rob Holmes did arrive, on foot, earlier than Sam had expected him. As he invited the DC into the house, Sam wondered whether the early arrival was deliberate; nothing about Holmes and his sergeant seemed to be straightforward.

'Sarge says you've been living here with Pharaoh,' said DC Holmes. 'How did that happen?'

'I know the family,' said Sam. 'I was looking for digs, and I think Frank's dad wanted someone to keep an eye on Frank, after his gran moved out.'

'He came down to the mortuary,' said Holmes. 'Pretty cut up apparently.'

What did you expect, Sam thought, but said nothing.

'Let's have a look, then,' said the DC. 'You've left things as you found them, right?'

'Apart from the jacket that I hung up. I've cleaned the kitchen and the bathroom. Couldn't leave them like they were.'

Holmes sniffed. 'Doesn't smell too bad in here.'

'Not now,' said Sam. 'Upstairs, at the back, that's Frank's room.'

They stood together in the doorway and looked at the mess.

Sam said, 'When his gran lived here the place was spotless apparently. She moved out a month or so ago, and he's obviously done nothing since.'

'I was married and a father at his age,' said Holmes. 'He was just a kid, expected people to clear up after him. Pathetic.' He stepped over towards the window and looked out onto the drying greens behind the houses. 'And now he's got himself killed.'

'Do you think so?'

'Figure of speech,' said Holmes. 'I mean he's dead.'

'What do you think happened?'

Holmes shrugged. 'Too early to tell.'

'Come in here,' said Sam, and led the way into the front bedroom.

'Grand view,' said Holmes, walking over to the window.

'Look at this,' Sam went on, standing by the wall. 'I've been collecting what I know. Some things are beginning to join up.'

Holmes stood back and stared at the wall, leaning forward

to read some of Sam's notes, then back again, to get the bigger picture.

'Where do these photos come from, the footprints and tyre tracks?'

'I took them,' said Sam, 'after we found Frank's body, before too many more people tramped around up there by the quarry.'

'Does Braithwaite know about this?'

'No, why should he? Couldn't get rid of me fast enough when I was up at the station this morning.'

Holmes looked again. 'What do you know about this Baldy bloke?'

'He knocks around with the man with tattoos, the one that had been to Arthur Paling's before they nailed him up. The woman next door, Mrs Barstow, she said she saw someone with tattoos round here too, shouting at Frank. I asked him about it but he just kept saying to leave him alone. I should have made him tell me more.'

'So you reckon that the tattoo man and this Baldy are debt collectors? They did for Paling and now they've done for Pharaoh?'

'Looks pretty obvious to me. Worth investigating anyway.'

Holmes pulled out his cigarettes, offered one to Sam, then lit up. The smoke curled out of his nostrils.

'Look, Sam, can I call you that, it's easier than the other mouthful? I can see you're caught up with all this, friend of the family and all that, but you're going to have to drop it.'

'Why?' said Sam. 'I'm getting somewhere, further than you two.' His frustration boiled over. 'For God's sake, Rob, you know these guys. You must do, you're a local copper and everyone knows them. The bald head, the tattoos, guaranteed to get them noticed and it works, except for you and Braithwaite who just shrug like a couple of kids and pretend to know nothing. What the hell's going on? It's like you don't want to know, don't want to do anything. Frank may have been just a pathetic kid to you, but he deserves better than this. I know you're blocking me, I know it. But why?'

Holmes turned again to stare out of the window, across the moving pattern of light and colour.

'OK, OK,' he said. 'I know who both those blokes are. Like you say, they're not making much effort to hide themselves. But that's what it's about. They want people to see what they do, what they can do if you get the wrong side of them.'

'But that makes you lot look like fools, or worse.'

Holmes was clearly annoyed, but Sam wouldn't let it drop. 'Look, Rob,' he went on. 'I know how it works sometimes. It only takes one who's bent and the whole force looks bad.'

Holmes shouted, spitting. 'Bent, who's bent?'

'Someone must be,' Sam was shouting too. 'How does it look to you? Known villains running round the place scaring the shit out of people, on your patch, and nothing gets done. They nailed a bloke to his garage door, for God's sake, and torched an old lady out of her home. They could have pushed Frank off the bloody cliff and you lot stand around sucking your teeth as if it's someone else's problem.'

Holmes' face was red. For a moment he stared, saying nothing. 'It's complicated,' he said finally. 'And anyway you've no authority to be doing any of this. I told you that, days ago, and you're too pig-headed to lay off.'

Sam knew he'd said enough; he couldn't afford to break the link with the police completely. He pushed past Holmes and went downstairs, and was making himself a drink when he heard footsteps on the stairs and Holmes appeared in the kitchen, still smoking. Sam waved his hand in front of him, and opened the back door. 'Do you know how those things stink out my kitchen?'

Holmes stubbed out the cigarette. "I'm prepared to ignore the accusations you're making,' he said. He waited, but Sam said nothing, and Holmes went on. 'Quite apart from the blokes Frank was with at the card game, you were the last person to speak to him, is that right?'

Sam shrugged. 'Could be. He was here on the Sunday before he died. He was in a mess, looked as if he'd been sleeping rough, and I made him some food and he had a bath.'

Holmes sat down uninvited and got out his notebook. 'Time?'

'Sunday, mid-morning' said Sam. 'Don't know exactly.'

'Did he tell you where he'd been sleeping?'

'No, I found that out from Dermot the croupier, from the Dog and Partridge.'

Holmes sat back and rolled his eyes. 'Dermot bloody Hennessey,' he said. 'We know him all right. Came from Cleator originally, then went off on the cruise boats. Got trained up as a croupier and now he comes back here to make some easy money when he's on shore. Always means trouble when those big card schools start. We're talking thousands of quid changing hands, big money.'

'Dermot told me Frank had been sleeping on his couch. Gave me Frank's bag, and I gave it to your boss. I tried to find him again this morning, after I saw Braithwaite, but he's scarpered.'

'Could be a coincidence,' said Holmes.

'Or he would have got wind of what happened to Frank and skipped to avoid you lot asking questions.' Sam hesitated, 'If you ever do ask any questions, that is.'

Holmes glared at him. 'Look, I know you think we're dragging our feet on this one, but we're not. Your lad Frank's getting all my attention. No one's making any assumptions, if that's what your good Catholic family's getting upset about. Looks like something happened on that cliff top, but we have to be methodical about it, not charging around like you. It takes time.'

Sam could have argued, but he thought better of it. He still had some favours to ask. 'There are a couple of things I'd like help with, and then I can keep out of your way.'

'Go on.'

'First, can you let me have the headlines off the PM report? I need to know whether there were signs of violence before he hit the beach. You know why, suicide's a big issue to this family, quite apart from them deserving to know exactly what happened.'

'And?' said Holmes.

'And I want to find out when someone's being released from Haverigg nick.'

'Name?'

'Ray, I suppose it's Raymond, Tennant. In for GBH, I think, and due out soon. I just want to know when.'

'What's that got to do with Frank?'

'It may not have any relevance, I just want to know. You'll have to trust me to tell you if it's connected.'

Holmes looked at him, and Sam didn't look away.

'Name doesn't ring any bells, but I'll check and let you know.'

'And the PM?'

'Scheduled for tomorrow. Can't let you have all the details but I understand what you want. Are you going to leave this alone any time soon?'

'John Pharoah's paying me to find out what happened to his son. So I'm a private detective for the time being. It's my job to keep on making enquiries.'

Holmes got up. 'Well, you'll get as much cooperation from us as any other private investigator would, which isn't much. And if we think you're holding out on us, we can charge you with obstruction.'

'I know that,' said Sam. 'So I'll share what I have, when I have something.'

Nothing more was said, and there was no handshake before Holmes let himself out of the front door.

There was no one in the *Furness News* newsroom when Judith knocked on the editor's door. Cliff Springrice was surprised to see her. 'Judith! We didn't expect you back yet. Come in, sit down.' He ushered her into the office and sat down beside her. 'I was so sorry to hear about your brother,' he said. 'What a terrible thing for your family. How are your parents? And how are you?'

Judith realised how hard it would be to say the same meaningless things to well-intentioned people, over and over again. 'We're all coping, you know, like you do. It's just such a shock, not like a very old person dying, or someone who's been ill. No warning, and Frank was only twenty-three.'

'Do they know what happened?'

She shook her head. 'My dad's asked a friend of ours who used to be a policeman to do some checking around for us. The police are involved of course, but I think Dad wanted to find things out more quickly.'

Springrice asked, 'Would that be the young policeman who was involved in your case, two years ago, wasn't it?'

'Yes, Sam Tognarelli. He left the force after all that happened, moved up to Whitehaven.' She hesitated. 'Dad thinks we need his help, but I'm not so sure. We'll see.'

'And the funeral?'

'Friday,' she said. 'It'll be at St Mary's in Kells. Father Price goes back a long way with our family.'

Springrice nodded. 'So you've come back to work until then?'

Judith smiled. 'There's nothing I can do at home,' she said. 'They have each other. I'd rather be here, keeping busy. My Dad understands that. My Mum's too upset to notice, and she's never approved of me working here anyway, living away from home.'

'Well, I hope your parents know how much we care for you here, Judith,' he said kindly. 'You've had a dreadful shock, so take it easy. You're in digs, aren't you, not on your own?'

'I'm with Sam's sister Elspeth,' said Judith. 'She's a good friend. She'll look out for me.'

'Someone else was asking after you, too,' he said. 'Harry Grayson, the new DS. I saw him over the weekend at the golf club. He was very concerned about you, when he heard what had happened to your brother. Left his number, asked if you would call him.' He looked in his wallet and pulled out a slip of paper. 'He said you could call him anytime, and his home number's there as well.'

Judith put the number away, and waited a moment, trying to decide whether this was the time to ask her question.

'Can I ask you something?' she said.

'Anything.'

'It's about a piece I'd like to do, a feature, beyond the usual stuff, something that the nationals might find interesting. But it may be too soon.'

Cliff Springrice put his head on one side. 'Too soon for what?'

'For a piece about Montgomery House,' she said. 'It's eighteen months since it all happened, and your predecessor took his own life over it. I'm surprised no one's picked up the story already, so why don't we do it? At least we'd get the facts right.'

Cliff Springrice grimaced, and got up from his chair beside her to look out of the window. 'I wasn't here,' he said, 'but it sounded a pretty nasty business. Police involved, obviously. Thornhill dead and his wife on the run.'

'But Montgomery House has carried on,' said Judith. 'Still looking after the boys that no one else cares about. Isn't that worth a story? "Good work carries on after tragedy" and so on. "Local hero undeterred, carries on his life's work".'

'Who's the local hero?' asked Springrice.

'Captain Edwards, the boss of Monty House. He was a war hero, wounded in Malaya, saw dreadful things, children needing help, came home and took over at Monty House. Bill Skelly thought he was a hero, many people round here do.'

Springrice thought for a few moments. 'Tell you what,' he said. 'Talk to Grayson about it. We can't get involved if the police case is still active. If they're happy that the criminal investigation is finished, then it might be a runner. I'll give it some thought.'

'Fair enough,' said Judith. 'I'll talk to Grayson. I never saw him as a DS but there he is, looking every inch the part.'

'He seems to like you,' said Springrice. 'And I'm sure he'd like to offer his condolences in person, if you can cope with that.'

It was the following evening, after Judith had finished work, that she met Harry Grayson in the back bar at the Victoria. The place and time were both her suggestions, and he'd seemed very pleased to hear from her. And pleased to see her too, she noticed as he got to his feet and smiled. 'So good to see you, Judith,' he said, giving her a peck on the cheek. 'I thought we might not have you back until the funeral was over. It must be so hard for you all, I'm so sorry.'

She smiled. 'Everyone's being very kind,' she said. 'I wanted to come back to work for a few days before the funeral. This job means a lot to me, and I've only been here a short while. Need to get my feet properly under the table.' She paused, sitting down beside him and unbuttoning her jacket. 'And to be honest, Harry, it's easier here than at home. My landlady in Roose and her son Tommy, they just take my mind off things.'

Harry went to the bar to buy his pint and the gin and tonic she'd asked for. 'How old's Tommy?' he asked as he put the drinks on the small table.

'He's eight now,' she said. 'It's a great age.'

'Did you ever wish you had kids?' he asked.

'Plenty of time for that yet,' she said, surprised at the question. 'Need to find the right man first.'

'Look no further,' he said, laughing. 'I'd be first in that queue, Judith, you know that.'

'When I start looking, I'll let you know,' she said. 'Cheers, and thanks.'

Suddenly Judith was very pleased at her decision to come back to work. The tensions of home seemed far away, and Harry Grayson's easy company was refreshing. She didn't want to think about Sam. She'd said some harsh things to him, although she couldn't remember the exact words. Harry was different, lighter, flirty: just what she needed. Her mother might disapprove, but that made it all the more enjoyable.

She was on her third drink, and already aware that she would have to leave the Vespa and walk home, when she remembered why she'd wanted to see Harry in the first place.

'I went to see the editor today,' she said, 'about a story I'd like to do, now I'm chief reporter.'

'I'll drink to that,' he said, raising his glass. 'Springrice must know a good thing when he finds it. Pleasant enough bloke, I see him at the golf club. What the story?'

'Montgomery House,' she said. 'The real story, the one that was overshadowed by all the business with Thornhill.'

He sipped his beer and looked at her. 'What's this "real story", then?'

'What a great job they've done with those kids over the years,' she said. 'Caring for boys who nobody wants, keeping them off the streets and out of trouble. And Mrs Robinson, the matron, do you know her?'

He shook his head. 'Only met her that night, when that bloke hanged himself, and me and Sam had to check his room. She was there then, but too upset to talk to us.' He hesitated, remembering something. 'That reminds me,' he said. 'Someone else I saw at the golf club, but never mind that now. What were you saying, about Mrs Robinson?'

'I think she's an amazing woman,' said Judith. 'And the captain has a story, wounded in Malaya, all that. Thornhill was there too, that's how they knew each other.'

'I think Sam told me that,' said Harry. 'What did your editor say?'

'He said I should check with the police about whether the criminal investigation of the Thornhills was over. So here I am.'

'That's why you're here,' he said. 'I'm disappointed, Judith, I thought you were here for my scintillating conversation, but you only want to know whether we're still investigating? Well,

Irene Thornhill's still wanted for questioning and she could be anywhere.' He took another sip of his beer. 'To be honest, I'm not sure doing a story about it is a good idea.'

'Raking it up again, you mean? Surely it might make people look out for her, if she is back in England.'

'I doubt she'll come back,' he said. 'Too much to lose.'

'But would we be within our rights to do a story about it?' she persisted. 'It's something the public have a right to know about, after all. Too easy to hide these problem kids away, pretend they don't exist.'

'Another drink?' he asked. She shook her head. 'You think I should pick something safer, more comfortable, don't you?'

'I'm surprised, I grant you,' he said. 'Not sure my bosses would approve.'

'You know me, Harry,' she said, finishing her drink. 'Never did care too much about people's approval. I think it runs in the family.'

Harry Grayson got up, pulling his coat round him. 'Freedom of the press, and all that,' he said. 'Far be it from me to get in the way of a good story. But I still think it's a bad idea.'

'My editor's not keen, either. By the way, I didn't think the golf club was your scene, Harry.'

He smiled. 'I've always believed that you have to meet people halfway, on their terms, if you want to get anywhere in this town. It's all about who you know. By the way, how's my old mate Sam these days?'

He saw the frown on Judith's face and smiled.

'Let's not talk about him,' she said. 'So, you've joined the club, literally.'

'It's a great game,' said Harry. 'I'm picking it up pretty fast.'

'Golf, you mean?'

'Yes, golf,' he repeated. 'What else? And when am I going to see you again, to get the next instalment of this thrilling tale of journalistic endeavour?'

'Same time next week?' she said. 'Funeral will be over, and I'll be clear to get on with something meaty. This is my chance Harry. You don't begrudge me that, do you?'

'Of course not, my sweet,' he said, taking her outstretched hand and squeezing it. 'But be careful, won't you? Can't wish you luck about the funeral, but I hope it's not too awful for you. Friday, did you say?'

She nodded. 'Better when it's all over. Have to see what Sam's managed to find out. Not much I imagine. He's so cautious, Harry, it drives me mad. My brother's dead and he pussyfoots around, afraid of upsetting anyone. I was really angry with him. Probably said too much, but it was all such a shock.'

'He'll recover,' said Grayson, smiling again. 'You have my number. Call me anytime. I'm on Walney, just a few minutes away if you want anything. Now give me a kiss.'

Judith reached up and kissed him. 'That'll do for now,' he said. 'Can you get home OK?'

'I'll walk, it's not far. Thanks, and thanks for the drink, and the company.'

A figure loomed at her side. She looked up. Detective Inspector Noel Cardine was looking down at her. She hadn't seen him since Doc Hayward's funeral, but the carefully combed white hair was unmistakeable, and the voice, too, with its permanent sneer.

'Leaving so soon, Miss Pharaoh? That's a shame. I was hoping for a little chat.'

He turned to Harry, who looked embarrassed. 'Good to see you getting on so well with the press, DS Grayson. So important in a close-knit community like ours.' He smiled.

'I've been watching you two for a while. This is a public place, after all.'

'DS Grayson and I are friends from way back,' Judith lied. 'Just friends, that's all.'

'Of course,' said Cardine. 'Chatting about old times, no doubt.'

'That's right,' said Harry, recovering, 'Old times.'

'I was just leaving,' said Judith. 'Are you coming, Harry?'

Harry edged past his boss, and took Judith's arm. Outside, well away from the open door of the pub, they both laughed. 'He's such a creep,' said Judith. 'How can you stand working with him?'

'It's my job,' he said. 'I don't have to like him, but he is my boss.'

'Good luck with that. He was Sam's boss too, and that didn't end well.'

'I'm different,' said Harry. 'You'll know that when you know me better.'

'I'd like to,' she said.

'We could do something now, if you'd like. Pictures maybe?'

She hesitated for a moment, then shook her head. 'Nice thought, thanks, but not tonight. Maybe after the funeral.'

'Yes, sorry,' he said. 'I'll be in touch.'

'Harry,' said Judith. 'Why don't you go back and buy old Cardine a drink? I won't tell Sam, if you don't. 'Bye.'

She smiled and waved, then turned and walked away. At precisely that moment, as Harry Grayson was imagining Judith Pharaoh in his bed, the phone jangled in the cheerless house at 23 West Row, Kells.

CHAPTER 16

The phone woke Sam from an evening snooze, fraught with dreams of lost bags and crumbling cliffs. 'Sam?' said Rob Holmes' voice. 'Thought you weren't in. Got some news about the PM.'

Sam shook his head to clear the fog away. 'What about it?'

'You asked for the headlines, remember. The report's in.'

Sam's heart bumped. 'Tell me.'

'Impossible to tell if Frank was roughed up before he went down the cliff. Obviously the fall left him pretty battered.'

'Frank could still have topped himself to get away from whoever was threatening him,' said Sam.

'True, but that's quite a different circumstance. He would have been forced into it, not the same as making a deliberate choice is it?' Holmes waited. 'I thought the family would want to have the body and see him buried. If there's no evidence of someone else involved, the coroner can let the funeral carry on.'

Sam thought about it, his eyes closed. 'What about the bloke in the house behind the quarry, Isaac Clegg?' he asked. 'He might know what was going on up there that night.'

'He's on my list of calls,' said Rob. 'There's a phone but no one ever picks up.'

'The quarry blokes said he'd been in hospital. Maybe he's still there,' said Sam. Or else he doesn't want to talk to the police, he thought.

'When's the funeral?' Rob asked.

'Friday, St Mary's, eleven.'

'We'll have someone there,' said Rob. 'Keeping an eye on things. Whoever hurt Frank might just want to see him in the ground.'

'Does that mean you think someone pushed him over?'

'Can't say that yet. Frank fell. That's all we know.'

'Well, Rob, as far as the priest and the family are concerned, this was a tragic accident. Let's give them that comfort for now. Will it be you at the funeral?'

'Could be. If I am, don't let on, right? Last thing I want is grieving relatives asking awkward questions.'

Sam was tempted to say that was what the police deserved, but he kept the thought to himself.

'Are you still investigating?' Rob asked.

'It's my job,' said Sam. 'The family want answers, and so far they've had none.'

Silence. 'Be careful,' said Rob, before he hung up.

The following day Sam was just getting up when the phone jangled again. Sam hurried down the stairs, hoping it was Rob Holmes, with more information.

'Hello,' he said.

There was no response. 'Hello,' he said, again.

'Sam?' The voice was scarcely more than a whisper, and was definitely not Rob Holmes, or Sergeant Braithwaite.

'This is Sam,' he said. 'Who's speaking?'

'It's Gloria,' said the voice. 'Can you hear? I can't talk much.'

'What is it? Are you all right?'

'There's a phone box, near the Co-op, end of Mirehouse Lane. Can you meet me? I need help.'

'Stay there,' he said. 'I'll come in the car, be about five minutes.'

The phone box was empty when he pulled up beside it. He drove slowly down the hill, turned and came back up. There were people around, but no sign of Gloria's small figure and white hair. When he stopped at the phone box again, he saw someone peep out from behind it, look up and down the street and then beckon to him. The woman was wearing a long coat and a headscarf pulled tight over her head although the May morning was quite warm. She ran to the car, opened the passenger door, got in and slid down in the front seat. Sam looked down at her. 'Gloria? What's the matter?'

'Drive on, anywhere,' her voice was little more than a croak. 'Can't let anyone see me, not round 'ere.'

This time he carried on up the hill to the top and turned left onto the old back road towards St Bees. Where the road widened under some trees he stopped the car. 'No one around,' he said. 'Do you want to sit up?'

Gloria pushed herself upright. As she turned towards him Sam could see the bruising round her left eye, and the blood on her dark eyebrow. 'You're hurt,' he said. 'What happened?'

Gloria swallowed painfully. Sam could see the bruises on her neck. 'He came out,' she said. 'Just turned up on the door-step. No warning. Must have come straight to find me.'

'And he did this?'

'Fucked me first. Then he just turned nasty, beat me, and fucked me again.' She sniffed. 'He's too big, I can't keep him off me. Then he went out, and I found your number. Didn't know what else to do.'

184

'Why didn't you call the police?'

She tried to smile. 'You're kidding, right? They have me down as a low-life prossie, gets what's coming to her, all that. Tried before to get them to do summat, waste of time.'

'What about PC Kelly from Kells, he seems like a good bloke.'

She shook her head. 'I know 'is mam. He wouldn't come near me.' She sniffed again, and took the hankerchief that Sam pulled from his pocket and offered to her. 'I think he's going to kill me,' she whispered.

'You told me you could handle him,' said Sam. She looked away.

'I tried to find out when he was coming out,' he said. 'Couldn't get any information about it.' He thought for a moment. 'When did this happen?'

'Yesterday, late. They release in the morning, don't know where he'd been but he smelled of drink.'

'Could he have been out last week?'

'He wouldn't wait that long for what he wanted. Down the pub first, then back to me for the rest.'

'Do you think he knew about Frank?'

'Frank with me, or Frank being dead?'

'You knew about that?'

'Course I did. No name in the paper, but news travels fast round here. That housekeeper at St Mary's, 'er mouth flaps. If she knows, everyone knows.'

'So your husband was still inside when Frank died.'

'Husband? Him? I was married once, but not to 'im. Once was enough for me.'

Something cleared in Sam's mind. 'So he's not called Ray Tennant?'

'Tennant's my stage name. My real name's Gloria Billings.'

'His name?'

'Raymond bloody Noakes. Bastard. Wish I'd never met 'im.'

Sam turned towards her. 'Did you say Noakes?' Images bounced in his brain. A bare interview room at Lancaster jail, a sullen man leaning back in his chair. 'Does he have a brother?'

'What? How do I know?'

'Think,' he said. 'It's important. A younger brother, called Bill.'

She looked puzzled. 'What about it?'

'I knew a man called Bill Noakes, couple of years back. He was in Lancaster nick.' He hesitated. 'I put him there.'

Gloria took off her headscarf, pulled down the sun vizor in front of her and looked at herself in the mirror. She took a powder compact from her handbag and patted the side of her left cheek gingerly. Then she turned towards Sam.

'Are you telling me you're a copper? You said you're a postman.'

'I was a postman, or I was when you asked me. Things have changed a bit since then. I was a copper in Barrow. One of the villains I put away was called Bill Noakes, but he was younger than your Ray.'

'He's not *my* Ray.' Gloria spoke firmly, but it made her cough. 'You got any cigs?' she asked. Sam shook his head. 'I told you, I like 'em young, or I did. Ray's thirty summat. In and out of nick since he was a lad. He might have a brother. We don't talk much about stuff like that. What about it anyway? Are you going to help me?'

Sam's mind was racing. 'What can I do, if you won't go to the police?'

'But you are the police, aren't you? Once a copper, always a copper. I can tell you what Ray's up to. The man's a villain, that's not going to change. When he's inside, I'm safe. But I've had enough. No more being knocked around, treated like a whore.'

'And you'll shop Ray to the police, to get him back inside?'

'Of course,' she said. 'Obvious, innit? He did this to me, and more that I'm not going to show you. He could kill me next time.'

'Was it about Frank?'

She shrugged. 'He's been inside for a while. I'm not a nun. Men like Ray, they're not like you. They've been hit and bullied since they were kids themselves, that's all they know. Don't care about who they hurt, and specially not women. Who cares about women like me? Just a punchbag or something to be screwed.'

'So why hook up with someone like that? Why do that to yourself?'

'Blaming me are you? Had it coming?'

'No, not like that. You're a good-looking woman, Gloria, bright, talented. You can do better than this.'

'The first one wasn't violent,' she said. 'Drugs, that was 'is thing. Got me into it. Nearly killed me. Can I keep this hankie?'

'I'll take you home,' he said, starting the engine. 'Will he beat you again?'

'Probably got it out of his system for a bit. Just had to remind me who's boss. Now he's off with his mates, might not see 'im for a while, with any luck. But I still want 'im back inside. I think 'e's up to summat, always is.'

'Up to something?'

'Summat to do with cigs. When he went out he said, "Don't buy any cigs, there'll be plenty when I get back," summat like that.'

'Theft?'

'Maybe, or they could be bringing them in from Ireland. They've done it before.'

'Smuggling, you mean?'

'It 'appens all the time,' she said. 'All up and down this coast for hundreds of years, since they put taxes on stuff that people didn't want to pay. Booze, cigs. And other stuff now. Cannabis, heroin. All sorts.'

'How does it work?' asked Sam, wondering what on earth he was getting into.

Suddenly Gloria slipped down in the seat, bending over to hide her head. A grey van passed them and on towards St Bees.

'Who's that?' said Sam.

She wriggled back and looked behind them, down the road, but there was nothing coming. 'Ray's mates 'ave a grey van,' she said. 'But so do loads of other people. I keep thinking 'e's watching me. If he knew I was 'ere with you 'e'd kill me.'

'It's all right,' said Sam. 'I can try to get Ray back into jail, and you'll be safe again.'

Even as he said the words, Sam knew he was using this woman just like everyone else did. 'How does the smuggling thing work?' he asked again.

'Never seen them do it, 'ave I?' She thought for a moment. 'There's a lad up Cleator, Michael Leary, Irish. Drinks like a fish. He's been round my place a couple of times. Ray treats him like shit, but he's always hanging round when there's cash to be made. Bet he'd know and he's daft enough to let on, if you get him drunk enough.'

'Cleator? Big place is it?'

'Try the Black Horse. Find 'im, and you'll find Ray and the others. They'll be planning summat they could get banged up for.' She looked up at him and moved a little closer. 'You get the glory, and you could get the Gloria, too. Make it worth your while.' Her small white hand inched towards Sam's trousers, and he flinched.

'I'm taking you home,' he said. 'By the way, do you know an older bloke with a shaved head?'

'Baldy? Yes, I know 'im. Who doesn't?'

'He has a mate with tattoos all up his arm?'

'Yeh, they call 'im Blue. Don't know why.'

'Proper names?'

She shrugged. 'Don't ask me. These blokes never use their real names. Don't need to, everyone knows who they are. Drop me back by the Co-op. I need some milk.'

Sam didn't respond. When Gloria got out of the car, he blew out a deep breath as he drove away.

Back in West Row, Sam wrote down as much as he could remember of what Gloria had told him, adding to the details on his wall. Ray Noakes went in there now, alongside Baldy and Blue the Tattoo. He looked at the emerging picture. Ray Noakes could be Bill Noakes' brother, it wasn't such a common name and the ages were about right. Bill Noakes. He sat on his bed, looking out at the sea, remembering.

Bill was a petty criminal in Barrow, thieving, taking cars. Morrison had given Sam the case to keep him busy. And the local bobby on the estate where Bill Noakes did his dirty work, what was his name? PC Farrell, that was it. Old school, knew his patch inside out. He knew where Noakes kept the stuff he'd nicked and it was all there when they raided it. Then Sam found out that Noakes had been at Montgomery House as a lad, and came close to getting information out of him that could have closed the place. That was the first time Sam realised that boys didn't want to talk about being sexually molested. Being beaten up, punished, that was part of life, but being touched up by old blokes, and worse? That couldn't be admitted without unbearable shame. Even an offer of lighter punishment hadn't been enough. Bill had preferred to stay in jail than tell Sam what really happened. That had been Sam's best chance of building a case against Montgomery House and Edwards, and it had gone. Edwards was still there, and maybe the 'visitors' were still molesting the boys. Surely, Sam thought, the men who did this couldn't be protected forever. But Cardine was still around, and Edwards could carry on.

Sam wanted to put all this on his wall somewhere, but where, and linked to what? He wasn't certain that Ray and Bill Noakes were related. It would have to wait a while. Tomorrow he had to go to Frank's funeral. Would John ask him for a progress report, and what could he say? That the inquest decision would probably be delayed? That the police were refusing to deal with him? He had to do something, to get the police to listen to him. The need to act made him think of Judith, and his face burned, remembering what she'd said to him. She'd accused him of exploiting John's grief to get an easy life. Was that what she really thought of him? He wished he didn't care. What was she up to in Barrow? Why did Grayson ask about her?

Downstairs he picked up the phone, dialled the Barrow police station, gave his name and asked for DS Grayson. Harry's voice was friendly. 'Sam, mate, how are you? Still hauling a big mail bag round Whitehaven?'

At least Judith hasn't told him everything, Sam thought.

'No, given that up for a while actually, doing a bit of unofficial police work.'

'Really? What does that mean? Sam Spade rides again?'

'Judith's dad hired me to find Frank, and when we found

him dead he asked me to find out how he died. Police don't seem to bother, as far as I can see. I told you. They're being really off with me.'

'Nothing we all hate more than a private eye', said Harry. 'You know that. Pain in the arse, get in the way. What do you expect them to do?'

'Try and find out how Frank died instead of writing it off as a suicide or a tragic accident. What the hell was Frank doing at the top of a cliff in the middle of the night? They don't seem a bit curious about that. I've given them everything they need to bring two blokes in for questioning about assault and intimidation, and they've done nothing.'

'OK, point taken. Can't help with that, though. Different county, different force, nothing to do with each other.'

'There's something else,' said Sam. 'From last year's case, to do with Montgomery House.'

'Monty House again,' said Harry. 'What is it with that place? Judith's going on about it and now you. It's finished. End of story. The place is still there, with splendid Captain Edwards and the saintly Mrs Robinson. Why can't you leave it alone?'

Sam ignored this outburst and carried on. 'Do you remember a bloke called Bill Noakes?'

'You nicked him for theft and cars, Upgill estate, right? Went to Lancaster?'

'That's the one. Did I tell you how close he was to telling me about what went on at the place we're not allowed to mention?'

'Can't recall, but nothing came of it, I assume.'

'No, he backed off, refused to make a statement.'

'Not surprising. Hard enough being in jail without rumours about being a perv.'

Sam ignored that, too. 'Can you check his record for me? I

know he was in Monty House when he was a lad. But I need to know if he's got an older brother called Ray who's about thirty.'

'And I suppose you want to know if he was in Monty House too?'

'Yes. He must have a record long as your arm. He's just come out of Haverigg, two years for GBH, and his name's cropped up here. It's a loose link to Frank Pharaoh's case, but I want to check him out. You've got a better chance of getting the info than I have. Call the collator at Whitehaven, give him some guff about the Noakes family and see what you can find out. Can you do that?'

'And you're not going to tell me what it's about?'

Sam thought about it. 'OK. Frank, the stupid boy, was seeing Ray Noakes' missus while he was inside. That gives Ray motive to go after Frank, even though he was still inside when Frank died. There are plenty of blokes he could have got to frighten Frank off the edge.'

Grayson took a moment to get the facts straight. There was more that Sam could have shared with him, but that he was still unsure about Grayson, so he decided against it.

'See anything of Judith?' Sam asked, as casually as he could manage.

'Ah, Judith,' said Grayson. 'What a girl, but I wish she'd give up this obsession with Monty House. She asked me if I thought she should do a feature about the place and I warned her off, for all the good that'll do.'

'I'll see her tomorrow, at Frank's funeral,' said Sam.

'Get her to drop it, will you?'

'Not easy, telling Judith what to do,' said Sam.

'True,' said Harry. 'We had enough trouble with that last time. Could her parents tell her to leave it alone?'

Sam laughed. 'You don't know her very well, do you? Judith's spent most of her life trying not to do what her mother wanted. Her dad might persuade her. Maybe that's because he's her stepfather.'

'Well, do your best. Judith could have a good future in this town if she keeps her nose clean.'

Sam wondered what kind of future Harry had in mind.

'Good luck with the funeral,' Harry said before he rang off. 'I'll get back to you if I find anything on Ray Noakes.'

Sam went to bed early, wanting rest before the stress of the funeral and conversation with John. But he dreamed of Judith having sex with someone else whose face he couldn't see.

Chapter 17

They followed the hearse from the house in St Bees along the ancient twisting road, under the bright green, leafing trees, beside old pit workings and the long fence of the Marchon plant up to the High Road where the church of St Mary's stood tall and proud among the houses on the ridge. Smoke and steam from the Marchon stacks streamed across in the southerly breeze, but there were no trees here to bend their branches or offer shade from the sun.

Judith was in the first car behind the hearse with her parents, grandmother Violet and Vince. She was glad that Sam had not come to the house. She didn't want to face him. As the cortege approached the church all the family looked with astonishment at the cars parked right down the neighbouring streets, the people thronging on to the road ahead of them. 'Are there lots of people?' Vince asked. 'Hundreds,' said Judith. 'Look at them all.' Maggie began to cry again, and John put his arm around her. When the car eased to a halt, John said, 'Wait. Let them move away a little. The undertakers will know what to do.'

They waited, and stepped from the car into the May sunshine. Maggie hung on to John, and Judith linked arms with her grandmother on one side and her brother on the other as they followed the coffin slowly into the church. Judith kept her head down as she walked. She had no idea who many of the people were and didn't want to look at them, see their sympathetic faces and their undisguised curiosity. Frank Pharaoh's death had been the talk of the town since it happened. 'Why don't they leave us alone?' she thought bitterly. Sam was out there somewhere, too, and she especially didn't want to catch his eye.

The organ droned, a choir of young boys sang, Father Price waited at the altar. They eased into the front pew and the service began. They would be there a while; Maggie had insisted on Mass as well as the funeral service. Judith tried to block it all out, just to focus on helping her grandmother to sit and stand. She didn't sing, or pray. Vince groped for her hand and squeezed it, but she didn't look at him. She felt numb, as if this was all a dream and she would wake and Frank would still be hovering on the edge of the family, grumbling and resentful. She'd had no idea about the Frank who had stolen Violet's pension, slept with a singer, lost money and died on a beach. It was if she were mourning a stranger. When it was time for Mass, she stayed where she was, refusing to stand humbly in line and take the wafer and the wine that meant nothing to her. John looked at her with a silent question, but she shook her head and let Vince squeeze past her to help Violet. People would notice, but she didn't care.

Two rows behind her, Sam did notice. He'd been waiting outside when the cortege arrived and had seen her pale face and the auburn hair pulled back under a black hat. Sam guessed the hat was Maggie's idea. Now all he could see was Judith's back, and the white of her neck as she bowed her head. She still looks angry, he thought, not just with me, with everyone. He'd noticed PC Kelly standing at the edge of the crowd outside, and another man with him, not in uniform, but unmistakeably a policeman. Sam remembered suddenly that this was the man he'd seen at the police station, who'd spoken to Sergeant Braithwaite.

After the interminable service some people drifted away, while others followed the hearse down to the cemetery, past ornate Victorian gateposts and flowering cherry trees, to the spot where Frank would lie. The breeze carried Father Price's familiar words up into the air, to mingle with the songs of nesting birds. Just a few minutes away from the windy ridge of Kells High Road, the cemetery was warm and smelled of newly mown grass and fresh earth. Sam stood quietly on his own, remembering the man in the coffin, and the dark curls plastered to his wet face on the beach. He hung his head. Frank was too young to go like this. He might not have killed himself in a deliberate act but he had courted trouble and it had finished him, alone and in pain. Sam felt his hands clenched, fingernails digging into his palms, and took a deep breath before shuffling forward to pick up a handful of earth and throw it into the grave, hearing the hollow thud on the coffin lid.

Groups of people made their way back to their cars, heading to the hotel in St Bees for the wake. Sam knew he had to make an appearance, and that he had to find a chance to speak to John, if only to arrange a time to see him on his own. He was part of this mourning family now, whether or not Judith wanted him there.

For her part, Judith was dreading seeing Sam, but when she saw his old car pull into the hotel car park she braced herself. At least she'd been able to take off the ridiculous hat and release her hair from too many pins and grips. In the mirror in the cloakroom she saw the tired eyes looking back at her.

It was nearly over, she told herself. Church, cemetery, now the hotel. Soon she could escape, for a walk on the beach, or a chat to Vince, and then back to Barrow and real life as soon as was decently possible. But before that she would have to see Sam. She knew she'd been harsh with him, and that he wouldn't return her anger, which made her feel worse. He would be reasonable and sympathetic, and she couldn't bear it.

As she emerged from the cloakroom to join the family greeting people as they arrived, she spotted Sam. He and her father were shaking hands, murmuring something to each other. John put his hand on Sam's shoulder, Vince gave him a hug, Maggie and Violet smiled. He was looking for her now, and she ducked back round the corner. What should she say to him? "Thank you for coming." It sounded trite, it was trite, but it was enough. Then she could move away and the worst would be over.

When she rounded the corner again, Sam was standing right in front of her. 'Judith,' he said, as surprised as she was. She put out her hand, and he took it and leaned towards her, kissing her on the cheek. 'How are you?' Suddenly her eyes filled with tears, and she wiped them away with her fingers, feeling for a handkerchief in her pocket while he stood looking at her. 'Bloody awful,' she said. 'I knew it would be bad, but the service was so long. Too long.'

'Father Price does go on,' said Sam. 'But it's what your parents wanted.'

'Not Dad,' said Judith, 'He won't even speak to Father Price.' She looked at him. 'What did he say to you just now?'

Sam looked away. 'We, you know, arranged to meet. Can't talk here, and I have some things to tell him.'

'Can you tell me?'

'You don't think I'm doing anything,' he said.

Judith was embarrassed. 'Did I say that?'

'Yes, and more. You were upset, I know. I was, too.'

She looked around. Food and drink made people relax, and there was a steady hum of conversation in the room. No one was looking at them. 'Is there a back door to this place?'

'Probably, to the car park at the back.'

'Let's get out for a while. They won't notice. We can get something at the café. I'm so hungry.'

At the café overlooking the beach Judith ordered tea, with beans on toast, and Sam had a bacon sandwich, neither of which would be on the polite hotel funeral buffet. Judith ate with energy and without talking. Sam watched the sun bouncing off the incoming tide and the slow movement of small white clouds across the blue. 'This is a great spot,' he said. 'Good idea.'

'I needed that,' she said, pushing her empty plate away. She wiped her mouth on the paper napkin and looked across at him. 'Was I really horrid the other day?'

He nodded. 'It upset me,' he said. ' You said I was taking advantage of your father, but I wouldn't do that. He's a good man.'

'Sorry,' said Judith, wondering again exactly what she'd said when she'd been so angry. 'It was such a shock. I know you're trying to help.'

He shook his head. 'Not achieving very much.' He remembered something. 'You know PC Kelly, don't you?'

'He's been around for years. He was there today.'

'Did you see someone with him, looked liked a policeman, shiny shoes, tweed jacket like mine?'

'What about him?'

'Has he been to the house at all, asking questions?'

She shook her head. 'I've been in Barrow most of the week.

Dad said a young DC came to ask some questions about Frank, but I know that bloke, and I haven't seen him today. They didn't mention anyone else. Vince would have told me. Why?'

'It's to do with the police in Whitehaven,' he said. 'They know more than they're telling me, I'm sure of it, and the man who's with PC Kelly hangs around the station there. Something odd about him.'

She shrugged. 'What have you found out?'

He hesitated. 'If I tell you some of it, will you keep it to yourself? I'm seeing John tomorrow and should really report to him properly.'

'I won't say anything, promise.'

'Well, Frank might have been hurt before he fell, which probably means he didn't do it deliberately.'

'That's good, isn't it, for Mum and Gran and Father blessed Price?'

'But it complicates the question of how he died. Did someone hurt him, and when, where? That's what I need to find out. And there's something else, about Gloria.'

Judith sat back and interrupted with a harsh laugh. 'Wouldn't trust that woman to tell the truth if her life depended on it.'

'Well, she told me her husband, or whatever he is, is out of jail, and knows about her and Frank.'

'Cried on your shoulder, did she?'

'Not exactly, but she's been beaten up and wanted me to help her.'

'Why should you?'

'Because she knows the people who might have been after Frank. Whitehaven's a small town. Villains know each other. She could be useful.'

Judith looked sceptical. 'Did she make a pass at you?'

He felt himself blushing. 'No,' he lied. He had a sudden urge to ask her about Harry Grayson, but stopped himself. 'Anyway, I'll tell your dad what I know tomorrow and take his advice about what to do next. He's my boss, and a much better one than that bastard Morrison.'

Judith poured herself another cup of tea. 'Talking of happy times in Barrow,' she said, 'I'm planning to do a feature on Monty House, now that things have settled down.'

'Settled down?' Sam was shocked. 'How can you say that? Cardine's still around, and Edwards.'

'I wanted to do a piece about the place last year and no one would let me, and then there was all that trouble.'

'Judith,' he interrupted, leaning forward to keep his voice down. 'That's a very bad idea. God knows what you could stir up. It's too soon. Wait till Cardine goes. He must be close to retirement.'

'That could be years,' she said. 'I need a story, something that the nationals might pick up. This is my career, Sam, I need to make a splash.'

Sam looked at the ceiling in disbelief. 'A splash? I can't believe you're saying that. It's a huge risk, Judith, can't you see that?' He knew where this was going. Grayson had told him to warn her off, and he'd said it wouldn't work. And it wasn't working. Judith had recovered her normal fight.

'You all think I'm some cub reporter, messing around,' she said. 'I'm a journalist, Sam, that's what we do. There's a story here, not about the Thornhills, but about the boys that nobody wants. Lads like Stevie Stringer – who tells their story?'

'Stevie ended up in a quicksand, poor little sod, and we never really knew how or why. But even if we had known, Cardine wouldn't have let it stick. He and Edwards are thick as thieves. There was nothing we could do, that's why I resigned.'

'I know you had no real choice about resigning after what Cardine said. But now I have the chance to say something good about those lads and people like Iris Robinson who care for them when no one else does. What's wrong with that?'

'Is that what you want to write about? The saintly Mrs Robinson?'

'Have you been talking to Grayson?' she asked.

Sam shrugged. 'I had to talk to him about the Whitehaven stuff. He mentioned that you wanted to do something like this.'

'And you boys decided I needed to be warned off, I suppose?'

She pushed back her chair. 'End of conversation. I'll pay for this, and then I'll go back to the hotel, to do my duty. I'm going back to Barrow tomorrow, to do my job. You can get on with yours, without any interference from me.'

She pushed her way across the room to the till. Sam watched her go and sat with his head in his hands. Why could they never talk without arguing?

The following day Sam drove to St Bees in the afternoon, and was relieved to find that Judith had already left. He met Maggie in the hall. 'Yes, Judith couldn't wait to get away again,' she said. 'I'm just glad that Elspeth is there, such a sensible woman, your sister.'

John ushered Sam into the front room as Maggie went to make them some tea. As far as he was able to, with the limited information he had, Sam went over what he knew. He told John the post-mortem had been inconclusive, but he wasn't specific, and John didn't ask. He mentioned Gloria, describing her as a friend of Frank's, but without the detail, and he said there was some suspicion that Gloria's jealous husband might be involved. No names, nothing about the potential for further trouble. John listened with care, but Sam could he see how distressed he was.

'It's haunting me,' said John, after Maggie had brought the tea and departed. 'Frank had another life completely unknown to us, and we had no idea. Violet said he was fine, just as normal, and that was all we knew.'

'Violet never wanted to see any fault with Frank, even if others might have done,' said Sam. 'That was the link to the family, and it was weak.'

John nodded. 'What do you think the coroner will say, when they finally get round to a proper inquest?'

'It'll depend on the police investigation,' said Sam. 'They must know more then they're telling me, and it's my job to help them trust me. An old colleague in Barrow reminded me that the police don't like private investigators, and he's right.'

'How much longer do you think you'll need?'

Sam thought about it. 'Two more weeks, at least.'

'That's fine,' said John. 'Don't feel rushed. We're clearer than we were already, and Maggie and Violet seem reassured that Frank hasn't condemned himself to everlasting purgatory, or what ever punishment suicides get. All seems pretty barbaric to me.'

'There's one other thing,' said Sam. 'It's got nothing to do with this, but I feel I have to mention it. It's about Judith.'

John looked troubled. 'Has she been rude to you again? I'll talk to her about it.'

'No, it's not about me,' said Sam. 'She says she wants to do a story about the boys' home near Barrow that she and I were involved with last year.'

John frowned. 'The one where that boy was drowned and

the man hung himself? I thought that was all over.'

'So did I, but there are still things that were never really cleared up, and I'm worried that Judith will rake it up again.'

'Why would she want to?'

'For a story, to make her name in this new job,' said Sam.

'Damn the new job,' said John with unexpected ferocity. 'I just buried my son, and she wants to put herself at risk? Is that what she's doing?'

'Maybe you could help her see that, from your point of view,' Sam said. 'I tried to put her off the idea. No joy, but she might listen to you.'

'I'll try Sam, but she can be terribly stubborn, like my mother, Jessie. She was a difficult woman. Not a blood relative, but they were very close when Judith was young and Jessie seems to have rubbed off on her.' He looked at Sam. 'Can you keep an eye on things, if she won't change her mind? Help her, if you need to?'

Sam blushed, and John noticed. 'You're fond of her, aren't you?'

Sam nodded. More than you know, he thought.

CHAPTER 18

Sam gazed at the wall of his bedroom, now covered with notes and scribbles and lines with arrows. If he'd been honest he would have invited John to look at it, but it might not make sense to anyone except himself. He tried moving the pieces around to put different bits of the picture at the centre, and when he moved Gloria Tennant to the centre, he stopped to think. She knew Frank, her 'husband' Ray knew of Frank, Ray was close to Baldy and tattoo Blue. Blue was probably the man seen at both Arthur Paling's house before his assault, and at Frank's before the arson at Mrs Barstow's house next door. Sam added a note to the list of things he needed to do. There must be some official report about the fire and he needed to see it. For some reason the police were either doing nothing about Baldy and Blue, or were choosing not to tell him about it. Now that Ray Noakes was out, were they keeping an eye on him, too? Another note was added to the list.

At the edge of the space surrounding Gloria's name he put a question: *cigarette smuggling*? Presumably it was from Ireland. The duty on cigarettes was lower there, and there were big profits to be made buying them cheap and selling here illegally, at a lower price than normal but still enough for a good mark-up. Sam knew how close the connection had always been between Whitehaven and Ireland. These days, the harbour was busy and full of equipment used by Marchon for loading and unloading ships carrying phosphates, and there were plenty of hidden corners for things to go unnoticed. There was no special security down there that Sam knew of, but it wouldn't be hard to find out. Another note on the list.

He thought about what Gloria had told him and went back to the wall for the details: Michael Leary, the Black Horse in Cleator – part of the group around Ray Noakes, not very bright and sometimes drank and talked too much. That was Gloria's information, and why should she lie about it? She wanted Ray to get caught, and was using Sam to achieve that. No point in sending him off on wild goose chases.

He fumbled through his clothes, regretting that Judith had taken the leather jacket back to Barrow with her. He needed to look less like a policeman and more like a redundant postman, resentful and bored. He put his hands through his hair to mess it up, found an old sweatshirt and a pair of jeans, left his face unshaven, dirtied his hands and fingernails with soot from the front room fireplace and looked at himself in the small mirror on the mantlepiece.

The effect was interesting; it made him feel disconsolate and detached. He looked at this image of a different Sam and rehearsed what this man could say about himself. He'd given up the postal service because he couldn't stand the poisonous atmosphere in the sorting office and the bag was too heavy. His wife had run off with a lover, taking with her everything they owned, and he hadn't had a woman since then. He had a bit of money, but it was running out fast, and he was living in someone else's house with the stink of smoke in his clothes. None of that's far off the truth, he realised. Now what he needed was a different name. Sam was OK, but Tognarelli was too memorable. Maybe a nickname.

The idea came to him from nowhere. Shorty. He would call himself Shorty. He'd always been aware of his short stature, so it fitted. It was Ray Noakes' nickname too, but this Shorty was new in town and wasn't to know that, was he? Maybe someone would comment, warn him off, and tell him why. If he needed a surname it would be Brennan, a good Irish name that would raise no comment in a community where many Irish families had settled. Shorty Brennan carefully checked all his pockets, put away his alter ego's driver's licence and left himself with some loose change, a tenner, and an old betting slip he found in a drawer in the kitchen. Before he went out, he took a swig of the whisky that Frank had been drinking before he left the house for the last time. Then Shorty Brennan climbed into his old car and headed inland, towards Cleator.

The Black Horse wasn't easy to find, and Sam decided to start his evening in the first pub he saw in Cleator. With the whisky and a pint or two he might be driving badly, but that was what Shorty Brennan would do. When he pushed open the door of the Black Horse half an hour later he was beginning to inhabit the person he'd created. The small bar was crowded, men standing around in groups and a few women sitting together in a far corner. No one took any notice of him, including the barman, until Sam pushed his way through, leaned over the bar and demanded a pint of Guinness in a voice that didn't sound much like him. He could do a good Lancashire accent. It was different from the local, but that didn't matter.

He stood alone with his dark pint, watching and listening. There was a pool table in a room at the back and he pushed towards it. It was quieter there, and a number of young men were standing around, two with cues, the others leaning against the wall, watching. A pound note lay on the side of the table, held down with an empty glass. The game ended, the pound note was removed, cheerful insults were exchanged and two more men picked up the cues. Sam realised there was an unofficial queue for a game, and parked himself at what he guessed was the end of the line. He exchanged glances with one or two of the other men, but nothing was said. Sam was beginning to doubt Gloria's information when another young man sauntered into the room. When he was hailed as 'Mick, lad,' Sam turned to look at him more carefully. The game continued. 'Mick' disappeared but left his drink and returned after a few minutes. 'You in, Leary?' someone asked. The young man nodded. He was thin, with a pock-marked face and spikey black hair. Sam left his place in the queue to get another drink and to give himself longer to watch.

When Sam got back to the poolroom, Mick Leary was playing, and not very well. He was drinking steadily, and had lost three games and three pounds before Sam was handed a cue, with a raised eyebrow that asked whether he wanted it. Years in the barracks paid off, as Sam was able to make mistakes that looked accidental but were quite deliberate. He wanted to give Mick Leary a hope of winning his money back, and Mick rose to the bait quite quickly. Sam lost the first game easily, surrendered his money, lost again, and gave up. He bought himself yet another pint, but he'd poured most of the previous one into the toilet, so he could appear more affected by the drink than he actually was. It was nine o'clock when Mick took Sam's third pound off him, stuffed the money in his pocket. 'I'm off to town,' he said. 'Too quiet here.'

'I'm off there meself, had enough,' Sam said. 'Want a lift? I could drop you in Kells.'

Mick Leary looked at the scruffy stranger. 'Why not?' he said.

'Name's Sam,' said Sam as he unlocked the car. 'People call me Shorty.'

Mick laughed. 'Shorty? Anyone told you that's not a good name?'

'Why not?' said Sam. 'I'm short, shorter than you any road.'

'I know someone else called Shorty,' Mick went on, as Sam fumbled with the keys. 'And 'e wouldn't be 'appy.'

'Tough,' said Sam, as the engine sputtered into life. 'Bloody thing's on its last legs,' he went on. 'Have to sell it.' He drove with exaggerated care down the narrow street onto the main road.

'Bloody 'ell, Sam,' said Mick, 'put your foot down. I'm meeting people tonight, not tomorrow morning.' He checked his watch. 'Time enough, though. Whereabouts in Kells are you?'

'West Row,' said Sam. 'Miserable digs, but the view's good.'

He was parking the car in a spot a few yards down from the house when Mick said, 'Need the bog. Can I use yours?'

Sam froze. The toilet was upstairs, his bedroom door was open, and the bedroom wall was covered with the details of Whitehaven's villains.

'Me first,' he said. 'I'm bursting.' He unlocked the front door, left Mick standing in the hall and took the stairs two at a time. He closed the bedroom door and left the light on in the toilet when he'd finished. 'All yours,' he said. 'Door's open, light's on.' He waited anxiously until Mick came back down the stairs.

'Think I'm going to nick summat?' said Mick cheerily.

'You in a rush?' Sam asked, as casually as he could manage. 'Couple of beers in the back. Might as well finish 'em off. Don't get much company these days.' Mick hesitated, and Sam pressed on. 'Go in the front room, I'll fetch 'em.'

Sam had just turned towards the kitchen, pleased with his progress so far, when the phone rang. He thought of letting it ring, but why would he do that? He picked it up. Judith said, 'Sam? Sorry it's late. I've been thinking.'

'Bloody daft time to ring,' Sam interrupted, loud enough for Mick to hear. 'I've had a few, and may 'ave a few more. Saturday night, for God's sake. Piss off.' He put the phone down.

Mick was smiling when he took the beer in. 'Who was that?' he said. 'Your mam?'

'Sister,' said Sam. 'She says I need "support".' He minced the word and Mick laughed. 'Lost me job, lost me wife, but I didn't really want either of 'em.'

Mick laughed again. 'What job?'

Sam was ready. 'Postman. Thought it'd be easy, after the strike an' all, but it was shite. They just moaned all the bloody time, and the bag was too heavy. Mug's game. I packed it in.' He hesitated. 'And the wife, what a bitch. Found her in bed, my bed, with some bloke and then she took every last bloody thing out of the 'ouse and buggered off.'

Mick laughed out loud. 'You signing on, then?' he asked.

'Suppose I'll 'ave to,' Sam said. 'Hate it. All that standing around, questions, having to turn up on time to get a handout. Don't want to do that again.' He got to his feet unsteadily. 'Found some whisky in the back. Fancy a drop?' Mick drained his bottle of beer and sat back. 'Why not?' he said again.

'Don't you 'ave to be somewhere?' Sam asked.

'Later,' said Mick. 'Just down by the harbour. Won't take long to get down there.'

When Sam came back with a couple of glasses of whisky Mick said, 'There's plenty of money around if you don't want to sign on.'

Sam feigned disinterest, staring into the glass. Mick went on. 'Got a cig?' Sam shook his head. 'None in the house.'

'Want some, cheap?'

'Where from?' Sam didn't look up.

'Come up the Black Horse, Friday. I could give you a deal, and you could make a bit selling 'em on.'

'How much?' said Sam.

'Enough.'

Sam raised his head. 'On the level?'

Mick tapped the side of his nose. 'Ask no questions. Friday, right? Should have it sorted by then. Tide's about right on Monday.'

Sam tried to look confused. His heart was bumping. 'Tide? You going fishing or summat?'

'No questions,' Mick repeated, enjoying his role as the man of mystery. 'Friday, Black Horse. Tell the barman you're looking for me.' He pushed himself out of the sagging chair. 'Got to go. And keep quiet about this, right?'

Mick finished his glass and left, weaving down the quiet cobbled street and disappearing round the corner. Sam breathed in and out slowly, going over what had been said. The man knew where he lived, but it wouldn't have to matter. Gloria was right. Mick Leary couldn't handle the drink, had taken Sam at face value and given away just enough to make himself look well-connected and savvy. For a few minutes Sam was exultant. He'd made a plan, seen it through, and it worked. Now all he had to do was get some more informa-tion about how it was done, and he could hand Braithwaite and Holmes something they couldn't ignore and would have to thank him for. Cigarette smuggling, through Whitehaven. Everything pointed to that, what Gloria had told him, and now this. Suddenly the euphoria collapsed and unaccustomed alcohol made Sam's head swim. He left the glasses in the sink, went upstairs, lay on his bed fully dressed and was asleep in minutes.

In Elspeth's house in Roose, the two women sat at the kitchen table with a bottle of Cold Duck. 'Tell me again what he said,' said Elspeth. 'Doesn't sound like Sam.'

'He's your brother, Elspeth,' said Judith, 'but he can be such a shit. And he was drunk.' She mimicked his voice. "I've 'ad a few". Then he told me to piss off.' She finished the glass of wine and poured herself another. 'Every time we seem to be getting on better, it goes wrong. He started lecturing me about my job in the middle of the funeral tea, for God's sake. Then I ring him to talk to him about it sensibly for once and he's drunk and foul-mouthed. Unbelievable!'

Elspeth frowned. 'Doesn't sound like Sam at all. He told me he'd got pretty drunk at his birthday party in March, but I don't think he'd want to do that again. Maybe he just didn't want to talk to you.'

There was silence for a few minutes before Judith said, 'What am I going to do with him, Elspeth?'

Elspeth put down her glass. 'You know what, Judith? I think you should just forget about Sam for a while. The last few months, ever since you were ill, you two have been up and down, all the time, and it's getting tedious. And now he's in Whitehaven and you're down here. Now that the worst is over and you can get on with your life, why don't you just forget about him? You live here, and Sam's my brother, but so what? Maybe you need a proper break from each other.'

'You haven't met Harry Grayson, have you?' said Judith, smiling. 'No, but I want to,' said Elspeth. 'You seem to like him.'

211

'I do. He's attentive, a bit flirty, but nice with it, and good-looking. Don't know why I didn't notice that last year. And he treats me like an equal. He and Sam don't get on, but that's not surprising. Sam was pretty down on him, said he didn't take enough care, all the things you'd expect Sam to say. He can be such a prig about work.'

Elspeth poured the rest of the wine into her glass. 'I don't think Sam has a clue about women. Christine was completely wrong for him, but he married her because she wanted the ring and all the etceteras. He thought getting married is just what people did when they'd been going out together for a while. Idiot. They were both too young, and then she was cheating on him right under his nose. When she left and took all their stuff he never said a word. She divorced him in the end, and that was a farce too. "Mental cruelty" she said, because he worked all the time and left her alone. She could have gone out to work like the rest of us, but not her. And after all that, he still won't say anything about her.'

'She gave him that leather jacket,' said Judith.

'Yes, but who earned the money to pay for it? He did. I love him dearly but he's an idiot about some things.'

She put her hand on Judith's arm and squeezed. 'Why don't you invite Sergeant Grayson over here for supper one night, so I can get a look at him? Do Tommy good to see a man around the place.'

'Does Tommy miss Sam?'

'I'm sure he does. Sam's so good with him.'

'Yes,' said Judith.

Sunday was clear and bright. Judith suggested a walk. 'Over the Walney Bridge, then round to Earnse Bay. If the tide's right we could paddle, or sunbathe in the dunes at the far end near the airstrip. Might be some planes going in and out too, Tommy would like that.'

Before they left, she found the home number that Harry Grayson had given her. thought about it for a while and then made the call.

It was Elspeth, not Judith, who was surprised when a smartly dressed young man walked into the café by the beach while they were eating tea and cake that afternoon.

'You sneaky thing,' Elspeth whispered to Judith when Harry introduced himself. He walked back with them to Roose and stayed for supper, played cards with Tommy and chatted amiably to Elspeth about her work at the school, and how happy she was to have Judith as a lodger.

'I'd be happy too,' he said, smiling.

When he left, having given Judith a kiss on the cheek, Elspeth turned to her friend. 'Well,' she said. 'He's a charmer, Judith. And obviously fond of you. Where's the problem?'

Judith shrugged. 'He's very friendly, I know, but there's something I'm just not sure about.'

'Is it something Sam told you?'

'No, well, yes,' said Judith. 'He's not said anything about him recently, but I know he wasn't sure about him last year, when Sam was struggling with Morrison. He thought Harry was too keen to keep his nose clean with the bosses. But now Harry is the boss, and he seems very keen on the golf club, keeping in with all the other blokes who hang out there.'

'Sam has every reason to feel jealous of him, doesn't he?'

Judith frowned. 'I don't see Sam as underhand like that. He's honest, too honest sometimes.'

'Well, I like Harry very much, and you should definitely make up your own mind about him. Are you going to see

213

him again?'

'He said he'd ring me.'

Elspeth squeezed her friend's shoulder. 'Give him a chance, that's all I'm saying. I think he's delightful.'

It took Judith a while to fall asleep later that night. Elspeth seemed keen for her to find a man, but the only thing she was certain of was that she was good at her job, and needed the chance to prove it. Everything else could wait.

CHAPTER 19

Sam always found weekends difficult, unless he was working. From noon on Saturday everything closed down, and people spent time with their mates or their families. This weekend, yet again, he was reminded that he had no one to whom he mattered more than anyone else. The loneliness was intense and wrapped around him like a cloud, blotting out light and warmth. He looked for the bottle of whisky that Frank had left in the kitchen but Michael Leary had finished it; a search through the cupboards revealed that they were as empty as the day that stretched ahead of him. At least the sun was shining, for the time being, and Sam opened the front door and sat on the step for a while, watching the sea. The strip of land opposite the house taunted him; with time and care it could give him some pleasure, and even some food, but the idea of working out there made him feel guilty. That wasn't what John was paying him for.

A van came down the street and stopped outside Mrs Barstow's house next door. A young man got out, pulled a bag of tools after him, dropped them on the doorstep and then opened the back of the van and pulled out a new door, struggling to hold it upright in the stiff breeze. Sam stood up to give him a hand.

'Thanks, marra,' said the young man. 'It's for our mam. She wants to get home and I promised I'd fix the door for 'er.'

'The firemen made a mess inside too, water everywhere,' said Sam. 'I should have gone to see her about it, but things got a bit complicated.'

'Aye, I heard,' said the young man.

'Funeral last Friday,' said Sam.

'Heard about that, too. I'm Colin, by the way. Are you the bloke who pulled our mam out? Police said she'd've been in trouble else.'

'Sam Tognarelli. Yes, I could see her feet,' said Sam. 'It was lucky I was there.'

'Well, thanks anyway,' said Colin. He put out his hand and Sam shook it. After helping to take down the boards and the old door, Sam was standing, holding the new one steady for Colin to fix the hinges, when Colin asked, 'They found Frank down on the beach, didn't they?'

'Yes, he must have fallen,' said Sam. He didn't want to discuss the other possibilities with someone he'd just met.

The unexpected work was a godsend. Colin chattered away about nothing very much, the sun shone, Sam's urge to help was satisfied, and while the first coat of primer was drying Colin insisted on buying Sam a pint. They stood in the yard behind the pub on the High Road drinking in convivial silence for a few minutes before Sam asked, 'Did you know Frank?'

'Not really,' said Colin. 'Mam knows Violet well enough, but Frank weren't there much, and kept to 'imself. Folk said he were down the betting shop a lot lately, but that was nowt to do wi' me. He sorted a few things for our mam, always respectful like, so no business of mine what he did.' He took a long mouthful of beer. 'In trouble, was 'e?'

Sam didn't respond. He suspected that both Colin and his mother liked to gossip, so he asked, 'Did you ever see a bloke around Frank's house with tattoos up his arm, since Violet moved out? I think they call him Blue.'

Colin put down his pint, and shook his head. 'I told you,' he said, 'none of my business. I live up Cleator, only come down this way if our mam wants summat.'

Sam wondered. 'I was up in Cleator last night,' he said. 'D'you know a bloke up there called Michael Leary?'

Colin looked at him. 'Mick Leary? Daft as a brush, like all them Learys. Give 'im a wide berth. Gets into all sorts of bother.'

Sam waited. Colin looked around before he said, 'Too many mates across the water, if you know what I mean.' He looked at Sam and raised his eyebrows. Sam's question was unspoken and went unanswered.

Thirst quenched, they walked back to West Row and Colin fitted the new locks before he disappeared to see his mother at her friends' house round the corner. For a while Sam had assumed that Eileen Barstow would move straight back into the house, but it hadn't happened yet. The street was so quiet that he could hear the waves on the beach far below and soon the cloud of isolation descended on him yet again, with even greater opacity than before. 'Across the water?' he wondered. What was that about?

When the fish and chip shop opened, Sam was first in the queue and ate his meal in the front room to make the most of the sunlight that streamed through the window. He wondered yet again about the reliability of the information he'd been given by Gloria Tennant. If Ray was as violent as she claimed, was he using her to pull Sam in and stop him poking around in Frank's death, which Ray himself could have engineered before his release? Judith didn't trust Gloria, and maybe her instincts were right. And now he was being offered hints about illicit cigarettes from 'daft as a brush' Mick from Cleator. The whole business smelled as suspicious as the smoke in Eileen Barstow's house. No wonder she didn't want to move back in. Sam felt he was sinking into a quagmire.

Some time later, standing in front of the information displayed on his bedroom wall, Sam asked himself what was the simplest way to explain what had happened? One: Frank owed money and was being warned to pay up. Two: Ray Noakes found out about Frank's dalliance with Gloria and used his contacts to punish Frank, or at least to threaten him. Three: Frank decided to avoid his persecutors, whoever they were, by taking the path to St Bees and the protection of his family, but he'd been overtaken by bad weather, slipped and fell to his death. 'That would have been enough for Harry Grayson,' Sam said to himself. 'But it's not enough for me. Too many guesses and easy assumptions, no hard evidence to take to the police.' He stared at the wall for a while longer. Then he put his camera and a long lens into a bag, put on the darkest clothes he could find, waited until cloud covered the darkening sky, and set off for the harbour.

The only way that any of what Mick Leary had said made sense was the possibility that he and others were buying cigarettes smuggled in from somewhere that didn't have such high taxes. 'Across the water' Colin had said. It was 1970, not 1770, Sam told himself, but if cigarettes could be bought cheap 'across the water' in Ireland and sold at a profit on the black market in England, where there was money to be made, someone would find a way to make it. Mick Leary was just a small cog in whatever operation might be going on, Sam was sure of that. But it was the harbour Mick had been heading for when he left West Row, so that was a good place to start.

Tonight he would have a good look round the harbour, and tomorrow he would go himself to the house by the quarry and not leave until Clegg had told him what he'd seen the night that Frank died. If he claimed he'd seen nothing, there would be little he could do, but at least the question would be asked. If that upset people, too bad.

By the time he reached the bottom of the steps that led down to the harbour it was almost dark, the setting sun obscured by a thick bank of cloud that loomed on the horizon and reached across towards the coast. Sunday night noise drifted over the water from the town and reverberated off old sandstone walls. Sam stood at the bottom of the steps as close to the wall as he could, pulled his hat well down over his face and looked around. On the far side, a few fishing boats were tied up, resting quietly on the black. No lights over there; the catch would have been unloaded and the crew gone to wherever their real lives took them. The trucks and engines that hauled phosphates onto ships were silent, too. The only light was in a hut on the quayside, and someone was standing outside, the light from a cigarette glowing in the darkness. Sam listened carefully. No voices.

He closed up the bag on his shoulder and walked slowly round the quayside towards the hut. The smoking man turned at the sound of Sam's footfall. 'Good evening,' Sam said, in the most casual off-comer tone he could muster. 'I wonder if you could help me?'

The man was wearing a heavy jacket and a cap, as if he'd just left the bridge of one of the fishing boats. He said nothing, and Sam continued. 'I just came down the steps over there,' he pointed behind him, 'and here's this huge harbour. No idea it was so big.'

'Used to be one of the busiest in England,' said the man. 'Close to the Atlantic.'

'Yes, of course,' said Sam. 'Fascinating. What are all these trucks and things for? Coal?'

'Some, but mostly phosphates, from Marchon, tha' knows. Goes all over the place.'

'And fishing too, by the look of it,' said Sam, warming to his 'geography teacher' persona. 'I had no idea. Seen the towns on maps and so forth, but it's all much bigger than I expected.'

'From away?' said the man.

'Just up for the weekend, from Manchester,' said Sam. Not for the first time he realised how easily lying came to him.

'Oh, aye,' said the man.

Sam knew he sounded like a buffoon, but that was fine. He ploughed on, accentuating the educated accent. 'Is this the kind of place that smugglers used, like in Cornwall you know, in the old poem, "Face the wall, my darling," all that?'

The man stared. 'You what?'

Sam laughed. 'I was just wondering, who keeps track of the ships coming in and out?'

The man pointed to one of the big buildings on the other side. 'Harbourmaster.'

'No one there now though, is there? No lights anywhere that I can see.'

'He'll be 'ere tomorrow,' said the man.

'Ah,' said Sam with a flourish, 'but what if I wanted to bring something in that I shouldn't? Smuggling, you know, like the old days.'

'What you on about?'

'Any police around?'

'Not special, not down 'ere. Station's just up the street. You going to hand yourself in or summat?'

Sam laughed merrily. 'Well, nice talking to you,' he said. 'Very interesting place, I must say. Can I get out into the town this way?'

The man pointed. 'Keep on this side, then head away from the dock and you'll come out near the market place.'

'Thank you so much,' said Sam.

He followed the man's directions, looking back at one point to wave. He'd risked being remembered, but it was worth it to gather some more information. No special police, not much supervision or security at night, plenty of places to watch without being seen. The pubs in the market place spilled noisy drinkers onto the pavements, but Sam didn't join them. He walked back to Kells up the long hill, and in the quiet of the kitchen he sketched a plan of the harbour with as much detail as he could remember. If Mick Leary's boast about the cigarettes was true, and if Whitehaven was the port of entry, then something would be happening there in the coming week. Mick Leary had mentioned Monday and Sam was already planning how he might see it for himself.

He sat back on the old chair and felt the legs creak. It was all too bizarre. And what did any of it have to do with his task of finding out about Frank? To reassure himself, he spelled out the convoluted logic that made this flurry of activity seem useful. All of it depended on Gloria, and Sam felt the story bending into a circle. It might come to nothing, but he knew from his albeit limited experience that if you kept looking for information something might make sense, eventually. He would plod on, working down the list of possible enquiries that was pinned to his bedroom wall. Next on the list was a talk with Isaac Clegg.

Early Monday morning might be a good time to find Clegg at his cottage behind the quarry, Sam reckoned, so he set off before seven in a steady drizzle. He took the car as far down the track from Sandwith as he dare without risking it on the ruts and stones, then pulled into a muddy passing place and got out. Fine rain blew horizontally into his face as he walked the rest of the way, and it was almost half past seven when he got to the cottage. He checked behind him. The two quarrymen he'd already met would be on their way to work, but he'd planned to be there ahead of them and there was no sign of anyone on the track behind him.

Sam stood at the gate and peered at the cottage, looking for signs of occupation. It looked almost derelict, but the windows and roof were intact. No sign of a car, and no tyre tracks that he could see. Whoever lived here was either not at home or came in and out on foot. He walked up to the door and leaned towards it, listening. Voices. He stepped back. The quarrymen had mentioned only one person living here. He leaned forward to the door again, listening for longer this time. The voice was low and even and didn't sound local. A radio: there was someone in the house, listening to the radio. As if to confirm the thought, Sam heard music start up, and then the sound of a closing door.

This time he stepped back towards the road for a few paces, before returning to the door and knocking sharply on it. Almost immediately the music stopped. Sam knocked again. 'Hello there,' he called out. Silence. 'Mr Clegg?' This time he heard footsteps approaching the door from the other side. 'Could I have a word, Mr Clegg?' Sam said, in his local voice. He wanted to sound as little like a policeman as he could manage.

'What is it?' called an old man's voice.

'It's about the man who fell down the cliff.'

'You the police?'

'No, the man was a friend of mine.'

For what seemed like several minutes there was nothing. Then the voice said, 'I'll get the key,' and footsteps receded into the house before returning. A key turned on the inside and the door creaked open. Blue watery eyes, a weathered face and grey hair appeared in the small gap.

'Mr Clegg?' said Sam.

'Aye, who are you? Bloody early, whoever you are.'

Sam smiled. 'Yes, sorry. I really hoped I would find you in. People start work early round here.'

'Aye, well, not me. Not worked these past two years. I'm a sick man, diabetes.' The old man was wheezing. 'They found me in a coma, month or two back, had to go to th'ospital.'

Sam looked sympathetic. 'Sorry to hear that, Mr Clegg. Is it all right for me to talk to you now?'

Isaac Clegg sniffed. 'About the man who fell?'

'Yes, that's it,' said Sam. 'Well, he was a boy really, only twenty-three. I'm a friend of the family.'

'Not police?'

'No.'

'They came and asked a lot of questions. I told 'em nowt.'

'Could I come in, Mr Clegg?' said Sam, 'It's pretty wet out here.'

Isaac Clegg looked him up and down, then stood back and pulled the door open a little more. Sam stood in the hall by the door, with the old man a few feet away. The house smelled stale and damp.

'That's far enough. What do you want?'

'The man who fell was called Frank Pharaoh,' Sam began.

Isaac interrupted. 'I know that already, in't paper. So what do you want?' he asked again.

'The police aren't interested in what happened to him,' said Sam. 'The family asked me to find out about what he was doing out here, how he came to fall.'

'They think he topped 'imself?' Ike asked.

'Well, that's a possibility, but they're hoping not. We just wondered if you – if anything happened up here that night that might have, you know…'

'You mean, did someone push 'im?'

Sam shrugged. 'We don't know. Did you see anything? He was found the next day but we're talking about the night of Tuesday May 19th, or the early hours of Wednesday.'

Isaac picked up a pipe off a small table, jammed it in his mouth and started to suck. Then he felt in his pocket, pulled out the tobacco and began to fill the pipe, laboriously tamped down the tobacco and lit it. Acrid smoke filled the small space and Sam began to cough.

'Clears me lungs,' said Isaac.

'Did you see or hear anything that night?' Sam asked once he recovered his breath. He was still standing by the door, with no sign of permission to move anywhere else. The old man pulled on the pipe and looked at him. 'Might 'ave,' he said. Sam wondered whether he was expecting payment. 'We'd be very grateful for any information,' he said. 'The family are desperate to know what happened.' He waited. 'Do you have children, Mr Clegg?'

A strange noise came from the old man, before he coughed again, long and loud. 'Not that you'd notice,' he said.

Sam waited. Another draw on the pipe that glowed in the dim light. 'It were in't middle of the night,' Isaac said. 'Lights. Car lights, or a van mebbe. And voices. Shouting. Didn't last long. Then the lights flashed, turning round like, and gone, back down the track.'

'Did you see anyone?' asked Sam.

'I looked out, didn't put the light on. Couldn't see much. Someone went past, maybe two people, men. It were dark, and raining hard, too.'

'Two men?'

'Maybe more. Hard to say. The van stopped a while with th'engine running before it turned around.'

'And what time was it, do you think?'

'I'd gone to bed, so after midnight, but I wasn't asleep when I heard them. Maybe one? Summat round then. Went back to bed. Up to no good, whoever they were. None of my business.'

'You didn't hear anything that was said?'

'Nay, just a lot of shouting.'

Sam waited. He knew that sometimes people added details if you waited long enough, but Isaac just sucked on his pipe.

'Anything else, Mr Clegg?'

Isaac shook his head. 'I told the police nowt. So that's for you and 'is folks, the poor bugger. If you're asking what happened to 'im, I don't know, do I? He could have run away and slipped, or they could have pushed 'im. No way to know.'

'Did you see any of the men carrying anything?'

'Nay. Told you, it were dark.' He paused, then stepped towards the door. 'What d'you say your name is?'

'Sam, I'm a friend of the family. One last thing, Mr Clegg, did you notice what colour the van was?'

'Hard to see, but it weren't black. That's it. It were dark and wet and that's all I can tell you.'

He pushed past Sam, pulled the door open and stood back. A fine veil of rain swirled into the space.

'Thanks anyway,' said Sam. 'You've been very helpful,' he added, but he knew that wasn't true. Even if the old man was prepared to make a statement, it didn't amount to much.

Sam trudged back to the car. No positive ID of any of the people, nor the vehicle. He couldn't even be certain it had anything to do with Frank's fall. Another door closed. He would pester the Whitehaven police again later, but he had no new information to offer and didn't expect to be made welcome. Then he remembered another question that had been bothering him since the funeral. Maybe he could find an answer today, and fill in at least one of the gaps in his evidence wall.

When he reached home and had dried out, Sam picked up the phone. He needed to talk to Judith, but when he'd rung on Sunday afternoon there'd been no reply.

'Is that you Sam?' said Elspeth. 'If you want Judith, she's at work.'

'I tried yesterday, but there was no answer.'

'We were out, having a lovely afternoon. We met your friend, Harry Grayson.'

'Oh,' said Sam.

'Why were you so rude to her on Saturday night, Sam?'

'I had to be,' he began. 'I had someone here with me, I couldn't talk to her.'

'Well, she got the message loud and clear.'

'But–' said Sam.

'But nothing, Sam. She's not here, and I suggest you leave her alone until you've sorted all this out. And don't bother ringing here tonight. Judith's got a date, a real date, with a very suitable man. Are you hearing me, Sam? You had your chance and you blew it.'

She hung up, leaving Sam staring at the lifeless receiver.

CHAPTER 20

For a long time after he hung up the phone, Sam stood with his forehead against the wall, his mind so full that everything merged into a grey formless mass, turning slowly, round and round. Judith was out with someone, probably Harry Grayson, and Elspeth was blaming him. Nothing he was finding out about Frank made sense. No one seemed to know or care how he spent his fruitless days. He could cross Isaac Clegg off his list of tasks, but what had he gained? Nothing of value, again.

What was he doing with his life? He thought of his father, working for years at mind-numbing manual jobs to put food on the family table, but at least he had been able to see his children growing, with opportunities that his work had provided. Compared to that effort, Sam's struggle through adulthood had scarcely started. He pushed his forehead harder against the wall, raised and banged it down again, harder. The pain cleared his mind. If Judith had found someone, there was not much he could do about it, but he had to tell her what she meant to him. It might not make any difference, but he had to do it. And he had to try again to make the police listen to what he knew. Why should they listen now when they'd already dismissed him as an interfering nuisance? But he still had to do that, too.

Upstairs in his bedroom he took a Polaroid picture of one section of the evidence wall, waiting and watching as the photo emerged from the machine and slowly resolved itself into a visible image. It was too dark. Standing on the bed, he pulled up the pink curtains and tucked them carefully into the curtain rail to let in as much light as possible and tried again. Morning sun gleaming off the sea helped and the second image was sharper, the tyre tracks and footprints from the cliff top standing out quite clearly. He worked his way round the wall, framing the pictures to align with each other and watching the damp prints as they appeared. Carefully he gathered the half dozen photos and numbered them in a sensible order. Next, he copied out sections from his notebook and records of his meetings and conversations with the various people who had contributed to Frank's story, realising as he did so that this wasn't just about Frank any more. A bigger picture was emerging, like a Polaroid image that had stuck halfway to clarity, an image of the underbelly of the town. All these neat handwritten notes were numbered, cross referenced with the visual items, and clipped together. He even had a folder for them. In fact he had ten folders, bought on that first heady morning of his work as a private investigator, when his hopes had been higher than they were now.

The idea of ringing the police station to make an appointment with Sergeant Braithwaite had crossed Sam's mind, but he'd decided against it. The only way to make sure that someone would see him was to turn up there, in person, and wait. If it took the rest of the day, no matter. He had reached the end of what he could do alone, except for one next step which worried him. He didn't want to take risks – it was not in his nature – but soon risk might be unavoidable, and he forced himself to come to terms with that. In any case, what did he have to lose?

It was the middle of the day when Sam carried his precious folder into the police station in Scotch Street. In the solid sandstone building there seemed to be little going on, except for a banging door and the distant sound of voices echoing from the cells. The duty officer carried on talking into the phone without acknowledging Sam's presence, although Sam knew that the man had both noticed and recognised him. When the phone call finally ended, Sam put his folder on the high counter and asked to see Sergeant Braithwaite, or failing that, DC Holmes. No, he did not have an appointment. Yes, he did know how busy they were, but he had information for them that they needed to see. At this point Sam tapped the folder and looked the sergeant in the eye, until the man glanced away and picked up the phone. 'Miss Marple's 'ere,' he said. The sergeant listened, said 'Right,' and pointed to the wooden bench to one side. 'Wait there,' he told Sam. 'When they're ready, someone will come and find you.'

Sam waited, wishing he had a newspaper to pass the time. People came and went, the phone rang, the shouting from the cells continued and the desk sergeant went about his business. A WPC brought the sergeant a cup of tea but didn't seem to register that anyone else was there, ignoring Sam's raised hand and his tentative 'Miss'. The large clock on the wall told him he'd been waiting nearly an hour when a door beside him opened and Sergeant Braithwaite looked down at him. 'In here,' was all he said, but it was enough. Sam picked up his folder and followed the sergeant's ponderous body up the stone stairs.

Braithwaite's desk was clear and shone with the innocence of a closed mind. To one side stood a rack of trays, with one or two items placed to indicate that work was done, systems were respected and conclusions would be reached after due consideration. Sam was pleased with the systematic order of the notes and pictures in the folder that lay in his lap. Braithwaite squeezed into his chair behind the empty desk and leaned back. 'What is it this time?' he asked.

Sam took a deep breath and opened his folder. 'I've been gathering evidence,' he said, 'to examine the circumstances of the death of Frank Pharaoh on the night of May 19th, or the early hours of the 20th. Everything's in this folder, and I'd like to take you through it.' Braithwaite rolled his eyes. 'Give it 'ere,' he said, holding out his hand. Sam hesitated, regretting suddenly that he hadn't made copies for himself. Braithwaite gestured with his fingers, 'Come on, haven't got all day,' and Sam reluctantly handed over the folder. Braithwaite snatched it out of his hand, opened it and tipped the contents onto his desk. One section of notes slid onto the floor, and Sam bent down to pick them up. 'Bloody hell,' said the sergeant, scooping the papers together, the careful sequencing already lost. 'Get yourself a typewriter, lad.' He squinted at the tiny neat print that Sam was so proud of, then fumbled in a drawer for his reading glasses before looking back at the notes with an exaggerated frown.

Sam leaned forward, trying to re-impose order on the scattered documents, but Braithwaite waved him away. One by one he picked up the notes and pictures, removed the clips, and began to spread things out on the desk. Sam watched. The man seemed to be looking at things randomly, picking up something, reading it, picking up something else, without paying any attention to the numbering and cross-referencing. After a few minutes Braithwaite put both hands on the arms of his chair, pushed himself up, manoeuvred round the side of his desk and left the office by the door behind Sam. 'Stay here, and don't touch that stuff,' he said, leaving the door open.

A few minutes later he was back and the puffing performance of sitting down in the chair that was clearly too small for his girth began again. Sam looked at his face, but read nothing there. Behind him he sensed movement. He turned and looked up at the face of the man he'd seen before, most recently with PC Kelly at Frank's funeral.

'Never mind 'im,' said Braithwaite. 'What d'you know about Gloria Tennant?'

Sam was surprised that this was the first question, which he'd expected to be about the night of Frank's death, or his debts, or the fire at the West Row house, all of which were carefully documented in the papers and photos now strewn randomly in front of him.

'Not much about her background,' Sam said. 'Frank's mates gave us her name, and Frank's grandmother confirmed that she and Frank had been seeing each other.'

Braithwaite snorted. ' "Seeing each other", is that what it's called these days? She's on the game, right, has been for years. She'd sell her granny if the price was right.'

Sam didn't respond, remembering the bruises and the cracked voice.

'And this bloke, Ray Noakes, we know 'im too. My DC said you thought he was called Ray Tennant. Just shows what a tale she must have given you.'

'She didn't tell me that name. I thought they were married, so I assumed…'

Braithwaite snorted again, and a sigh came from the figure behind Sam.

'Who is this?' said Sam, pointing over his shoulder.

'Never you mind,' said Braithwaite. 'It's me you're talking to.

So our friend Gloria mentioned another of our local villains, young Mick Leary from Cleator. And you went up there to flush 'im out. He must be thicker than we thought. Right in the lions' den up there, weren't you? Daniel sounds better than "dickhead".'

The man behind Sam laughed and Sam felt himself flush with anger. Braithwaite was showing off shamelessly for this bloke, but why? Who was he and how did they know he'd met with Mick?

Sam said, 'I think there's a connection. All this information tells me that there are people in this town, already known to the police, who are running illegal gambling, collecting debts with intimidation and violence, and possibly involved in smuggling cigarettes, probably from Ireland. I've done this work myself, with precious little help from you lot, and brought it to you. All I've had from you is rudeness and a flat refusal to act on matters that you should be dealing with.'

Braithwaite smirked and said nothing. Sam was determined to say his piece. 'The man who hired me to do this work is one of this area's most respected people. Ask anyone in this town about John Pharaoh and they'll tell you. He's been one of the big shots at Sellafield for years and probably knows most of your bosses. I'll be reporting to him later today, and what do you think I can tell him about the co-operation I've had from this police force in the investigation of his son's death?'

Sam got up and began to pull the notes towards him, until he was seized from behind by the shoulders and pulled back into his chair. The unknown man stood at his side, looking down. His face was pale, with a dark stubble and big ears, and oily hair combed close to his head. 'John Pharaoh, my arse,' he said. 'Doesn't mean a thing to me sonny, 'cos I'm from London, not this godawful town.' He carried on, exaggerating the London accent. 'Local heroes mean nothing to me, right? All I know is, you've been poking around in things that ain't your business and getting on my tits, right? All this stuff stays here, and you, my son, are going home. Give him a receipt, George, and we'll get back to proper work.'

'You 'eard the man,' said Braithwaite. 'Leave the folder an' all. If we've got questions, we'll find you, right?'

Sam sat still, trying to think what to do. The London man had already gone and Braithwaite didn't move, sitting with his elbows on the arms of his chair and his fingertips together, and the same fixed grin on his red face. With as much dignity as he could muster, Sam stood up, added the folder to the disarray on the desk, pushed back his chair and stepped out of the office. DC Holmes was standing close by, but Sam was too angry to acknowledge him or see the hint of sympathy in the young man's face.

The walk back to West Row helped to calm him down. By the time he got home, a plan was clear in his head. First he would recreate the folder that had been taken from him, and put it somewhere safe. Then he would write a detailed report for John, referencing the documentation, explaining his efforts to share with the police, and naming names, although he still didn't have a name for the man from London who bossed Braithwaite around and got away with it. Maybe Rob Holmes could help with that. The last thing on Sam's list was clear to him, now that his efforts to go by the book had been thrown back in his face. Whatever doubts he'd had about checking the harbour at night had gone. He was certain that all the things he knew were linked and would take him back to Frank's sad story.

And something else was on his mind, too. Two men called Noakes. If they were related, Ray Noakes might have some information about Montgomery House. If Ray was involved in the smuggling business Mick Leary had told him about, and if they were caught, then he might be persuaded to talk. Too many 'if's and 'maybe's, but Sam couldn't let it go.

He wanted to sleep before what could be an eventful night, but sleep wasn't easy. The room was light and his head was full, not just of villains and bastard London coppers, but of a woman with long red hair and pale skin, a sharp tongue and a brave soul. He loved her. He couldn't hide it from himself any longer. The thought of her with someone else was eating into his heart.

Waking with a start in the pink glow of his room, Sam panicked that he'd slept for too long, but it was not yet nine and there was time to have some food and plan what to do while he waited for darkness to fall. The sky was overcast, for now at least, which meant less light, and less chance of being seen. He looked at the plan of the harbour, made after his last visit there, thought about where a ship might tie up and where he could hide to get a decent view of it. Any number of things could go wrong, but he could not pull back now. He needed to redeem himself, and the thought of what lay ahead excited him. As before, he prepared by putting on his darkest clothing and checking his camera equipment for any photos that might be possible. In the spirit of danger that had already raised his heart rate, Sam took soot from the front room grate and smeared his face, breaking up the pale features under an old cap he'd found in the cupboad under the stairs. A balaclava would have been better, but he didn't have one. He looked at himself in the mirror above the fireplace and smiled. Sam Tognarelli, commando, primed for action.

He stood for a while at the front door watching the light fade and, having checked his bag once last time, drove the car to the edge of the town and waited, thinking, picturing what he would need to do, pleased that he had come this far, but still fearful. People who smuggled cigarettes weren't your average hopeless burglars. They would have to be well organised and determined; the stakes were high and there was a lot to lose. Sam had hoped to have some backup to surprise a criminal act in the making but his encounter with the police had deprived him of any protection. He was on his own, and surprised that part of him relished it. He was responsible only for himself, and only to himself.

By eleven, with an overcast, moonless sky, the darkness was complete and Sam decided not to wait any longer. The car was parked down a side street out of sight, and he locked and left it, skirting down more side streets in the shadows, trying to end up as close to the bottom of the Kells steps as he could, remembering the layout from the last time he'd been there. He knew to avoid the little cabin where he'd met the smoking man and wondered again about this man, and his role in any operation involving movement in the harbour at night. He guessed that someone had paid him to turn the other way, or simply disappear while the work was done. When Sam crouched in the shadow at the bottom of the steps and looked across, the cabin was in darkness, and there was no sound save the lapping of water and the cry of a nocturnal bird out on the black surface of the inner harbour.

He found a spot on the landward side of the wall beside the steps. It was muddy and smelled of urine, but he could peep over the wall and see most of the wharf. It was still cloudy, but dry, with a faint breeze that ruffled the water. He made himself as comfortable as he could and waited, feeling his heart thump and the damp seep through his trousers. Nearly an hour passed and his knees and shoulders were getting stiff when he heard the quiet throb of an engine. Sam peered over the top of the wall and saw the outline of a boat slipping along the far side of the harbour, its engine cut to the minimum, no lights on board that he could detect.

With a flash that made him jump, lights flickered to his right, from the corner of the wharf. On, off and on again. It could be a torch, or headlights, but he couldn't hear anything except the soft thud of the boat's engine as it turned and slid slowly towards the wharf in front of him. Now another sound, a vehicle this time, moving down the wharf from the other direction. Still no sign of life or interest from the little cabin. Sam shrank back into the shadows and waited. His breath was shorter, his heart throbbing in his throat. He was too exposed. How many people would there be? Four, maybe five. If they found him, he couldn't fight them off. It was too dark to use the camera. Without evidence, who would believe him?

Voices. First from the boat, a hoarse low shout. 'Over here you useless git, catch the fucking rope.' To his right a door slammed and someone jumped down. It was a truck, Sam thought, coming for the boat's cargo. Suddenly it occurred to him that Mick Leary would probably be here. Did it matter that he would recognise Sam if he was caught? Maybe he could pass himself off as another villain trying to get in on the action. Why hadn't he thought this through before? Even as he shrank down out of reach of the torchlight flashing around the wharf he heard Mick Leary's whining voice for the first time – and there was another voice from the truck, lower, older, local. The urge to look over the wall was strong, but he knew he had to stay hidden and use his ears not his eyes to follow what was happening.

Someone jumped across from the boat on to the wharf. The voice was unmistakeably Irish. 'You out already, you auld bugger.' Sam heard a back being slapped, laughter.

'Turn that fucking light out,' said the local man. The torchlight went out.

'Who's the eejit?' said the Irish voice.

'Pain in the arse, Paddy,' said the other. 'Me sister's lad. Come 'ere Mick, meet the big man.' More insults traded to and fro, and cigarettes were lit. Sam smelled lighter fuel and then tobacco mingling on the slight breeze that danced round his hiding place. He pressed himself further back against the wall, hardly daring to breathe.

'Plenty more where these came from,' said another Irish voice. 'About fifty boxes, got enough room on the truck?'

'Got this one specially from the docks up Workington a couple of weeks ago. Plenty big enough.'

'Good man, Shorty,' said the Irishman.

Sam froze. Shorty, Ray Noakes, the man who clutched Gloria's neck until her voice shrank to a croak, the man who could have given the order that sent Frank over the cliff edge.

'Tek us a while, so we'll get started,' Shorty said. 'Mick, see if you can get the truck a bit closer, save us carrying too far. Where's Bomber?'

'He'll be 'ere in a bit,' said Mick, in his boy's voice. 'Something to do in town.' Shorty cuffed him. Sam heard the blow and the squeak of protest. 'I told 'im to come down 'ere but 'e's bigger than me.'

'These boxes are light, man, no bother,' said Paddy. 'Best thing about cigs. Stuff we're taking out's heavier. Where is it?'

They turned away and lowered their voices. Sam had to strain to hear them, piecing the audible and inaudible sections together in his mind to make sense of them.

'Six of the best,' he heard, and mention of Yorkshire. Then the Irish voice, a little louder, said, 'A bent squaddie, eh? He could have an accident sometime soon, am I right?'

'Right,' said Shorty.

What were they taking back to Ireland that mattered so much?

Intent on the conversation, Sam didn't hear the footsteps coming slowly down the stairway behind him, but he sensed a rush of air as the butt of a pistol arced down. The back of his head burned briefly before the lights went out.

CHAPTER 21

'Again!'

Cold salt water poured over Sam's head, catching in his nostrils and throat, making him choke. He spat, and a boot hit his ribs. He doubled over, trying to protect himself.

'One more.' This time Sam heard the bucket splash into the harbour before the sluice of oily water hit him again, knocking him down to the streaming flagstones. He was shivering, and couldn't see. His head throbbed.

'Who the 'ell's this?' said Paddy.

Someone said, 'I saw 'im from the top of the steps'. Sam didn't recognise this voice. The accent was different again, Scottish, he thought. Someone pulled Sam's bag out from under his shivering body. 'There's a bloody camera in 'ere. What the fuck's going on? Anyone know who 'e is?' There was silence for a moment, then Sam was pushed onto his back, and the hat pulled from his head. 'I know 'im,' said Mick Leary. 'He were in the Black Horse, playing snooker. Said 'is name were Shorty.' Another kick. Sam doubled over to protect his stomach. 'I told 'im,' Mick whined. 'Told 'im what, you moron?' Sam couldn't see, but he heard Mick wheeze as Shorty picked him up. 'I told 'im 'e shouldn't call 'imself that, because of you.'

'Wait on,' said Paddy. 'Tell us what you said to 'im. Who is 'e?'

Mick was snivelling now, fear leaking out of his eyes and nose. 'Nowt. Told 'im nowt. 'E said 'e were a postman, and his wife ran off.'

'For fuck's sake, Mick. What's 'e doing 'ere, with a camera? Must be police or Specials.'

'On 'is own?'

Sam sensed the men stand up and move away from him. They're looking for the backup that's not here, he thought. Then hands searched his pockets, pulling out the driver's licence he'd meant to leave at home. A torch flared. 'Samuel Tognarelli, what kind of name is that? Address in Barrow.'

Sam was hauled to his feet, his head pulled back. 'Talk, you little shit. Who sent you?' Sam closed his eyes, expecting the blow that came quickly to the side of his face. He tasted blood on the inside of his mouth.

Paddy said. 'Can't waste time on this. There's some rope on the boat. Tie these two up, chuck 'em in the truck. The kid's no use to us, don't care who 'e is.' Mick began to wail. 'And get the stuff unloaded before this bastard's mates turn up, whoever they are.'

'Give me the driver's licence,' said Shorty. 'Phone box back there. I'll find out who 'e is.' Sam heard footsteps receding before he felt himself being tugged and trussed like a carcass and thrown into the truck. Something landed on top of him, whimpering. Nothing was said. A heavy tarpaulin that smelled of fish was pulled over and the darkness was complete. Sam slipped into the black hole of oblivion that opened underneath him.

❖ ❖ ❖

The noise of the engine and movement made his head throb. He had no idea how long he'd been unconscious or where they were. Beside him, Mick was still whimpering, bumping against him as the truck bounced on the road. Then the engine died. Sam strained to hear voices from the truck's cabin, through an open window. He could smell cigarette smoke. 'A cop?' said an Irish voice. 'On 'is own?' An unintelligible reply. 'Pharaoh? You 'aving me on?' Sam wondered how they'd connected him with Frank. He'd told Mick nothing about this. Paddy said, 'We'll get 'im to talk. Have to know who he's working for.' There was more indecipherable muttering, impossible to hear who was speaking or what was said. Then Sam heard, 'Fucking kid must've said something, to get this bloke down here.' A pause. More mumbling. The truck started up again. Sam tried to concentrate but he could see nothing, and the engine noise masked any more conversation in the cabin. Who had Shorty called on the phone?

Sam guessed they were going to drop off the cigarette boxes that were sliding from one side of the truck bed to another as they rounded corners, and maybe pick up whatever it was that the Irish boat was taking back. It seemed an age before the truck stopped again, but this time the engine kept running. Sam was fully awake now, his heart thumping. The taste of blood was strong in his mouth and exhaust fumes made him retch. He wanted to shout but there was no point. It was better if they thought he was unconscious and he lay still. Mick was quiet, too. Sam poked at Mick with his tied feet but there was no response. He inched nearer to the top end of the truck's bed, where the air was slightly fresher. Then the engine stopped. Thank God.

Paddy's voice came again. 'This'll do. Leave 'im at the side of the road. Someone will find him. Use your pistol, not one of ours, then throw it away.' Sam tried to swallow, but fear had dried his mouth. Was this it? He thought of Judith. He should have told her that he loved her. Someone was fumbling at the side of the truck near Sam's feet and he drew himself up, braced like a foetus in the womb but waiting for the end not the beginning. Cold air swirled around him as the cover was pushed back. Someone clambered in and pulled up his head. He kept his eyes closed.

'The kid first,' said Paddy.

Sam heard Mick start to cry and felt him wriggling as they pulled him out of the truck. Mick's cries rose to wail and then stopped suddenly. A shot, a scream, another shot, another scream, then silence. Sam clenched his eyes tight.

Paddy's voice, raised. 'Wipe the pistol. Now throw it. Not this side, the other side.'

'What about the cop?' Shorty asked.

'Need to get him over the border. How far to the drop-off? An hour? We dump the cigs, pick up the other stuff. It's all there, right? Then we'll think what to do with 'im. What a mess. It'll come back to you, Shorty. Your patch, your fucking lad. Start praying.'

Sam tried desperately to free his hands, but they were tied tight and the skin on his wrists was raw and probably bleeding. He could splay his knees, but his ankles were crossed and crushed together. He gave up trying to hold in his urine and let it go, feeling the warmth. He didn't know how long he had, but thought he would not see another dawn, unless they wanted to keep him alive for someone to beat the truth out of him. He remembered his army training: name, rank and serial number, no more. What did he have to tell them? Nothing worth dying for. Would Judith grieve for him? He pictured her, standing by his gaping grave as she'd stood beside her brother's, hair blowing in breeze off the sea. Where would they put him? How long would it take to find him? Would he rot where he lay? Thoughts and questions rolled in his head, softly, like distant thunder on a quiet evening. The truck was moving again, but he had no way of knowing where they were. Through a crack in the tarpaulin he could see that the sky was still dark, but as they turned a corner a pale gleam appeared on the right. Still heading north, and it had to be around three in the morning.

Not long afterwards the truck pulled off the road and stopped again. Lights flashed. Another vehicle, he thought. Beyond Sam's trussed feet the tarpaulin was pushed back and unseen hands pulled out the boxes of cigarettes, carrying them away, returning for more. There were no words close by, but voices further off. Sam heard doors creak and close. Then something else was loaded into the back of the truck. Wooden boxes this time: he heard them scratch on the floor, not slide like the cardboard. The men worked with care, tying the boxes down tight to stop them moving. They ignored him, until someone pulled on his hair. 'Pissed himself,' said Shorty. 'Dirty git.' Sam's head was slammed down and pain hit him hard before fading to a pounding ache. 'Hurry up, for God's sake,' said a voice.

Moments later, Sam heard a car coming closer, then stopping. Light seeped under the tarp. 'They're here,' said Paddy. 'Thank Christ. It's gone three already. Get him out, into the boot. They'll take him from here.'

Salmon light was streaking the horizon as they pulled Sam half-conscious from the back of the truck and dropped him onto the ground. Cold air smelled of pine trees and blood. He opened his eyes and faces peered down at him, silhouetted against the grey. The faces turned as someone else approached.

Sam couldn't see the newcomer who was greeted by Paddy. 'Stinking parcel for you,' he said. 'God knows what he was doing at the harbour when we dropped off the cigs. Some eejit must have said something, we've taken care of that. Shorty reckons he's a cop, but if he is, he's on his own. No back-up, no radio. He had a camera but we smashed it – too dark for photos anyway. Seamus needs to work on 'im, and well away from here, over the border, out of reach. He's all yours, we're off. Our stuff's more valuable than this piece of shit.'

Sam felt himself lifted and carried a few yards. He heard the boot of the car open, and he was thrown down before the boot lid slammed shut and he was in darkness again, helpless, while all hell broke loose around him.

Voices faded in and out. Someone breathed close by, sweet minty breath. A light shone in one of Sam's eyes, then the other. A voice said, 'He's still with us. Taken quite a beating. May have a problem where he got kicked. You can talk to him, but don't expect much response.' Another face loomed over him. This one looked familiar. 'You've been a bloody nuisance, mate. But we got them, and the guns. If we hadn't moved in when we did we might have got the big fellers, but then you'd be dead by now.'

It was the London voice of the man from Whitehaven, the one Braithwaite deferred to. Sam tried to speak. The face came back into view.

'Mick,' said Sam. 'Mick.'

'We found 'im. Kneecapped, poor bugger, both legs. E's in surgery.'

Sam tried again. 'Who are you?' The man laughed. 'Still hasn't a clue,' he said over his shoulder. The man's face disappeared and a woman said, 'That's enough. You'll have to wait, both of you. Now, out.'

Sam sank back into darkness.

When he woke again, his head throbbed and his mouth tasted vile. He swallowed, but it hurt. He turned his head. There was light behind a curtain and someone was talking. He cried out. The talking stopped. The curtain moved, light flooded in; he closed his eyes, and heard a woman's voice 'He's awake, tell Sister. Don't let that man come in.'

Someone took his bandaged wrist and held it gently, feeling the pulse. 'That's better. Can you hear me, Sam?'

He opened his eyes and saw the woman smile. Tears flooded his eyes, and she wiped them away. 'There now,' she said. 'Heaven knows what you've been up to. There's a big burly policeman outside the door. Sister Knowles can't wait to get rid of him.' She smiled again. Sam searched for words. 'Don't try to talk,' she said. 'We've given you something for the pain. It'll make you drowsy. You'll be fine, once the bruises and swelling settle down. Here's the alarm buzzer, in your hand. If you press it, like that, someone will come. OK?'

Next time he opened his eyes, there was no one near him and the curtains were open. Sunlight flooded through the window. He turned his head and tried to sit up. 'Nurse,' came a voice from the next bed. 'He's awake.' The smiling woman came towards him. 'Well, well,' she said. 'let's have a look at you.' For a few minutes she checked him over, pulse, eyes, then the curtains came round and she pulled back the covers to check something on his side. 'Good, good,' she said. 'I'll get Dr Roberts to have a look at you, before that other policeman comes back to bother you again. He's been on the phone already this morning, pestering.'

An hour later Sergeant Braithwaite peered into the ward

and walked over towards Sam's bed. 'You look a bit better. Nice bruises,' he said. 'Thought we might lose you. Summat about your kidneys. Lucky you've got two, eh?'

'Where am I?' Sam asked. His voice sounded odd.

'Carlisle,' said Braithwaite. 'You were almost over the border when we got you, and this was the closest hospital. Good job too. Bad enough being here, without dealing with Scottish police.'

'What happened?'

'You don't know?'

'I was in the back of a truck,' said Sam. 'I heard them shoot Mick. I thought he was dead.'

'One in each knee cap,' said Braithwaite. 'Wheelchair job, likely.'

'Then I heard more shooting. How did you find me?'

'We were right behind you, all the way up,' said Braithwaite. 'Inglis wanted to trail them right to the source, Glasgow he reckoned. But we couldn't risk it.'

'Inglis?'

'Sergeant Inglis, Special Branch, to you, lad. Stationed at Whitehaven, from down south. He was here a while ago, and he'll be back later. Anyway, when we saw them dump you in the boot of the car we moved in. Quite exciting for a while. One or two injuries, nothing fatal.'

Sam said nothing, trying to work things out.

Braithwaite smiled at Sam's confusion. 'Special Branch have been in Whitehaven for weeks, watching that ciggie racket. Cigs in, guns out, back to Belfast and the Provos. We knew Shorty Noakes was involved somehow, and Bomber Harris, and that idiot Leary.'

'And someone called Baldy?' Sam asked, beginning to piece things together.

'Yeh, 'im and all, and Blue with the tattoos. They fleece poor bastards; like your mate Pharaoh, who owe money, money buys cigs, and the ship that brings the cigs in from Ireland takes out the guns that the Provos pay for. Big business, lad. Too big for amateurs like you.'

Sam stared. Braithwaite enjoyed the power of knowing more. 'And there's you in the middle of it bleating about sodding Frank Pharaoh falling off a cliff. Oh dear, oh dear.'

'What about Gloria?'

'Chicken feed. We've been watching her, too,' said Braithwaite. 'She's the link to Shorty while he were inside. Messages in and out. They even had her lobbing stuff over the prison fence down by the sea, poor cow.'

'Is she OK?'

Braithwaite shrugged. 'Who cares? She's not important now that Noakes is out. Anyway, it's none of your business, lad. You've caused us enough trouble already.'

'Where's Ray Noakes now?' Sam asked.

'Locked up tight,' said Braithwaite.

Sam struggled, holding onto Braithwaite's sleeve. 'He, he…'

A woman in a dark blue uniform came briskly into the ward. 'That's quite enough, sergeant. Time to leave my patient alone now. And take that big policeman away with you. He's causing havoc.'

'Why is he here?' asked Sam.

Braithwaite leaned forward, tobacco fumes strong in Sam's face. 'They won't be pleased that we've got those guns, and their precious legmen. You'll need some help getting out of this one.' He stood up, holding up his hand as the nurse gestured for him to leave, then turned to speak to Sam again. 'We warned you off, God knows, but you took no bloody notice. And we arrested you, to make it look better, but that won't fool them for long. You're a marked man, laddie. Watch yourself.'

'Sergeant!' said Sister Knowles. 'That's enough. I'm sure you have other important work to do, well away from here.'

Braithwaite turned away and clumped out of the ward.

Sam breathed the fresh soap of the blue uniform as Sister Knowles re-established control over her patient. She was clearly annoyed by the disruption to the normal routines. 'I don't know what you've been up to Mr Tognarelli, to cause all this fuss. Are you a policeman, too?'

'I used to be,' said Sam. It was too hard to explain further. 'I've been trying to find out how a friend of mine died.'

'Well, we'll be glad when you're well enough to transfer to Whitehaven,' she added, pushing Sam forward as she straightened his pillows. 'That should be tomorrow, all being well. Dr Roberts will have a look at you on his rounds today and hopefully we'll get back to normal after that.'

'Is there a phone I could use?' Sam asked.

'There's a public phone down the corridor,' she said. 'But we'll see whether the doctor says you can get up. Patience, Mr Tognarelli. You've been very lucky so far, no serious damage, but you took quite a beating. How old are you now?'

'Thirty,' said Sam.

'Not as young as you were. Healing takes a bit longer, you know.' She looked at him. 'Is there anyone you'd like us to call?'

'My sister Elspeth in Barrow. Can you tell her where I am, and that I'm all right?'

'Write her name and telephone number down and we'll do that. No wife, then?'

Sam shook his head.

'Will your sister be able to look after you? You'll need a

week or two more rest before you're fit to be at home on your own.'

'Maybe,' said Sam. 'I'll think about that later.'

Sister Knowles smiled her thin smile, then her presence faded and he sank back to sleep.

Waking later, Sam lay still in the quiet room, trying to work out what had happened. Too many unknowns, too many questions. And Judith. Sam squeezed his eyes shut, trying to block out the image of her. He could have died, and she would never know how he felt.

Chapter 22

Judith watched Harry Grayson as he stood at the bar, and then as he walked back to their table carrying his pint and a lime and lemonade for her. She liked the look of him, no doubt about that, and the way he smiled at her. 'Sandwiches will be out in a minute,' he said. 'At least they should be fresh, not yesterday's. Cheers.'

'Thanks for this,' she said, raising her glass to him. 'It's been a tedious morning. "Chief Reporter" sounds good, but it feels like I'm doing more than my share of the work.'

'How are you getting on with Cunningham these days?' he asked. 'Still the same slime?'

'Better,' she said. 'We'll never get on well, but that doesn't matter, so long as he does his job and let's me do mine without all the sneers and insults I used to get from him.'

'And Springrice?' asked Harry, clearing a space on the table for the sandwiches.

'He's OK, too. Nothing very exciting going on, but that's not his fault. Sometimes the news is just slow, and I'm still finding my feet.' She sipped her drink. 'Sounds awful to say it now, but I think Thornhill was a better journalist, even if he did turn out to be a monster.'

'I always thought it was the wife who was the monster,' said

Harry. 'She was the one who wanted you dead. Lucky for you he didn't have the guts to go through with it.'

She shuddered. 'True, but he'd let her do those dreadful things and not challenged her, until then. They deserved each other.'

'And she's still out there, that's what galls me,' he said.

She looked at him carefully as he tucked into the sandwiches. He liked her a lot, that was obvious, and she was warming to him too.

'How's Sam?' Harry asked. It sounded an innocent enough question, but any mention of Sam seemed to have several layers. She took a moment to decide what to say.

'He's still up in Whitehaven, chasing around and getting nowhere. The police up there have frozen him out, and he seems to be going round in circles.'

Harry nodded, but said nothing.

'He loved being a detective, you know,' Judith went on. 'I think he regrets giving it up.'

'He could apply again,' said Harry. 'Different county, different force. He's trained, experienced, they should be glad to have him.'

'Even after what happened with Morrison?'

Harry shrugged. 'No one in Whitehaven probably knows or cares about Morrison. There are some bent coppers, we all know that, and a few of them get away with it.'

'Or get shipped off to Hong Kong, out of the way.'

'Here's to faraway places,' said Harry, raising his glass again. 'And here's to you, Judith. We should do this more often.'

She smiled. 'Thanks,' she said. 'Being with you makes me feel like a grown-up.'

'And a lovely, grown-up woman you are, Judith,' he added.

A few minutes later, when the sandwich plate was empty

and Harry had finished his second pint, he said, 'You know I have my own house now, on Walney, out near the golf club.'

'Good for you,' she said. 'Finished? I need to get back.'

'Nice lunch?' said Hattie, raising her eyebrows, when Judith came back into the office. 'I wasn't sure where you were, so she had to leave a message.'

'Who did?' said Judith.

'That lady you live with,' said Hattie, 'Elspeth. She rang about half an hour ago wanting to speak to you. She wants you to ring her at school. The number's here.'

'At school? What about, did she say?'

'No, just said it was important.'

Judith sat down at her desk and dialled the number. There was a delay, then Elsbeth came to the phone.

'Are you all right? Is it Tommy?' said Judith when she heard the anxiety in Elspeth's voice.

'No, it's Sam, he's in hospital.'

'Sam? What's the matter with him?'

'The nurse who rang just said he was in Carlisle hospital recovering from an accident. No, she said an *incident*. What does that mean?'

'What was he doing in Carlisle?' Judith asked.

'If she knew, she didn't say. Just that Sam had asked her to ring and tell me where he was, and that he's all right.'

'Is that all?'

'Could Harry find out a bit more, maybe?' Elspeth asked. She knew Harry would enjoy helping Judith any way he could. 'Could you ask him?'

Judith thought about it for a moment. 'I'll call him at the station,' she said. 'Do you want me to call you back?'

'Not until afternoon break at two-fifteen, if you know anything by then. The Head is really snotty about me getting phone calls here. Let me call you, that's easier.'

'Harry couldn't find much out,' said Judith, when she spoke to Elspeth an hour later. 'Either they wouldn't tell him the details or he's not allowed to tell me. Apparently Sam was rescued by the police just before they crossed the border into Scotland.'

'Rescued from whom, how?'

'I don't know Elspeth, honestly. The Whitehaven police just said he'd been roughed up and was being checked over. He should be taken down to Whitehaven hospital tomorrow.'

'When will they let him out?'

'You'll have to ring them to find that out. They won't tell me anything, but you're his sister. Harry said to try the hospital at Whitehaven about this time tomorrow.'

A bell rang in the background. 'I'll have to go,' said Elspeth. 'Is that all he told you, Judith?'

'Don't worry, Sam's OK. I'll see you later.'

Judith sat at her desk for a while, trying again to piece it all together. For some reason Sam had been taken north, presumably against his will, and the police had managed to get him out of whatever predicament he'd been in. He must have been hurt to be in hospital for a few days. Why would no one tell her anything? She wanted to walk straight out and catch the train to Carlisle, but she couldn't, and what good would it do anyway? Tomorrow, if she could clear the work by late afternoon, she could be in Whitehaven by evening visiting time. Then she could see for herself.

Later that evening she rang her mother in St Bees. It took a while to explain: Maggie insisted that Sam was at the West

Row house, working alongside the police, finding out what happened to Frank. 'He would have told us if he was going to Scotland,' she said, as if Judith was making it all up. 'It doesn't make sense. And why is he in hospital? Has he had an accident?' Judith could hear her granmother's questions in the background. 'Be quiet Mam, please,' Maggie said in exasperation.

'They're taking him to Whitehaven hospital tomorrow, apparently,' Judith added. 'I'll come up tomorrow after work and see him myself. Can I stay overnight? I'll sleep on the couch and get the early train back.'

'Of course you can,' said Maggie. 'This is your home, Judith. I don't understand what's happening these days. First Frank, now this. We need you here, dear.'

'See you tomorrow, Mum,' said Judith. She'd learned not to respond to maternal blackmail.

The phone on her desk rang immediately after she ended the call. 'Mum?' she said, assuming that her mother hadn't finished piling on the guilt.

'No, it's Harry. Do I sound like your mother?'

Judith laughed. 'No, thank heaven. Does your mother keep asking you to come home?'

'I think she was glad to see the back of me. Anyway, I've winkled a bit more detail out of Rob Holmes. That's several pints I owe him now. Turns out it was Special Branch who picked Sam up. They'd been tailing whoever he was with, and didn't want them to cross into Scotland. Pretty "hush-hush" by the sound of it. I told Sam a while ago there could be something going on, when he was having so much trouble getting the police up there to play ball. He's probably as popular there now as he is in Barrow.'

'I'm going up to see him tomorrow,' she said.

'Oh. How long for?'

'Just overnight.'

'Are we still OK for dinner on Friday? I've booked a nice place.'

'One night at my mother's is enough for me right now,' she said. 'And Sam's being looked after. I'll be back.'

'Good,' he said. 'I'll pick you up Friday at seven.'

It was only when she'd put the phone down that Judith let herself think about Sam being hurt, frightened and alone, and about how much she wanted to see him.

Sam felt every bump in the road as the ambulance took him down to Whitehaven the following day. He could sit up, which was better than bouncing helplessly on a stretcher, but as they turned up the final hill towards the hospital he'd had just about enough. He hadn't been carsick since he was a child, but the smell of diesel fumes had leached into his nostrils, making his stomach churn. That took his mind off the throbbing bruises on his back as the painkillers wore off.

He was sitting up in bed finishing an unattractive breakfast and weak tea when a familiar figure appeared at the end of the ward looking for him. He raised his hand, and Rob Holmes walked towards him with the unmistakable gait of a policeman. The room was warm, and Rob loosened his tie before he pulled up a chair and sat down.

'Good trip?'

Sam grimaced. 'No, but it's good to be back. Carlisle feels like the end of the earth.'

Rob Holmes looked at him carefully. 'Bruises on your face are pretty colours,' he said. 'Have you seen yourself?'

Sam shook his head. 'Don't want to. Is it gruesome?'

'Not quite your usual handsome self. How's the back? Braithwaite said something about your kidneys.'

'They gave me a good kicking at one point. Can't remember much about it now. When I heard them shoot Mick Leary I thought I'd had it.'

'We did too, that's why we had to get you out. Inglis was cursing you for getting in the way.'

'I don't like him,' said Sam.

'Join the club.' He looked around, and lowered his voice. 'We've been stuck with him for weeks. Braithwaite's had his nose right up his arse. With any luck Inglis and his equally nasty chum might bugger off back to London now they've closed this gun smuggling thing down, and we'll get our office back.'

Sam had too many questions, and not enough energy to ask them.

'Is there somewhere else we can go?' said Holmes. 'I have to take a statement, and there are too many ears flapping round here.'

They went to the day room where Sam sat uncomfortably, answering DC Holmes' questions as best he could. Apart from the occasional expletive and some eye rolling, Holmes laboriously wrote down Sam's answers in silence and gave the pages back to Sam to read and sign. It sounded much more ordinary than it had felt at the time. Sam leaned back and tried to blot out some of the more painful memories and the sounds of a man's kneecaps being shattered by two carefully aimed bullets.

'Bit of a mess,' said Rob. He hesitated. 'Sorry I had to piss you about. Nothing personal. Inglis said we couldn't trust you, and we had to shut you down, but you kept going.'

'I had to,' said Sam. 'The family needed to know what happened to Frank.' He thought for a moment. 'They still do.'

'We're getting as much as we can out of the blokes with the cigs, and another couple of villains we picked up last night. Do you still think they were the ones threatening Frank?'

'The bald one, and his mate with the tattoos? I'm sure of it, and they got Arthur Paling, too. You might get some more out of Paling now, enough to get them into court for what they did to him.'

'I still won't be able to tell you much about all this, you know that, don't you?' said Rob.

'I just want you to keep on at them about Frank. Accuse them of murder, that should frighten them. They're bullies, not killers. Is Ray Noakes talking?'

Rob shook his head. 'Not a word. He's an arrogant sod.'

'I know someone who'll be happy to see him back inside.'

'Our Gloria? Is that what she told you? I'll bet you a tenner she's on the defence witness list saying what a great guy he is.'

'Could someone check she's OK?'

Rob snorted. 'We're police, not social workers. I'm not chasing around after miserable tarts like her.'

Sam said nothing more. After Rob left, he walked slowly back to his bed, left the lukewarm lunch uneaten and slept.

He was asleep when Judith walked hesitantly down the ward towards him later in the evening. She touched his hand and he opened his eyes to see her eyes filling with tears.

'Oh, Sam,' she said, 'What happened?' She touched his bruised face gently with her fingertips. 'Who did this to you?'

He tried to sit up, and she leaned forward to help him. He sensed the warmth of her, and the smell of her hair.

'Thanks,' he said, leaning back on the pillow that she'd pulled up behind him. 'I still don't know all of it. Rob Holmes, the DC, was here, but it's Special Branch's case really and they won't tell me more than the bare details.'

'I thought you were finding out about Frank.'

'I was, I am, but some of the people who were bothering Frank were involved in another racket, smuggling cigarettes. I went down to the harbour to see what was happening, and they caught me.'

'Do the police know who did this to you?'

'Yes, they're all in custody. Holmes knows I want some answers about what happened to Frank, and they may get them as part of the investigation.'

Judith wanted to know more. When Sam told her about Mick Leary being shot, she reached out and took his hand. 'That could have been you,' she said. For a moment he wanted to tell her how he'd longed for that touch, so many times, but the words didn't come. 'Can you pass me the water?' he said. 'Talking's making my mouth dry.'

'Do you want me to go?' she said, handing him the glass.

'No, no, stay, please. I've felt very lonely the past few days. It's lovely to see you.'

Judith smiled at him, then looked away, breaking the spell.

'How's Elspeth?' he asked.

'Shocked,' said Judith. 'She wanted to come up here straight away, but it was easier for me to come while she stays with Tommy. I'll ring her when I get home.'

'Are you staying in St Bees tonight?'

'On the couch. Vince will want to hear all about it. He'll want to visit too, I expect, if Mum or Dad could bring him. How long will you be here?'

'Just a day or two, I think. They want to check my kidneys are OK.'

'Your kidneys?'

'I got kicked.'

She grimaced. 'Painful?'

He nodded. 'I'll be OK.'

'You can't go back to West Row on your own until you're properly well. I'm sure Mum will want you to stay with them until then. Vince would love that. I'll talk to them about it. Is that OK?'

Sam wanted to ask about Harry Grayson, but he didn't dare. Instead he said, 'Judith, can you do something for me?'

'Anything.'

'One of the men involved in the smuggling racket was called Ray Noakes. He's Gloria's boyfriend – Gloria Tennant.'

Judith made a face. 'That woman. I knew she was trouble.'

'Do you remember, last year, I arrested a bloke in Barrow for car theft and it turned out he'd been in Monty House as a boy? He was called Bill Noakes, and it could be the same family. If it is, this man might have been in care as well, and willing to talk about Montgomery House, if I can persuade the Whitehaven cops to ask the right questions. I need to know more about his background.'

Judith's face was suddenly animated. 'I told Harry Grayson that story wasn't finished.'

'When was that?'

She blushed. 'We've been out, you know, a few times.'

Sam felt his stomach churn at the thought. 'What did he say?'

'He told me to drop it, or at least tread carefully.'

'Do you trust him?'

'Why not?'

Sam shook his head. 'Just a feeling.'

'You don't like him do you?' she said.

'It doesn't matter whether I like him. He's too close to Cardine. You need to be careful with him.'

Judith paused before she said, 'Anyway, what do you want

me to do?'

'Go and see Iris Robinson, at home, away from Monty House. See if she remembers the Noakes boys, both of them. I may be wrong, but it's worth asking.'

'What should I do about Harry?' she asked.

He shrugged. 'Whatever you want. None of my business.'

Judith looked down at her hands. 'I have to go,' she said. 'Don't want to tire you out. I'll talk to Mum and Dad about you staying there a few days. I know that's what they would want.' She hesitated. 'Do you know for sure what happened to Frank?'

'No, not yet. I don't think he killed himself, and that was your mum's first concern. Beyond that, it's still not clear. Sorry. Is she very distressed still?'

'Very shocked, I think. She's strong, but this has been a nightmare, for all of us.' Her eyes welled up again. 'You think I'm a hard-faced cow sometimes, don't you?'

'Oh Judith,' he said. 'You know I don't think that.'

She sniffed and blew her nose. 'Well, I'm not as hard as I pretend. And I'm trying to do this job…'

'I know,' he said. 'Give me a few days, then I'll come down and see you all. I miss you.'

Judith stood up and picked up her bag. 'I'll ring Elspeth and give your love to them both, shall I? And I'll see what I can get out of Iris Robinson, if she'll talk to me at all.'

'Thanks, and thank you for coming,' he said.

She leaned forward and kissed the top of his head. 'Bye, Sam.'

He watched her walk towards the door and out of his sight, then turned his head away, closing his eyes tight against longing and regret.

❖ ❖ ❖

It was nearly nine when Judith opened the front door of her parents' house. She could hear the television in the front room, and found her mother standing in the kitchen waiting for the kettle to boil. John was out with Vince at the cricket club, and the two women talked more calmly than usual; uncertainty had lowered the wall of hurt that so often stood between them. Judith explained what Sam had told her, and that they would have wait for more details to emerge.

Maggie shook her head. 'It's all too much,' she said. 'I can't take it in. Sometimes I want to be like your gran and let it all wash over me and then forget. You know, she asked me the other day if you and Sam were married.'

Judith laughed. 'Not much chance of that,' she said.

Maggie sat down suddenly, her head in her hands. Judith put her arm round her mother, feeling the sobs. 'That's all I've ever wanted for my children,' Maggie said after a few minutes. 'I just wanted you all to be happy, to settle, to stay close. Frank was never easy, but he was, you know, a normal man, working hard, living nearby, looking after Mam. I don't understand. Was it me, was it something I did?'

Judith pulled up a chair and held her mother close. 'You did everything for us,' she said. 'You and Dad, we couldn't have hoped for better parents. But we grew up, and things happen. If we'd known Frank was in trouble, we could have helped him, but he kept everything to himself. You can't blame yourself for that.'

'And you? Did I drive you away?'

'I needed to be away, Mam. After being away at school, and at university, I couldn't just come back home. I need to have my own life.'

261

Maggie sat up and held her daughter's shoulders, looking at her. 'I just want you to be happy,' she said. 'What about that nice policeman in Barrow? Harry isn't it? He sounds like a steady man, good job. Does he have a house?'

Judith smiled. 'Yes, he was very keen to tell me about his house. It's on Walney, near the golf club apparently.'

'Well then,' said Maggie. 'That's important. Your Dad had his own home when we met. He was a real catch.'

'And he loves you so,' said Judith. 'That's the important thing.'

'It helps,' said Maggie. 'But it's not enough. You can't live on fresh air, Judith. If a man looks after you, you can give him a family. That's what makes the world go round.'

'That's your world, Mum,' said Judith. 'I'm not ready for it yet.'

'Don't leave it too long, dear,' said Maggie. 'Let yourself be happy.'

Chapter 23

Judith knew roughly where Iris Robinson lived, but had to check the phone book and then a street map to find the small house in Attercliff not far from Montgomery House. She parked the Vespa near the Post Office, out of the way, and walked down to the house. When she knocked on the front door it opened almost immediately. Iris Robinson took a few moments to recognise who was calling on her. When she did so, she stepped back and was starting to close the door again when Judith held out her hand.

'Judith Pharaoh,' she said. 'You may remember me, Mrs Robinson. I'm sorry to visit you unannounced, but could you spare me a few minutes?'

'Of course I remember you. I'm getting on a bit, but not completely gaga yet. What do you want?'

'Could I come in, please? I won't be long, I promise.'

'My father's just been taken out for lunch by his friend, like every Thursday,' said Iris. 'I don't have strangers in the house normally, it upsets him.'

'But I'm not a stranger, am I?' said Judith, trying to smile.

'No, more's the pity. We're trying to forget all that unpleasantness. What is it you want? You'd better come in. Don't want the neighbours taking an interest.'

She ushered Judith into the small room at the front of the house, picking up a newspaper off the arm of a chair as she did so. Iris remained standing, so Judith did the same. 'Well?' said Iris.

Judith had prepared what she wanted to say. 'I'm gathering information about boys who've passed through Montgomery House over the years, and what's become of them.'

Iris looked puzzled. 'Not about, you know, what happened?'

Judith shook her head. 'That's all over now. Life goes on, doesn't it?'

'Not for some,' said Iris. 'That nasty editor of yours, Mr Thornhill, life ended for him, didn't it? And that wife of his, that Irene. She might as well be dead, too. I'm surprised at you, Miss Pharaoh, wanting anything more to do with us after that.'

'That was a long time ago,' said Judith brightly, although she remembered every second of it. 'The new editor, Mr Springrice, is very keen to have some good news stories to counteract all the bad news from last year. That's why I'd like to see what a positive difference you and the captain have made to the lives of some of the boys. It's such important work, isn't it?'

'Mmm,' said Iris, dubiously. 'So that's why you're here? Why come here, not to Montgomery House?'

'Oh, I wouldn't like to disturb you there, just to talk to me. I've got one or two questions, if you don't mind.' She delved in her bag for her spiral bound notepad, to make it look more official. 'Now then,' she said. 'Could you tell me, do you ever have boys from the same family at Montgomery House?'

Iris sat down and gestured to Judith to do the same. 'Well, of course,' she said. 'Same problems at home, and the boys are often better off away from it all.'

'Yes, indeed,' said Judith. 'And I expect they sometimes turn out quite differently, don't they?'

She listened for a while as Iris reeled off a list of boys who'd 'made good', as she put it. 'Did you ever have one brother who 'came good' while another struggled?' she asked, scribbling notes into her pad. 'I remember one boy I came across in Barrow last year,' Judith went on. 'In trouble with the law, I'm afraid. He had a older brother, I believe, who may have spent time with you.'

'Who was that?' said Iris.

'The older brother was called Ray Noakes, it must be quite a few years ago now.'

Iris raised her hands and smiled. 'Raymond Noakes, well, well,' she said. 'Yes he was with us, about three years ahead of the other one, William was his name. He was a bright boy, the older one, that is. William, well, he didn't thrive. Was he in trouble, did you say?'

'Yes, I think he's in Lancaster jail at present. Nothing serious, but repeat offending, you know. The courts don't like that.'

'Nor should they,' said Iris. 'Thieving, I suppose.' She lowered her voice. 'We had trouble with him too, from an early age.'

'And Raymond?' asked Judith.

'So different,' said Iris. 'Hard to believe they were brothers. Raymond was always going to make something of himself, I thought. And he worshipped the captain like a father, you know. They were very close, and they've kept in touch over the years. Very gratifying.'

'How interesting,' said Judith. 'Do you happen to know where Raymond is now? It would be good to talk to him.'

'The captain got a note saying Raymond was going to work abroad, as I recall. That was a year or two ago, but so many men travel overseas to work these days, don't they? I think Raymond was living up Whitehaven way, the captain would remember. He's always pleased to hear from Raymond.'

She smiled again. 'I remember now, Raymond told me once that the captain was the father he never had. Wasn't that nice?'

'Lovely,' said Judith. 'No need to mention any of this to Captain Edwards at the moment. I'll have to decide who I want to interview. There's no rush. Features can wait, you see, not like real news.'

The memory of Raymond Noakes had obviously cheered Iris up, and Judith was not about to tell her that he had not been abroad but a little closer to home, in Haverigg prison.

'I'm sorry I was a little frosty earlier,' said Iris. 'It was an unhappy time, and seeing you reminded me of it all. You must have worked hard to put it all behind you, dear.'

Judith smiled bravely. 'Some bad dreams,' she admitted.

'And that dreadful woman, did they ever find her?'

'Irene Thornhill? No, she escaped to Spain from what I heard, and they can't get her back. That was a relief in a way. I really didn't want to see her again.'

'The captain told me all about it,' said Iris. 'How she bullied that poor husband of hers and then left him, taking all their money. No wonder he felt there was nothing left to live for. But why should he want to harm you, that's what I couldn't understand? Dreadful business.'

'Yes, so it was,' Judith agreed. 'But you and the captain are still going strong aren't you?'

Iris shook her head. 'We soldier on, you know, but we aren't getting as many boys as we used to. I'm not sure how much longer we'll be able to carry on the good work.'

'Talking of good work,' said Judith. 'There was another boy I wanted to catch up with. Such a nice young man. Called himself Mikey, he was friend of poor Steven Stringer.'

Iris frowned. 'Oh yes, Michael Bennett. Such a pleasant boy when he was with us. Cheerful, co-operative. I heard he was

266

doing so well after he left. One of the captain's old friends, Inspector Cardine – do you know him? – got him a job at the golf club. A steady healthy job, working on the greens, meeting nice people, you know, and the members can be very generous, I'm sure. But something must have gone wrong.'

'What makes you say that?'

'Well, I met Michael in town one day, not long ago, quite by accident. It was a Friday, and I was going to the fish stall. I hardly recognised him, but there he was, looking terribly dirty and dishevelled. I think he tried to avoid me, but when I called his name he came over. He told me he goes out fishing with his uncle and brings the catch on Friday to sell to the fish man himself. I made sure he had a proper wash in the toilets at the market, and I bought him a cup of tea. Looked as if he hadn't had a decent meal in weeks.'

'That's a shame,' said Judith. 'Did he tell you what had happened?'

'Just said he'd lost his job and was living out at Lowsy Point.'

Judith looked puzzled. 'Where's that?' Iris held up her hands to explain. 'Here's Walney Island,' she said holding her left hand out straight, curving the fingers around a little. 'And here's the mainland,' holding her right hand in a fist. 'There's a channel between them and Lowsy Point is on the land side of it, opposite the north end of Walney.' She pointed to the end of her fist. 'It's a pretty bleak place. When the tide's high, the water spreads right across the road. Michael said he was living in one of the huts out there, doing a bit of fishing while he looked for another job, but who'd want to employ someone who looked so unkempt?'

Judith shook her head. She was remembering how keen Mikey had been to talk to her about his friend Stevie's disappearance. Surely she would have seen some signs if he had been abused, but she wasn't sure of anything any more. She smiled at Iris with a confidence she didn't feel. 'Well, I must be off. Thanks for your time, Mrs Robinson. And if you remember any more success stories, do get in touch,' she said, giving Iris one of the new business cards she'd had printed. 'Very nice to see you again.'

They were at the front door when Iris said, 'How that's young man, the policeman with the Italian name? He seemed a cut above the average, but I've not heard of him recently. Is he still in Barrow?'

Judith smiled. 'Sam Tognarelli? I hear he went to White-haven, looking for promotion I expect.'

'So both of you are doing well,' said Iris. 'That's good news, anyway.'

Judith walked down to the gate and turned towards the village to pick up her scooter. A dark blue car was parked outside the Post Office, with one of its wing mirrors cracked. Who'd want such a big car on these narrow roads, Judith thought, as she pushed the Vespa carefully out of its way. On the road back to the newsroom she wondered yet again about Iris Robinson's unquestioning loyalty to Captain Edwards.

In the office she could tell Cunningham was busy in his cubbyhole by the smoke that was leaking out and spreading in a blue haze across the room. 'Know anyone at the golf club?' she called, knowing that he would hear.

'Load of tossers,' came the reply.

The rest of the afternoon passed in a satisfying succession of necessary tasks completed, and for once the phone didn't ring. It was only at the end of an unusually peaceful few hours that Judith realised that Hattie had unplugged the phone by mistake. As soon as Judith plugged it back in, it rang.

'Is that you, Judith? Where have you been?'

'The phone's been off, Elspeth, Are you all right?'

'No, I'm not all right, and nor is Tommy. Are you coming home? We need to talk.'

'What's wrong with Tommy?'

'Just come home,' said Elspeth. 'Now.'

The back door of Elspeth's house opened as Judith parked her bike in the yard. 'You need to hear this,' Elspeth said. 'I've been worried sick. Where's Sam? Is he out of hospital yet?'

'Slow down,' said Judith. 'Let me get in and start at the beginning.'

'Just a minute,' said Elspeth. 'I don't want Tommy hearing us.' She opened the door to the front room and Judith heard the familiar jingle of Tommy's favourite TV programme starting. Elspeth shut the kitchen door and pulled out a chair for her friend to sit down.

'Someone talked to Tommy on his way home from school,' she whispered.

'Yes,' said Judith.

'It was a man', Elspeth continued, 'someone Tommy didn't know. He knew Tommy's name, Judith. A stranger, who knew who he was.'

'What did the man say?'

'He said that I'd sent him, to pick Tommy up and take him for a ride in his car.' She put her hand to her mouth. 'Oh Judith, he might have taken him!'

Judith leaned forward to comfort her friend, who was breathing heavily, clearly upset.

'Where was this?'

'Just round the corner, not far from the school, about five minutes after they came out. He always comes home on his own, it's so close. I never thought...'

'It's all right, Elspeth, he's safe here. Is he hurt, or scared?'

'Tommy's fine. He said some other people came along and the man got into the car and drove away.'

'Did he see the car again?'

'No, he came straight home.'

'Did the man try to get hold of him?'

Elspeth shook her head. 'Thank God we had that talk about not talking to strangers,' she said. 'I could have lost him, Judith. I couldn't bear it.'

'But you didn't,' said Judith. 'Have you told anyone yet?'

Elspeth shook her head. 'That's why I was trying to find you. I didn't know what to do. The police might think I was just some hysterical woman. I thought you might phone Harry, then at least they'd believe me.'

'Of course they'll believe you. Why shouldn't they?'

Elspeth shook her head again. 'I wasn't thinking straight. And I didn't want some strange policeman to come and frighten Tommy.'

'But Tommy's OK?'

'Yes, it's me who's a wreck. When I think about it … he could try again, couldn't he?'

'But who's the man?' asked Judith, 'and why go after Tommy?'

Suddenly Elspeth was angry. 'I don't know. To get at you, or Sam? You're as bad as each other, running around, stirring things up. This is a warning, Judith, don't you see?'

'We don't know that. You're just guessing. You're upset.'

'Of course I'm bloody upset! This is my son we're talking about. Maybe if you two had any kids you'd understand.'

Judith began to protest, but Elspeth waved her away. 'Just do something useful, get that policeman who fancies you round here, right now. Someone's getting at you and using us to do it. You'd better sort this out.'

Judith made a cup of tea for them both, to calm Elspeth down. When she called the police station looking for Harry, Sergeant Clark recognised her voice straight away. 'Why it's the lovely Judith,' he cried. 'When are you coming to see us, instead of that spotty youth who turns up every morning? Too posh for us now, eh?'

Elspeth was fuming; she could hear what was being said and wanted Judith to get on with the business.

'Do you know where Harry Grayson is?' Judith asked.

'Aye, aye,' said the sergeant. 'Love's young dream is it?'

'Please Clarky,' said Judith. 'This is serious. I need to talk to DS Grayson, is he in the station?'

'He just passed the desk, going out,' said Clark. 'Hang on, I'll give him a shout.'

A minute later Harry's voice said, 'Judith? Just on my way home. What's up? Clarky said you sound upset.'

'It's not me, Harry. I'm fine. Could you call round here, at Elspeth's, on your way home? There's been a bit of trouble and Elspeth wants to tell you about it.'

'On my way,' said Harry.

When he rang the bell, Judith answered and ushered him inside, where Elspeth was waiting. Elspeth repeated her story, more calmly this time. Harry took out his notebook and took her through it, piece by piece. 'What did the man look like,' he asked, 'and what kind of car? Do you know?'

'Tommy couldn't remember,' she said. 'I asked him of course, but he just shrugged and said the man was old and the car was new. Do you want to talk to him?'

'If you stay here, that should be fine,' he said. 'I'll see if I can jog his memory a bit. Don't worry, I won't upset him.'

Judith and Elspeth stood back and let Harry talk to the child at the kitchen table. Judith was impressed; Harry just chatted about school, getting the boy talking more freely, without asking any questions for quite a while. Then he said, 'Your Mum tells me you talked to a man on your way home today, is that right?'

'I'm not allowed to talk to strangers.'

'That's right, Tommy. What did the man say to you?'

'He knew my name. He said Mum had asked him to pick me up.'

'Did he know your full name, or just Tommy?'

'My proper name. But I hadn't see him before.'

'Was he a tall man? Taller than me?' asked Harry, standing up. Tommy shook his head. 'Not as tall as you, but bigger than Judith.'

Harry wrote something on his pad. 'Black hair?'

'No, brown, like Mummy's, but shorter. He had little eyes, and a fuzzy chin.'

'Do you think you could tell all this to someone who will draw us a picture?'

Tommy nodded. 'Shall I draw you a picture of the car?'

Harry looked at Elspeth. 'Any crayons in the house?'

Elspeth rushed upstairs and returned with a boxful, and some paper. Tommy sat at the table and drew with great concentration, until he put down the crayons and held the picture up for Harry to see. Judith could see it too and she gasped. The car was the same shape and colour as the one she'd seen in Attercliff that afternoon. Harry noticed her reaction, but she shook her head and put a finger to her mouth. Harry thanked Tommy and took the paper that the boy proudly handed to him. He looked very carefully at the drawing, and folded it into his notebook.

'Can I go back to my programme now?' Tommy asked.

'Sure', said Harry.

The adults stayed in the kitchen looking at each other until the front room door was shut again.

'There was a car like that near Iris Robinson's house in Attercliff this afternoon,' said Judith. 'One of the wing mirrors was cracked.'

Harry looked at her curiously. 'Let me ask Tommy about that,' he said, and went into the front room. When he came back he added something to his notes. 'Yes, Tommy noticed it,' he said. 'Very likely the same car, but it may be just coincidence.'

He put away his notebook.

'So you went to see Mrs Robinson,' he said to Judith. 'I thought we talked about that.'

'Talked about what?' Elspeth interrupted. 'What have you been doing, Judith?'

'Nothing. I'm doing a feature about boys who've been to Montgomery House, that's all. Harry thought it wasn't a good idea.'

Elspeth stared at her. 'After all that trouble last year, and you're poking around that place again? What's the matter with you?'

'She's right, Judith,' said Harry. 'There may be people who don't want you asking questions about Montgomery House. They may know you live here. They might even think Tommy is your son.'

Elspeth turned to her. 'You see? For God's sake, Judith, listen to the man.'

Harry held up his hand. 'I don't want to alarm anyone,' he said. 'But this could be a warning for you, Judith. That's what I've been worried about all along.'

Judith looked from one to the other. 'What do you want me to do?'

'Drop the Monty House questions, right now,' said Harry. 'Leave the rest to me. Do you hear me, Judith? No more.'

When Judith talked to Sam on the phone later that evening she told him all the details of her visit to Mrs Robinson and what had happened to Tommy, but didn't mention the warning she'd had from Harry Grayson. There were some things she wanted to keep to herself.

CHAPTER 24

The following day, Dr Roberts pronounced Sam fit to leave hospital, so long as he had someone to look after him, and in the afternoon John drove up to Whitehaven after work to take him back to St Bees. John suggested they check on the West Row house and pick up Sam's things on the return journey.

'Is it OK if we stop off at the harbour and pick up my car first?' Sam asked. The wet weather made him all the more keen to be able to drive, rather than stand on windy stations, or walk the steep streets.

John looked doubtfully at Sam's battered face, 'Well, we can take a look.'

Sam's car was where he'd left it, the windscreen smeared by the gulls, but still a welcome sight.

'Are you sure you're up to this?' John asked anxiously 'You're obviously uncomfortable and your face looks a real mess.'

'Plenty of painkillers,' said Sam. 'It probably looks worse than it feels. And I might need the car over the next few days.'

They drove slowly to West Row, where Sam gathered a few things into a bag to take with him. Not for the first time, he realised how few possessions he'd accumulated, and what that said about his rootless life. He stood once more in the front bedroom, looking at the display of information he'd recreated with such care and that now seemed so dated. Some of the links and clues he'd looked for seemed obvious, but others taunted him still.

'Something I need to do, John,' he called downstairs. 'I won't be long.' Carefully, Sam took the items down, one by one, numbered them so that he could recreate them if needed and placed them in the file he'd kept. He couldn't find a suitable box for all his supplies, so he pulled out a drawer and put everything into it: file cards, pins, pens and paper, photographs, the Polaroid. His other camera was lost, smashed in anger by the thugs at the harbour. Dr Roberts had told him to rest, but how could he, with so many questions unanswered?

While Sam pottered and fretted around the empty house with the wind whining through the window frames, John went to call on Mrs Barstow next door, who was safely settled back in her home after her enforced stay round the corner. A small fire crackled in the kitchen range, and a wisp of steam curled from the spout of the blackened kettle. 'Neighbours were very good and all,' she confided to John, 'but there's nowt like your own home, is there?'

'Very true, Mrs Barstow,' he agreed. 'I don't think you'll have any more trouble now.'

'That poor lad of yorn,' she said, 'I was very sad to hear about it. No one wants to live longer than their own children. Do they know what happened to him?'

'It seems it was an accident, when Frank was trying to take a short cut back home. One slip, and down he went. Sam has been helping the police. He used to be a policeman himself, you know. And they've already found the two men who set that fire by your door. You should be safe now. I'm only sorry you were involved.'

'Is that Sam I can hear next door? I wanted to thank him

for getting me out that day. I could have gone, the firemen said, with the smoke and everything.'

'Sam's coming to stay with us in St Bees for a while,' said John. 'Just for a few days.' He didn't want to share any more details that might alarm the old lady even further.

'Very nice, I'm sure,' she said.

Driving slowly and painfully back to St Bees, with John following behind, Sam went over the latest news from Judith in his mind. Who was the threat to Tommy truly aimed at? Most of the Whitehaven gang were in custody, but Ray Noakes would have contacts all around the area who feared or owed him. Sam had asked Judith to visit Iris Robinson, so if that was the trigger for the approach to Tommy, he felt responsible. Elspeth and Tommy were dear to him; guilt and doubt buffeted his mind.

He still felt that there was a link between what had happened to him in Whitehaven and the events in Barrow of the previous year, but what was it? Judith had established that Ray Noakes had been at Montgomery House, but so what? Not all the boys there had been abused. Mrs Robinson had told Judith that Ray and Captain Edwards had been very close, but what did that really mean? Iris had been determined from the start to refute any suggestion of wrongdoing at the home, and they couldn't rely on her memory, distorted as it clearly was by her loyalty to the captain. Round and round the questions seethed in his head. By the time they arrived at the house in St Bees, Sam was more confused than ever and the pain in his back was almost unbearable.

An hour or so later, after a good meal and some more of the pills that Dr Roberts had prescribed, Sam lay on his good side in his bed, turning the same question over in his mind. Who had Shorty Noakes rung that night at the harbour, after they'd found Sam's driving licence? Who had told Shorty that Sam was a policeman, and put his life at risk? And how did the name of Pharoah come into it? He'd mentioned the phone call to Rob Holmes, but neither he, nor Braithwaite, nor the ghastly Inglis, cared about that piddling detail, now that Sam was safe, the smuggled guns captured and the villains locked away. He fell asleep and dreamed that he was locked in the boot of a car, falling down a never-ending cliff to the beach below.

The following morning he lay awake, listening to the sounds of the household. He heard John's goodbye to his wife and the car leaving the garage behind the house. When someone tapped on his door he called 'Come in,' without wondering who it might be. It was Vince, carrying a cup of tea. 'Gran can hardly remember her own name, but she insisted that you have your tea like this,' he said, putting the mug down by the bed. 'Milk, no sugar, right?'

'Spot on,' said Sam.

'So what's happening?' Vince asked eagerly, sitting on the bed uninvited. 'No one will tell me anything now our Judith's gone. Sounds like you got kidnapped by the mafia and James Bond had to get you out.'

Sam laughed, and the pain in his back made him wince. 'Something like that,' he said. 'I'll be fine in a day or two. I can't tell you much about it, Vince, honestly. Special Branch are involved, and they want everything kept dark.'

'Impressive,' said Vince. 'Was Frank mixed up in all that as well?'

'No, but we think that the men who bullied him were part of the gang who were picked up the other night. It's a bit complicated. Frank was just unlucky, really.'

'But he got into the mess in the first place, didn't he?'

'True, but he certainly didn't deserve what happened to him. Don't think ill of him, Vince. Don't get into debt, that's the lesson learned from all this.'

'And what's our Judith up to?' Vince pressed on. 'Getting off with some bloke with a big house, from what Mum's being telling Gran. That right?'

Sam thought for a moment. What chance did he have? 'Could be,' he said. 'I'd be the last to know about that.'

'Got to go,' said Vince. 'College today and the bus will be here soon. See you later.'

John had told Sam to use the phone as much as he wanted to, but that felt awkward, so Sam went to the shop for change and then occupied the phone box near the station for a while. The first call was to Sergeant Clark in Barrow, for the benefit of his encyclopaedic memory. 'Bill Noakes? Aye, still in Lancaster, but due out soon. I'll check. Yes, I remember the brother. Bailed Bill out once or twice in the early days. God knows where 'e got 'is money from but 'e allus 'ad plenty. Ill-gotten gains, no doubt. Last thing I 'eard, 'e were back inside. Nasty piece of work, that one. Collator at Whitehaven, Albert Frodhsam – Einstein they call him – d'you know 'im? Have a word if you can. Knows all there is to know about the villains up your end… You OK, by the way? Rumours floating around about some big Special Branch shindig up your way. I asked Grayson but he wouldn't say 'owt. Canny lad, knows when to keep quiet. Oh, and by the way, more rumours about Cardine retiring. Keep your fingers crossed.'

'No sign of Morrison coming back?'

'Not that I've 'eard. Keep 'em crossed about that, too.'

Sam was just about to put the phone down, but he remembered the other thing he wanted to ask about.

'Do you remember Doc Hayward, Clarky?'

'Aye, he could be a grumpy old sod, but I liked him. Morrison never 'ad a good word to say for 'im.'

'Do you know what happened to his widow?'

'Ann, wasn't it? Haven't seen her since the funeral.'

'Could you ask around, see what you can find out? Bit difficult for me to do it at the moment, away from my own place.'

'You want to see her?'

'Just to ask about something that happened, before the doc died.'

'Leave it with me,' said Sergeant Clark. 'I'll let you know.'

Walking back to the house, the warm air felt good on Sam's face. House martins twittered and dived round his head, still building their mud nests under the eaves of some of the houses. There were swifts around too, in and out of the crannies of the old priory tower across the fields. It felt like summer. Sam promised himself a walk to the beach later, but before then he had a call to make.

Gloria Tennant's house in Mirehouse looked as closed as it always did, curtains drawn across the windows. Sam revved the car engine outside a couple of times to see if the sound caused any movement, but there was no reaction. He looked at the notes he'd made earlier, after laying all his information from the West Row bedroom wall carefully over his bed and staring at it for a while. He hadn't noticed a phone at Gloria's the last time he'd been there, but he'd be surprised if Shorty hadn't installed one there, if Gloria was as central to his network as Braithwaite had implied. Without authority, he couldn't check what calls Gloria might have had on the night of his kidnapping, but she might just tell him herself, now that Shorty was out of the way again. He wanted to trust her, but someone had told Shorty about Sam's identity and she was top of the list.

Before knocking on the front door, Sam tried the gate on the side of the house that led towards the back door. It was open, but the uncurtained kitchen window revealed a chaotic but empty room, and the back room curtains were as impenetrable as the front. He knocked quietly on the back door, and put his ear towards it. At least the neighbours wouldn't see him. Nothing. He knocked again, and listened. He heard something. Was it a cat, like the one at Mrs Barstow's? No, this sound was lower, more sustained, and sounded like words. He strained to hear. 'In here. Help me!' He pushed at the back door as hard as he could, but it stayed firmly shut. Looking up, he saw a bedroom window open, the latch hanging loosely down, but how to get to it? The back yard was a mess of overgrown bushes, weeds, sacks of rubbish and bits of old concrete. In the far corner, almost hidden behind a pile of bricks, he saw the end of a ladder. 'I'm coming in upstairs,' he called through the back door, but there was no response.

The ladder was too short and the old wood rotten in places, but the upper rungs seemed solid enough to hold his weight. Sam clambered up, pulled the window wide open and hauled himself over the sill, dropping down on to the floor hands first. The bruises on his back protested, but the pain abated as he lay on the floor for a while, breathing heavily. There was still no sound from downstairs. The house smelled of tobacco and urine, like a rough pub toilet on Saturday night. Sam knelt by the open window, pulling clean air into his lungs. Then he heard it again. 'Help me!'

Downstairs he followed the sound into the dim front room. Gloria was lying by the fireplace, which was dark and sticky with blood. 'Fell,' she groaned. 'Can't move.'

'Is there a phone?' he asked.

'Kitchen. By the door.'

He dialled 999 and told the operator to send an ambulance. 'Don't know where she's hurt, but could be her head. Yes, she's conscious, but hurry, please.' Back in the front room, Sam knelt beside Gloria, trying to ease her bent legs from under her. She groaned, but gradually he was able to lie her flat on the floor. Gloria's hair lay like straw round her shoulders, the purple housecoat was stained, and the stench of defecation overpowering.

'It's Sam,' he said. 'Do you remember?'

Her lips moved. 'Sam.'

'Where does it hurt?'

'Head,' she said. 'I fell. Fireplace.'

Sam looked at the corner of the tiled fireplace that was sticky with blood. 'It's Friday,' he said. 'How long have you been here?' It was too hard a question for a half-conscious woman, but the smell told him she'd been there a while. Sam brought water from the kitchen and poured a little into her mouth. 'More,' she said. He was fetching more from the kitchen when he heard the ambulance coming closer. By the time he'd opened the front door they were there, and he let them do their work, giving whatever information he could, which wasn't much.

'I found her lying by the fireplace, her legs under her as if she'd just collapsed. Must have hit her head.'

One of the men sniffed. 'Drugs? Alcohol?'

'Possibly,' said Sam. 'Are you taking her in?'

'Follow us up there, can you? They might need some more details. Do you know her?'

'A little,' said Sam, but not enough, he thought, to guess the answer to the question he wanted to ask her.

'You here again?' said one of the nurses in Accident and Emergency when Sam followed the stretcher. 'You were on the men's ward upstairs weren't you? Do you find trouble, or does it find you?'

'Not sure,' said Sam.

Gloria disappeared into a curtained cubicle, and Sam waited, wishing he had his painkillers with him, but not daring to ask for some. Eventually a young man appeared, his white coat stained and a stethoscope hanging casually round his neck.

'Are you with Mrs…' he checked his notes, 'Mrs Tennant? Next of kin, any idea?'

'No, sorry,' said Sam. 'I needed to see her about something, heard her calling for help and got in through an open upstairs window.'

'Like the Milk Tray man,' said the doctor.

'Sorry?'

'Never mind. So you found her and called the ambulance?'

'That's right.'

'Not the police?'

'I am the police,' Sam started to say, but stopped himself. 'No, I could see she needed help fast.'

'That's true. Could be some bleeding inside the skull from the fall or a blow on the head. We've informed the police. Someone called Holmes? Good name for a detective.' The doctor smiled, but his second attempt at humour brought as little reaction as the first.

'Do you need me here?' Sam asked.

'I don't, but I think the police will need to talk to you.'

'Can I have a word with Mrs Tennant? It could be vital.'

The doctor looked carefully at him. Then he turned away, and spoke to one of the nurses. 'Nurse Evans will be with you,' he said. 'Just a minute, mind. She's very weak.'

The nurse opened the curtain and ushered Sam in. Gloria was lying still, tubes in her arm, her eyes half open. He leaned towards her, to speak into her ear.

'It's Sam. I need the truth, Gloria, OK? Did Ray call you, last Monday night, late, and ask about me?' He leaned back to see her face. She could see him, he was sure of that. She knew who he was. 'Did Shorty call you?' he said again. 'No,' she mouthed. 'No.'

He glanced at the nurse who was pursing her lips in disapproval, and leaned forward again. 'Who did this?' he said. Gloria closed her eyes and said nothing more. 'That's enough,' said the nurse sharply. 'You're not family, and you're not police. Time to go. Out.'

Sam left the cubicle and sat on a plastic chair, hearing but not seeing what transpired behind the curtains. They wheeled Gloria out on a stretcher towards the lifts, and only moments later when Sam was heading towards the door Rob Holmes appeared.

'Too late,' said Sam.

'She's dead?'

'No, I think they're taking her to theatre. Something about a bleed under the skull.'

'Did she tell you anything?'

'Nothing,' he said, truthfully.

Rob looked around. 'Must be somewhere we can talk,' he said. 'Come on.'

The relatives' room was empty. Holmes pushed Sam into a chair, and closed the door, standing over him.

'Are you crazy? What the hell are you doing here with her?'

'I went to see her, and found her like this. What was I supposed to do, just leave her there?'

'But why did you go to see her?'

'Something I wanted to ask her about.'

Rob Holmes rolled his eyes. 'You don't get it, do you? Ray Noakes is banged up, but it didn't stop him making sure that Gloria was done over. That's what he does. And you'll be next, if you hang around here any longer. I thought you were going to St Bees.'

'I did, I'm staying with Frank's family.'

'So what the hell were you doing at Mirehouse?'

'I can't rely on you lot finding anything out, so I had to ask Gloria myself, about a couple of things.'

'And they are?'

'First, I wanted to know if Noakes rang her the night I got kidnapped. He rang someone, I know that, and came back knowing that I was a copper, and connected to Frank Pharaoh. I've been trying to work out who told him that, and Gloria was one of the people on my list.'

'You think she shopped you?'

'She said he didn't ring her, and I believe her.'

Rob stood with his head raised staring at the ceiling, then looked down at Sam again. 'You think Noakes doesn't know everything she gets up to? He'll have people who tell him every time she blows her nose. He couldn't have done this to her, could he, while he's banged up, but someone did. Has it occurred to you that you could be the reason for this? That's what comes of amateur bloody meddling. You're into things you know nothing about, blundering around, getting people hurt. If you were working for us, we might be glad of your pig-headedness, but you're not. We want you out of here before you do any more damage.' He leaned down, close to Sam's face. 'Are you hearing me, Hercule Poirot? Leave it alone, for God's sake.'

Sam had nothing to say. Someone had attacked Gloria in

her own home, and it was sheer chance that he had found her. Was it because of him?

'You said there were a couple of things,' Holmes said, lighting up a cigarette just below the 'No Smoking' sign on the wall. 'What else?'

Sam had to think for a moment. 'It was about Ray Noakes' childhood,' he said finally. 'Gloria might have known whether he'd been in care as a kid.'

'What on earth's that got to do with any of this? You're off your rocker.'

'It's not do with this, what's happening now,' Sam said. 'It's about another case I was working on, last year in Barrow.'

'You know what, Sam? The sooner you get out of here the better. First, because your life is probably in danger, and second, because we're sick and tired of seeing you around. If you're poking around some old case in Barrow, then just go to Barrow to do it. Don't even bother telling me what it's about, I don't want to know. OK?'

Again, Sam sat silent. There was no point in trying to explain anything.

Holmes ranted on. 'When Gloria comes round enough to give me a statement, I'll ask her the questions and probably get no response. We've got enough to put Noakes away again for a long time, but that won't make her any safer, and she knows it. That's her problem. And if I see you around again, I'm going to charge you with obstruction, or wasting police time or any bloody thing I can think of to shut you up. Are you quite clear about that?'

Sam nodded.

'And one more thing, St Bees is too close. Get further away from Whitehaven, stay there, and change your name too, if you've got any sense. The Provos are busy boys these days, hopefully too busy to bother about idiots like you, but don't make it too easy for them. Disappear.'

Sam didn't look up but he heard the door open and close, leaving behind the acrid scent of Holmes' cigarette.

Chapter 25

'Back to Cannon Street?' said Elspeth when Sam rang the following day with his decision. 'What do you want to go there for?'

'I checked,' said Sam, 'and Judith's old flat is still vacant. It seems like the best option.'

'How come? Why do you have to come back to Barrow?'

Sam took his sister through some of the conversation he'd had with DC Holmes, telling her just enough to explain why he needed to be away from Whitehaven for a while. 'Just until things settle down up here,' he said. 'St Bees is too close, and after what happened with Tommy I want to be closer to you two.'

There was a short silence before Elspeth spoke again. 'Is this about Judith?'

'Of course not. You keep telling me how keen she is on Harry Grayson these days. I reckon she's given up on me.'

'You could stay here.'

'No, Elspeth, that wouldn't work. And it's not for long. The landlord of the Cannon Street flat is still trying to sell the house, he's happy for me to be there for a while, nothing long term.'

'Are you any nearer knowing what happened to Judith's

brother?'

'It's still guesswork,' he said. 'But now the people I think were involved are in custody the police might be able to get the truth out of them. We'll have to wait and see what happens in the next few days. I still don't think they murdered Frank. Dead men don't pay their debts. But I'm sure he didn't get to that cliff top on his own. The Whitehaven police have got all the evidence I gave them. It wouldn't be official of course, but it might help them get closer to the truth.'

'Does Judith know that, or her family?'

'I haven't talked to Judith's dad about it yet, but I will.'

'All sounds a bit of a mess to me.'

Sam was about to ring off when Elspeth said. 'I know it looks as if Judith and Harry are all fixed up, but she's still fond of you. Why don't you talk to her about it?'

'Leave it,' he said. 'Please, Elspeth. Just leave it alone. It'll take me a day or two to sort things out up here. Then I'll just pack up here and drive down. I'll let you know.'

'Shall I tell Judith?'

'If you want to. I have to talk to John Pharaoh first. I'll call you later.'

John was surprised when Sam told him what had transpired. 'You think the police will find out more about how Frank died?'

'I'm sure of it, now they've finally got hold of the people involved.'

'And you still think you need to get out of the area for a while?'

'I do. Sorry to leave the West Row house unoccupied, but DC Holmes was right about me being too obvious, after what happened to the woman in Mirehouse.'

'They think she was attacked by someone linked to all this?'

'Yes, although I think she'll be too afraid to press charges. She's had a rough time.'

'How long will you stay in Barrow?'

'Just a few weeks, while the police do their work. They obviously want me out of the way.'

John smiled. 'And you still want to get back into the police force?'

'I think I do,' said Sam. 'I know it seems strange, after all the aggravation, but it's a job that needs doing, and I know I can do it well when I get the chance. It may take a while, but I'll be back.'

'You'll probably hear before I do if anything happens,' said John. 'Keep in touch. We're reassured that Frank's death was more likely an accident than anything else, but we still need to know. Let's leave our arrangment in place for another month, and see how far it's got by then. That OK with you?'

They shook hands.

It was nearly a week, and several phone calls later that Sergeant Braithwaite finally deigned to ring Sam and tell him what was going on. 'Those photos and measurements you took were quite useful,' he said grudgingly, 'although they wouldn't have held up in court. We were able to match the tyre tracks on the truck they used in the smuggling caper to the ones you found on the track outside the quarry, and Holmes persuaded that lunatic with the tattoos that the boot prints you found matched his, too. He was spilling the beans about the whole thing before his lawyer could shut him up. His story was that they picked Frank up after that last card game and were explaining how they would get the money off him when he broke away from them, slipped, hit his head on a wall, and knocked himself out. They thought he was dead, so they slung him in the back of the truck, drove it down to the cliff, carried him along to the edge and pushed him over. Job done. Post-mortem couldn't tell us whether he was dead before he went over the edge, but he could have been. All very handy for getting them to cough to the other offences, where the evidence is stronger. Anyway, that's as far as we've got.'

'What about Gloria Tennant?' Sam asked.

'You've really got a thing about her, haven't you? Still in hospital as far as I know. She's another one who needs to get the hell out of here, for her own good, if she recovers.'

'Is there a chance she won't?'

'God knows. Serious head injury by all accounts. Holmes might know more, but I doubt she'd testify against whoever beat her up.'

Sam put down the phone. They didn't care about Gloria, with her white hair in the dark, drab house.

Harry Grayson's house near the Walney golf club was anything but drab, the windows glowing in long evening light. Sam sat in his car outside for a few minutes, looking at the comfortable semi with its fresh paint and colourful front garden. Harry had been most insistent that Sam should visit him at home, 'for old times' sake' and he could see why. It was all for show, a display of worldly success for Sam, and no doubt a prospect of security for Judith. The man was as subtle as a brick.

'Thanks for having a word with Judith about that Montgomery House obsession of hers,' Harry said, as he put a cold beer into Sam's hand. 'She's getting back into real newspaper work by the look of it, not chasing old stories. That Springrice bloke probably talked some sense into her as well.'

'Did she ever tell you why she wanted to do that story?' Sam suspected that Judith hadn't dropped the idea, but he was keen to know Harry's take on it.

'Some guff about finding out how well the Monty House old boys had done. She'd be struggling with that, most of them just go from bad to worse.'

'Or end up dead, like Stevie Stringer.'

'All the more reason to let it go. Even if some of those Monty House lads had been fiddled about with, or whatever the local pervs get up to, it's almost impossible to prove anything. Who's a jury going to believe, a rat-arsed kid with no family and a history of lying, or pillars of the local community?'

'So that's all that matters, is it? Who's more powerful?'

'Don't get high and mighty with me, Sam. I'm just stating the obvious, even if you don't like it. No newspaper editor worth his salt would dare publish accusations like the ones Judith has in mind. I know that's what she's after, all the stuff about good news stories is just a smokescreen.'

'If that's what you think, you'd better tell her yourself, and good luck.'

Sam sipped his beer, wishing Judith could hear Harry's cynicism for herself.

Harry grinned at his old mate. 'Come on Sam, you're a good copper, one of the best. You know there has to be evidence, real evidence, not just a few kids complaining after the event. There's nothing. No evidence, and some pretty powerful people who think Captain Edwards is the bee's knees. He's a war hero, for God's sake, devoting his life to helping wayward boys whose families don't want them, etcetera etcetera. He doesn't play golf with that bad leg of his, but the blokes down the golf club all think very highly of him.'

'Cardine?'

'Yes, Cardine, and all his mates. And me too, actually.'

Sam hesitated. He had something to ask. It might be risky, but Harry might be able to help.

'That business with Tommy,' he began. 'It reminded me of what happened in '69, when Judith was being followed by a strange car, and then Stevie Stringer's brother was killed when he started asking questions about Monty House.'

'That was two blokes in a red Landrover, wasn't it?'

'I know, the vehicle's different, but it got me thinking. They used that vehicle to dump Stevie's brother out on the sand.'

'And left our Judith out there to nearly drown,'

Our Judith? Sam thought, but now wasn't the time for a discussion about that. 'After they dumped Stringer,' Sam went on, 'they left the Landrover at Hest Bank and torched it, but the forensics blokes got some prints and matched them.'

Harry shook his head. 'Morrison never mentioned that, not to me at least.'

'I remember it clearly,' Sam insisted. 'We checked the prints and got a name.'

'Who was it?'

'That's it, I can't remember. It'll be in the notes somewhere, unless…'

'Unless what. You reckon someone at the station would get rid of evidence?'

'Not deliberately,' said Sam. 'But think what happened immediately afterwards. I resigned, Morrison buggered off, and as far as I know no one followed it up.'

'Do you want me to ask Clarky?' said Harry. 'He's been there for ever, and doesn't miss much.'

'Could you do that?' Sam didn't want to go back to the police station again, and he was curious to see whether Harry would follow through.

'Leave it with me,' Harry said. 'Oh yes, Clarky said to ask you to phone him, by the way. Something else you're on?'

Sam lied, and changed the subject. 'Nothing special. But there is something else for you, while we're catching up with things, and you mentioned the golf club. It's about a kid from Monty House – don't mention this to Judith by the way.'

'You can trust me,' said Harry. 'Judith's hearing nothing more from me about Monty House.'

'Do you remember Mikey Bennett, the cocky lad from Monty House? He got a job at the golf club, didn't he?'

'Yes, doing the greens. Cardine got it for him.'

'He's not there now, though, is he? Do you know what happened?'

'They caught him going through people's pockets in the locker room. Instant dismissal.'

'What did Cardine say about that?'

'Nothing. Open and shut case. The boy had to go.'

'I'm curious why Cardine got him the job in the first place. How did he know him?'

Harry shrugged. 'Through Edwards I guess. They go way back.'

Sam thought for a while. It was time to fan the embers a little.

'Cardine's not married is he? I never heard him mention his family.'

'What's that supposed to mean?'

Sam shrugged.

'Cardine's a career cop,' Harry said. 'Married to the job. Morrison was the same, come to think of it. Those two were always close. I was surprised when Morrison just upped and offed. I heard he had a nice car he might have wanted to sell quick, but nothing happened about that… Anyway,' he slapped his knees and got to his feet. 'Enough talking, we need to eat. I've got some of that sausage everyone raves about.'

The following morning Sam needed three cups of tea to deal with the sour taste in his mouth left by the beer, or perhaps the conversation with Grayson, or both. It was well after nine before he got through to Sergeant Clark.

'The lady you were asking about,' said the sergeant, with unusual discretion. 'I hear she's gone to live with her daughter in Milnthorpe. The daughter's name is Andrews and she's married to a GP. I don't have an address, but it shouldn't be too hard to find. OK?'

It wasn't hard to find, and Sam stared at the phone number and address, thinking, before he picked up the phone again. 'Can you meet me, now, it's important. Bruciani's, I'll wait for you.'

'What is it this time? I haven't got long.' said Judith, sitting down opposite him. The coffee machine screeched and hissed before suddenly falling silent. Sam lowered his voice. 'It's about Monty House. I need your help.'

She looked at him quizzically. 'Hang on, wasn't it you who told me to drop the whole thing? And now you want my help?'

Sam looked around. 'We can't really talk here,' he said. 'How long have you got?'

'Half an hour, that's all. Deadlines, you know? Forget the coffee. Come on.'

They walked down to the end of the Walney Bridge and leaned on the wall, watching the tide creep up the channel to lift the small boats off the mud.

Sam's mind was full, as if a rising tide was lifting his memory to float free and clear. He turned to Judith and spoke into the wind that was sweeping in with the tide. 'It was a few years ago,' he said. 'There was an accident on the coast road and one of the boys from Monty House was thrown from the car and died. The driver was a man called Feversham, a friend of Captain Edwards.'

'And the boy was Eddie Stretch. I know all that, the story was in the archives.'

'But that's not the story. Hayward did the post-mortem on Eddie Stretch and found the same tranquiliser in his body that he found in Steven Stringer's. Diazepam. That's what they used on the boys, to make them more compliant. Morrison made Hayward fake the PM report, to cover it all up and make it look like just an unfortunate road accident. They said Feversham had been giving Eddie driving lessons.'

'How do you know about the diazepam, and what Morrison did?'

'Hayward told me himself, and his wife and I wrote his final statement down, just before he died. Ann even typed it up, and we got him to sign it. She had to help him write his name. It must have been one of the last things he did.'

'So where is it now?'

'Ann kept it. I thought it would be safer with her.'

'So where is Mrs Hayward? Does she still have it?'

'She's moved to live with her daughter. I've tracked her down, but even if I see her, she might want to bury the whole business. None of it does much for her husband's reputation.'

'Sam,' said Judith, putting her hand on his arm, 'If that statement's out there, we can use it. Two boys we know of have been poisoned by people who should have been looking after them. And both those boys are dead.'

Sam ran his hand over his face and blinked into the wind. 'The police should be handling this, but I don't know who we can trust.'

'What about Harry?' said Judith. 'He can't be involved, surely?'

Sam shook his head. 'I know you like him, Judith, and he's very fond of you. But I went to see him last night, and he's too far in with Cardine.' Judith frowned. 'Look, he may be straight,' Sam went on, 'but I can't be sure. We need more evidence, from people who are still around.'

'Iris Robinson,' said Judith. 'She must have known what was going on. She's here, she's respected, people would listen to her.'

'But if she knows, she's said nothing so far. You've talked to her. She still thinks Edwards is a hero, devoted to his boys. If we want to break that down we'd need something pretty solid to convince her.'

Judith took a moment to think, while Sam watched her intently.

'What about Mikey Bennett?' she said. 'He's still in Barrow, we could talk to him. And Bill Noakes. And his brother, Raymond. The police have him, couldn't they get him to talk about Monty House?'

'They'll all know something,' said Sam. 'I'm sure of that, but they may not want anyone else to know. They're terrified of what other men will say and think. That's what's kept them quiet all these years, and why should that change?'

Rain began to fall, rattling into the shallow tide. Sam took Judith's arm and they ran back across the road towards the shelter of the neighbouring streets. They leaned against a wall, side by side, breathing hard, watching the rain obscure the tall houses on the other side of the bridge. Sam turned to face Judith. 'Here's what I have to do,' he said. 'First I find Mrs Hayward and see if she still has the statement. Anything on paper and signed is good, even if a lawyer could question its truthfulness. Then I need to take the statement back to Iris Robinson and persuade her to stop denying everything. She's the key. If she's prepared to acknowledge what was happening and say so publicly, that would open everything up.'

'The saintly Mrs Robinson,' said Judith. 'You keep talking about you doing all this. What about me?'

'It's too risky for you, Judith. Think what happened to Tommy. That could have been a message for you.'

'But whoever it is could be watching you as well.'

'I know, but let's hope not. I'll have to keep under the radar as far as I can. They may not even know I'm around.'

'Lots of maybe's,' said Judith. 'Don't you need me to talk to Iris?'

'I always got on well with her,' said Sam. 'But it might need to be you who talks to Mikey. I'm pretty sure he wouldn't deal with me.'

Judith nodded. The rain was abating. She looked at Sam, the intensity in his face, and the fading bruises, She wanted to touch him.

'What about Harry?' she asked.

'We leave him out. We have to.'

Judith looked away. 'You don't like him, do you?' she said.

He put his hand to her face and stroked away a strand of hair. 'Do you really like him, Judith? Honestly? I need to know.'

She met his eyes, then looked away again.

'I like him, but...'

'But what?'

'I don't trust him, not really, not like I trust you.'

Sam leaned across and kissed her. She pulled away and smiled. He kissed her again.

CHAPTER 26

Judith was very quiet when she got back from work that night and she pushed Tommy away when he tried to show her a picture he'd done at school. What she really wanted to do was hug the boy and tell her best friend Elspeth that she was in love with Sam. But she was afraid, fearful that Sam's determination to continue with the case against Montgomery House would threaten all of them. And she was afraid of herself, too. Did she trust Sam enough to tell him how she felt? Did he really like her, or was he trying to prove something to himself, and to Harry?

'Off you go, Tommy,' said Elspeth, and when they boy had left the room, her irritation with Judith spilled over. 'What's up with you?' she said. 'Is it Harry?'

Judith laughed, 'No, why should it be?'

Elspeth persisted. 'You need to talk to him again. Someone has to follow up what happened to Tommy, Judith. You and Sam just go your own way, chasing shadows, and no one seems to care that Tommy has been threatened by strangers just round the corner.' She turned to the sink. 'I thought Harry liked you, Judith.'

'He does,' Judith began. 'But I don't know what's happening, Elspeth. Why don't you talk to Harry yourself? Tommy's your

300

son. Don't put me in the middle.'

Elspeth threw down the tea towel she was holding and burst into tears. 'That's it,' she said. 'I'm sick of the pair of you, you and that precious brother of mine. He's no use either.' She picked up the towel and wiped her eyes with it. Judith regretted what she'd said and tried to make amends. 'It's complicated,' she said. 'There's so much going on. I'm sure Harry's doing what he can, but I don't want to talk to him about it right now. I can't explain.'

Elspeth sniffed. The two women sat silent for a while, both feeling aggrieved. Elspeth reached for a tissue and blew her nose. 'We have a week off school next week, Tommy and I,' she said, 'and it'll be just the two us, again. I love him dearly, you know that, but I get lonely, Judith. I want to get out and do things, like everyone else does. And I want to get Tommy away from here. I hate the thought of someone watching us.'

Judith thought of something. 'I'm not working from Saturday lunchtime till Monday night,' she said. 'Why don't we go to see my folks, the three of us, on the train? I could come back to work after the weekend and you could stay on a while. It'd be a change of scene, at least. You and I and Tommy could have Vince's room, and Vince could go on the sofa. He'd be OK with that, he gets bored if things aren't happening.'

'What about your Mum?'

'It'll be fine,' said Judith. 'She loves having people around to help entertain Gran. We can take Tommy to the beach. Come on Elspeth, let's do it.'

At lunchtime on Saturday, Sam took Elspeth and Tommy in the car to the station and Judith met them there. She was late, and they had to run for the train. Sam noticed that Judith didn't look directly at him, even before she kissed him on the cheek. He cursed himself for assuming that things had changed between them. Now he had no idea what was going on. He stood, watching the train pull away, confused and unhappy.

Outside in the street he was almost too preoccupied to notice the blue car pulling out of the car park, until a squeal of its brakes made him look up and notice the broken wing mirror. He froze, trying to see the registration plate, but the car was away down the street, and by the time he reached the corner it was gone. He closed his eyes to see if there was any image of the driver in his brain, but all he could remember was that the car was the shape of either a Jaguar or a Daimler.

Back at the Cannon Street flat Sam rang the police station, but Harry was out, and he didn't want to leave a message. Since their conversation about the identity of the red Landrover man, he'd heard nothing more from Harry. What was he up to?

In his new flat, Sam had started another information display about the continuing puzzle of Montgomery House. As he added the information about the car, it was still clear to him that Mrs Robinson was their best hope, and to break her persistent denial they needed whatever Mrs Hayward could give them. He found the Milnthorpe number and went back downstairs to the phone in the hallway. It was the daughter, Christine, who answered. 'Who?' she asked. 'A friend of my father? He passed away over a year ago, didn't you know? And why do you want to speak to my mother? She's just beginning to feel better, I don't want her upset.'

'I understand,' said Sam. 'It's about something that happened just before your father died and I think she'll want to talk to me about it. I wouldn't be asking unless it really mattered. Could you check with her? She'll remember me.'

'Wait a minute,' she said. 'No, don't wait. I'll ask her when it feels right. Is it urgent?'

'Yes, it is,' said Sam. 'Can you ring me back, please, as soon as you can?'

It was the following day, Sunday, when Christine Andrews rang back. 'Can you come today?' she said. 'Mum was very agitated when I told her last night that you had been in touch. She does want to talk to you, but I don't want her upset like this for too long.'

Ann Hayward opened the door herself when Sam rang the doorbell of the large house in Milnthorpe that displayed the doctor's name and the opening hours of the surgery. At least there wouldn't be any patients coming and going today.

'Sam,' said Ann smiling. 'How lovely to see you. Come in, please.'

How she's aged, Sam thought.

Christine brought them fresh coffee and biscuits and left them alone in the comfortable sitting room. 'I'm just in the kitchen,' she said to her mother, 'if you want anything.' Her look to Sam said, 'Don't upset her.'

Ann poured the coffee, and Sam made himself wait and calm down. 'Do you remember when I came to your house, just before David died?' he asked. She nodded. 'That awful cough he had,' she said, 'and the wheezing. I heard it in my dreams for weeks afterwards.'

'You told me how Morrison had blackmailed David, for years,' Sam went on. 'And you'd kept notes about it.'

She nodded. 'And you asked him to tell you about that car accident, and that boy who'd been drugged.'

'That's right,' said Sam, excited that her memory seemed so clear. 'You typed it all up and helped him sign it. Then you put it with your other notes.'

'In the sugar jar,' she recalled suddenly. 'That's where I kept everything. It was like something out of a spy film.'

He smiled, relieved. 'I thought it was a great idea,' he said.

Ann Hayward's face clouded. 'But then I moved here,' she said. 'Where's that jar now?'

Sam looked at her. Surely, all that precious information couldn't have been thrown out? ' Don't you know where it is?' he asked. She shook her head. Sam had to press for more. 'Who helped you move?'

'Christine and Eric,' she said. 'And my grandson, Ian. He came home for the weekend. They all helped. I was in a bit of a state.'

Sam sat back, his hopes fading. 'When was it?'

'Before Christmas, in 1969,' she said. 'It was a rush, so soon after the funeral, but they said I couldn't be in that big house on my own, so they organised everything really quickly. The house was finally sold in April. It was the best thing to do. I was exhausted by the whole business, and I do enjoy living here after those dreadful years. David was never himself after Morrison threatened to get him struck off. The drinking got worse and worse.'

'Does Christine know about any of this?'

Ann shook her head. 'I was too ashamed to tell her, and with Eric being a doctor himself... You won't tell her, will you?'

Sam looked away. How could he get them to remember what happened to an old sugar jar without telling them why?

'Leave it to me,' he said. 'Christine's in the kitchen, right? Is there any chance that the sugar jar is still there?'

'But why would it be? Christine has her own storage jars.'

'Think, Ann, please. Do you have any idea what might have happened to it?'

Ann closed her eyes tightly, trying to remember. 'Eric and Ian were dealing with the big heavy stuff,' she said. 'Christine and I dealt with the curtains, and the kitchen. We had big orange boxes. She wrapped up the things I thought I might want to keep. All the rest was left for the house clearance people.' Sam couldn't bear to think of an old sugar jar being chucked onto the tip, and the truth about Morrison going with it.

'Wait a minute,' said Ann suddenly. It was a really big jar, quite hard to find these days. And it had belonged to my mother, too. I don't think we would have thrown it out.'

'Can you think where it might have gone?'

'I'll need to ask Christine. Please Sam, don't tell her everything. I couldn't bear it.'

Sam picked up the tray of coffee cups. 'I'll just say there were some papers that David was keeping for me, notes about what was happening at the station.'

She nodded.

In the kitchen, Sam said, 'Mrs Andrews, I wonder if you could help me. I brought some papers to your parents' house, just before your father died. They were about things that were happening at work, and David was the only person I could trust to look after them for me. I don't want to say any more about that, but I need those papers now. Ann and I think they may have got lost during the move, when she came to live here.'

Christine looked hard at him. 'Are you the young policeman who lost his job? Mum told me about that.'

Sam hung his head. 'I resigned. I had no choice.'

'And these papers are to do with that?'

'I can't tell you any more, I'm sorry.'

Ann Hayward smiled at him.

'Where were the papers?' Christine asked.

'In an old sugar jar. Your mother tells me she hid them

there for me. It was a big jar and belonged to her mother. She doesn't think it would have been thrown away, but she can't recall where it went.'

Christine frowned. 'A sugar jar? Well, it's a good hiding place. Who'd think of looking there?'

'Exactly,' said Sam.

They all began to glance round the tidy kitchen, in case by some miracle the jar was sitting on a shelf, in plain sight. Nothing.

'It's big,' said Ann, demonstrating with her hands. 'Plain glass, quite thick, with a silver coloured lid.'

Christine's face brightened. 'Oh, *that* jar,' she said. 'I thought it would make a good flower vase. It's in the cupboard with the others.'

'Did you empty it?' Sam asked, his heart sinking again.

'Of course I did. Not much use for flowers if it's full of sugar.'

'Did you find anything inside?'

Christine thought for a moment, frowning. Ann and Sam watched her. Sunlight flooded into the room and a robin sang just beyond the open window. Suddenly Christine walked to a large sideboard and began opening drawers. She looked through one, then another, and then stopped. 'No, not here,' she said. 'I can remember finding a load of papers wrapped up in a plastic bag. I could see they were handwritten and I knew they had to be important.' She hesitated. 'I think I put them in an envelope, and in a drawer, but not here. I don't know where you were, Mum, or I would have asked you at the time. But it was all such a rush, just before Christmas. Can I go and look in your room? It might come back to me.'

'Go, go,' said Ann.

They followed Christine up the stairs and into a large room

at the back of the house that overlooked the garden. In the corner by the window was a desk with a roll top and drawers on each side. 'In there,' said Christine, pointing. 'Must be. That's where I'd put personal papers, isn't it?'

Ann pushed past her daughter without a word, rolled up the desk top and began opening the small drawers that lay inside. 'No, too small.' She closed the lid and started opening the larger drawers. Sam could hardly bear to watch. Suddenly she turned towards him, smiling, holding an envelope above her head. 'That's it,' said Christine. 'I knew I'd put it some-where sensible.'

Ann passed it on to Sam. His hands were shaking. Finally he managed to prise back the flap and look inside. 'Is everything there?' Ann asked. Sam pulled the papers from the envelope, turned his back on the two women and looked through them. Many of the pages were in Ann's own handwriting, but right at the back were several typewritten pages. He leafed through to the end, and there was David Haywood's spidery signature. This was it.

'Sorry,' he said, turning back to them. 'Confidential stuff. I think it's all here.'

Ann Hayward put her hand to her mouth. 'It will have to stay confidential, won't it?' she asked.

He nodded. 'They'll be safe with me now.'

'Well,' said Christine. 'That was worth your trip over here I hope, Sam?'

'Oh yes,' he said. 'And thank you. This means a great deal to me.' More than you could ever know, he thought.

Ann Hayward walked down the drive to the car with him. When they were well away from the house, she said, 'You never said what happened to that awful Sergeant Morrison. Is he still away?'

'Yes, still in Hong Kong, as far as we know,' said Sam, although he was beginning to have his doubts.

'I hated that man,' she said. 'I had to listen to him being unbearably rude to David, and there was nothing I could do. Every time I saw his car outside the house my heart sank.'

Sam turned towards her. 'What was it like?'

'A Daimler maybe, something expensive like that. Blue, I think. Nice colour.'

Sam stared.

'Ann,' he said. 'Can I use your phone?'

'Are you all right?'

'Yes, it's just… I need to check something. It's important.'

He ran back to the house where Christine had left the front door open. Ann followed him in and pointed to the phone on the hall table. Christine opened the kitchen door. 'It's all right dear,' said Ann. 'Sam just needs to ring someone urgently. Let's leave him to it.'

Sam dragged the phone number out of his memory and dialled. His heart was racing.

'Hello,' said Vince.

'Vince, thank God,' said Sam. 'Where's Judith? Can I speak to her?'

'They've all gone to the beach,' said Vince. 'You just missed her.'

Sam felt sick. 'Vince, can you still recognise cars by their engine noise?'

'Good trick, isn't it,' said Vince. 'Why?'

'Have you heard a strange car near the house, since yesterday?'

'Actually, there was one last night,' Vince said. 'Just outside, only for a few minutes, but I knew it wasn't one of the usual cars. Posh engine, very smooth.'

'Is your dad there?'

'Yes, he's reading the paper. Do you want him?'

'Please, Vince, hurry.'

There was a rustling sound, then, 'Sam?' said John. 'What's wrong?'

'Did you see a car outside the house, last night? Vince says he heard it but I need to know what it looked like.'

'Yes, I saw it, a beauty,' said John. 'A Jag or a Daimler, blue I think. Quite new I'd say. Must have cost a bit.'

'Have you seen it today?'

'No, why? What about it?

'The girls are out with Tommy, aren't they?'

'Yes, and Maggie and Violet are at church. Why Sam, what's this about?'

'John, please, I can't explain, but I need you to go and find them.'

'What? Why?'

'Please, John, just do it. If you see the blue car, it's important I have the number plate. And when you find the girls, stay with them, and bring them all home. Can you do that?'

'And then what?'

'Ring me back on this number.' Sam peered at the phone and read off the number, then repeated it for John to write down. 'Try and get the car registration. I'll tell you why later.' The phone clicked as John put it down.

Less than twenty minutes later the phone rang again and snatched it up. John was out of breath. 'They're here, they're OK,' he said. 'The number?' said Sam. 'I've got it,' said John. 'The car was in the beach car park, no one in it. Judith's upset. She wants to know what's going on.' Sam wrote the car number down and checked it. 'Tell her I'll talk to her later. Got to go. Thanks.'

Ann and Christine were hovering at the kitchen door. Sam ignored them, picking up the phone once more without asking and dialling the familiar number of Barrow police station. 'Clarky, it's Sam. Is Grayson there...? At home? Do you have the number? I need to talk to him. It's important. No, no, better still. Can you check a car number plate for me, please? I know you shouldn't but it's important, I wouldn't ask otherwise. Here it is.' He read the number carefully into the mouthpiece. 'And when you find it, give the name of the owner to Grayson. It's a car he's been looking for... Tell him it's about Tommy, he'll know. Thanks Clarky. I owe you a pint. And can you keep all this to yourself, please?'

Sam put down the phone and leaned back against the wall. His heart was thumping and he felt sick.

CHAPTER 27

'It's Morrison's car,' said Sam to Judith on the phone from the Cannon Street flat, after she'd calmed down. 'The car that you and Tommy saw. Ann Hayward mentioned that Morrison had a big blue car. That's why I needed the number plate, to be sure. I've passed it on to Harry and asked him to call the police in St Bees. They can keep an eye on the house. Elspeth and Tommy should be fine.'

Judith was silent. 'Are you still there?' he said.

'I'm here,' she said. 'I'm thinking.'

'What's Morrison got to do with it when he's on the other side of the planet?'

'But he left his car here, Grayson told me that. Someone is using it, and they're following you around.'

'But if it's because of me asking about Monty House, how do they know about that? Mrs Robinson wouldn't have told anybody, would she?'

Sam's mind was working hard. 'She could have mentioned it to Edwards. And your editor, Mr Springrice, knows, doesn't he? Or Harry could have said something, at the golf club maybe, about you looking for good news stories on the Monty House boys. He worked out you were digging for dirt, and other people probably worked that out, too.'

'What about Cardine? He saw us together in the pub one night. He commented about it.'

'Maybe he asked Harry straight out.'

Judith was quiet for a while. 'So it's me they're after, again?'

'Could be,' he said.

'We have to do something, Sam. This can't go on.'

'I know. And I've got what I needed from Ann Hayward.'

'You did? All of it?'

'All of it. All her notes and the statement about Eddie Stretch's post-mortem. I can take them to Iris. She'll have to admit that something was wrong.'

'I need to come too,' she said. 'This is my problem, Sam. I'm coming back tomorrow. It's the bank holiday. Let's see if Iris is at home.'

'I'll pick you up,' said Sam. 'Can you be back by three?'

The following day, Sam and Judith sat on a wooden bench on the coast road by the shore for a while, thinking about what they had to say to Iris. It was mid afternoon, and the tide had reached right up to the top of the shingle, covering the mud and winding channels that took the rivers out to the mouth of Morecambe Bay and into the Irish Sea. Sandy bubbles marked the edge of the water, and two oystercatchers stood among them, motionless. Sam shielded his eyes from the glare bouncing off the shallows. A breeze ruffled the trees behind them. Judith pushed her hand between his elbow and his body, feeling the rough tweed of his jacket. Sam didn't move. Neither of them spoke for a while.

The oystercatchers rose suddenly and wheeled away into the pale blue of the afternoon sky, settling again a few yards away. Judith turned to Sam, leaning towards him. She was surprised by her need to be close to him.

'How old is Iris?' Judith asked.

'Hard to tell. In her fifties probably. Not old enough to retire. And she's got her father to look after. She must need the money.'

'But it's not just about the money, is it?' said Judith. 'She's put her life into that place, and she can't believe Edwards would let anything happen that harms the kids.'

'She's no idea. Surely she'll believe us now. We need her, Judith. She's our only hope.'

'She might just shut the door in your face,' said Judith.

Sam turned to her. 'She might, but I don't think she will. There's a habit of politeness in her,' he said. 'Bred in, you know. She won't be hostile, but she might not let us in the house.' He smiled. 'You knock on the door. Tell her we were passing and you suddenly felt faint. She's a nurse. She'll have to help.'

Judith stared at him. 'That's sneaky,' she said, smiling.

'Needs must,' Sam said. 'We have to get in there, and we're running out of time. Whoever wants the Monty House business kept quiet must be panicking by now. Why else would someone be following you?'

He looked around. A car was approaching along the coast road, coming closer. Sam pulled Judith to him and put his arms tightly around her head as the car passed by. She pulled away, gasping.

'Sorry,' he said. 'I just wondered about the car... you know.'

Judith looked at him. 'Was that all?' she said.

Sam blushed and smiled. 'Not now,' he said. 'Come on. When we get to the house, you knock, tell her you don't feel well, ask if we can come in for a few minutes, get a glass of water, you know what to say.'

'And what will you do?'

'Just chat. Get her to relax a bit. She was so close last time. I'll show her the papers, or read them to her if I have to. I need to hear her say what she knows, and then she'll have to write it all down. That might be harder. But I have to try, Judith. She's the key to all this, I'm sure of it. If I can nail Edwards then Cardine's next.'

They went back to the car and headed further down the coast towards Attercliff.

Sam was out of sight behind the beech hedge when Judith knocked at the front door of Iris Robinson's small terraced house and waited. The curtains at the front window were half closed. A basket with purple and yellow anemones hung by the door. After a few minutes the door opened and Iris peered out into the light. 'Miss Pharaoh?' she said. 'Is it you?'

Judith smiled. 'I'm so sorry to bother you again, Mrs Robinson. We were coming down from Barrow in the car and I suddenly felt dizzy. Something I ate maybe. I had to stop, and then I remembered you live just here and I wondered if I could get a drink?'

'Is there somebody with you?' said Iris, following Judith's glance towards the gate.

'Yes,' said Judith. The lies were bothering her already, but she had to go on. 'My friend Sam is here.' She raised her voice. 'Sam,' she called, and he appeared at the gate.

'But,' said Iris. 'He's the policeman who…'

'Yes,' said Judith quickly. 'It was he who suggested we call on you. He came to see you didn't he, last year?'

Iris looked hard at Judith, who felt herself blushing. Some people were hard to lie to.

'Well,' said Iris. 'If you need my help, of course you must

314

come in. And you too, Mr…?'

'Tognarelli, Sam Tognarelli,' said Sam. He stretched his hand towards her but she ignored it. 'I was a detective constable then, the last time we met.'

'Yes, of course,' she said. 'Come in, both of you. I only have a few minutes, though. Father will need his tea at four, as always.' She walked ahead of them, into the house and through to the kitchen at the back. 'Father lives in the front room these days. He's too frail for the stairs. Someone else sits with him while I'm at work. I keep to the routines. Four o'clock is tea time.'

The kitchen was spotless and frozen in time: pale green distempered walls, with various cupboards, a deep sink and old-fashioned cooker, and in the centre of the small space was a square table covered in a cloth, and two chairs. Sam glanced at the clock on the wall. He had less than twenty minutes before she would have a reason to ask them to leave.

'Would you like a cup of tea, Miss Pharaoh?' said Iris, 'or water?' Judith tried to look ill. 'Call me Judith, please. Miss Pharaoh sounds like someone else. A cup of tea would be grand, thank you. And may I use your bathroom?'

'Top of the stairs,' said Iris, turning to fill the kettle.

'This is very kind of you Mrs Robinson,' said Sam. 'Do you remember the last time I was here? You made tomato sandwiches for me, and chocolate cake. That was one of the best lunches I had in all my time on the force.'

Iris didn't acknowledge the memory or the compliment. She put the kettle on the stove and lit the gas under it.

'Yes, I heard you moved on,' she said, still with her back to him. 'Workington was it?'

'Whitehaven,' said Sam. 'And you?' he asked. 'Are you well?'

Iris took a handkerchief from the pocket of her apron and

blew her nose.

'Mustn't grumble,' she said. 'But I've not been at my best…' her voice trailed away. 'Things have been difficult, you know.'

'I'm sorry,' said Sam.

'That awful business with the Thornhills,' she said. 'Dreadful. The captain was so shocked. We all were.'

'I'm sure,' said Sam, hoping that Judith would take her time upstairs.

'Have they found that woman?' Iris asked.

'Mrs Thornhill? No, I don't think so. Looks like she's in Spain, probably changed her name. And they'd struggle to get her out. Plenty of criminals go to Spain.'

Sam heard the flush of the toilet and Judith's step on the stairs. Mrs Robinson busied herself making a pot of tea. 'Are you feeling any better, dear?' she asked, when Judith came back into the room. 'Tea won't be a minute.' Judith looked across at Sam, who shook his head.

'Mrs Robinson was asking about Irene Thornhill,' said Sam.

Judith shuddered. 'I don't know, and I don't want to,' she said.

'You poor dear,' said Iris. 'I only heard bits of the story, but it sounded terrifying. And to be there, when he…' She gestured vaguely towards her head.

'We reached her just a moment or two later,' said Sam.

Iris put the teapot on the table and took four cups and saucers down from a shelf. She looked at Judith, and then at Sam, a question in her eyes.

'Sam's just come down to visit his sister,' said Judith, smiling. 'As a matter of fact,' she went on, as Sam glanced at the clock, 'there's something I wanted to ask you, about another of the Monty House boys. Would you mind, while I'm here?'

'Iris looked puzzled, and Judith presssed on quickly. 'It was about one of the boys who died in a car accident, quite a while ago now. I wondered if you remembered him.'

Sam waited. If Iris wanted to get rid of them, she could do so anytime. They didn't have long.

'One of our boys?' asked Iris.

Judith nodded. 'His name was Eddie Stretch.'

Mrs Robinson put her hand to her mouth. 'Edward. Oh dear. Such a tragedy. Not far from here. They were taking a bend and they skidded, I understand. Edward was thrown out, hit his head. So sad.' She reached for the handkerchief in her pocket.

From the front room a man's voice was calling. The sound cut across Mrs Robinson's sniffles and the slow relentless ticking of the clock on the wall. Iris and Sam glanced at the clock simultaneously. Just after four.

'It's Father,' said Iris. 'He wants his tea.'

'I'll take it,' said Judith quickly. 'You stay here with Sam.'

'But Father will want to talk,' said Iris. She was pouring the tea, her hand shaking slightly. 'And he likes me to read to him.'

'I can do that, too. It would be my pleasure.'

Sam smiled brightly. 'Judith used to work in an old people's home, didn't you, Judith?' he said. She looked across at him. 'While you were at university, in the holidays,' Sam went on, raising his eyebrows. 'You told me how much you enjoyed it.'

'Oh,' said Iris. 'How interesting, dear. Father can be quite, you know, demanding at times. Are you sure you don't mind?" She reached for a large square tin and opened it. 'He'll have a piece of cake, and shall I cut one for you, too?'

'Lovely,' said Judith. 'I'm feeling much better, thanks. It'll be a pleasure to sit with him for a while.'

'Not for long, mind,' said Iris. 'He has a rest soon. You'll need to leave him if he starts to droop.'

'Of course,' said Judith. 'Won't be long.'

They were alone again. Sam said, 'Do you mind if I sit down Mrs Robinson?'

'Iris, call me Iris.'

Sam pulled one of the chairs out from the table and sat down carefully. He feared that any sudden movement might break the spell of the quiet room, the ticking clock. He leaned forward as she sat down opposite him.

'Forgive me, Iris,' he said softly, 'but you don't look quite as well as you did the last time I was here. Have you been poorly?'

Iris pulled out a chair and sat down, turning slightly away from him.

'It's been a difficult time,' she said. 'And I'm not sleeping well. And Father, as I said, he can be rather demanding, especially at night.'

'And you have your work as well,' said Sam quietly. 'That's a lot to deal with.'

Iris was looking down at the embroidered tablecloth. She stroked out a crease with her fingers. The clock ticked more loudly. From the front room they heard the low murmur of Judith's voice.

'How is the captain?' asked Sam. 'It must be difficult for him, too. First Stevie Stringer, then Mr Harries. And the Thornhills. I know how much Montgomery House means to him. How can he carry on?'

'He has to,' she said, without looking up. 'Things are changing. We have two new teachers. He has to stay at the helm.'

'He's a remarkable man,' said Sam.

She looked up. 'Yes he is,' she said. Her eyes were full of tears. 'But…' she hesitated. 'I think sometimes other people have not been so dedicated. Not just the Thornhills. They were evil. Other people…'

Sam waited. She knows, he thought. It's just the captain she's protecting.

'Do you think some people may… may…' he hesitated.

Iris looked down again, and wiped her eyes.

'Iris,' he began.

From the other room an old voice began to wail, calling her name. She got up quickly. 'Oh dear,' she said. 'I must go to him.'

Sam was on his feet. 'Please,' he said. Judith appeared at the door. 'He'd like some more cake,' she said briskly, cutting another piece as if this was her own kitchen. 'We're having such a good chat in there.' And she was gone, cake in hand, closing the kitchen door behind her. Sam breathed out, and sat down again, willing Iris to do the same. She stood for a moment looking at the closed door, and then at Sam.

'What do you want from me?' she said quietly.

Sam leaned forward. 'I know you care so much about those boys, and you want the best for them. And you have so much respect for the captain, too. This must be very hard for you.'

She sat down and lowered her head.

'Iris, we think that some people who have visited Montgomery House may have hurt some of your boys. They've given them presents, I know, but some of those could have been bribes, to keep the boys quiet.' She didn't move. 'Do you understand me, Iris?'

She nodded.

'We keep finding out things, little things, but when you add them up it doesn't look good.' He waited. Still she didn't move.

'There was that car accident, wasn't there, just down the

319

road from here? Eddie Stretch was killed. We know that, don't we?'

Iris Robinson nodded her head, the faintest acknowledgement.

'We have reason to believe that Eddie had been given something before he died. Some drugs. The police doctor, Dr Hayward, found them, when he did the post-mortem.'

'But that wasn't in the report, was it? The captain asked to see it, and he would have told me.'

'Someone made Dr Hayward change the report, leave out any mention of the drugs.'

'That's not possible, surely. Why would he do that?'

'Dr Hayward was being blackmailed. He told me so himself, just before he died. He made a full statement about it, and he signed it.' Sam took the envelope out of the inside pocket of his jacket. 'I have it here, Iris. It tells the whole story. Eddie had been given diazepam, to make him,' he hesitated, 'more compliant. Do you know what I mean, Iris?'

She stared at him, alarm in her eyes. Sam pushed on. 'And the same drugs were in Stevie Stringer's body, too. That's probably what killed him.'

Iris put her hand over her mouth.

'We need to know what happened, what really happened to them both.'

There was silence in the little kitchen. They could both hear Judith's quiet voice reading to the old man in the neighbouring room. Iris Robinson closed her eyes. 'Poor Stevie,' she said. 'It was the teacher, Mr Harries,' she whispered. 'He killed Stevie and put his body in the quicksand, and then he hanged himself, that's what the captain told me.'

'But Mr Harries wasn't at Montgomery House when Eddie Stretch died, was he?' He waited, holding her gaze. 'So what happened then?'

Iris dabbed at her eyes.

'These were your boys,' Sam said. 'You looked after them, every day. They came to you. They remember you fondly. Bill Noakes, he told me that himself.'

She looked away, but Sam pressed on.

'Bill's in prison, angry and afraid. He told me what happened here, but he wouldn't let me tell anyone else. He wouldn't write down what he knew.'

'I need to go to Father,' Iris said, struggling to her feet.

'No, Iris,' he said. His voice was too loud. 'You can't turn your back on these boys, not now. They need you, more than ever, even the ones who are lost. Who else can speak for them, if you don't?'

She crumpled, leaning her elbow on the pristine tablecloth, holding the handkerchief to her mouth and sobbing into it. He wanted to stop, but he could not. Everything that he'd fought for since he came to Barrow rested on this woman and what she knew. He thought of Doc Hayward, and Bill Noakes, and Morrison and Cardine bullying him, and his own weakness, giving in and walking away.

'Iris,' he said. 'Please. Tell me. You know, I know you do. But you've buried the truth all these years. Let it go.'

Iris Robinson took a deep breath, and another. She turned to look at the small window, and the yellow laburnum tree outside.

'I wasn't there, the night Stevie died,' she said. 'But I knew it didn't happen like they said. I'd seen what was happening to him. It was hard to wake him sometimes. He slurred his words. It was drink, or drugs. I told the captain about it and he said the boys smuggled drugs in for themselves, and that he would deal with it. Then when you asked about Bill Noakes, I remembered what else I'd seen. The marks on him, you know. The sore places.' Iris looked at Sam, pleading for him not to ask. He didn't.

'I asked the captain if anyone might have hurt the boys, but he said it was from their families, that's why they came to us. He kept saying how important it was to have these people visiting, supporting the house. That TV man came. I never liked him, but the captain always spoke up for him. Even when...'

'When what?' Sam asked.

'When Bill told me, what that man did to him.'

She covered her eyes again, not wanting to look at him.

Sam held his breath. He wanted time to stop, and prayed that Judith could keep the old man quiet for a few more minutes.

'Iris,' he said. 'Tell me about Eddie Stretch. It was Mr Faversham who was driving, wasn't it?'

She nodded.

'And he was injured, wasn't he?'

'Yes, he broke his ankle.'

'So who called for help?'

She looked at him. 'It was the other man in the car, who wasn't hurt. He came back here to use the phone.'

'There was another man?' Sam's mind was racing.

'He came here. He was upset. He said there'd been an accident and the captain called the police. He went out to meet them but the man stayed here. I suppose he didn't want to go back there.'

'Who was it?' Sam asked.

'The other man was Inspector Cardine,' said Iris. 'He was your boss, wasn't he?'

Sam was stunned, then – exultant. If she would stand by this story, he could nail Cardine in a lie, a big lie, and link him directly to what happened at Montgomery House. He said nothing, thinking what to do next. He had to keep her talking. Out of the blue, another question came to him.

'Two weeks ago, Iris. A Monday night, were you at Montgomery House overnight?'

'I'm usually there on a Monday, to give the captain a night off.'

'Do you remember a phone call, it would have been late, around midnight?'

She looked at him, her eyes bright with distress, and nodded. 'Someone did ring, to speak to the captain. How did you know?'

'Did they give a name?'

'No, it was a man's voice. But he knew my name. I was surprised. I didn't want to wake the captain, but the man said it was urgent, so I went to tell him and he took the call in his office.'

'Do you know what they talked about?'

'Oh no, of course not. Phone calls are private, aren't they? They talked for a few minutes. I heard the captain go back to his room.'

'Did he say who had called him, or what about?'

'No, and I didn't ask.'

Another piece of the puzzle in Sam's mind dropped into place.

He stood up. 'Do you want to see Dr Hayward's papers, Iris? They're all here, everything he told me before he died.'

She shook her head. 'I knew...' she shook her head again. 'But the captain is a good man. I couldn't believe he would let such things happen. I still can't.' She hesitated. 'What are you going to do?'

'I don't know,' he said. 'DS Grayson is involved. It's up to him now. Do you remember him?'

'He was with you, wasn't he, when Mr Harries died? He seemed such a nice young man.'

'Yes, he's the sergeant now and it's him I need to talk to. He'll have to decide what to do.'

'I see,' said Iris. She looked up at Sam. 'Judith wasn't feeling ill, was she?'

He blushed. 'We weren't sure you would speak to us. I'm sorry.'

She seemed strangely calm. 'It doesn't matter. You'll have to go now. I must be with Father.' She hesitated. 'Will they arrest me?'

'I don't know. Perhaps.'

'And what will happen to Father?'

'I don't know. I'm sorry,' he said again.

CHAPTER 28

'I couldn't have done that without you,' Sam said to Judith as they walked back to the car. 'If the old man had been pestering all the time I'd never have reached her. Poor woman. She must feel terrible.'

'But she could be relieved.'

'I don't think so,' he said. 'This has been her worst nightmare. She's kept going all these years by trusting that Edwards wouldn't let those boys be hurt. Now we're telling her that he's lied to her and betrayed the boys. Her reality is falling apart.'

'She wouldn't do anything drastic, would she?'

'Not while her father needs her.'

Judith sat silently as the car wound along the coast road. The mud flats uncovered by the ebbing tide stretched away towards the horizon and the open sea. Grey blue haze obscured the far shore of the bay.

'What are you going you do?' she asked after a while.

'I don't want to talk to Grayson about it, not yet. He's already given me a lecture about evidence, or the lack of it, and we're not there yet. Hayward's statement and Mrs Robinson's memory could both be challenged. And Edwards might still be able to talk her round. We've got most of the pieces of the picture, but it's not enough. We have to keep going.'

'And what about Frank?' said Judith suddenly, taking Sam by surprise. He turned towards her, but she was still facing away from him, out across the bay. 'You may have a good idea about exactly what happened, but no one's ever talked properly to my mum and dad about it, have they? The police seem to have forgotten about him, with all the fuss about the guns and what happened to you. Dad didn't say much while I was there, but I could tell he was upset about it.'

Sam thought about it. 'You're right,' he said. 'Frank's case has been playing second fiddle to Special Branch all the time. I've done my best, but the Whitehaven police have been distracted. Is that what John feels?'

'I'm sure he does. And I don't know what he's told Mum, or Vince.'

'What do want me to do about it?'

'Talk to the DC you worked with at the start, Holmes. They need to talk to Mum and Dad, properly.'

It took Sam a full day to track Rob Holmes down on the phone. Even when he did, Holmes seemed rushed and offhand. Sam insisted that they should meet. It was a nuisance having to drive to Whitehaven, but there was no other way. They met in a café round the corner from the police station, which wasn't ideal but better than another frustrating conversation on the phone, or being closely watched at the police station.

During the drive north, Sam had decided that he should say exactly what was on his mind.

'You've not done right by Frank Pharaoh, or his family,' he said, as soon as Holmes sat down.

Holmes bridled, 'Wait a minute,' he began, but Sam persisted, leaning forward and keeping his voice low, despite the anger he was feeling.

'Hear me out,' he said, 'and don't forget I'm one of you. I know how relatives get fobbed off, may have done it myself before now, but this has gone on long enough. Some families don't care what happens, or don't want to know, but the Pharaohs aren't like that. They didn't ask the right questions, I grant you, or see the signs that Frank was in trouble. They relied on the grandmother, Violet, to keep them connected to Frank and her mind was going. Did you hear about Frank's Christmas club? He was taking her pension money, how low is that? It's come as a terrible shock to them. Can you imagine? You've got kids. There must be guilt, shame, remorse. John Pharaoh's a steady bloke, and he's been trying to protect his wife. I've tried to tell him what I know, but I'm not on the inside. It's not enough.'

Sam sat back, surprised at himself, waiting for the comeback from the other side of the table. The reaction was not what Sam expected.

Rob sipped his coffee. 'OK,' he said. 'Point taken. We've relied on you to keep the family in the picture and that's not what should have happened.' He looked round and lowered his voice even further. 'Bloody Inglis, he's an arrogant git. Couldn't give a shit about some local bloke who got into debt. What do the Yanks call it in Vietnam? "Collateral damage." Him and his mates have been camped in our office for weeks, bossing everyone around. And Braithwaite lets them do it. What's that about? Nothing else matters except the bloody Provos and who they're working with over here, where the guns came from, where they're going. Inglis called you all the names under the sun when we had to come and get you out. You could have been collateral damage too, for all he cared. Bastard.'

'So will Inglis and his mates stop you sitting down with the

Pharaoh family?'

'I'm not even going to ask. Frank died on our patch, at the hands of people known to us. This is our case, and we deal with it. I should have spoken up about it before now.'

Sam smiled, remembering how hard it was to stand up to an overbearing sergeant. 'I've been there,' he said, 'I spoke up, and look at me now.'

Rob didn't smile.

'So what are you going to do?' Sam went on. He had to press home the advantage before it disappeared.

'Do the right thing. Tell the relatives as much as we can without compromising the case.'

'They just need to know that Frank didn't kill himself and didn't suffer too much at the end. Isn't that what you would want, if it was one of yours?'

'Post-mortem couldn't be absolute about that, but we can piece it together from what Baldy and his mate told us.'

'Unless they're lying. Murder's worse than manslaughter.'

'I don't think either of them are bright enough to make it up, and we got the same details from both of them separately. Looks like Frank's original head injury was an accident, part of a scuffle or when he broke away from them. If he wasn't dead when he went over the cliff, he certainly wasn't conscious.' Rob looked round the quiet café once more.'

'We can't talk properly in here,' he said. 'Walls have ears. Come on.'

They paid for their coffees and walked down the main street towards the church and the garden beside it. On a seat away from the bustle of the street, Rob sat and lit a cigarette. 'The old bloke in the bungalow behind the quarry, Clegg, he told us more when we interviewed him again, after all that fluffing around. He said he saw two men that night dragging something off the back of the truck, 'like a sack of potatoes', he said. Those drag marks you found on the path outside the quarry, Frank's feet most likely. Poor bastard. But at least he probably didn't know much about it. I'll tell the parents what we know, without all the nasty details. Can you set that up?'

The following day, Sam sat with John and Maggie in the front room of the St Bees house listening to Rob Holmes explaining as much about Frank's death as he was able to share. He'd picked up Rob in Whitehaven and driven him to St Bees, and the conversation on the way had helped to clarify what the family really wanted and needed to know. Rob did it well, Sam thought; his opinion of Rob as a policeman and as a person was improving. Maggie was quiet and calm. 'Did he suffer?' was her only question. It was impossible to answer with any certainty, but she was looking for reassurance as much as the truth. 'Do many young men get into debt like this?' asked John. It must be incomprehensible to him, Sam thought. 'Young, old, mostly men,' Rob replied. 'Gambling's an addiction for some people.' John shook his head. Maggie stared at her hands.

'Thank you for telling us all this,' said John, as he shook Rob's hand. 'We owe it to Frank to know what happened to him.'

Afterwards, Sam drove him back to Whitehaven along the old road through Kells. They stopped for a lunchtime drink before dropping down into the town. The air was unusually still and humid. Sea and sky merged with no visible horizon to the west. 'Bad weather coming,' said Rob. 'You can feel it.'

Sam made a decision. He needed to ask Rob a favour. 'There's one thing still bothering me about the case – not the Pharaoh case – the Special Branch affair. When the Noakes gang found me that night at the harbour, how did they find out so fast that I was a copper? Even when they knew my name, none of them could know I had any connection to Frank Pharaoh or to the police, but when Noakes came back from making that phone call, he knew it all.'

'Gloria,' said Rob. 'Had to be.'

Sam shook his head. 'I don't think so. She swore to me that Noakes never asked her. And there's something else. This is where it gets complicated.'

As simply as he could, Sam told Rob Holmes about Montgomery House, and what had happened the previous year. Rob listened carefully and nodded. 'You're right, it's complicated. And what's any of it got to do with our case?'

'Ray Noakes,' said Sam. 'I think his phone call was to Captain Edwards at Montgomery House. The matron said someone rang that night and spoke to Edwards, just for a few minutes.'

Rob was puzzled. 'But why would Noakes call Edwards? He was a hardened crim and Edwards was a pillar of the community, by all accounts.' He hesitated, remembering something. 'Hang on. In your statement, the one I took in the hospital, you mentioned something about Frank. It should be in my notes.' He fumbled in his inside pocket for his notebook and flipped back through the pages. 'Here it is. You said that when Shorty came back from the phone call he talked to someone in the truck. You couldn't hear Shorty, just the bloke he was talking to, who said something like, "Pharaoh? You gotta be kidding".'

'Well, it is a strange name.'

'But it was just that, no mention of Frank, just Pharaoh.

Sam thought for a minute, then banged his fist down on the pub table, making the drinks wobble and neighbouring drinkers turn to look.

'That's it,' he said. 'I thought it had to be Gloria because she knew Frank, and Edwards couldn't have mentioned Frank because he didn't know him. But Edwards *did* know Judith Pharaoh. That's who he must have mentioned to Shorty. Judith, not Frank.'

Holmes nodded. 'But that still doesn't explain why a career criminal should ring Edwards in the middle of the night and ask for advice. Doesn't make sense.'

'But it does,' Sam insisted. 'Edwards never knew what happened to Ray. Mrs Robinson told me they both thought Ray had fulfilled his promise, that he was a hard-working young man, who'd made something of his life with their help, all that. Ray knew Edwards was well-connected, in with the police. And he genuinely admired the man. Probably the only authority figure in Ray's life who ever supported him.' He leaned forward, 'It fits, Rob. It all fits.'

Holmes thought about that, then asked. 'But does Mrs Robinson know for certain it was Ray who called?'

'No. She just said that the caller knew her name, and that she recognised the voice.'

'So, that wouldn't stand up. Defence brief would take it apart, unless Edwards had a brainstorm and admitted to giving you up.'

They both leaned back, staring at their drinks. Sam looked up at the clouds racing from sea to land, then back at Rob.

'You're going to interrogate Noakes, right? I want you to ask him, straight out. What's he got to lose now? He's going down, for a long time. Could you trade something with him, just enough for him to give this information up? I need to build the case against Edwards and this is one more piece.'

Rob shook his head. 'Trading's out. No one wants to give this scumbag anything. And you must be pretty desperate if this is the best you can get. These cases never work, you know that don't you? Unreliable accusers, middle-class defendants, sceptical juries. It takes years to bring any charges and then they usually fail.'

'Could you ask Noakes anyway? And doesn't Inglis want to know what made them kidnap me?'

'No, he's only interested in where they were going to take you. And he never got the chance to find out, did he, because we had go in too early. Inglis couldn't care less.'

'Could you?'

Rob shrugged. 'No harm in asking the question. Noakes isn't going anywhere. Chances of getting him to tell us anything at all are pretty slim, but if it might help, I'll give it a try. What's he like, this Edwards bloke?'

'Old soldier type, single, apparently dedicated to "his boys". I think he's bent as a nine bob note, but a lot of people think he's God's gift.'

'Well, Noakes is still in our cells,' said Rob. 'They don't want him back in Haverigg, too many connections there. I can get him into an interview room, if you want?'

'Please, I'll write down what I need to know.'

'On the night of Monday, May 31st,' Rob began, after the usual preliminaries, as Ray Noakes sprawled in the chair in front of him, 'you were at the Whitehaven harbour around midnight, when one of your men discovered a man watching you, covertly.'

'Covertly,' Noakes scoffed. 'Christ.'

Sam sat quietly in the observation room, watching through the viewing window and listening on the intercom.

'The identity of that man was revealed by the driver's

licence you found in his pocket.'

Silence.

'How did you discover that this man was linked to Frank Pharaoh, and had been a policeman?'

'No comment.'

'Do you know a man called Captain Edwards?'

Sam saw the flicker of reaction in Noakes' face.

'You were in the Montgomery House boys' home for three years, is that correct?'

'It's in my record. Why ask me?'

'Captain Edwards was the director of that home while you were there, and still is, isn't he?'

Noakes shrugged, feigning boredom.

'And your brother, Bill, he was there too, wasn't he?'

More reaction. Noakes leaned forward, looking straight at Sam through the glass but seeing only a reflection of himself. 'Leave my brother out of it.'

'So I'll ask you again,' said Rob Holmes. 'Do you know Captain Edwards?'

'No comment.'

Holmes looked down at his notes, then back at Noakes. 'Your brother, Bill, claims that he was molested at Montgomery House by friends of Captain Edwards. Abused, buggered, repeatedly, is that clear enough for you?'

Noakes sprang to his feet. 'It's a lie. He's made that up. Edwards is a good man.'

'Ah,' said Holmes. 'So you do know him.'

'And 'e's a good man,' Ray Noakes said, lowering himself into the metal chair.

'Who did you call on the phone that night? Who told you about Tognarelli?'

'No comment.'

Sam hung his head. Ray wouldn't let it slip, not now.

'And where were you taking Tognarelli when the police stopped you?'

'For a little ride, what do you think?'

'You were taking him to people who would get the truth out of him.'

'No comment.'

'You were instructed by the two Irishmen who'd brought the cigarettes across and would take the guns out.'

'I don't take no orders from no one,' said Ray, now almost completely in control of himself once more. He leaned forward. 'Look, copper, you got nothing. I'm telling you nowt. Why would I? I can do the time. Done it before. Piece of piss. Now get me back to my nice cosy cell. I know my rights.'

'Nothing,' said Sam when he rang Judith later that evening. He had all the windows open in the Cannon Street flat but the upstairs rooms were stuffy and sweat ran down his back after the tiring drive from Whitehaven through the Sellafield traffic. 'We're running out of leads. What did Iris tell you about seeing Mikey at the market?'

'It was a Friday. Mikey was bringing fish he'd caught to sell to the fishman, I've forgotten his name. He has a stall there every Friday.'

'That's tomorrow,' he said. 'You need to find Mikey, Judith, talk to him. He trusts you, right?'

'We got on OK, but that was a long time ago.'

'You've got more chance than me. Can you go down there tomorrow?'

'I'm working Sam. I have a job, remember?'

'You take a lunch break, don't you? It's just down the street. Spend an hour down there.'

'What are you going to do?'

'Cardine. We have to link him to Morrison's car. I'm going to watch his place tomorrow.'

'If Mikey is at the market, what do you want me to do?'

'Talk to him if you can, follow him if you have to. Iris Robinson thinks he's out at Lowsy Point but he could have lied about that. We need to know where he hangs out.'

Judith sighed. 'The things I do for you. I spend Friday afternoon chasing Mikey around some God-forsaken salt marshes while you sit on your backside in leafy Barrow watching Cardine's house? Sounds like you get the best of this deal.'

'Please, Judith. We're nearly there. You want to nail these blokes as much as I do. We just have to keep going.'

'I know,' she said. 'It's OK.'

'Thanks. Meet me at Cannon Street, when you've finished at the office, around five?'

There was so much more to say, but neither of them wanted to say it.

Judith had to start work early on Friday morning to make some time for her lunchtime excursion to the market. She'd slept badly and the day looked like she felt: the sky to the west had the colour and menace of a bruise. After a busy morning she drove the Vespa down to the market, parked on a side street and walked through to the fish stall, which was bustling, as ever. This end of the market seemed to be home to all Barrow's lost litter, rustling in lazy eddies across the concrete. 'Flanagans', that was it, she remembered. They'd been there for years, and local fishermen sometimes brought their catch to sell.

She waited in the queue, bought a piece of sea bass that she didn't really want and took the chance to ask Mr Flanagan a question. 'D'you know a young lad?' she asked. 'About my height, calls himself Mikey.'

'Aye, what about 'im?'

'You know him, then.'

'Brings me a few dabs every now and then. Skinny little runt.'

'Seen him today?'

'Not yet. Is that all, love? I'm busy.'

Judith stepped away from the stall as the people behind her jostled forward. Someone stepped on her foot and as she turned to protest she caught sight of Mikey walking towards the stall. She dropped her bag and bent to pick it up, hiding herself as the boy joined the end of the queue. Glancing round, she walked away to the side of one of the stalls nearby to watch and wait. Mikey handed over the paper parcel, and waited while Flanagan opened it, sniffed the contents and handed over some coins. The boy was standing beside the fish stall, counting the coins intently, when Judith came to stand next to him.

She put out her hand and touched his shoulder. 'Mikey,' she said, 'do you remember me?' He started, his eyes full of panic. 'It's all right,' she said quickly. 'You're not in trouble. I just wanted to say hello.'

'Go away,' he said.

'I hear you lost your job,' she said quickly. She could see that he was ready to bolt.

'Who told you that?'

'Inspector Cardine,' she said. The reaction was instantaneous. Mikey spat on her shoes. 'He can fuck off,' he hissed. 'And you, too.' People in the queue looked across curiously.

'Wait,' said Judith, but he was gone, running towards the main road. She ran after him, saw him heading for the bus stop and doubled back to the street where she'd parked the scooter.

She took a short cut through to the main road out of Barrow to the north. There was no bus ahead of her and she waited at the side of the road, the scooter's engine purring. A bus came into view. She let it go past, waited for a couple of cars moving slowly behind it and followed them, stopping when the bus did at various stops along the road. She'd guessed right. The bus stopped at the end of the road that led down to Lowsy Point and she saw Mikey step down and set off walking down the road towards the railway line. Now what? She still had work to do, a wind was blowing in from the sea, and she feared they were chasing shadows. She turned the scooter round and headed back to the office.

But she couldn't settle. She picked up the phone and called Sam's flat. No response. She sat for a while, thinking, then picked up the phone again. This time she said, 'Is Sergeant Grayson around? Judith Pharaoh would like to speak to him.'

CHAPTER 29

Sam sat well down in the seat of his car, parked about fifty yards from the gate of Inspector Cardine's house. This was the kind of stakeout that he'd seen in the films, and he'd come prepared. Resting on the passenger seat was the notebook and pencil that he always had with him. He had the Polaroid ready too, and a flask of coffee and some of his favourite biscuits. This end of the street was quiet, but he'd brought a newspaper to hide behind, just in case. The two biggest problems facing him were how to stay awake, and how to relieve himself if the need arose.

Time dragged. He was unbearably tired. He tried to read the newspaper but the print blurred. He wondered whether Judith would do as he had asked and track down Mikey Bennett. If Grayson was ever going to help them, the case had to be strong. And he wasn't even sure that Grayson would help them. Ambition and fear were a powerful combination, and Harry Grayson had them both.

The postman trudged down the road, disappearing at each gate as he made his way towards Sam's car. That could be me, he thought, feeling the heavy bag get steadily lighter as the round progresses, looking forward to the end of the familiar route and the smoke-filled sorting office, eating lunch, talking to people, heading for home. Easy, uncomplicated, no responsibilities. He buried his head in the newspaper as the postman passed by. Drowsiness crept up his body to his head, his eyes.

A rumble of thunder woke him with a start. Outside the air was still and the trees along the road drooped, leafy branches sagging towards the pavement. He'd been dribbling and his mouth felt dry and sour. As he looked at his watch, a movement in the street made him stop and peer into the gloom of late afternoon under the darkening sky. Cardine's car was approaching from the other end of the road; it turned into his driveway. Sam ducked down instinctively, and as he did so, another car passed him from behind, moving slowly. The profile of the driver was clear. It was Harry Grayson. The car stopped at Cardine's gate. Grayson emerged and walked into the drive, disappearing behind the high beech hedge.

Sam sat for a moment, his mind a jumble of conjecture, suspicion, anger. He knew it. Grayson and Cardine, they were in this together, using Judith to get information. What had she let slip? What were they planning? Sam pulled his rain jacket from the back seat and struggled to put it on, pulling the hood over his head. He checked in the rear-view mirror that his face was well shadowed, and got out of the car. As he approached the start of the beech hedge he could hear voices; he stopped, straining to hear what was being said. They must be talking on the front doorstep. Then the voices faded and Sam heard the front door close. He crept a little nearer but the hedge was high and thick and he couldn't see through it. He checked his watch. Christ, how long had he slept for? It was five-thirty. Judith would be waiting for him, but he couldn't leave, not yet.

Minutes passed. The front door opened. Cardine's voice was raised but indistinct. Grayson was leaving. Sam turned quickly and walked away from the house, down the road towards his own car, praying that Grayson wouldn't recognise his retreating back. He'd just reached the car when he heard Grayson's car door slam; the engine revved and the car accelerated down the road, braking hard to take the corner at the far end. Sam turned and walked back towards the house. He could hear footsteps crunching on the gravel driveway. Just by the fence that bordered Cardine's garden there was a small gap in the hedge and Sam peeped through. Cardine was opening the garage that stood at the side of his house. One door, then the other. Inside was a blue car with the unmistakeable Jaguar on its bonnet and a familiar number plate. The car's engine started and Sam ran, reaching the safety of his own car just before the Jaguar nosed into the street, turned away from him and disappeared. He sat, breathing hard. The only certainty he could find in his jumbled mind was that Judith would be waiting for him at the Cannon Street flat, and that he was late.

The red Vespa scooter was parked at the kerb beside his house and Judith was sitting on the step reading the evening edition of the paper. 'You're late,' she said.

'I saw Harry Grayson,' said Sam.

'What about him?'

'He was at Cardine's. And Morrison's car was there, in the garage.'

'Are you sure?'

'Certain. I told you, we can't trust Grayson.' Judith looked away but said nothing. 'Did you find Mikey?' She nodded. 'I asked him about Cardine and he swore at me and ran. I followed the bus. He set off walking down towards Lowsy Point and I went back to work.'

'Why didn't you follow him?'

'I couldn't, Sam. I had to go back to work. And I didn't

sleep much, and I'm tired, and hungry.'

He bent down and pulled her gently up off the step by her shoulders, holding her to him, speaking softly into her ear.

'We can't stop, Judith, not yet. Come with me, there's some biscuits in the car.'

'Where are we going?'

'Lowsy Point. I need to talk to Mikey.'

By the time they reached the level crossing where the track to Lowsy Point began, it was raining heavily, large drops of water bouncing onto the windscreen and streaming down. Light flickered on the horizon and the rumble that followed was louder than before. They rounded the first bend in the rough track and stopped. Ahead of them remnants of light were reflected on an expanse of water where the bay curved round to the point. Lightning leaped horizontally across the sky, bleaching the landscape for a second or two, and the boom of thunder shook the car.

'The tide's nearly up to the road, did you see?'

'It could be going down,' said Sam. 'Weather's pretty bad out there. Are you OK?'

Judith nodded, unnerved by the storm and uncertainty. The car bumped painfully along the track, grinding through every pothole that the wheels couldn't avoid. The potholes were full of water and there was no way to guess how deep they were. Sam gripped the steering wheel, swearing. The car lurched to a stop and stalled, rain hammering on the roof. He started the engine again and revved it hard to heave the wheel forward out of a rut before it stalled again.

'This is hopeless. We'll have to leave the car here,' he said. 'There's a bridge just ahead of us, across the stream. I saw it in that last flash. If we can get across, we can run to the shacks to shelter.'

Judith said 'I want to stay here,' but her voice was drowned by the rain and thunder that beat against the car.

Sam pushed open the car door, pulled up the hood of his rain jacket and began to pick his way towards the bridge. After a moment's hesitation, Judith followed him, not wanting to stay there alone as the apocalypse raged over their heads.

An old stone pillbox, a remnant from the war, loomed at the side of the track, its door and windows rectangular shapes in the old concrete. 'In there,' she cried, but her voice was lost and Sam didn't wait. When they reached the low bridge the stream was already backing up, meeting the incoming tide and flowing backwards, flooding the track on either side. They splashed through. Another burst of light showed the track ahead of them running with water. Sam took Judith's hand and pulled up her up onto higher ground. 'Through the dunes,' he shouted. 'If Mikey's in one of those shacks, we'll find him.'

The first two shacks they tried were locked, but the third one was open and they burst into the dark space beyond, pushing the old door shut against the storm, before they both bent over, gasping for breath.

'We must be mad,' said Judith. Her hair was dripping in long curls. As the next flash lit the room Sam looked around, found a towel hanging by the sink in the corner, and handed it to her. 'Probably filthy, but better than nothing.'

'No thanks, it smells of fish,' she said.

Sam pulled a small torch from the inside pocket of his jacket but the light started to dim almost at once and he switched it off. 'Paraffin lamp here,' he said. 'Not seen one of those in a long time. It might do, if I can get it to work.' Several matches later, the lamp produced a steady glow, while the lightning spiked white light into the room at regular intervals and the walls of the little shack shuddered.

'Is this where Mikey lives?' Judith asked. Her tiredness had gone, dissipated by anxiety.

The paraffin lamp sputtered and went out. They both groaned. For a moment they could see nothing, and then lightning lit up the room for an instant. 'Someone's been living here. Look,' Sam said, pointing. A newspaper from two days before was spread across a table. On a shelf by an old couch several packets of cigarettes were stacked neatly, next to an overflowing ashtray. There was a cigar box too. Sam picked it up and opened it. At first he thought it was empty, but he felt something, and recognised the feel of a photograph. Sam took it out. It was impossible to see in the darkness, so he carried it to the small window, held it up and waited. Light seared into the room. 'Look,' he said. The light was gone as suddenly as it began. 'Use the torch,' said Judith. 'There may be enough battery left, it's better than nothing,' Sam switched on the torch and Judith held it as close as she could and peered at the photograph. 'It's Mikey,' she said. 'Driving a car.'

'Look at the car,' said Sam. She stared. Mikey was sitting in the driver's seat of Morrison's car. The window was down and he was smiling. 'I wonder who took the photo?' she said. 'He looks happy.'

The torchlight faded to nothing. Sam put the photo carefully into his inside pocket.

'Evidence,' he said. 'Leave the rest. Mikey isn't here, so we need to find him. Are you ready?'

Judith hesitated. 'I have to tell you. I phoned Harry this afternoon.'

Sam stared. 'When?'

'When I got back from the market. Must have been about two.'

'What did you tell him?'

'Nothing, he wasn't there.'

'What were you going to tell him?'

'That we need help. We do, Sam. We can't deal with this on our own.'

'Was that all? Did you leave him a message?'

'No, why?'

Sam shook his head. 'Never mind. We need to get back to the car.'

The path back through the dunes was less exposed than the main track, and without the potholes on the road that had now flowed together into a flood. The worst of the storm had passed over but lightning continued to flash, illuminating the scene like a flickering old movie. The tide was still rising. Sam was ahead, holding Judith's hand. Suddenly he stopped. 'Down, get down. There's a car coming. Over there.'

Headlights jerked in the distance as the car bounced up and down over the rough surface. They squatted in the shelter of the dunes, watching.

'The bridge has gone,' Sam said. 'They'll have to stop.'

The headlights stopped moving but stayed on. Sam shielded his eyes. Then the lights went out. The driver's door opened. The man who emerged was tall, with white hair that glowed in the gloom. He had a powerful torch that lit his way as he splashed towards the flooded stream. 'Cardine!' Sam whispered. Another clap of thunder crashed around them. The man stopped, turned his head. The beam of the torch followed his eyes, towards the pillbox where a figure stood silhouetted in the doorway.

Cardine turned off the torch and walked towards the figure. Sam and Judith watched and heard a voice, but not what was said. The figure stepped forward. It was Mikey. The two of them stood quite close together, the dark head and the white. They seemed to be talking. Then Cardine slowly raised his hand to the boy's cheek. It was a gesture of affection, not violence. Sam gasped.

Mikey stepped back suddenly, pushing Cardine's hand away. He was shouting but the words weren't clear. Cardine gestured towards the car, but the boy didn't move. Cardine pointed again towards the car, but Mikey stood motionless as Cardine walked to the car, opened the driver's door and reached in. A sheet of light flooded the sky. He was standing straight, facing Mikey, his arm raised, something in his hand.

'He's got a gun!' said Sam. He stood up and shouted, 'Stop! Stop!'

Cardine turned towards the sound and raised his arm again. As Sam ducked down, Judith saw Mikey launch himself onto Cardine's back, shouting, pushing them both down into the flooded stream. They rolled into the water, locked together. Sam slipped down the sliding sand, but before he could reach them, Mikey struggled to his feet, picked up a stone from the bank and struck down hard at Cardine's head, once, and again. Judith stood and screamed. Mikey looked up, dropped the stone and staggered backwards towards the far side of the flood. Sam plunged into the water, found Cardine's shoulders and began to haul him out.

Judith slid down to the water's shredded edge, losing one of her shoes as she fell. She could see Mikey's distorted face staring back at her. 'Go!' she screamed. 'Go!' She pulled her wallet from her pocket and hurled it across the watery divide between them. 'Take it. Go!'

Mikey waited an instant, picked up the wallet, turned and stumbled away into the darkness.

❖ ❖ ❖

Judith sat by the ebbing stream, holding Cardine's head. Her hands were sticky with blood, but she didn't dare let go. Sam had left her there and gone for help. If he could have taken Morrison's car it would have been easier, but he wouldn't touch it. Maybe his own car wouldn't start, or was stuck fast. She didn't know. The storm had passed, and a half moon rose into the clearing sky. Reeds rustled in the dunes, and from the inland fields she heard a fox bark. The stream had subsided as fast as it had risen and now gurgled innocently past the broken bridge, across the salty marshes and out into the bay.

Cardine was still breathing, very slowly. He stirred, moving his mouth. Judith dipped her fingers into the edge of the stream and wet his lips. Time passed, and she stopped imagining what Sam was doing, or where, or who he was with. He would come, when he could. There was nothing she could do except wait, and hope.

She heard the rumble of an engine before the lights appeared, bobbing down the track. A car came first, then an ambulance. Suddenly Harry Grayson knelt beside her. 'Are you all right?' She nodded. 'He's alive, I think.' One of the ambulance men checked Cardine's neck for a pulse and nodded. 'Still with us,' he said, calling to his mate for a stretcher. Together they prised the long body away from Judith and away into the ambulance, which bumped away towards the town. She rested her aching arms but couldn't get up.

Harry stepped away to examine the ground around the stream and it was Sam who helped Judith to her feet. As they picked their way across the sodden ground she whispered to Sam, 'Did they get Mikey?' He looked around. Grayson was watching but couldn't hear them.

'No,' Sam said. 'I waited as long as I could before I told them what happened. He has a good chance.'

Grayson called across. 'The constable will take you home. Tell him to come back for me. I'll be here a while. There's a tow truck coming down for Cardine's car, and yours, too. Get some rest.'

Sam helped Judith into the back of the car but didn't get in himself. 'Won't be a minute,' he said. She watched as he walked back to where Grayson was searching. Sam took the photo of Mikey in Morrison's car out of his jacket. Grayson looked carefully at it, and put it into a small bag that he took from his pocket. The two men shook hands. As they returned to town in the back of the police car, Sam rubbed Judith's cold hands, and put his arm round her shoulders.

'Lean on me,' he said.

Tears ran down Judith's cheeks. She wiped them away, then put her arm across Sam's chest, warming her hand inside his jacket.

CHAPTER 30

Sam lay in his bed listening to the house sparrows chattering in their nest above his window. Damp muddy clothes littered the floor of his bedroom and he was cold. It was already light, but his watch said that it was not yet five o'clock. He groaned. Morning after morning, once he was awake sleep eluded him, and layers of exhaustion were accumulating, day after relentless day. He cursed the innocent sparrows, who had now fallen silent. Perhaps if he lay still for a while, he might drift off again.

Memories of the previous night played across his mind, flickering, shredded by the storm. He could see the white-haired man, the shiny pistol in his outstretched hand, and the boy's bright, defiant face. What had there been between Mikey and Noel Cardine to bring them both to this? Sam wanted to know, but Mikey was gone, and Cardine's life was hanging by a thread.

It was almost eight o'clock when he woke again, still feeling wretched. He needed to speak to Judith. Elspeth had been awake when they reached her home in the early hours. She had eased Judith into her arms and waved Sam away. Now he longed to hear Judith's voice, to see her face. Today was Saturday. Elspeth and Tommy would be at home and he could phone the house without Judith having to answer. He pulled on his dressing gown and went downstairs to the telephone in the hall. The air was cool. Light from the fragments of stained glass over the front door refracted into colour on the pale walls.

The phone rang for a long time. It was Tommy who answered. 'Mummy's gone to get milk,' he said. 'I have to look after Aunty Judy.'

'Is she still asleep?' Sam asked. There was silence. Sam regretted the question, knowing that Tommy would check and in doing so probably wake her anyway.

'That you, Sam?' her voice was husky. 'I was asleep.'

'I'm sorry,' he said. 'Are you all right?'

'My arms ache, from holding him. How long was I there before you came back?'

'Maybe an hour. I couldn't get the car to move, so I had to walk back to the road and flag down a car to get to a phone.'

'Harry was there, wasn't he? It feels like a dream.'

'Yes, they called him at home and he picked me up.'

'And you brought me back here?'

'Yes. You were very cold.'

'Elspeth put me in the bath. I don't remember much.' She hesitated. 'Is Cardine dead?'

'He was still alive when they took him in, just. You kept him warm, Judith, holding him like that.'

'I don't want to think about it.'

'Go back to bed.'

'No, I'll get up now. Come and see me later.'

'I will,' he said.

As he drove into the hospital car park, Sam saw Harry Grayson talking to an ambulance man outside the Accident Department. He stopped the car and waited. He didn't want to see Harry, not yet, until he'd sorted out the jumble of suspicions in his mind. He found the room where Cardine was, and noticed a constable in uniform sitting by the door reading the paper. The man didn't recognise Sam and Sam ignored him. He wasn't ready for questions. In the ward sister's office a nurse was sitting at the cluttered desk, writing notes. Sam knocked quietly on the open door and she turned towards him.

'May I see the patient?' he asked.

'Are you a relative? It's relatives only I'm afraid. There's a policeman here making sure that no one goes in.'

'I'm with the police,' said Sam.

'You as well? The place is crawling with you lot today.' She got up and looked past him towards the main door of the ward. 'Can you tell me what's going on? Nobody will tell me. I'm not even supposed to know the patient's name.'

Sam shook his head. 'I can't tell you anything, sorry.'

'At least you're polite about it. That other man who was here snapped at me. You just missed him. He looked pretty awful, I have to say. Said he'd been up all night. Looked like it too.' She straightened her nurse's cap. 'Well, back to work. My mysterious patient needs a bit of a tidy up.' She lowered her voice. 'Daft thing is, he's not a mysterious patient at all. I know who he is.'

'How?'

'My dad knows him. I think they play golf together. He's a police inspector isn't he?'

'I can't say,' said Sam.

'Well, his brother should be here soon. I hope that constable lets him in.'

'Whose brother?'

'The patient-who-has-no-name's brother. I talked to him earlier on.'

Sam stared at her. 'What do you mean?'

'Bit thick for a policeman aren't you?' said the nurse, smiling. 'People have brothers, you know, who come and see them. Happens all the time.'

'You said you talked to him, this brother?'

'On the phone. The anonymous patient whose name I know anyway gave me the number and asked me to telephone, so I did. I'd do the same for anyone. People need family at a time like this, don't they? Now, I have to go.'

'No,' said Sam. He grabbed at her arm.

'Excuse me,' she said, loudly. 'Just watch your manners, young man. I have a job to do.'

'No,' he said again. 'Sorry, but, I need –'

'Look, he just asked me to ring and give his brother a message. What's wrong with that?'

'What's the brother's name?'

'He didn't tell me, just wrote it down. The message looked funny. He said it was Latin, something from when they were kids. I didn't know what it meant. He told me how to say it, and he wrote it down for me.'

'Where? Where is it?'

'What? Oh, I put it down somewhere,' she waved towards the desk. 'Haven't got time to look for it now. Is it important?'

'Do you remember the number? Tell me.'

'That's on the piece of paper, too. Sorry, I have to go, and so will you. Come back later. Maybe they'll send that constable away. Can't see what good he's doing here, anyway.'

She stood by the door of the office, waiting for him to leave. He did so, walking towards the lift for long enough for her to go back to the ward. Then he turned and retraced his steps, checking that the nurse was no longer around. The door to the office was shut. Please, he said to himself, let it not be locked. It wasn't, and Sam went in, closing the door behind him. He could be discovered at any moment but there was no choice. He began to sift through the papers on the desk, looking for numbers and a few words among the official records and forms. Nothing. Another pile of papers lay on a shelf. He picked them up. There, on the top, was a handwritten note. He read it, put it in his pocket and left the office, running back to the lift. He pressed the button, waited, then found the stairs and took them two at a time.

Out in the car park he looked across to where he'd last seen Harry, but there was no one there. Just outside the Accident and Emergency main door was a telephone. A woman with grey hair was using it. He glared at her and gestured her to hurry up, but she turned her back to him and carried on talking. Sam waited until he could wait no longer. 'Police,' he said, 'I need to use the phone, madam, right away. Important business.' He snatched the phone out of her hand and replaced it to break the line.

'You can't do that,' said the woman. 'Don't care who you are. Haven't you got a radio or something?'

Sam ignored her and dialled three nines. It was the quickest way. He felt the panic rising in his chest.

'Emergency, which service please?' said the calm voice.

'I need the Barrow police station, it's urgent,' he said. 'Sergeant Grayson, I need him now.'

'Your name, sir?'

'Tognarelli, Sam,' he said.

'Can you spell that?'

Sam shouted into the phone. 'Tell him it's Sam. He knows me. I'm at the hospital. Have you got that?'

'No need to shout, sir,' said the woman. 'You're at the hospital in Barrow?'

'Yes, in the car park, outside Accident and Emergency. Please hurry. Tell him it's urgent.'

'Stay where you are, sir, I'll do my best.'

Sam put down the phone. He had no more change. He held his head, trying to think what to do, then ran to the newspaper shop in the hospital main entrance to get more coins. He made another call.

Sergeant Clark said, 'Oh it's you. They were on a bit ago looking for Grayson, to go to the hospital. Cardine dead, is he?'

'No, Clarky, but get Grayson out here. Something's cropped up. Tell him I can't do it on my own.'

'He was 'ere all night apparently,' said Sergeant Clark, 'making calls, running around with files. What's going on?'

'Can't tell you, sorry. Just tell him I need to see him. And tell him to ask the nurse about Cardine's brother.'

'Didn't know Cardine had a brother.'

Sam rang off.

Another coin, another call. This time Elspeth picked up the phone. 'I've sent her back to bed, Sam. You said you would come and see her, and she's been waiting for you. Where are you?'

'I can't explain, not now. But I have to do something and I need Judith with me… Yes, now. It can't wait. I'm sorry to mess you around, but it's important. Tell Judith I need her. I'll pick her up in twenty minutes.'

'But —' Elspeth began.

Sam put the phone down. He could wait ten minutes for Grayson, no longer. Impatience overcame him before the ten minutes was up and he drove across to Roose too fast.

'This is ridiculous,' said his sister, opening the door. 'Whatever it is could wait, surely. She needs a bit of rest, not more running around.'

Sam persisted.

'I know she'll want to do this, and it can't wait. Is she ready?'

Judith came down the stairs. She was pale, her hair pulled back, wearing old tracksuit trousers and a T-shirt. He grabbed her hand and pulled her out of the door.

'Shoes, cried Elspeth, throwing Judith's sandals after them down the path. Sam picked them up and pushed Judith into the passenger seat.

'What is it?' she said.

'Monty House. We have to get there.'

'Why, what's happened?'

'Cardine asked the nurse to make a phone call for him and she wrote it down,' he said, rummaging in his pocket for the note. He found it and handed it to her, then started the engine as Judith peered at the tiny writing. 'Eddie, who's Eddie?'

'Look at the number.'

'The Monty House number,' she said. 'Is Eddie Captain Edwards?'

'Must be.'

'And what does this say?'

'It's Latin. *Carpe diem.*'

'What does it mean?'

'It means: *Seize the day.*'

'Like: Get on with it?'

'Yes. That's why we have to go. Don't you see?'

They drove as fast as the Saturday morning traffic would allow. Just outside the town a herd of cows blocked the road and Sam swerved down a narrow lane to avoid them, branches from the hedge scraping against the car. When they reached the long drive towards Montgomery House, the back wheels of the car skidded on the loose gravel.

'Sam,' said Judith. 'Calm down. What are you going to do?'

'We have to find him, stop him,' he said.

He hammered on the door of the house and they waited. The air was cool and Judith shivered. He took off his jacket and gave it to her. Iris Robinson opened the door. She seemed to be expecting them, but didn't smile.

'Where is he?' said Sam.

'The captain's busy,' she said.

'Is he here?'

She hesitated. 'No, he had to go out. You can wait for him.' She looked at her watch. 'It could be an hour or so. Can I make you some coffee? The boys will be having lunch soon. We have it early on Saturday so the cook...' She didn't finish. Sam took hold of both her shoulders. 'Iris,' he said. 'Did someone telephone here this morning, early?'

'Someone from the hospital, yes. I wasn't here. Captain Edwards told me when I came on duty.'

'What did he tell you?'

'Just that Inspector Cardine was in hospital. He seemed quite upset about it.'

'May I use your phone, Iris?' he asked. 'Just a local call.'

'Of course,' she said. 'Judith and I will make some coffee, shall we dear? Cook's gone home, so we won't have to worry her with a stranger in her kitchen.' Judith followed Iris towards the kitchen, hearing Sam's breathless voice on the phone.

'Clarky, it's Sam again. Can you hear me? Did you find Grayson? Tell him I'm at Montgomery House, and can he get here as soon as possible? OK? Thanks. No, sorry, I can't. 'Bye.'

The house was quiet, just a murmur of voices from upstairs and the sound of a football thumping a wall somewhere outside. The quiet was shattered by the jangling of the telephone, and Sam picked up the receiver. Sergeant Clark told him that Sergeant Grayson would be there as soon as he could, less than half an hour. Mrs Robinson emerged from the kitchen. 'Was that the phone?'

'Wrong number,' said Sam. She looked carefully at him for a moment. 'We'll bring the coffee through. In the boys' sitting room, I think. I don't use the office when the captain isn't here.'

''Where is he, did you say?'

'I'm not sure. Sometimes he goes to Broughton at the weekend to see one of the trustees. He'll be back soon, I'm sure.'

'Are you all right, Iris?' Sam asked. 'You don't look very well.'

She smiled brightly, 'I'm fine, really. My father, you know, it can be difficult.'

Mrs Robinson's hand shook slightly as she poured their coffee, which they drank in silence. Judith was watching Sam, knowing that something was brewing but not wanting to ask. They all heard the sound of the car outside. Sam held up his hand as Iris got up to open the door. 'I'll go,' he said. Harry was standing on the doorstep and Sam put his finger to his lips before he took Harry's arm and led him down the steps, out of earshot. 'Cardine got a message to the captain this morning, don't ask me how. It said *Carpe diem*. It's either a signal, or just a warning.'

'Where is he?'

'Mrs Robinson says he's out, but I think she's lying. She's upset about something.'

'Have you searched the place?'

'No, I was waiting for you.'

'Did Clarky tell you I was at the station all night?'

Sam nodded.

'I went through everything we have about Montgomery House. Morrison had hidden most of it away, but there's enough. Things have been going on here for years, I'm sure of it now. Cardine will deny everything.'

Sam said, 'I saw you there yesterday, at Cardine's house. I was watching. What were you doing there?' He hesitated. 'Did Judith tell you something?'

Harry's eyes opened wide. 'I didn't speak to Judith yesterday. I was determined to get to the bottom of what was going on with Morrison, and this place, and I wanted to give Cardine the chance to tell me what he knew. It was a courtesy, no more. And he might have been willing to co-operate.'

'Was he?'

'He threw me out. I was only there a few minutes. You saw me come out, didn't you?'

'I think Edwards is up to something, destroying evidence probably, having got that message this morning. I don't know why she's covering for him, but I think she is.'

A bell rang in the house. Grayson pushed past Sam and ran inside. Boys were clattering down the stairs heading for the dining room and their cold Saturday lunch. They looked at Sam and Harry, some of them knowing from long experience in their short lives that something was up. Iris Robinson was standing by the dining room door, checking the boys' hands. She looked up, her face pale.

'Mrs Robinson,' Grayson began, but she held up her hand, ushering the last of the boys into the room.

'One moment, sergeant, if I may. Come along boys, hands together eyes closed, 'For what we are about to receive...' The boys joined in, mumbling the familiar words. 'You may start,' she said.

Iris stepped back into the hall. Grayson stood close and

looked at her. Her eyes were full of tears. 'Mrs Robinson,' he said quietly, 'I have a warrant to search this house. You can wait until the full team arrives and turns the place upside down or you can tell me now where Captain Edwards is. Make up your mind now, please.'

She took a deep breath. 'He's in there,' she said, pointing towards the office. 'The door is locked.'

'Can you open it for me, please, or I shall have to break it down.'

Iris closed the door to the dining room and took a key from the pocket of her apron. She unlocked the office and stood to one side. She looked close to collapse and Judith went to her.

Harry Grayson opened the door and went into the room. 'Sam,' he called. Edwards was sitting at his desk, leaning forward, his head resting on his hands. On the desk beside his head were two small bottles, both empty. The room smelled strongly of whisky and burnt paper. There was another larger empty bottle on the floor.

Sam took a step into the room. Harry held up his hand. 'Wait.'

He placed his fingers carefully on Edwards' neck, waited, and shook his head. Then he took two pairs of gloves from his pocket. One pair he pulled on, the other he threw across to Sam who was still standing by the door.

'Judith,' Sam called. 'Can you take Mrs Robinson back to the kitchen, please, and stay with her?'

In the kitchen, Iris put her head in her hands. 'He's gone. I knew when I saw his face this morning.'

'Did you say anything to him, about what you told us?'

'I said that we would have to tell the truth about some

things that had happened. We talked. He was a fighter. He denied anything was wrong. But this morning, when he heard that Inspector Cardine was in hospital, he just seemed to shrink away. He knew it was the end. He said I should take over here, and that he didn't want to be disturbed before lunchtime. He shook my hand.' She sobbed, tears spilling over her hands. 'Then he went into the office and locked the door.'

'When was that?'

'Just before eight. There was a pistol locked in his wall cupboard. I knew it was there, and I knew he wouldn't use it. The noise might upset the boys. He took the pills for the pain in his leg. He must have kept some aside.' She wept again, then wiped her eyes and blew her nose. 'He asked me to take over, and I must see to the boys. I'll take them out to the school-room across the yard. I'll tell them the captain's been taken ill and we must stay out of the way for a while.' Judith nodded. 'Let me check with Sergeant Grayson. He may want someone to come with you.'

Iris looked up. 'Will you stay with me, Judith, please?'

Judith squeezed her hand. 'For as long as I can,' she said.

CHAPTER 31

For several hours the residents of Attercliff watched with interest as events unfolded at Montgomery House. They saw an ambulance arrive, and later the mortuary van. Two more cars joined the two already parked carelessly by the front door, and a coach took the boys away to various destinations. Judith went back to Roose for a while, but insisted that she would stay with Iris once the police had let her go home.

The search team turned Montgomery House upside down. A policewoman looked after Mrs Robinson's ageing father while Iris showed Sergeant Grayson where records and papers might be kept, and opened locked drawers and cupboards before she was allowed to go home. By the time darkness finally fell and the empty house was left quiet, several large boxes filled with papers had been loaded into the boot of Grayson's car to be taken back to the station.

Sam and Harry leaned back against the car, looking at the improbable shape and colour of the dawning moon. 'It was the Eddie Stretch business that got me thinking,' said Harry in response to Sam's question. 'I checked the accident report, got the details of the man who was injured and checked him out. Maurice Feversham. Partner in a law firm in Preston. It took a few phone calls, but one of the collators I talked to remembered the name. There was another complaint against him, last year, from the father of a boy who claimed he'd been drugged and assaulted by Feversham. Police thought that the father was dodgy, just out for what he could get. Feversham was bailed, but he skipped, went abroad, not been seen since. That's a drastic step for an influential man to take. He had a lot to lose. So I just kept digging. I knew that you and Judith were sure something was going on. There were too many coincidences, accidents, questions. Now we have to see whether there's a credible paper trail implicating Monty House in the systematic abuse of boys living there. Looks like Edwards had been burning papers in his office.' Harry hesitated. 'I'll have to get someone from another force to get the truth out of Cardine. He has a lot to answer for, and I can't have the old boys' club rallying round to protect him, or Morrison, if we can get him back from Hong Kong.'

Sam said, 'Mrs Hayward's papers will help with that, filling in some of the missing pieces. By the way, she doesn't want her daughter to know how Hayward fell into Morrison's clutches. Can you manage that?'

Harry nodded. 'I'll try.'

'And Iris will give you a full statement, which will probably cover the rest. Names, dates.' Sam closed his eyes. 'You don't need me now, do you?' He wasn't sure how much longer he could stay on his feet.

'Nothing more to do tonight. I'll be in tomorrow, but no need for you to stick around. Are you still at Cannon Street?'

'For now. The business in Whitehaven is settling down. I may go back there, I'm not sure.'

'Still planning to get back in the force?'

Sam shrugged. 'Still thinking. Unofficial policing isn't my style. I like the feel of the warrant card in my wallet.' He hesitated. 'I wasn't sure about you, you know. All that stuff about the golf club, and what a good guy Edwards was.'

'And you thought Cardine gave me Morrison's job to carry on doing his dirty work?'

'Sorry, but it could have happened that way.'

'Something else to tell you, talking of Morrison and Cardine. You remember I was checking on the man whose prints were on the red Landrover, in the 1969 case?'

'I'd forgotten all about that,' said Sam. 'You were going to ask Clarky.'

'I did. Memory like an elephant that bloke. He knew where to look, and he found it. The bloke's name was, – hang on –' He took a notebook from his inside pocket and leafed through it. 'Colin Peter Jackson, date of birth, April, 1928. Record as long as your arm. We've got a warrant out for him, for the job two years ago and possible links with either Cardine or Morrison or both. With any luck he'll shop them to save himself a few years. We have to find him first. I'll see if Tommy identifies Jackson as the man who stopped him on the way from school.'

'That's good,' said Sam. 'Another loose end tied up, hope-fully.'

Sam turned to go, taking his car keys out of his pocket. 'Before you go,' said Harry. 'I did check with you about Judith, remember, before I asked her out.'

'Yes, you did,' Sam said, after a pause. 'But she's not a parcel to be handed around. It was up to her.'

'Well, I know her heart wasn't in it, not with me.'

Sam looked at him and smiled. 'We'll see,' he said.

At Mrs Robinson's, Sam found Iris and Judith sitting at the kitchen table. He sat with them for a while before they left Iris alone and went out to the car.

'She knows that the hard times are just beginning, but she says she's ready,' said Judith. Sam took the coast road, and they saw the rising moon reflected in a shining ladder of light across the channels of the bay.

'Stop here,' she said. 'I don't want to go back yet to all Elspeth's questions. Can we just sit here for a while? We haven't had a chance to talk.'

'What about?' he asked.

'Everything. Us,' she said.

Sam pulled off the road and turned off the engine. Silence lay between them for a moment before Judith spoke, looking straight ahead, not at him. 'There was never really anything going on with Harry, you know that, don't you?'

'I do now. He has a lot to offer, Judith. The house, steady job, prospects.'

She nodded.

'And he's a good man,' he added. 'I could see why you might go for him.'

'Dear Sam,' said Judith, turning towards him. 'This is me, remember? I want my own life, with someone I love, not just the big house and the husband with prospects.'

He smiled. 'I know.'

'Can you take me home?' she asked. 'Not Elspeth's, your home.'

'You want to come to Cannon Street?' He stroked her hair. 'Are you sure?'

'I want to be with you, and I want us to be alone together for a while.'

'We're both tired, but can I take you to bed?'

She leaned over and kissed him.

He pulled back and looked at her. 'Is that what you want?

Are you sure?

'Yes,' she said, 'Oh, yes.'

The phone downstairs was ringing. Sam stirred. He was warm and unbearably happy.

'The phone,' Judith murmured.

'Let it ring,' he said.

She smiled. 'You'd better get it.'

'Sam? Rob Holmes here. Sorry to disturb you so late. Rumour has it you've been busy down there.'

Sam smiled. 'You could say that. What've you heard?'

'Just that something happened at that boys' home, the one you told me about, where the Noakes brothers were.'

'Yes, it's been busy,' said Sam. 'Most of the action's over for a while. Tons of paperwork for someone else to do.'

'Thought you might like to know,' said Rob. 'It's about Gloria Tennant.'

'What about her?'

'She's gone.'

'Dead?'

'No, not that sort of gone. She walked out of the hospital against doctor's orders, picked up a bag and went. I needed a statement and went round there, and one of the neighbours told me. She worked on cruise liners, right?'

'That's what Dermot told me.'

'Well, maybe she's gone back to that. The neighbour said someone arrived in a taxi and picked her up. It could have been Dermot. You said they were close.'

'If she's skipped, it's probably the best thing,' said Sam, surprised at his reaction. 'We didn't protect her, did we?'

'We got that nasty piece of work away from her and back

inside, which is what she wanted, wasn't it?'

'She set it up,' said Sam. 'She put me on to Mick Leary and the smuggling herself, to try and Shorty got nicked. Clever.'

'Actually,' Rob went on, 'there's something else I wanted to ask you about. Are you still thinking of re-applying for the force?'

'Maybe,' said Sam.

'And not going back to Barrow?'

'Probably not. Cardine is finished, but I've offended too many other big shots round here. Can't play golf, not in the Masons, and my name sounds like a Catholic. No chance.'

'Could be the same up here,' said Rob. Sam could hear him smiling. 'But things are changing a bit, don't you think? Anyway, word is that Braithwaite's going for retirement in a year or so.'

'Whoopee,' said Sam.

'And I've been shoulder-tapped by Special Branch. Don't laugh. If I go for it, there'll be space for a DC here. You could give it a year, then go for sergeant when Braithwaite packs it in. You've done the exams, got the experience, they'd be mad not to take you. Braithwaite's already checked you out with the DS in Barrow, Grayson is it? Said you were the best copper he's ever worked with. Even Braithwaite was impressed, although he'd rather cut his throat than admit it. Just thought I should tell you.'

'Thanks. That's useful.'

'What about, you know, the domestic stuff?' Rob asked.

'Are you referring to my friend, Miss Pharaoh?'

'Who else? I reckoned you two were pretty serious, despite all the ups and downs.'

Sam hesitated.

'Well, you may know more than I do Rob. I'll let you know.'

365

'And about the work decision?'

'That too. Thanks for the call.'

'What was it?' said Judith when Sam climbed back into bed.

'Someone being nosey.'

Judith sat up. 'Elspeth?'

He smiled. 'No, not Elspeth. Would that worry you?'

'I don't want to share this with anyone, not yet.'

'Do you want to go back, so she doesn't guess where we've been?'

'We can do this again, can't we?'

'Any time you like.' He kissed her. 'She's bound to know sometime.'

'I know. What time is it?'

'Just gone eleven.'

'Another hour,' said Judith.

'Amazing what you can do in an hour,' said Sam, as he put his hand to the back of her neck and drew her down into the warmth of the bed.

Elspeth eyed Sam suspiciously later in the morning when she opened the front door to him.

'What time did you get her back last night?' she asked. 'Or was it this morning? She's still asleep.'

'It was very late.' he said. 'You and Tommy were asleep.' That much was true.

'And?' said his sister. 'Are you going to tell me what's going on?'

Sam was trying to think what to say when Judith pushed open the kitchen door, wiping the sleep from her eyes. She was wearing a dark green dressing gown, her hair was down and Sam thought she had never looked so beautiful.

'Sam,' she said. 'Been here long?'

Elspeth looked at Judith carefully, then back at Sam. 'OK,' she said, 'Tommy and I are going to the park. You'll be here for a little while, right, Sam?' She went to the foot of the stairs and called up, 'Tommy, get dressed, we're going to the park.'

As the front door closed, Judith turned to the sink to fill the kettle. Sam put his arms around her from behind and kissed the side of her neck.

'You OK?' he asked.

She left the kettle in the sink and turned to face him. 'More than OK,' she said. 'You?'

'The same. Why did we wait so long?'

'Too complicated.'

'And what do we do now?'

'Enjoy it,' he said. 'Plenty of time to think about what to do. I'm as happy as I've ever been, and I want it to sink in. And I'd like to take you out tonight,' he said.

'What shall we tell Elspeth?'

Sam kissed her again. 'We can tell her the truth.'

'Now that we know what it is,' said Judith.

Sam kissed her again and they stood holding one another for a while before he said, 'Can we go back to my place?'

'Now? Again?'

'Why not? We can leave Elspeth a note.'

And they did.

Hours later, Judith asked 'That phone call last night – who was it?'

They were sitting side by side on a bench overlooking the Irish Sea, on the far side of Walney Island, watching the sun slip towards the horizon. The fish and chip supper had been

367

welcome after a day spent making up for lost time.

'That seems a long time ago,' Sam said. 'It was Rob Holmes. He just wanted to tell me that Gloria discharged herself from the hospital.'

'Will she be all right?'

'Looks like it. Neighbours said she went off in a taxi with a suitcase. Probably back to the cruise job. She needs to be away from Whitehaven. Noakes is back inside like she wanted, but she's probably not safe, even so.'

Judith scrumpled up the chip papers and held them on her lap. 'I thought you were keen on Gloria,' she said.

Sam looked at her, smiling. 'Really? No, I felt sorry for her. I still do. She's had a rough time.' He kissed the side of her head. 'The only woman on my mind for months has been you. All the time I was away I dreamed about you. I told myself that you would never really care for me. I was too dull, you'd want someone more exciting.'

Judith took his long chin in both her hands and looked at him closely. 'You're a passionate man, Sam. I can vouch for that. And you care about your work, and doing it properly. Nothing dull about that. I love you for it.'

'That was the other thing Rob told me, about the work. He said they want me to go back as a DC in Whitehaven and that I should go for the sergeant's job when Braithwaite retires in a year or so.'

Judith turned towards him, shielding her eyes from the low sunlight that shimmered on the ebbing tide. 'Is that what you want? Back into the police force?'

'I think it is. I'm good at it, Judith. But I need to know what you think.' He put his arm round her and held her close to him. 'I want to be with you, you know that. I've wanted it for a long time. Could we do it, Judith? Could we live together?

Get married? What about your job?'

'I want to be with you too,' she said. 'I'm sure of that now. But…' she hesitated, 'I don't want to get married, not yet.'

'Until I'm earning more?'

'No, silly, until I am. If I stick at this job for another year, then I can go up again, or sideways to a bigger paper, further north maybe. But I need a bit longer. Could we wait?'

Sam thought for a moment. 'There's no rush,' he said. 'We could have a long engagement, like people used to.'

Judith leaned against him, and together they watched the sun fade to a golden glow in the northern sky.

If you've enjoyed this story, you may want to…

- Order another copy of *Fatal Reckoning* to pass to a friend. *Cruel Tide* and *Fatal Reckoning* together make a great gift!

- Read the full backstory of the Pharaoh family in Ruth Sutton's trilogy, entitled *Between the Mountains and the Sea* shown on the last page of this book:

  > *A Good Liar* tells the story of Jessie who risks career and independence with a love affair, whilst her secret past draws ever closer.

  > *Forgiven* is set among the coal mines and fells of the Cumberland coast. Jessie's struggle for happiness continues.

  > *Fallout* features the nuclear disaster at Windscale, which brings a compelling stranger into Jessie's world.

- Check Ruth's website at *www.ruthsutton.co.uk*

- Follow her on *Twitter@ruthsutton* and on Facebook.

Titles by the Same Author:

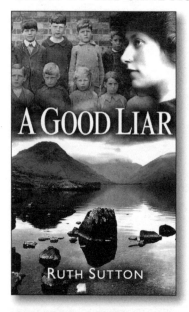

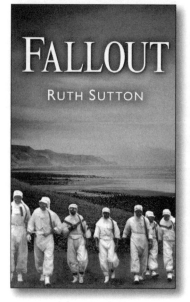